To Gordon

all the Best!

Michael Ruhlman

THE SAVIOR VACCINE

A Novel

Michael Rushnak

Also by Michael Rushnak

DENIED

TERMINAL NEGLECT

THE SAVIOR VACCINE
Copyright (c) 2012 by Michael Rushnak.

Published in the United States of America

Rushnak, Michael - Author
The Savior Vaccine
First Edition, 2011
Second Edition, 2012,
Create Space 9781463628673

Testimonials

"Twists and turns abound in this second novel of the Health Club Mysteries by Michael Rushnak, with our old friend, Dr. Jonathan Rogers back to lead the way through this break-neck page turner. Murder, terrorists and world holocaust are just a few of the intrigues brought to light in this story and it's a race to the terrifying finish. Rushnak has done it again and you won't want to miss this horrifyingly true-to-life novel by this medical thriller writer."

- 'DJ Weaver for WebbWeaver Reviews'

"Nuclear attacks, a potentially lethal vaccine, cover-ups, corruption and revenge. The Savior Vaccine captivates and intrigues - A medical thriller with more twists than a small intestine."

- Michael Balkind, Author of *Sudden Death & Dead Ball*

Dr. Michael Rushnak's book, The Savior Vaccine, is one of the best books I've ever read. It was so real and as I turned the pages, I kept wanting to see what was next. The book is pure genius and I recommend anyone who wants to read a book, that not only has a terrific story, but holds true in the real world MUST read this book.

- Dr. Joyce M. Knudsen, PhD, AICI CIM

"Terminal Neglect is a white hot thriller, tightly plotted and full of terrific twists. This is one of the very best medical thrillers I have read--not recently, EVER! Michael Rushnak's first novel hits with the force of a runaway freight train. The tension starts on page one and never lets up. I am so impressed. His imaginative, fast-paced thriller gave me paper cuts from turning the pages so rapidly. But then I was too wary to trust any doctor to fix them. This is one terrific read. The genre of medical suspense has been needing some new blood. We have found it in Michael Rushnak. I loved this book, and the friends I have turned on to it are loving it, too."

- Michael Palmer, NY Times Best Selling Author

I dedicate this book to all readers who have been thrilled, engaged and hopefully inspired to think about the deeper questions raised in my medical mystery thriller trilogy that began with TERMINAL NEGLECT and now moves on with THE SAVIOR VACCINE

THE SAVIOR VACCINE

A Novel

PROLOGUE

The President of the United States, Jane Williams, felt numb. Her confidential national security binder slipped out of her hands. The highly classified report fell to the floor with a thud. Yet, Williams barely batted an eyelash. She stared vacantly, through the Oval Office window out at the Rose Garden. Silently, she prayed that her younger sister wasn't at home during the nuclear catastrophe in Minneapolis. *Please let Maryann be all right!*

From behind, a couple of sharp knocks caught her attention. She swiveled her chair toward the hand chiseled oak door of the Oval Office. It swung open. Chief of Staff, Mackensie Pitnar, her trusted advisor, stood in the doorway. Eerily glued to her face, his puffy reddened eyes blinked repeatedly. His feet shuffled forward in her direction as if he wanted to delay as long as possible a dreadful message to the Commander-in-Chief.

Williams hung her head. A coarse tremor, on both of her arthritic hands, out of nowhere, erupted like a volcano, and as seconds ticked by, significantly increased in intensity. Fear of what he would say triggered a quickening of her heartbeats. With downcast eyes, she sensed that he was drawing nearer; increasingly terrified that he would deliver heartbreaking news. As his footsteps grew louder, she looked up and met his unsettled gaze.

Her Chief of Staff came to an abrupt halt in front of the presidential desk, constructed from oak timbers of a nineteenth century warship. In almost a whisper, he uttered her worst horror. "Madame President, it is with my deepest regret to inform you that your sister died in the latest terrorist attack."

In a flash, she felt the air sucked out of the room. Mac suddenly became a blurry image. She gasped, "Maryann!" The muscles of her throat tightened. Williams stammered, "Do—we? Do we kno---?" She brushed away a budding tear from her right cheek. "Do we know?"

Mac looked away, eyes slammed shut.

Struggling to gain control of her emotions, she jutted her quivering jaw in his direction. Williams tightly gripped both sides of her desk. She blurted out, "Did my sister suffer?"

He stiffened, realizing that he had just detonated a live hand grenade upon raw nerves. His eyes broke open. "No, Madame President."

"How do you know?" she snapped.

Silence!

She thundered as quickly as a lightning bolt. "Prove to me that Maryann didn't suffer!"

Mac painfully returned his line of sight to latch on to her darting eyes. "Madame President, I'm profoundly sorry." He scanned her contorted face. "Your sister and thousands of others were instantly vaporized by the nuclear blast."

With her heart racing, she rubbed away the heavy chest discomfort that her recurrent palpitations were causing. "Tell me details," she asked, though her tone came out as if it were an order given by a five star general on an open battlefield during a full-scale war.

After a brief period of shifting his feet, Mac assumed a military attention stance. He began to speak in a matter of fact manner. "Tens of thousands, who were not at ground zero, are severely burned and critically injured. All survivors are currently being transported to eighteen hospitals within a fifty mile radius of Minneapolis."

Williams raised her shaky right hand above her head. She felt every muscle fiber tensing throughout her body. Unable to hold back her building rage, she smashed her fist down on her desk. Instantaneously, shooting pains radiated from her fingers up her right arm when her fist violently touched down. Venom exploded from her mouth. "These terrorists are heartless killers who will burn in hell! I'll make them pay dearly for what they've done to our nation."

His eyes darted--in the direction of the open Oval Office door.

"You know our protocol," she barked. "Let's implement the plan."

Mac took a half step toward leaving her presence but suddenly froze in his tracks. "Madame President, may I speak freely?"

"I have always respected what you contribute. You know that!"

The Chief of Staff knitted his bushy black eyebrows. "As you well know, the American people are extremely angry."

Her nostrils flared. "I am furious! If I get my hands on any one of these terrorists, I'll break their neck," she shouted.

Mac winced as his words gushed out, in a torrent of revealing passion. "Pardon my bluntness, Madame President. That's not what I meant."

"Look, we have a lot of work ahead of us. Just say what's on your mind."

He fired away. "The American people are angry at you---Madame President. And, although it pains me greatly to say this, national polls show that the majority of Americans no longer believe that you have acted appropriately to protect the homeland."

The President sprang to her feet as if she were a tightly wound spring that had just uncoiled. She folded her arms across her chest. "Mac, you have always been loyal to me. This is no time to start casting blame."

He cleared his throat. Pulling back his shoulders, his posture straightened to a rigid form. Mac's steadfast eyes locked on hers. "In Gulf War One, I've served my country in battle." His voice began soaring-- higher and higher with each spoken word. "I placed my life on the line for my country. It was right for me to follow my Commander in Chief's orders. I deeply respect the office---through our democratic process—of the Presidency of our great nation."

She shot him a quizzical look. "Why the hell are you going on about what *you* have done in Iraq?" Williams plopped down in her chair. She slapped the side of her desk. Her much needed focus on next steps-- inexplicably high jacked by what she took as a totally out of character pointless diatribe from her own Chief of Staff.

"I'm sorry Madame President. You are right. This is not about me. This is about *you!*"

The President grabbed her left hand, attempting to smother the tremors. "Mac, I am in no mood for whatever you think that you are doing." Williams paused a second or two. "And, you need to get back to work. Pull together my national security team for an emergency meeting. Call me when it's assembled."

Pitnar swiped a series of beads off his forehead. "Forgive me at this most tragic moment. I have one more thing to say. There are rumors of mounting pressure on Congress to hold-----impeachment hearings."

Williams shuddered upon hearing his words. She pointed toward the door. "Get out! I have heard enough of this political rhetoric."

Pitnar took a step backwards and with great difficulty held his tongue. He squared up to her, waiting for the right moment to strike again.

"The American people will again come to trust me." She coiled her aching fingers into a tight fist. She thrust it forward—directly at him. "I will do whatever it takes to save America!"

He frowned, vigorously rubbing his mouth. "Madame President, with all due respect, it was your decision that there would be no consequences for the Taliban's attack last year on our consulate in Peshawar. Who knows---?" He stopped himself in mid sentence.

The veins in her neck pulsated. "Enough," she barked. "Unless you stop your counterproductive Monday morning quarterbacking, I will demand your immediate resignation."

Mac stood motionless for several seconds. He uttered, "I understand the rules." He squinted as a ray of brilliant sunlight streamed through the window, landing squarely on his face. He nodded, almost imperceptivity, before pivoting and taking several quick paces through the open door.

Williams held her forehead in both hands. She began saying the *Our Father* prayer in complete silence. She concluded by actually speaking aloud the closing words, "…deliver us from evil."

***

Jane Williams, an extremely slender woman with a sallow complexion and sagging wrinkled facial skin, had celebrated her sixtieth birthday just weeks before the initial terrorist attacks began nearly one year ago. She rocked back and forth in her soft leather chair, her chest still heaving like pistons revving up a turbo-charged sports car.

Needing to release her pent up ire, the President ripped out the first two pages from her national security executive summary. Williams crumpled the torn out pages into a tightly knit ball. She flung the paper missile toward the Ben Franklin clock, situated on the far side of the room. Today's nuclear disaster in Minneapolis had embedded itself among her neurons. *It will never again be the same!*

Since the first "dirty bomb" detonation of one year ago, the first woman commander in chief's migraines had markedly worsened. She massaged away the flaring muscle spasms in the area of her right temple, just behind her earlobe. The President flipped open an opaque two ounce bottle that she pulled from the upper drawer of her desk. She downed a couple of ibuprofens, unable to blot out of her mind the embedded ghastly pictures of disfigured faces and an endless train of coffins.

When the mass murders first began, her cardiologist started her on treatment for recurrent palpitations—atrial fibrillation. Medications usually did the trick although once she required an electrical current to shock her heart back into a normal sinus rhythm. For the President, a restful night of sleep had clearly become a long lost art.

She glanced down at the photos near ground zero that lay on her desk and plucked out a gruesome shot. Just seconds after the nuclear mushroom cloud had showered its deadly brew on Minneapolis; a badly burned survivor with a smart phone had captured the carnage.

Maryann. Flashbacks to the last time she had seen her sister alive cascaded throughout her troubled mind, tripping brain cells, sending out irrepressible impulses of intense guilt and revenge. Nevertheless, she knew that no matter what action she would take from this moment on, one haunting fact would never change. Maryann Williams was gone--- gone forever, in the blink of an eye. *Mac was right! It is my fault!*

Her eyelids grew heavy. The rhythmic ticking of the Franklin, with each sweep of the second hand, seduced her into a light daze. Imagined demons began swarming toward her in the form of upright marching human shaped skeletons. *Clang! Clang! Clang!*

Three piercing chimes of the Franklin clock jolted the President's mental fog. The throbbing within her brain took center stage as tens of millions of neurons connected with each other—hammering out a strategic plan of what she needed to do.

She spotted an embossed pencil, protruding as a placeholder in her six-inch security binder, lying on the carpet. Williams bent over and picked up the pencil. She clutched it tightly at each end. Her mouth twisted into a snarl. Gritting her teeth, she snapped it in half.

The President spun her chair and looked out again at the Rose Garden. Despite a gorgeous mid-September sunny day, the gathering dark clouds on the horizon, just beyond the Washington Monument, were a troublesome metaphor for the mounting demand of revenge by American citizens. Unable to dismiss this reality anymore, an escalating series of widespread outrages by a panicked public had engulfed her every waking moment. Talk of impeachment, an unlikely possibility that had begun as mere gossip inside the beltway just six months ago, was now taking firm root along many main streets across the land.

The forty-sixth President of the United States pushed down on the mahogany arms of her chair. Weary to the bone, she struggled to rise but unable to sustain her feeble effort, she landed hard on her seat. "I will do this," she said to herself. With a forced thrust of her hips, the first term leader sprang to her feet.

Williams walked with conviction toward Madison, seated just outside her office. She acknowledged her appointment assistant before plodding forward. Within the last year, she had compulsively begun counting the number of paces to the Green Room. It was always between sixty-four or sixty-six strides. Yet today, her journey to the twenty-foot high door at the far end of the hallway seemed endless, conceivably hundreds of agonizing steps away.

After a series of wobbly strides, she found herself veering toward the right wall. She grazed several of the protruding ornate frames that circled a half dozen hand -painted portrayals of the Founding Fathers. Yet their portraits did not budge from their well-entrenched moorings.

Soon, she approached the tall hulking Secret Service guard who stood to one side of the imposing floor to ceiling lime green painted door. The President came to a sudden stop. She fired off a commanding glance in his direction. The sentry drew back the massive oak with a powerful twist and pull on the gold plated doorknob.

Williams peered through the opening. The Green Room was buzzing with lively conversations. She took two steps forward, entering the huge chamber. Heads of dozens of captains of industry turned toward her. Seconds later, the clamoring ended amid widespread whispers of---*Ssshhh!*

A sea of CEO's from Fortune 500 companies began standing in a string of cascading waves that began in the rear of the room. Over the last year, she had felt increasing isolation from this powerful business constituency. Feeling vulnerable, the President felt their hostile vibes. She forced a half smile, intentionally avoiding any direct eye contact.

Williams hastily walked over a light green canvas floor cloth placed in the room two centuries earlier during the Jefferson administration. Just before she reached the head of the forty-foot long maple wood table, she allowed herself a momentary glimpse of the hand painted canvas masterpieces of Washington and Lincoln. Their immortal images dominated the emerald painted sidewall. Awed by her revered predecessors, she felt puny despite her above average five foot ten stature.

After arriving at the head of the conference table, the President turned slowly to face her invited guests. Subtle grimaces seemed to be screaming back at her to do something to save the country from its long lasting trajectory toward further chaos and ruin. She brushed aside a water glass and began to speak in a hurried manner. "Good morning. Please take your seats."

While she waited for her invited guests to come to order, she thought of Christian James, her Secretary of Health and Human Services. James had wanted to accompany her to this meeting. However, she had insisted on doing this meeting alone, emphatically telling Secretary James that she alone possessed the mettle to get the job done. *This is my ballgame! James understands*, she thought.

"I want to thank all of you for coming in today." Her throat felt like sandpaper. "I've invited you to the White House to obtain your counsel at this gravest of moments." Williams paused and reached down to take a sip of water.

"As you well know, despite our selective tactical retaliation on high value military targets within Pakistan and Afghanistan, the jihadists remain undeterred." She smacked her parched lips. "As a result of the direct and indirect effects of their nuclear strikes in our metropolitan centers, we are seeing massive levels of human suffering and deaths in America not seen since the days of the European Black Plague. From this past year's nuclear fallout, radiation induced diseases and cancer have become epidemic in America! The incidence of malignancies due to primary strikes on cities and secondary to the down -wind radiation from the cesium "dirty bombs" have been skyrocketing. Sadly, we can expect many more cancers as a result of the uranium bomb that recently struck Minneapolis." She configured her right hand in the form of a claw and pointed toward her guests. "We must act to stop these terrorists and we must act to prevent these nuclear radiation induced diseases--- and make no mistake about it, we will act!"

The silence was deafening. Williams scanned their faces. The business leaders appeared dubious and fearful. Their eyes darted, landing on hers, before quickly shifting in another direction. Her jaw muscles tightened, along with the reappearance of an old habit. Unable to stop the nightly grinding of her teeth, this recent exacerbation of her right sided TMJ syndrome had only added to her worsening migraines.

She latched onto the sullen looking face of Tony Lowman, CEO of General Restaurants of America. While listening to her, his facial features had solidified as if he was posing for the fifth spot on Mount Rushmore. He raised his hand. Williams pointed her left index finger at him.

Lowman promptly launched himself to his feet. "Madame President, with all due respect, before we contribute our ideas," he said with a caustic edge to his voice, "I believe all of us would like to hear your solutions to this unprecedented crisis. It has added to the soaring health care costs that we all bear for our employees. I know that I am stating the obvious but our businesses are no longer competitive in the world."

The President pulled back her sagging shoulders, locking her gaze on Lowman's stiff upper lip. "Tony, you are correct. Our heath care costs are spiraling out of control. Prior efforts at reforming our healthcare system have not taken root. Our five trillion dollar health care expenditure this past fiscal year, driven to a disproportionate degree by the medical and psychiatric costs of treating radiation induced illnesses and cancers, has propelled our country toward the brink of economic depression."

Williams allowed her eyes to roam the room for a couple of moments. She dug her low-heeled shoes into the nineteenth century cloth covering the floorboards beneath her chair. "Earlier today, I consulted with my Secretary of Health and Human Services and the Surgeon General. We have calculated that the short and long-term costs of caring for untold hundreds of thousands of radiation-induced cancers alone may soon approach our aggregate spending on all other health care problems combined. Moreover, not even one scientist, not any health care professional whom Secretary of Health Christian James and Surgeon General Jonathan Rogers have consulted, not one single public health expert harbors any doubt that this already severe situation will soon escalate ten- fold unless we dramatically do something."

Williams stopped to gulp in a huge breath. Her parched throat felt as though she was speaking from the middle of the Sahara desert. She drained her water glass, wishing that it had been a double Scotch.

"I am proposing a new strategy." The President pointed skyward. "We've accomplished the near impossible before. It has been more than a half century since JFK galvanized the will of this country to land a man on the moon in less than a decade. American can succeed and America will succeed. So, in addition to our ongoing campaign to root out and kill the terrorists, I am launching a full scale war on preventing all forms of illnesses and cancers secondary to nuclear radiation."

Re-focusing on Lowman, the outspoken CEO argued from his seat. "President Nixon proposed a war on cancer over forty years ago. Therefore, I must ask you, are there any well respected and independent scientists who truly believe that what you're suggesting is even possible?"

Williams shook her head in the affirmative. She walked toward Sean Parker. Seated near the front of the room, the tall blond middle aged CEO of Doctors Choice Products straightened his red paisley tie while she approached his seat.

"Mr. Parker, please tell us about a promising vaccine in your drug company's pipeline."

"Thank you Madame President," he said, slightly bowing his head toward her. "Our scientists at DCP have recently concluded their testing of a compound on a cohort of Rhesus monkeys who were exposed to high doses of radiation that would mimic a sizable nuclear explosion. Over time, every monkey who did not receive our vaccine has developed a malignancy at the expected rate. However, the good news is all monkeys receiving our vaccine before exposure to the radiation have remained cancer free for more than a year since this experiment began." Parker held his hand out in the direction of the President, deferring to her to take it from here.

"Tell us more," Williams added while she progressively inched toward the door in the rear of the Green Room.

The CEO puffed his muscular chest. "Scientifically, we have clearly proven that our cancer preventing vaccine is completely safe in monkeys. This was a critical first milestone. After we receive FDA approval based on the overwhelming success of our monkey trials, DCP will begin the first phase of human clinical trials."

Out of the corner of her eye, Williams noted that the entrance to the green door was now slightly ajar. She wondered whether someone was listening, outside in the corridor. A moment later, the door creaked open a couple of inches. *Secretary of Health James?*

"Please continue Mr. Parker."

"Once our product achieves FDA approval for human deployment, DCP intends to call our vaccine by the brand name ---*NeoBloc.*"

"Thank you for that critical briefing on what we will be using." After confirming that there were no intruders on her meeting, she stood by the open door and he proclaimed, "Tomorrow morning, I will instruct that the Secretary of Health and Human Services as well as the Surgeon General to take the lead in what I have dubbed Project Moon Shot. Our goal will be to inoculate every American with this savior vaccine within the year. May God be with all of us!"

***

As the President confidently re-entered the Oval Office, she was surprised to notice a routine event that had not been on her radar for many months. Almost miraculously, the clouds had disappeared. The sun blazed. A wide grin broke out on her troubled face, having almost forgotten what it was like to feel the soothing warmth from the center of our solar system

Sitting down at her desk, she repeatedly scribbled the name of the DCP vaccine on her presidential pad. *NeoBloc. NeoBloc. The Savior of America!*

CHAPTER ONE

Dr. Jonathan Rogers squirmed impatiently in a wobbly pine wood captain's chair. Twenty minutes earlier, he had chosen this isolated seat in the back of the dimly lit pub. Hidden on a narrow cobble-stoned alleyway in Georgetown, the tavern was barely noticeable from the main thoroughfare.

From the outside, the local watering hole looked like an old horse stable in the shape of an early twentieth century hay barn. The dull gray paint on the pub's siding, pealing in random spots, added to the weathered appearance. Rogers ogled the inside roof peak before dropping his eyes to the splinters protruding from the wall adjacent to his rickety pine wood table. *Where is she?* With each irritated shuffle of his mug of draft beer, the table rocked back and forth.

With mounting boredom, he looked up again at the empty lofts. The din of the tavern's rowdy patrons clanged in his eardrums. Proud of his widely acclaimed skills as a problem solver, he wished the owners had retained something in the tavern rafters, maybe a few dozen bales of hay to absorb the noise. Checking his Timex watch, he grew increasingly restless. His wife would be expecting him for dinner within the hour. Kim would not be pleased if he arrived later than his usual time.

Rogers glanced over at the bartender. Mikey, a six foot six inch strapping chap with numerous red scaly looking islands of actinic keratosis patched on areas of sun damaged skin around his neck and a +well worn face, leaned against the inside rail of the bar. He wiped off the alcohol spigots with a drenched tan cloth. Above his head, the establishment sign, *Hurleys*, flashed green and white. *Established 1860.* A perch of half-empty Vodka, Scotch, Rum, and Bourbon bottles lined a shelf that was easily within his reach. Mikey scanned the tavern, seemingly always at the ready, on the look -out for any customer wanting to order another round.

Rogers cursed inwardly for agreeing to meet with Laura Timmons at *Hurleys*. She had called him earlier that afternoon at his office at Health and Human Services. He agreed to meet with her at Hurley's tavern this evening. Yet, if she had not been married to Adam Timmons, Governor of Michigan, he chided himself that he would have declined her last minute demand to meet on such short notice. He shook his head. Since becoming the nation's Surgeon General, through last year's appointment by President Jane Williams, he frequently blamed himself for being far too accommodative of politicians, who for the most part, he despised.

He remembered hearing about Timmons from his previous near death experiences at the hands of the prior CEO of her Company, Doctor's Choice Products. Since then, he had seen her name many times in the state newspaper. Lauren was certainly no shrinking violet. She had a penchant for the limelight. In fact, the word on the street was that she would do almost anything to further her own career, possibly even at the expense of her husband.

Back home, near the company's corporate headquarters in Michigan, Lauren enjoyed a public persona reputation as a dutiful wife, embracing her husband's meteoric rise in his political career. Yet, it came as no shock to political insiders to read in the newspapers that she had recently filed for divorce.

Days later, the whole truth came out. News of Governor Timmons's sexually explicit adulterous scandal turned public opinion against him. Folks in the Wolverine state began to empathize with her plight as the faithful wife, a wife who inadvertently let on to the media that she knew many secrets that could bring down her husband, a political rock star until word of his seedy affair leaked out through social networking media.

With his eyes glued to the entrance to the tavern, Rogers grew increasingly impatient. The Surgeon General reached into his pocket to pull out his wallet. He grabbed a ten spot to cover his beer and tip for Mikey. In grabbing for the bill, he spotted his own wedding photo in one of the well-worn leather slots.

For sure, he thought, he had savored every year of his close relationship with Kim. Thirty years later, Rogers still cherished their close bond. He chuckled at a thought that ironically sprang to his mind. Both of them often referred to themselves as two peas in a pod. He laid the bill on the unsteady wooden table while internally beating himself up one last time. He vowed never again to let Lauren or anyone else for that matter to sway him into last minute meetings at unlikely venues.

In speaking with her no more than three hours earlier, she had identified herself as the Vice-President of operations at the pharmacy of DCP, a Michigan biotech company that he had known all too well. In his brief conversation with her, she claimed to have vital information; data that he --as the country's Surgeon General--the "top doc"--needed to know. When he had pressed her for details, she told him directly that he would have to wait until she was face to face with him.

Rogers countered with an offer to meet with her in his office the following morning. She declined, offering a plausible excuse for this evening's urgent meeting. Lauren was going to be in DC only for the night. Early the next morning, she would be flying out of Reagan Airport, back to Michigan, to assist in the move to her new bachelorette apartment.

Rogers cracked his knuckles a few times. Lauren was now more than thirty minutes late. He peered out the side window. Through crisscrossing fractures in the white and yellow stained glass panels, rays of the setting sun bounced off the slanted lamppost at the corner of Mill Road, projecting a source of streaming light through the window cracks. Twenty feet to the rear of the seldom-traveled intersection lay hundreds of tombstones in Oak Hill Cemetery. Bored, he began counting the headstones. *Fifteen in the first row. Twenty in the next.*

He took a final swig from his mug, tapped his finger several times on the table, and seriously began to think about heading home to see Kim. While Rogers was staring at the front door of the tavern, it creaked open. A half- dozen men barged in, yelling to Mikey for a full set up at the bar. Distracted by the rowdy behavior of the latest arrivals, Rogers hadn't noticed until now a tall heavily bearded man at an adjacent table next to his. The well-tanned man yelled out for table service. Seemingly, on cue, the bartender appeared at his table with three whiskey shot glasses that the customer grabbed, draining each in successive gulps.

Mikey headed back to the bar just as Rogers' neighbor shouted out for another round of three. Curious, mainly out of the monotony of the evening, the Surgeon General found himself gawking at the man, taking note of the deep crow's feet harboring near a pair of reddened slits and an elongated narrow nose. His dark blue overalls and a freshly pressed red lumberjack shirt were remarkable for how spotless they appeared, given the numerous red paint stains that adorned the smooth looking skin of both of his hands. Half- way slumped on his chair, the apparent painter was vigorously typing in several text messages on his cell phone.

The patron cast a wary glance over at Rogers. The Surgeon General averted the direct eye contact and promised himself to give Lauren just one more minute to appear. *Fifty-nine, fifty-eight.*

With his countdown down in the single digits, a middle-aged woman wearing huge dark sunglasses and a form fitting navy blue dress sauntered through the front door on her way to the bar. Her three-inch heels clanked across the wood flooring. As most heads turned in her direction, Rogers was clearly not the only man in the tavern who had taken notice of her striking good looks.

She tugged along a colorful *DC Sports Club* bag under her arm as she strolled up to the bar. The woman seductively grazed her hand over the bartender's hairy forearms. Leaning forward, Mikey gave her a quick peck on her cheek. She gingerly lowered the pink and white stripped bag to the floor planks below her three-inch stilettos. A martini swiftly appeared in front of her. The woman snatched her drink off the bar and held it firmly in her right hand. She promenaded toward the rest rooms in the tavern rear. While she seemed to be casually surveying each of the gawking men, she conspicuously yanked off her large sunglasses.

Near the rest room door, she sharply spun around, walking straight toward Rogers. She sat down on a chair on the opposite side of his table and plunked down her martini and sunglasses.

Feeling extremely uncomfortable, he pushed back his chair. He rose to his feet, his eyes still drawn to her deep cleavage.

She asked in a hushed tone, "Come here often?"

He slouched back down on his seat. "This is my first time here."

"First of many opportunities," she said coyly.

Rogers frowned. "I'm supposed to meet a business woman. But she's late."

She dipped her index finger in her drink and stirred the martini. Withdrawing her finger, she placed it on her lips and sucked on it. "What about your wife?"

He remained silent and toyed with his watch while uncomfortably looking over at Mikey.

The bartender flashed him a thumb up sign despite casting a jealous expression toward him.

"You know what I think." She pursed her lips. "I think you're stepping out on your wife and looking for someone else to enjoy the evening." Taking an unhurried prolonged swallow from her martini, she added, "Actually, I could use some personal attention myself. My husband is bad news."

Rogers shook his head. "Look, I need to go."

She winked. "Listen, I'm here to meet a doctor—a big shot doctor."

"Is that so?"

"Actually, I need a checkup." Her eyes sparkled. "Know of any good doctors?"

Intrigued, he curtly asked, "What's the name of the doctor who is supposed to meet you?"

"You're such a tease." She giggled. "Come on, Dr. Jonathan Rogers."

The Surgeon General leaned back in his chair, saying nothing. *Lauren Timmons?* Suddenly, the painter at the adjacent table began to snore loudly, diverting his concentration. The Surgeon General uneasily surveyed the other patrons in the tavern before returning his rapt attention back on her.

"You still haven't told me your name."

The woman laughed. "Hey -doc. I'm just playing with you. I've seen your picture on Facebook, Twitter, and the *Washington Post*."

Annoyed, he said, "What's your name?"

She leaned across the table and spoke softly, "Look, Dr. Rogers, Surgeon General, I spoke with you earlier today."

He said nothing, waiting for her to continue.

"To be frank, reaching you was not very easy. I had to use up a favor from my ex-husband. Actually, it was more of a threat to expose him. In any case his office contacted you so I could be patched in to speak with you—the famous Surgeon General of the United States of America. I told you that I had news to share with you."

She looked at his expressionless face. "OK, I'll give you more. I work at Doctor's Choice Products. Yes, it's me, Lauren Timmons."

"I'm sure you can understand why I need to be cautious."

She lightly placed her hand on his. "So, can we be friends?"

He pulled his hand away. "So, Mrs. Timmons, what exactly did you want to share with me?"

"Call me Lauren. I hate my last name—more to the point, I hate my husband. But, I guess I'm stuck with my surname until my divorce comes through." Timmons sent a flirtatious look his way. She cocked her head. "Who knows the future? I could even be Lauren Rogers. Get my drift?"

"Look, I'm happily married. Please stop playing games." He folded his arms on his chest. "Let's get down to why you wanted to meet me here. And, since you're already very late, I don't have much time." While he spoke, he sensed the senior at the next table periodically awakening from his slumber, sneaking furtive peaks at them. The painter yawned and stretched before reaching for his cell. He began texting, fast and furiously.

Rogers pulled a notepad from the inner pocket of his navy blue suit jacket and began scribbling. He pushed it toward Lauren.

Let's write down our conversations. There is a possibility that we're being watched.

She responded with a knowing look. Lauren began printing in large letters and turned the note to face him. *I know everything about NeoBloc.*

His eyes widened. Abandoning the game he had just established, he leaned toward her so that their faces were no more than a foot apart. He whispered, "Know what?"

"My company, Doctor's Choice Products, is working on a vaccine to prevent cancer in monkeys exposed to lethal doses of nuclear radiation.

Rogers noticed that the painter had stopped texting and was leaning toward them. Covering the side of his face nearest the painter, Rogers pointed toward the note. "Write"

Lauren picked up the ballpoint and wrote her message. *There is a deadly problem with the vaccine. We shouldn't start the human clinical trials.*

Reading her reply, he covered his mouth. His eyes darted to her hardened looking face.

Once again, Timmons began writing furiously. She pushed him the latest note. *In the monkey trials with NeoBloc, every monkey died within a year. The vaccine is a killer.*

Rogers's mind whirled back to that morning's meeting with President Williams and his own boss, Secretary of Health and Human Services, Christian James. The President had just charged both of them to evaluate the safety of *NeoBloc* as part of Project Moon Shot. Stunned by her revelation, the Surgeon General sat speechless.

Lauren pulled the paper toward her and flipped it to face her. She began writing again.

At that moment, Rogers felt a hard tug on his left shoulder. Spinning around, he saw Mikey towering above him. The Surgeon General glanced over at the painter. The man was in the middle of downing the second shot in his latest row of three whiskeys.

The bartender shouted down at the Surgeon General, "Another beer?"

Focused on the fear erupting on Lauren's face, Rogers waved him off. "No thanks."

The bartender lowered his voice several octaves. "Passing love notes I see." Mikey bent over, grazing Rogers's ear with his shoulder length unkempt tousled hair. "You're a lucky guy. Usually when she comes in here, she sits alone."

"I'm about to leave."

Rogers watched Mikey march away. The bartender shrugged his shoulders. Looking back at Lauren, her latest directive faced him. *Take my gym bag when you leave. It's by the bar. I need to leave for an appointment. Someone else is opposed to NeoBloc. That means we have an ally. That someone wants to discuss this matter with me—TONIGHT!*

He wrinkled his forehead. Rogers took the pen. *Who?*

Lauren shook her head. She grabbed the pen, completing the next verse in their mutual communiqué. By now, he noted that the painter had vacated his seat and was leaning against the bar talking with Mikey. The Surgeon General thought about calling Secretary James. He checked his watch. *Kim will not be pleased.*

He glanced down at her last message.

I'll be walking through Rock Creek Park to catch a subway at Dupont. In case we have to meet again, I'll leave you a voice message in your office with a code letter. P for Park. D for Dupont. Wish me luck.

Rogers scratched out a reply. *The park is dangerous this time of night. I'll call you a cab.*

Lauren's leg was shaking and her jaw began to quiver. She began writing again, looking around nervously every few seconds. Once again, she flipped the notepad toward him.

I'll call you in your office tomorrow after you've had a chance to study what's in my gym bag. Please tell your administrative assistant to put my call through to you.

Apprehensively, he covered the well-worn note with his hands. As if she was reading his mind, Lauren scooped up the page and rolled it up into a one-half inch round ball. She moistened it with a hefty wad of her saliva. Swallowing it in one forced guzzle, she murmured, *"Guard my gym bag with your--- life."*

He looked over to the bar. Mikey stood in front of it. His bulbous abdomen protruded from his tight blue tee shirt. His right foot rested on the *DC Sports Club* bag. Without another word, Lauren rose and began walking toward the back door of the tavern.

Rogers looked back at the bar. Mikey was now holding the gym bag, motioning for him to come and get it. The Surgeon General stood and began walking to claim the bag. He heard the back door of the tavern slam shut. Along with many men in the tavern, his attention was now on the rear of the bar. Oddly, the seemingly drunken painter was methodically pacing the floor, near the rest room, speaking excitedly into his cell phone.

He threw down the ten-dollar bill on the bar and then reached for the gym bag. Smiling a wry grin, the bartender held on to the pink and white stripped bag tightly before several seconds later finally surrendering it to Rogers. Mikey then unleashed a wicked sounding laugh that unnerved the Surgeon General. Timidly, he waved to the bartender and ambled out of *Hurleys*. Lauren's gift hung securely from his right hand as he made a sharp left out of the front door.

Rogers spotted the main entrance to Rock Creek Park behind the tavern. Straight ahead was P Street. The gym bag appeared to weigh a few pounds. He hailed a passing taxicab. After hopping in, he commanded the driver to head toward Pennsylvania Avenue. *I'm late. Kim is not going to be happy.*

In the rear view mirror, he watched the driver's right eye twitching. It would be better to wait, he decided, until he got home before he would open his gift from Lauren.

The taxi sped off. He reflected on his encounter with Lauren and wondered why she would be taking the Dupont Circle subway by crossing though the pitch-dark park, alone! He thought about Mikey's bizarre laugh when the bartender handed him the gym bag. *Who is she meeting in the park?*

The two story brownstones flashed by him as the taxi picked up speed. The Surgeon General made a snap decision. *I need to find her— now.*

Rogers tapped on the glass separating the driver from him. "Please turn onto Rock Creek Potomac Parkway. Take me through the park."

The driver complied. Rogers reconstructed in his mind her written messages. *Lauren said she was late for an appointment. She was meeting a guy who was also opposed to NeoBloc. An ally!*

Rogers spotted the sign for the Parkway. The cab zoomed through the sharp turns in the park as though the driver was competing in the *Tour de France*. He tapped on the window. "Please slow down." The driver grunted but followed orders.

He recalled his meeting earlier that day with the President and Secretary of Health Christian James. The President had wanted *NeoBloc* tested as soon as possible in humans. Furthermore, Secretary James certainly didn't mention any safety issue with the monkeys in the *NeoBloc* trials.

He pressed an automatic window button. The rear right window powered open. The warm summer breeze felt good. Back and forth, he looked, to both sides of the Parkway roadway, hoping to spot Lauren walking through the park. Listening carefully, he heard a single high-pitched scream. Rogers banged on the windowpane in front of him and shouted, "Stop. Turn off the engine."

The cab came to a dead stop. He heard only the constant chirping of crickets. His ears perked up. A second scream, more muffled came from his left—in the distance, over by the tree line. Just beyond that area, he surmised; laid the rear entrance to the tavern.

Rogers grabbed his prize package and tucked it under his right armpit. He ran in the direction of the second scream and stumbled down a grassy slope. He caught his balance just before falling. Slowing his pace, he kept a close eye on the rolling terrain while intently listening.

A half moon was shining down. He scanned the horizon. *Nothing!* A series of shrill chirps from the crickets seemed to be getting louder. Believing that he heard fast-paced footsteps hurtling across the open field in front of him, he came to a halt. His eye caught a reflection of the moonlight on a yard long shiny image—in motion--about thirty yards ahead. *It's a tall man running toward the Georgetown entrance to the park. He's carrying something.* A familiar smell hit Rogers in the face. *Not a skunk.* The footsteps were now gone. The sky grew darker as clouds covered the limited amount of moonlight.

He looked back at the taxi. Rogers was thankful that the cabbie was still there, standing, peering out into the darkness, keeping a watchful eye on him. *Need a light.* Rogers fumbled to find his key chain in his pants' pocket. He grabbed it and flipped on the attached penlight. He aimed the dim beam but saw only rolling hills of freshly mowed grass.

The pungent smell grew stronger. *A hospital type of smell.* With each step, he sensed that he was ascending a graduated slope. The flickering beam outlined what looked like a drop off, up ahead, to a lower clearing. He took another long whiff of the evening air. A breeze whipping toward him smacked him in the face with an overpowering odor, an almost metallic aroma. It reminded him of his days as a practicing gastroenterologist. He recognized the smell. It was the aroma of the iron in the red blood cells that when mixed with air gave off that unique scent.

Reaching the edge of the grassy knoll, he pointed the small beam of light down at the small ravine below his feet. The stench was now unmistakable. The cricket chirping became intense. Looking back, he noticed that the cabbie was frantically waving his arms. *Something is wrong! Time to leave!*

He scanned the ravine below his feet one last time. A reflection of several pools of bright red blood came into view---seemingly strung together over a six-foot area. He methodically followed the lighted trail inch by inch until he saw it.

No cadaver medical school dissection had ever prepared him for this moment. *Oh my God!* Rogers recoiled in shock upon seeing what lay in the weeds, just six feet below his black wingtips. There it was. Nestled between two sharp edged stones was the fully detached head of Lauren Timmons. A quick scan of the area showed that the rest of her body was nowhere in sight.

Waves of nausea smacked him. Rogers recoiled upon seeing moonbeams eerily bouncing off her motionless bright blue eyes. Bright red blood flowed from the bottom edge of her skull onto the dark green grass. He twisted his head away, no longer able to hold in his Hurley's beer.

He wiped away the vomit from his mouth, horrified that someone snuffed out her life, in such a horrendously violent manner, simply because she knew confidential information about *NeoBloc*. There was now no turning back. He felt compelled to follow her lead—wherever it might lead. *What's in this gym bag?*

CHAPTER TWO

Just after he dialed 911 on his cell, Rogers punched in a text message to his boss. He revealed to the Secretary of Health a brief description of the repulsion that he had just witnessed. Within a minute, his Blackberry rang. Pulling it out of the inner pocket of his jacket, he saw the name of Christian James on the screen. He flipped it open and listened. Not able to hear anything that Secretary James was saying amid the deafening police sirens approaching him, he powered down his mobile device.

Three squad cars with a half dozen DC cops were racing toward him—toward the crime scene. A plainclothes dressed detective, who had just closed his cell, approached Rogers. The detective inquired only about what he actually saw at the crime scene. After a few cursory questions, he was free to leave.

While walking back to the cab, he was incredulous that the detective in charge never asked his name. All he remembered saying was that he had known about Lauren from the past and they had met just fifteen minutes earlier at a local bar. Yet, the detective seemed completely disinterested in anything other than what the Surgeon General saw in the ravine where he discovered Lauren's head.

Slipping into the back seat of the cab, it dawned on him that Christian James must have intervened on his behalf with the police. *Why?* Just as perplexing to him, the detectives never even spoke to the cab driver. He looked out the back window of the taxi--in the direction of the bloodbath that he had just witnessed. Rogers then laid down the gym bag on the seat beside him and shivered despite the warm summer air, streaming in from the driver's open window.

He mumbled his destination and buckled his rear seat belt. His hand rubbed up against the polyester gym bag causing a static electrical shock to pinch him. The blood-curdling image of Lauren's head kept flashing before his eyes. The image of the razor sharp edge around the circumference of her mid-neck haunted him. *She was guillotined.*

He tried to distract himself. Kim would ask why he was so late. Not wanting to alarm her, he would tell her about a last minute meeting related to public health. He stared out the cab's side window. As the cab snaked through the streets, he counted the multi-colored fast food restaurant neon signs. The fifth sign flashed by him, closely followed by thoughts of the ghastly scene in the Park. *Kim will be furious. I*

*promised her that I would resign as Surgeon General if any danger
surfaced.*

It was clear that his family had already suffered more than needed
because of his carrying out official duties when he previously served as
the Commissioner of Health in Michigan. Now, he thought to himself,
his wife would go ballistic once she learned of matters that would suck
him into yet another potentially lethal vortex. If he told Kim what had
just happened to Lauren Timmons, she would insist that he resign as
Surgeon General. *I can't do that*, he thought. *Lauren gave her life for
what was in that gym bag. I have a duty to the American public to find
out if she was telling the truth about NeoBloc!*

Nothing would stand in his way. Not even Kim, his best friend and
closest confidant.

***

In a moderate state of nausea, he arrived in front of his two-story
brick faced townhouse. He snatched Lauren's package off the seat. The
cabbie slid open the bulletproof plastic window separating the back of
the cab from the front seat. Rogers handed him two twenty dollar bills.

Exiting the taxi, he caught a glimpse of Kim in the front window.
She was gaping down at him, her hands resting on both hips. A deep
frown creased her forehead. Her eyes protruded outward, sending out a
cold stare. It was not the first time he had seen her look that way.

While standing underneath the street light on Decatur Place, he
found himself holding the gym bag tightly against his chest---as if it
were filled with rare coins. His back to Kim, he thought of what he
would say when he greeted her. *Lord knows, I can't involve her. It
could be dangerous!*

Still facing the driver, he wondered why the cabbie did not pull
away. The front window of the cab lowered. The dark skinned middle-
aged husky man turned his neck to Rogers.

"Hey doc, got a second? I need to talk with you," the cabbie said in
a gravelly voice with a distinct Middle Eastern accent.

He bent down on both knees to be eye-level with the driver. "Who
said I was a doc?"

The bald headed rotund driver turned his back on the Surgeon
General and seemed to be fumbling with something on the passenger
side of the front seat. In one rapid blurry motion, Rogers caught just a
glimpse of a hand-held object. Caught by surprise, the camera flash
temporarily blinded him. Stars blinked before his eyes. The burning
rubber of the speeding cab gave off an odor. He glanced up at the front
window of his home. Kim was no longer watching.

******

Rogers poked his head inside the front door of their townhouse while leaving his precious cargo on the outside landing. Kim was nowhere in sight. He heard her footsteps moving about the kitchen, twenty feet down the hallway. With the coast clear, he snatched the gym bag and safely deposited it in the back of the foyer closet. He quietly closed the front door.

"Honey, I'm home." Upon entering the kitchen, he saw his wife's face. It was a mass of knots. Without a doubt, she was in a mood to pounce---on him.

"Jonathan, where the hell have you been?"

"I've been working." He tried to plant a kiss on her cheek but she swiftly pulled away. "I left a voice message on our landline to tell you that I was working late."

Kim backed away from him and returned to preparing her nightly green tea. Once the cup was in the microwave, she turned on her heels to face him. Sarcastically, she snickered, "Working late, my eye! I called your office an hour ago. There was no answer on even your private line."

"Something came up at the last minute. I had an emergency business meeting in Georgetown." He cornered her and gave her a weak embrace, from which she clumsily slipped away for the second time.

"Jonathan, with your job, there's always something." Her mouth twisted a hard right turn. "I'm sure that it's got something to do with confidential government business and you can't tell me anything."

He kissed her tenderly on the side of her neck. "It is top secret."

Squirming away from him once again, she asked, "Have you had dinner?"

"I'm not very hungry."

Kim half cocked her head in looking at him. "Now, I know you're lying."

Rogers grinned. "Honey, I didn't want you to bother but now that you mentioned it, could you please fix me a cup of soup? I'm not that hungry. Maybe I can stomach something light. It's been a really rough day."

"Chicken soup OK?"

"Sure." Rogers felt his stomach rumble. "So, is there anything worthwhile on TV tonight?"

"I'm sure that you'll want to catch the end of the baseball game. The Yankees are in town." She plopped down on the couch. "But then, I've also been in town all week myself," she said sarcastically. "Baseball games appear to get more attention---than me."

Not taking the bait, he walked into the den to turn on the TV. His face brightened once he saw the score. "I love to root against them."

"Forgot to make your soup," she said in an off- hand manner. "I'll make it now. It will be ready in a few minutes."

I have to see what's in the gym bag. Just before leaving the living room, he peeked back over his shoulder to see Kim grabbing a can of soup from the kitchen cabinet. While heading toward the foyer, he hollered, "I just need to finish up a few minutes of work in the study. Then I'll get the soup and join you in the den to watch the game. "

He back pedaled down the hallway and plucked the gym bag from the closet. After tip toeing another half -dozen steps to his study, he softly closed the door behind him. *Not much time.*

Rogers sat behind his antique maple wood desk and anxiously opened the gym bag. He pulled out several two-inch manila folders. He stacked the three folders on his desk. The one on top was titled *DCP market plan for pipeline products.* He perused it quickly before flipping through the second folder. After his eyes glazed over reading an endless string of numbers in the DCP financial projections for pipeline products, he dropped it on his desk.

The last folder at the bottom of the pile displayed large red capitalized letters. *Confidential.* The title of the report was *DCP Monkey Research Summary on NeoBloc.* He flipped through a few pages before reading it. However, he did make a mental note of a hardly readable doctor's signature. At the bottom of each page in the right lower corner, he confirmed a doctor's signature, scribbled in blue ink.

About to read the monkey research summary, he heard a squeak of the hallway floorboards. As fast as he could, he stuffed all three folders into his side desk drawer. Just as the door was opening, he yanked the gym bag from the desktop to the floor. Looking up, he met her mistrustful gaze and felt his face turn flush.

Kim's voice had an accusatory edge. "Where did you get that cute little *DC Sports Club* gym bag?"

He smiled sheepishly.

"Don't give me that look. I saw you before. You were trying to hide it from me when you got out of the taxi."

"A colleague gave it to me to carry my work papers."

Kim snickered, "A bag with pink and white stripes. I don't think they are your colors dear." She sighed deeply. "We'll talk about it in the morning. I'm very tired. So, are you finally done working for tonight?"

He nodded.

"Your soup's waiting for you."

"I'm coming. Let's watch an inning or two of the game before we go to bed. I'm pretty wasted myself"

She headed back into the den, next to the kitchen. In the meantime, he locked his desk drawer and placed the key underneath the desk lamp. Before leaving the room, he shut the slightly ajar front window and fully drew the blinds. He headed for the den. Upon seeing him walk into the room, Kim stared at his empty hands.

"Forget something?"

He smiled. He pivoted back into the kitchen and after a quick pick up of his dinner, he joined her on the couch---bowl in hand. After taking two sips, it felt as though a vice had gripped his stomach. He put the bowl on the side table and began watching the game.

"Not very hungry, I see."

"Guess not." The gruesome sight of Lauren's head kept flashing before him. His mind wandered. He stood to stretch; doing anything to divert his mind from the reoccurring flashback. "I have some early meetings tomorrow."

"You're acting pretty antsy tonight. Is anything wrong?"

"No, it's just the usual pressures at work."

He began pacing around the den. Glancing back at the TV, he clapped loudly when a Yankee batter struck out. He faked a yawn. Kim followed in short order.

"Just so you know, I was really worried about you when I couldn't reach you earlier."

He reached out for her hands, pulling her up and toward him. He hugged her and whispered in her ear, "Don't be. I can take care of myself."

She snorted, "Who will take care of me?" Kim broke the embrace, pulling back. "I'm picking up vibes that I don't like. You better not be starting up again with anything that will put our lives at risk. We went through enough of that last year! We are not going down that road anymore."

"Kim, that's all behind us."

She shot him a look of disbelief. "Then why can't I forget those awful days? When you were the Commissioner of Health, you were always on some kind of crusade to save Michigan –to save the whole country. You were lucky to have survived. Actually, we're all lucky to have survived, our daughter, me, and you."

"Things are different now. I feel it in my bones."

"Listen to me. No one is safe when you go against the flow—even now when you're working with an honest President."

"Especially-- the time when I was shot while working for a President who was less than honest."

"For starters---you were just walking along Pennsylvania Avenue after meeting with our not so nice former President. And a few minutes later, you're lying on the sidewalk---bleeding profusely, shot in the chest twice by a high powered rifle."

His eyes flashed. "Those who did despicable things to us are still in jail or dead!"

Kim fired back. "Are they?"

He softened his voice. "Believe me; things are different under President Williams."

She began walking toward the staircase leading up to the bedrooms, holding the TV remote in her hand. "In my opinion, all political leaders are mixed up in some way with unsavory characters." She looked over her shoulder at him. "And, let's not rehash all the other times you were almost killed. And let's not even mention what happened to our daughter or me."

He gently placed his hand on her shoulder. "Those days are over. We're safe now."

Kim ascended the staircase. He was barely a half step behind her. As if it were a baton, she passed the TV remote to him behind her back.

A roar from the Yankee game stopped him in his tracks. He looked at the set and saw the final score. After a pump of his fist high into the air, he shouted, "Now, I can sleep in peace," and clicked off the remote.

Already at the top of the stairs, Kim looked down at him. Hearing his comment, she asked, "What the hell does that supposed to mean?"

He let out a huge guffaw. "The Yankees just lost."

"Jonathan, it's not funny. We are having a serious conversation. You know I worry about these things. If I see anything like what we experienced last year, you're resigning your post as Surgeon General and we're going back to Michigan. Do you hear me?"

He trotted up the remainder of the stairs and grabbed her hand. "Of course, dear." They walked toward their bedroom. His hand tickled her side. "Bet I'll fall asleep seconds after my head hits the pillow."

She sighed. "You always do."

***

Lying down beside her, he worried that she was all riled up over him coming home late with the crazy colored gym bag and would have trouble falling asleep. He turned to his side and lay motionless. His thoughts were racing. *I must read that confidential NeoBloc report.* Every minute seemed like an eternity. She tossed about, snuggling close to him. He flipped over to face her and after massaging her back, he kissed her shoulder. Kim's breathing cadence began to slow.

He kept his eyes wide open locked on her, lest he would himself fall asleep. Careful not to stir until he heard her rhythmic breathing, the confidential folder revealing the DCP research on *NeoBloc* would be his late night reading. He could hardly wait.

Rogers quietly slipped out of bed. In his mind, the legacy of a dead woman was calling his name. A Doctor's Choice Product insider beheaded just minutes after speaking with him at *Hurleys*. *Who else knows what Lauren told me? President Williams believes the vaccine is the savior of America. What if Lauren is right?* Rogers carefully closed the bedroom door.

******

Rogers headed straight for the front room study, tip toeing in his bare feet, careful to avoid a few well-known squeaky hardwood steps at the end of the staircase. He entered the study. Closing the door was an option that he rejected; not wanting to risk making the slightest of noises that might awaken his wife.

Kim was a light sleeper. She would frequently hear all sorts of house noises at night. Many a night, she had awakened him--asking him to check out the house. For each of her requests, he always complied, holding a small hammer that he always kept under his side of their bed as a weapon-- just in case she was right. For added protection, Kim insisted on keeping an unloaded shotgun on the high shelf in the downstairs hall closet, next to a box of shells.

He clicked on the desk lamp and sat down facing his desk. A cool breeze struck the back of his neck. Whirling around, his eyes popped. The front window was open by six inches or so. The blinds on the window were now raised. He thought back, retracing his steps. His heart began pounding. Fear overtook logic.

Instinctively, he picked up the receiver to dial 911 but he dismissed his impulse and gently placed it back in its holder. *I can't let the police come and confiscate this gym bag before I even know what's in these folders.*

Uneasily, the Surgeon General walked toward the open window. He lowered the blinds and peeked through a slat. Decatur Place seemed as normal as any other night. With the nearby streetlight burning brightly, he saw no one. He looked downward. *What the--?* Below his window, eight feet higher than street level, was a four-foot wide trampoline.

To his left, down the street, he heard a motorcycle engine revving up. The top of his head began to throb. He backpedaled toward his desk. *Got to call 911!* Before he could turn toward the desk phone, he heard a thunderous crash. Propelled at him were shards of glass. Instinctively, he shielded his face with both hands. The razor-sharp glass fragments tore into the skin on the back of his hands and forearm. He bit his tongue—keeping silent.

In his bare feet, he continued backing away from the window, careful not to step over any of the jagged glass rubble, carpeting the floor. Blood dripped from the back of his hands and from the front of his neck. A second later, he heard a squeak outside the study.

The door opened fully. It was Kim. She was standing in the doorway, holding a Remington pump action shotgun. It was pointed directly at him. Her eyes seemed distant, unfocused and her face seemed clearly contorted.

He swallowed hard. "My God, what are you doing?"

Tears were cascading down her cheeks. She screamed, "No more. I'm ready to pull this trigger." Visibly shaking as if she were buck naked in a freezing rainstorm, Kim waved the shotgun in an erratic arc. She aimed the barrel at his chest.

Rogers felt his gut twisting. He pleaded slowly, "Honey, put the shotgun down. Everything is OK." Blood dropped every few seconds from his wounds onto the floor.

She shouted, her voice cracking, "Are you crazy?" Her eyes darted to the glass strewn around the floor and the cracked window. "Do you call this OK?"

"I was about to dial 911."

"Jonathan, I can't take this anymore. Our marriage is a never-ending dramatic movie. This has to end---it has to end! Whatever it takes, I'm going to make it end---NOW."

His chest heaving, he tried to slow his breathing cycles. "I'm so sorry that I've put you through all of this."

"Look at you, covered in blood." She advanced toward him. She began hollering, "Since you can't make this crap stop then I WILL---- STARTING NOW."

"Please put the shotgun down," he quietly repeated. He gently patted the air in front of him, palms facing downward. "It's OK."

The gun barrel was now pointing at his genitals. He took a step toward her. Kim turned her head away. Her finger tightly held the trigger. She began to tremble. "Jonathan, I can't---"

Her knees buckled. The shotgun slipped from her grasp, landing with a loud thud. He glanced at the shotgun on the floor and staggered backwards before yelling out in excruciating pain. *My foot! My foot!* While balancing on his right leg, he pulled his other foot toward him. He looked down. A two-inch triangular shaped glass fragment had become lodged in his left heel. Scrunching his face, he plucked out the glass sliver.

His eyes drifted toward the shotgun. "Help me!"

She seemed to stumble forward. Her voice was threatening. "Don't move."

He froze, trying to balance himself on his right leg. The sharp barking of a dog pierced the air. With each passing moment, the howling grew louder, coming from the street behind them. Watching her bend down on one knee toward the shotgun, his pulse raced. "Leave the shotgun where it is---do not pick it up!"

Despite his plea, Kim picked up the weapon and pointed it at the shattered window. She looked at where he was standing and yelled out, "Don't move. Your right foot---"

Rogers glimpsed downward. A half- inch from his right toe laid a stainless steel razor blade broad head. He looked up at Kim. An inch hole on the near wall behind her caught his eye. *The broad head must have struck something at an angle and bounced off.* Instantly, he jerked his right foot up and painfully balanced himself on the ball of his bleeding left foot. Kim grabbed the feathered end of the bolt and held it out in front of her, with the Remington still dangling from her left hand.

Black masking tape circling the shaft of the arrow caught his attention. He peeled the tape back; unwinding it with each turn. He discovered a white scrap of paper glued to the body of the projectile. A message printed in red ink caught his eye. He read it aloud, 'Kim Rogers, we hope this arrow finds Dr. Rogers's punctured heart. Death to the both of you!'

Kim cried out, "Last year they used an Uzi against you. Now they're shooting a crossbow bolt at you. What's next? A bazooka? A nuclear warhead?"

Rogers grabbed the shotgun as it began to slip from her weakening grip. "When you first came in here, I thought that you saw something and shot at the window."

Shaking her head, she fired back, "It had to have been the arrow that crashed through the window."

He shot her a guarded sideways glance. "I must say, for a moment or two, I thought you were going to shoot me. I've never seen that chilling look in your eyes before—like a lion about to pounce on its prey."

"Are you nuts? I woke up and reached over for you. When I realized you were gone, I ran down the stairs toward the study, not knowing what to expect. I grabbed the shotgun from the hall closet when I heard the window glass shattering." Kim put her arms around his waist, resting her head on his chest. "I love you."

Rogers kissed her head. "Of course, honey, of course you would never do anything to hurt me. I must be losing it."

Kim glanced over at the window. "Why are the blinds drawn?"

"The window was open. I thought about calling 911 but I couldn't because----"

Then, he remembered. Rogers broke from her grasp and walked quickly over to his chair, carefully avoiding the strewn pieces of glass on the floor. Leaning forward, he tilted the desk lamp to uncover the key. After unlocking it, he pulled out the drawer. Only two folders remained. *The file on NeoBloc research is gone!*

CHAPTER THREE

The following morning, Rogers found himself almost jogging through the complex of federal buildings of the Department of Health and Human Services. He carried the DCP marketing and financial folders in his briefcase.

Despite Kim's vehement protestations, he had steadfastly refused to report the robbery of the data and this latest attempt on his life to the authorities. His wife had suggested a local detective, Mr. Ryan Darden, whom they knew from their past ordeals. However, Rogers's gut told him to trust no one at this time. Not even the police. He had been down this road before—far too many times.

Yet, he felt guilty for not mentioning Lauren's tragedy to Kim. Usually, telling her anything that was not confidential, this time he held back and begged her to have faith in him. Though the recurrent tension between them kicked up several notches at this morning's breakfast, he insisted that his wait and see approach was the best for both of them.

One thing was certain. The Surgeon General knew that he needed time to gather further intelligence—to find the stolen DCP *NeoBloc* Research file. In the meantime, he cranked up his personal antennae—placing his senses on full alert for anything—from anyone!

Just a few steps outside of his office, he greeted his long time assistant. Sally told him that his boss, Secretary of Health Christian James, was on his way over to speak with him. He hustled to his office and quickly deposited the two DCP folders in his file cabinet. After locking the drawer, he trotted back to his desk. Just as he sat down, he overheard Sally speaking with the Secretary outside his office.

He looked up just as the well-built, handsome Secretary of Health pranced through. "Morning Jonathan," he chimed. Closing the door behind him, the boss appeared to be his typically relaxed and outgoing self. Yet, given the circumstances of their somber conversation about Lauren the previous evening, James's current demeanor perplexed him.

His boss threw down the morning edition of the *Washington Post* on his desk. Rogers cringed at seeing the headline. An old picture of Lauren Timmons in her college gown filled the top right side of the front page.

The Secretary sat down on the other side of the desk, directly facing him, eyes locked. His boss vigorously rubbed his chin but remained silent. His vacant gaze centered on the far window, behind Rogers's desk.

Rogers broke the palpable strain of the moment. "Christian, I had just spoken to this poor woman only fifteen minutes before I found her. I'm horrified that she was beheaded!"

James's voice was measured, reassuring. "Look, you heard a woman scream. You stopped to help. You stumbled upon a murder scene. You acted as a Good Samaritan. You called 911. Her death has nothing to do with you or this administration. In case you are wondering, there was no reason to get your name involved. You're the Surgeon General. Don't worry; I took good care of you. And, after talking with me, the DC police believe that they are working on a random homicide."

The Secretary stood and began walking toward the far side window. Rogers swiveled his chair, tracking him. "Jonathan, this day is gorgeous." He turned and leaned against the windowsill and said crisply, "Case closed."

"*We*. . . I mean *I* can't just forget about it." He thumbed through the newspaper pages, searching for the end of the story. "Does the story in the *Post* give any leads?"

"No suspects. It did mention that the police found the rest of her corpse, in several pieces, deeper into the woods. They also found the presumed murder weapon----a foreign made machete. There were no fingerprints. Probably a professional hit."

He recoiled. "Why would anyone want to kill her?"

"Jonathan, forget it. Things like this happen all the time. It could be a dozen reasons. We all have enemies."

He felt an uneasiness mounting within him, catalyzed even more so by the profoundly nonchalant attitude of his boss. "Don't you think that it's more than coincidental that a high ranking employee of Doctor's Choice Products is murdered on the same day that President Williams announces that DCP's pipeline vaccine *NeoBloc* is going to be the savior of our country."

James ignored his statement. He added a new wrinkle. "Did you know that she was recently divorced from the Governor of Michigan? Her husband may have had motive."

"I think she---." Stopping himself in mid-sentence, Rogers added, "I mean -I think the *Post* mentioned that."

A surprised look surfaced. "I must have missed that." He narrowed his wide set eyes. "To be honest, I heard about it through private sources."

His jaw tightened. "Where do we go from here?"

"What do you mean?" James began strolling back across the Surgeon General's office, toward the door.

"Where do we go with Project Moon Shot," he fired back.

His boss came to a dead halt and turned toward the Surgeon General. "We have our orders from the President. We've been instructed to do whatever it takes to facilitate the human trials for *NeoBloc*. As we discussed yesterday morning, we need to be ready for mandatory inoculation of the entire population of our country in less than twelve months."

"Christian, I understand what our mission is." He rose slowly from his seat. "But, how do we know the vaccine is safe to even test in humans?"

James, without a second of hesitation, squared up to him. No more than three feet separated them. The Secretary of Health peered deeply into his eyes. "We went over this ground at our meeting with the President. Safety checks on the monkeys revealed no problems with the vaccine."

"To be precise, that's what we were told by the President."

Rogers noticed that the Secretary's carotid arteries were rapidly pulsating. His boss began to backpedal toward the door. "Apparently, the monkeys that were exposed to radiation haven't developed cancer and all are reported to be doing fine."

He flashed back to what Lauren had told him. Softening his face, he asked, "Have you actually seen the monkey data?"

"No. However, Sean Parker, the CEO of DCP, shared the executive summary with me. Everything appeared in order."

He persisted. "But what if the monkey data that Sean Parker showed you is inaccurate?"

James stopped on a dime. His eyes danced wildly. "Hey doc, our job is to follow the President's lead."

Exasperated, he ran his right hand through his closely cropped wavy silver tinged brown hair. "Our job is to seek the truth so we can do what is best for the American people."

"We already have the truth."

Rogers raised his voice. "What we have is hearsay and opinion. We must ask for proof."

His nostrils flared as his breathing took on a rapid cadence. "Jonathan, understand what I'm telling you. The CEO of DCP would know if there was a problem."

"Then, I think that I should meet with him and his top scientist." He held out his hands in front of him. "I mean----just to be sure."

James rolled his eyes before nodding in agreement. "Look, if it makes you feel any better, just do it. Let me know what you find. Talk to no one else about this. Is that clear?"

"You have my word. And, Christian; one more point."

The Secretary looked down at his watch. "Make it quick."

"The President has asked me to go along with her to see hospitalized victims in one of the cities that suffered a nuclear attack."

"Thanks for telling me that. I didn't know. It's a great idea. What city?"

"The one hit with the full nuclear blast--Minneapolis."

"Better you than me." James grimaced and walked out of the office.

He pressed the intercom. "Sally, please set up a meeting for me to meet as soon as possible with the CEO and his top scientist at DCP."

"Will do, Dr. Rogers. I just hope their management has changed for the better compared to last year. Their former CEO, Zach Miller, was insane."

"For sure. Well, the good news is Zach Miller is dead. And, I'm sure that DCP is the better for it."

"When do you want to fly up to Michigan? As you know, you and President Williams will be leaving for Minnesota tomorrow. I arranged your full itinerary. You'll board the Presidential helicopter at the White House at nine. You'll then fly to Andrews where Air Force One will take you and the President to the Minneapolis-Saint Paul airport. A train of limos under Secret Service Protection will drive you and the President to the Medical Center."

"Tomorrow will be rough. I'll need a short break after traveling with the President before going to Michigan. Set up a late morning meeting for my visit to DCP –about three days after I return from Minneapolis."

******

Rogers understood the politics at the Department of Health. It was apparent to him that Christian James was not about to upset the President. His boss would deliver the *NeoBloc* vaccine to the American population as directed. The Secretary would do everything in his power to surpass the President's twelve-month deadline for full inoculation of all citizens.

Taking a notepad from his top drawer, Rogers began formulating questions for Sean Parker. Lauren Timmons had given her life to make sure that he was aware of what she claimed to be the vaccine's lethal effect on the monkeys in the animal trials. It would be up to him to prove whether she was telling the whole truth.

CHAPTER FOUR

Rogers buckled himself into a well-padded leather aisle seat aboard the US 101 Lockheed helicopter. With three high-powered engines and a state of the art communication system, he fully appreciated why one Texas Senator had once labeled the helicopter, "An Oval Office in the sky."

He had climbed aboard Marine One only a few minutes earlier. Rogers noted the intentionally built clone of Marine One off to the side on the south lawn. He was keenly aware that both well-armed helicopters always flew in tandem to try to hide the exact whereabouts of the President. Trying to distract himself from the disheartening business that lay ahead of him and the President, he began reading a book about how to live a longer and more productive life through lifestyle changes. He pinched his belly fat and promised himself that he would shed twenty pounds before the holidays. Rogers thought about the Christmas cheesecake that Kim served every holiday. He slammed his book shut and chuckled just before he heard a fleet of footsteps approaching him.

Several naval officers walked in single file down the aisle. He tossed his book onto the empty seat next to him and spotted President Jane Williams heading toward him. After a brief nod, she unloaded her manila folders onto the adjacent seat before she strapped herself into the seat directly opposite him.

He observed a slight tremor of her hands and an unsettled look on her face. She leaned over to the unoccupied seat closest to the window and fumbled with several of her folders. After selecting a particular one, she placed it on her lap while staring straight ahead, appearing to be looking right past him, lost in thought. A minute later, she seemed to emerge from her self-induced fog and began reading the first page of the folder in front of her.

While he thought of saying something to the President, the helicopter blades revved up. The rapid lift off from the pad sent his heart racing. Acrophobia was still on his bucket list of fears to overcome. Fretfully, Rogers looked out his portal and saw the sister "Marine One" helicopter a quarter of a mile off in the distance, chopping alongside the real number one. As Marine One banked hard left, Williams dropped her folder onto the adjacent seat and finally focused her troubled gaze on the Surgeon General.

"Dr. Rogers, I'm sorry that I've been so preoccupied. Thank you for joining me." She paused, glancing for a moment out her window. "I hope you had a full breakfast. I believe as this day unfolds that you and I will need every ounce of energy that we can both muster."

In the reflection of the sun on her face, he observed deep wrinkles that mimicked miniscule moon craters under her weary looking eyes. "Madam President, you are to be commended for your compassion and commitment to do what's right for our citizens."

She bent the fingers on her right hand so that it resembled a claw. Williams used her newly formed tool to point at him. "No, it is the American people who are to be applauded for their forbearance in not impeaching me. At least, Congress has not called for a vote as yet."

He smiled. "You're doing your best. It's all anyone can do."

She dismissed his compliment by repeatedly waving her hand, palm down, in front of her chest. She then picked up another binder---the manila colored thick folder. He had seen the same glossy cover before. It was easily recognizable to him. It was her daily national security briefing. Christian James had once shown it to him when there was an initial confidential report of Anthrax found inside a letter mailed to a Montana post office box.

The President twisted her mouth toward the window and seemed to have developed a habit of smacking her lips. Saying nothing further, she remained glued to her national security reading for the rest of their Marine One trip.

***

Rogers obsessed on his gaze of the three-story control tower at Andrews Air Force Base. A long time ago, he remembered speaking face to face with air traffic controllers on his Boy Scout troop's trip to the JFK International airport. He was nine at the time. From where he stood in those days, the control tower had seemed even taller than the Empire State Building. The tower brought back memories---good memories.

The flight to the Minneapolis-St Paul airport would take less than two hours. Seated in the rear of Air Force One, he reviewed his clinical notes. Through personal research of the medical facts related to nuclear blasts, he confirmed the veracity of the subject matter. While turning the second page of his notepad, he felt a light tap on his left shoulder.

He looked up to see a burly Secret Service agent. "Dr. Rogers, the President will see you in her office once the pilot gives us permission to move about the plane. Please be prepared by gathering your belongings at this time."

He read the nametag a tad before the agent strapped himself into the adjacent seat. Minutes later, Air Force One rolled down the tarmac as Rogers engaged in small talk with Agent Greg Lockwood.

***

After being escorted the twenty feet or so down the corridor to the Presidential office, Agent Lockwood opened the door for Dr. Rogers. Williams was strapped at her waist in her bucket seat, sitting behind a conference table on the far side of the mahogany paneled room. Her expression was pensive. The President looked over and waved him to come toward her as Agent Lockwood locked the door from the inside.

"Doctor, please take this seat next to me."

He followed her command.

She began as soon as he pulled the safety harness tightly around his waist. "As my Surgeon General, I expect your office to be my clearinghouse for what is called 'Medical NBC.' As you know, Congress uses the term to denote the biomedical effects of nuclear, biological, and chemical weapons and agents. As such, I hold you accountable to keep me, the nation's physicians, as well as the general public, informed of any clinical issues related to these weapons of mass destruction."

"I understand Madame President."

"Please brief me on what I should expect to see at the hospital---and don't hold back anything."

He tried to avoid gawking at the fatigue bags under her eyes, so prominent in the well-lit room. "It will be grim. And, please feel free to interrupt me at any time for questions."

Williams issued a stern order. "Agent Lockwood, please wait outside the door."

Folding his hands on top of the glass covered table, the Surgeon General waited for the President to speak.

After the Agent had departed and she heard the door lock, she motioned toward him. "Please begin," she said crisply.

"We'll be visiting the Regional Medical Center of Minnesota. It is thirty-five miles from where a five-kiloton uranium nuclear device exploded under the arch of the Intercity Bridge. The Medical Center is upwind from the detonation but there are no current dangerous levels of radiation in the area."

Williams narrowed her eyes. "Dr. Rogers, you don't know this but my sister died in this attack. This particular attack is extremely personal for me. Please accept that I need to help many others in her memory."

"I believe that I understand how you may feel."

She lowered her head, staring at the conference room phone in front of her on the desk. "Please continue."

"Several patients who have survived the nuclear blast have agreed to meet with us. They are suffering from acute radiation syndrome."

She gestured with her right hand, seemingly inviting him to tell it like it is. "Doctor, just let me know what to expect medically when we see these people."

"Madame President, these patients were directly exposed to the gamma rays from the nuclear fallout. They received approximately three hundred rems of radiation. To put that into perspective, they received a dose similar to those within one to two kilometers from the epicenter at Nagasaki. At that distance, from scientific analyses on the data from Chernobyl and Hiroshima, there is an overall thirty-five percent fatality rate within several months."

"In human terms, just tell me what we'll see." Her upper lip stiffened just as the teeth parted. "I don't want arcane scientific facts. Tell me what to expect to actually see."

"Madame President, these patients have suffered from skin burns, nausea, vomiting, diarrhea, bleeding from the nose, mouth, and rectum, loss of body hair, and overwhelming fatigue. They have also experienced a massive loss of white blood cells in their blood so they can no longer fight off life threatening infections. In just the last week alone, the Regional Medical Center reported seventy-five deaths in a cohort of ninety-eight patients who were much closer to the blast than the patients who we'll see today"

The President held up her hand and interrupted. "How far from ground zero were these patients who died within hours to days of the blast?" Williams grabbed the side arms of her seat, bracing for his response.

"They were all less than one kilometer from ground zero. They all received at least twice as much radiation as the ones we will be seeing today."

"How did they die?" She leaned forward, focusing on every word.

He noticed a coarse quivering of her jaw and a series of repetitive blinks. "Most of them suffered from massive infection and internal bleeding unresponsive to intense supportive care."

Williams closed her eyes for a moment. "Go on." She kept them shut, seemingly, as she was picturing what he was describing.

"It's a very painful death although I'm sure they received heavy doses of narcotics to make life as comfortable as possible."

Opening her eyes, Williams wiped away a tear. "That's not how my sister died. I learned that she was exiting off the Inter City Bridge the moment the nuclear device exploded."

The President covered her face with both hands. He remained silent. Seconds seemed like minutes. She grabbed a tissue from her pocketbook and blew her nose. "I've been told that she was vaporized. She was gone in a second." Williams sucked in a deep breath. "At least she didn't suffer."

To his surprise, her eyes looked as though they were on fire. Each capillary in the conjunctiva surrounding her brown pupil appeared gorged with blood. A second flow of tears did not put out the blaze. She looked back at him, composing herself while blinking wildly.

"I'm sorry."

"No need to be. It's completely understandable."

She picked up a glass and took a long drink of water. Williams wiped her face with a tissue. "So, where were we?"

Rogers nodded, giving her a few more moments.

Williams cleared her throat. She folded her hands on the table. He noticed how tightly her fingers were interlocked. She began, "What's being done for the survivors that we'll see today?"

"They are being supported with intravenous fluids, nutritional feedings, and antibiotics. Each of them is receiving a specific medication to raise their white count. In addition, everyone received potassium iodide to reduce their chance of developing thyroid cancer from the radiation exposure." He paused, waiting for the information to be absorbed.

Rogers continued, "Each victim also received a new drug which is in the class of drugs called protectans. This type of medication suppresses the effect of radiation to cause cell death, especially to fast growing cells in the gastrointestinal tract. Some patients may require around the clock pain killers."

"That's heartbreaking!"

"Recovery can be quite painful. One of the most gruesome effects of this type of nuclear exposure is that the uranium replaces the calcium in their teeth and bones. There have been reports that several patients have had a tooth snapped off like a dried twig just eating their morning cereal."

Holding her chin up with folded hands underneath as support, she asked, "What about the risk of these people developing cancer at a later time from the radiation?"

"Research from the Life Span Study of people exposed to atomic bombs that were dropped sixty years ago on Japan is archived at our National Academy of Sciences. The percent of those exposed to radiation that went on to develop cancers varied according to how close they were to the explosion. Within one kilometer from the center, of those who did not die instantly from the blast wave that can approach a wind gust of four hundred miles per hour, almost one in five survivors went on to develop cancer during their lifetime. For those victims within two kilometers from the blast, one in ten survivors developed cancer."

Williams sat up straight. "Remind me again. How close to ground zero were the people that we're going to see today?"

"Each of them was approximately two kilometers from the blast. If any of them survive their severe radiation sickness, they'll have a one in ten chance of developing leukemia within the next three years or a similar likelihood of having a malignant solid tumor sometime in their lifetime."

"Tell me about the so called "dirty bombs" that were exploded in the other nine cities before the uranium bomb that struck Minneapolis."

"The cesium that was released from that type of bomb is also highly radioactive and substantially increases the rate of developing cancer. The prevalence of cancer in populations exposed to cesium is less than populations exposed to isotopes that are more dangerous like uranium and plutonium. Hopefully, we won't see further exposure of our population to any further nuclear fallout."

"Unfortunately another nuclear attack is not only possible, but likely. We must utilize all technologies at our disposal to vaccinate all Americans against developing cancers. It's too late for those already exposed. My understanding is that the *NeoBloc* vaccine only works if received prior to exposure to radiation. We must protect the remaining ninety five percent of the population who have not yet been exposed before America is hit again."

"The issue on who should receive the vaccine is complex. Effectiveness of a safe vaccine might depend on the degree of prior nuclear exposure. Therefore, the benefit of giving the vaccine to folks already exposed to lower doses might be possible. My concern is that the risks of taking a vaccine such as *NeoBloc* outweigh the benefits for any population, given what we know so far."

Her lips formed a snarl. "Why are you so skeptical? This is not new science. Isn't there already another vaccine that has been approved by the FDA to prevent cancer in people exposed to a specific type of virus?"

"Correct."

"So the technology exists."

"The scientific answer to your question is that it depends. Dealing with the effects of nuclear radiation on cells is much more complicated and has not been as fully tested as it is for the effects of viruses on cells."

"I'm certainly no medical expert nor is the Secretary. James is a political bureaucrat. However, he is very good at what he does. On the other hand, you're a physician and an experienced former State Commissioner of Health. You are the Surgeon General. You are my expert in these matters. I'm charging you to collaborate with Secretary James to ensure that the *NeoBloc* vaccine is safe in humans. And the final recommendation on whether to approve the vaccine for mass deployment to eligible Americans will be yours even if the FDA approves it."

"I won't disappoint you, Madam President."

"This is not about me. I'm talking about a couple of hundred million Americans. Make no mistake about what is at stake here."

"You can count on me to do what's right."

"That's why I appointed you to your critical position. In the final analysis, our decisions will decide their fate. We must not fail them."

***

Rogers donned his long white coat just outside of room four twenty two. Walking into the semi-private room a few yards ahead of the President, Rogers noted that the bed nearest the door was unoccupied. Fresh white sheets, neatly tucked in, indicated to him a recent vacancy of the bed. Exclusively dedicated in caring for the victims of the nuclear bomb, he knew what the empty bed had signified.

A blue striped white curtain separated the two beds, pulled around to cover the bed closest to the window. He heard two voices, almost whispering to each other. After turning to face the President, she signaled for him to take the lead in the introductions. He loudly cleared his throat to give the patients several seconds of advance warning. "Excuse us," he added while pulling the curtain back to reveal the origin of the voices.

A young woman in her early thirties and a child of no more than five were huddling under a gray and white hospital sheet that covered them up to their necks. Rogers met their soulful eyes with a broad smile. Two bottles of fluid hung on an intravenous pole, each dripping into separate plastic lines that disappeared under the sheet, into each patient's veins. A white paste covered the left side of each of their faces, surrounded by what appeared to be a severe case of sunburn on remaining patches of skin. Crusty blackened scabs were scattered around their high cheekbones. A sterile gauze pad covered the center of the child's forehead. Several jagged lacerations were scattered about the neck and face of both. The woman had a deep cut covered with a clear colored ointment, sewn with six stitches, just below her left ear. A moment later, the young girl pulled the sheet completely over her head.

The Surgeon General began softly, "Good Morning! My name is Dr. Rogers." He turned toward his chief. "I would like you to meet President Williams."

The young girl poked her head out from beneath the sheet. Tears began to flow down her reddened cheeks. The child pressed her face into the woman's chest.

"Mommy, no more needles. No more doctors."

He took a step forward and presented his empty hands. "See. No needles." He softened his face, forcing a smile. "We're only here to talk with you."

She made a face at him. Sadly, she asked, "Do you promise?"

He covered his heart. "I promise."

The young girl surfaced a fluffy teddy bear that she had been hiding beneath the sheet. Gradually, she seemed to be finding her comfort zone. The woman managed a slight grin.

Williams asked, "What's your teddy's name?"

"Waggels"

"That's a nice name. He looks like he loves you very much."

The girl giggled. "I love him."

The President reached out to shake hands with the stuffed animal. The girl held up her teddy as Williams shook the right furry paw of Waggles.

She smiled. "Mr. Waggles, I hope you voted for me in the last election."

The girl laughed and tightly hugged her teddy. "He seems to like you."

The woman put out her right arm and shook hands with the President. "I'm Cassie. This is my five-year-old daughter. Her name is Emma."

He asked, "How are you both feeling?"

"We're hanging in there. Some days are better than others," she huffed a bit as if she were struggling to catch each breath. A moment later, Cassie grabbed her stomach. She was now grimacing. Rogers pressed the nurse call button on the side rail of the hospital bed. He motioned to the President to take a seat on the chair next to the bed, just as he heard footsteps coming into the room.

"Cassie, what's wrong?" the twenty-something nurse asked. "You look like you could use a pain-killer shot."

"I'm OK." Cassie managed a weak smile. "Jody, can you take Emma for a walk around the hallway? I need to talk to the President and Dr. Rogers in private."

The nurse beamed at Emma. Holding out her hand, she asked, "Want to get some cookies at the nurses' station? I think I can drum up some milk."

Emma's face brightened. "Do you have animal crackers?"

"Just lions, tigers and elephants."

Emma laughed a second but then settled into a serious mood as the nurse carefully pulled back the sheets. Jody avoided touching the girl's arms, covered with a pinkish medication, and pockmarked with sores covered with a brownish ointment. The nurse reached out for the young girl's hands, pulling her gently to her feet. Jody pushed the IV pole ahead of them. Emma walked alongside with Waggels in tow.

Before leaving the bedside, the nurse glanced at the woman. "Cassie, let me call another nurse to get you something for your pain."

"Not yet. It's only been an hour since my last shot."

The nurse smiled. "You're a trooper. Call us if you need us."

Williams waited until the pair was out of sight. "She's so cute. I'm sure that you are so proud to have a daughter like Emma."

"She's all I have left. Before the nuclear blast, I was six months pregnant." Cassie forcefully blew her nose.

"My husband was killed instantly. Joe was swept away by the nuclear blast wave into the street where a pickup truck hit him so hard that his broken body flew twenty feet in the air." Cassie slammed her eyes tightly shut. Rogers noted her contorted face; the deep pain she was enduring was self-evident.

He glanced back at the President. A tear rimmed her lower lid. Seconds later, Cassie's eyes flashed open, directed like a laser beam at the Surgeon General. Her breathing cycles seemed to double in frequency. He gently put his hand on her shoulder. "We are so sorry to hear about your losses."

"You're sorry. Everybody says they are so sorry that half of my family was wiped out in a second." She inhaled deeply, slowing releasing the air. "Doctor, Emma and I have a one in three chance that we won't make it out of the hospital. My doctors told me this morning. My white count is so low that without these antibiotics, I'd probably already be dead as well. My daughter and I might only have a ten percent chance of developing cancer even if we live. Those are the cold hard facts."

Rogers spoke in a quiet tone. "I understand. Life is not fair."

Cassie screamed back at him. "You're damn right that it's not fair."

He craned his neck toward the President, hoping that she would say something. Williams spoke up quickly.

"I promise you that the Surgeon General and I will do everything that we can do to get you and Emma out of this hospital."

"Why did this happen to us?" Cassie pulled the sheet over her face. Her sobbing grew louder.

He felt his hands growing moist. "We want to help you?"

Cassie stuck her face out and glared up at him. "We had no life insurance on Joe. Soon, I'll have no health insurance. Joe's company paid for it. We can't afford it on my factory worker's salary. I spoke with the insurance company yesterday on the phone. They also said that they're sorry." She looked down at the intravenous line running into her forearm. "The bills will be mailed shortly. We'll lose our home." Cassie sobbed. "Everyone is sorry. But how do I pay the hundreds of thousands of dollars in bills. I'll have to declare bankruptcy. "

"I'll do my best to help you and Emma," he said.

Cassie shook her head. "President Williams, I need help now, not pity."

"I'll get it for you."

She tried to catch her next breath but labored somewhat. "So, how exactly are you going to help Emma and me?"

The President turned back, facing her directly. "We'll find a way, dear. We'll find a way."

"Thank you, Madame President. By the way, I voted for you in the election. I believed in you."

Williams gulped hard. She understood the past tense of the verb that Cassie just used. No words came forth from the President's mouth.

Rogers noticed the orange blossoms and pine flowers on the night table. He could see that the patient noticed his sudden floral interest.

She said sadly, "My cousin gave me those flowers. Do you know what they mean?"

Williams spoke up. "The orange blossoms signify eternal love. Pine flowers mean hope."

"You're a smart lady." Cassie reached out her hand for both Rogers and the President. "President Williams, please do whatever it takes to save us. If I die, Emma is all alone."

Williams opened her arms for a hug, holding on for almost a full minute. "I'll instruct our good doctor here to track down your insurance company. We will ensure payment of all your bills. I give you my word."

He ran his hand over the bed sheets that covered her feet. "I'll follow up with your doctors every day. As the President stated, you and Emma will walk out of the hospital as survivors with no bills."

Cassie looked at the ceiling, seemingly in prayer, not responding to the President's assurances It was hard to avoid thinking about the thousands of Cassie's that were injured during the terrorists attacks. *How many can we save?*

He ushered Williams out to the nurse's station. Jody and Emma were dunking animal crackers into a glass of milk. He glanced over to Williams. The President's face looked blotchy, beat red. She wore a forced smile, tinged with pain. Emma waved at her, laughing aloud as if she didn't have a care in world, giggling as only a child can do. She held Waggels tightly and fed him an animal cracker.

The President softly patted the child's hand. "Don't worry Emma. You and your Mom will be fine."

"What about Waggles?"

"Invite me to his next birthday."

"I'll tell Mommy."

"Take care, my child."

The Surgeon General pulled the chart of the patient in the next room that they were about to visit from the rack. After reading the living will and the do not resuscitate order plastered on the front of the chart of the thirty eight year old man, he wondered what the President would promise next. His face tightened. From a quick review of the clinical situation documented in the chart, it was doubtful that this patient would even make it another day or so.

Glancing down at the rack of the dozen or so remaining charts of victims that they would meet on this grim day, he offered, "There are thousands of Cassie's and Emma's out there. God speed that we can save as many as possible."

She replied firmly, "*NeoBloc* is our answer. It will be our Savior for millions of Americans!"

His gut twisted. *Savior vaccine? Lauren Timmons is dead. Lauren said the vaccine is a killer.* "Thank you, Madame President, for your leadership. I sincerely hope that you are right."

"For the sake of Cassie and Emma, let's all pray that I'm right."

"I'm planning a surprise visit to DCP. I'll be flying to Detroit in a couple of days."

"Please find out if this vaccine is on track to help us save America."

He whispered, "Consider it done," as he and the President walked reluctantly into the room of another gravely ill victim.

CHAPTER FIVE

The fugitive enjoyed the absolute security of living in the tiny remote village for more than a year. A dense rainforest just outside of Belmopan, Belize encircled the mile square center of the fortress. Ten dilapidated wooden buildings constructed by a former tribe who had deserted this village, formed a complete circle, surrounded by innumerable types of fauna and flora.

The two dozen inhabitants worked solely for the boss. Except for the carefully chosen medical team who had been imported to stay for only two months, the daily responsibility of everyone else was to simply to supply and maintain adequate supplies of fresh water and food as well as doing their part to uphold the highest level of security to protect the singular lord who dictated their every act.

Great planning became the hallmark of the location of his hideaway video cameras, strategically placed at the entrances of the only two narrow footpaths leading to the village captured all activity. A staff of six formed the dedicated security team charged with guarding the American renegade. They rotated twelve-hour shifts with two sets of eyes always staring at the security monitors every second of the day. Ever since the military like takeover of this stronghold, no one had ever entered the village without an explicit invitation from the fugitive. Based on the realities, as repeated many times in local lore, no one would even dare to barge in—certainly not if they ever wanted to get out alive. Several explorers, challengers to the rules, met their Creator. Dropped into unmarked graves, eaten by the termites, earthworms, and fungi on the forest floor, the slain explorers set an example that no one else dared to follow.

Accessing the village by any means other than by foot, donkey, or cycle was virtually impossible. By using these modes of transportation, the time needed to enter the inner most sanctum, from the perimeter civilizations of larger rural communities bordering the thick forest, ranged from a minimum of four hours to a maximum of eight. Even for invited guests to meet with the ruler of the citadel, it clearly was no easy task to make their way to the hideaway.

Today was an important day. The boss led the planning efforts over a period of several months. All details needed to be in perfect order so that he could undergo the major surgical procedure that would enable him to return to America. His entire future depended upon the outcome of the operation. Staffing the state of the art sterile air-conditioned suite were world-renowned physician specialists. The latest medical equipment stocked the operating room. Donkeys were the taxis of this enclave.

Rainy season had ended several weeks ago. A blazing sun broke through the early morning haze. The sweltering heat index had already reached triple digits by the time Dr. Villani sauntered into the scrub room. Around eight o' clock, an orderly wheeled the strapping middle-aged man into surgery. Fortunate to have survived a massive explosion of his Ferrari before coming to Belize, he clearly needed this plastic surgery to give him a physical appearance that even his most hated enemies would not even recognize.

The patient looked into his surgeon's eyes just before the anesthesia mask was about to be applied. "Hey doc, just do what you have to do." He put on a wry smile. "I hope you don't think that your own life depends on me making it though surgery"

"Just breathe normally, Mr. Lucas."

For one of the rare moments in his life, the soon to be Connor Lucas followed orders. He chuckled inwardly upon hearing his fake moniker. Dr. Villani promised that the swelling would be down in six weeks. In three months, the fugitive would return to Michigan as Connor Lucas. Laughing raucously just before he fell asleep, Zach Miller could hardly wait to implement a wicked plan that would poison everything that he would touch, enabling him to become one of the richest men on earth. But, most of all, Zach looked forward to carrying out his final acts of revenge.

"Nurse, hand me the scalpel."

"Yes, Doctor Villani."

The surgeon looked over at the doctor administering the gas to induce the patient to enter a deep sleep. "Is everything OK? I'm set to begin!"

The anesthesiologist replied, "Vitals are stable. You can begin cutting the facial skin whenever you want."

Villani peered over his surgical mask. "I'm glad this man is in such great shape. He asked me to completely re-do his face."

"Doctor" the nurse asked, "How long do you estimate the operation to take?"

"Six hours. Please put on a tape of some classical music. It will help to pass the time."

The surgeon swayed as he waited for the nurse to turn on Beethoven's Fifth Symphony. He cocked his head, puffed his chest and proclaimed, "In order to make such dramatic changes in his chin, nose, and forehead, I'll need to take a few chunks of bone from his hip. Then, a complete face lift to accommodate his newly enlarged features will be performed."

A Beethoven classic began blaring from the loudspeaker in the corner of the operating room. The anesthesiologist clapped. "Your incision was flawless. You're a master craftsman."

"It's no big deal. Gives me a rush knowing a man's life is in my hands."

The head nurse asked, "Was Mr. Lucas just kidding when he said to you that you should not believe that your own life depends on his survival of the surgery?"

Dodging the question, Villani narrowed his eyes on his target, using his scalpel to slice through several layers of skin, tracing around the ear lobe. He then separated the tissues using a finely honed stainless steel instrument. "I'll also take some loose skin from his neck area to attach around his ears before stitching the grafted skin onto his new face." Blood spurted out onto the operative field. Calmly, the surgeon cauterized the blood vessels before looking at the gas doc.

"Vitals remain stable," added the anesthesiologist.

"Can someone please move the x-ray view box closer?" Villani stepped back from the operating room table, holding his gloved hands in front of him. "From time to time, I'll need to refer to the facial picture the patient gave when he first consulted with me. It helps me sculpt."

The nurse stared at the patient's pre-op picture. "Why would he want to trade his rugged good looks for this new appearance? It looks like he wants to be a little puffy in the face."

The surgeon glared at her for several moments. He then looked down at his patient, achieving a deft maneuver with his scalpel. "The patient decides, not us. We are paid, we live, and he is pleased. Are there any further questions?"

******

After a month of relative calm, the monsoon season was about to strike. The former DCP pharmaceutical baron inserted his new contact lenses. Admiring himself in the full-length mirror, he stroked his full sized beard. "Hey Haley, what do you think?" He plopped down on the bed and rolled on top of her. "Am I better looking than the old Zach?"

She reached over to the night table, putting her non-filtered cigarette in the ashtray. She pulled down his briefs. Haley Tyler planted a long wet one on his newly surgically enlarged lips. His short-cropped graying hair attracted a tender caress. She wiggled her hips, pressing her thighs together.

Haley moaned. "Blue eyes are sexier than your old brown ones babe. Your muscles are tighter than ever since you've been working out. My favorite one is so much bigger. Oooh, I can feel it."

Playing with her long red hair, it felt so good being inside her. After pulling her closer to him and sucking on her nipples, he completely released his passion for the second time that afternoon.

While passing through United States customs, Connor Lucas felt completely confident that his passport would pass muster. Connections with influential power brokers back in the States had helped create a new persona for him.

A man named Connor Lucas used to be a field agent for the CIA. After two decades of living abroad, the forty nine year old intelligence officer had no surviving family, let alone any friends in the US. Missing ever since a Middle Eastern sting operation, his name came to life-- resurrected--this time by Zach Miller. Not seen for over three years, no one was asking anymore what had happened to Agent Lucas. He was no longer on anyone's radar. His identity was available on the open market. Zach Miller submitted the winning bid.

More than a year after Dr. Jonathan Rogers had exposed his heinous schemes; Miller's high-ranking friends took care of everything, including getting him out of the country and taking care of the paperwork to have him assume the use of Mr. C. Lucas's old social security number. The newly minted Connor Lucas smiled amiably as customs approved his passage without a hitch. After losing a couple of bowling balls of excessive weight in his core, he could hardly wait to get back in the game. He felt like a million bucks.

Walking toward baggage, Haley asked, "So, what's the plan Connor?"

"Why are you always asking questions?"

She smiled playfully. "Just curious, I guess."

He yanked out a Cuban cigar from the inside pocket of his blue blazer. He chomped on one end. "I'll be getting to work right away. My friends have set me up with a middle level sales position at Sunview Pharmaceuticals."

"How long do you think it will take you to get back to Doctor's Choice Products?"

"Six months, depending on circumstances. Of course, Sean Parker will need to go. There can't be two CEO's of DCP. I made it to the top at that company once before. I can do it again."

Haley blurted out, "Zach---I mean Connor, nobody does it any better than you."

He drew her close, his face now no more than a foot from hers. He whispered, "Always think before you speak. Listen carefully. I'm going to have to eliminate anyone who ever knew me as Zach. That's the plan. Got it?"

"I'm sorry. You're right."

"Understand this as if your life depended upon it, Connor Lucas didn't skip the country on bail. Zach Miller did. And, I'm not spending the rest of my life in jail. From this point forward, I will leave no witnesses. Make no mistake, Haley, I'm deadly serious about this. OK?"

She turned up her nose. "I told you that I'm sorry. It will never happen again."

He pushed her away from him. "Just make sure. Remember, I don't give second chances to anybody unless I absolutely need them. And, I--." He held his tongue in mid-sentence and jutted out his enlarged jaw line.

"You can always count on me. I predict that you'll be back as CEO of Doctor's Choice Products in less than six months?"

Grinning widely, he said, "I'll make it happen. I always do." He flexed his bicep muscle. "First, I'm going to make Sunview sales soar so high that they'll have no choice but to quickly promote me up the ladder. However, in my spare time, I have a few old scores to settle. Just stay out of my way."

While waiting for their bags on the rolling baggage rack, Connor pulled out a copy of the *Washington Post* from his carry-on briefcase. He re-read the story on the follow up investigations into Lauren Timmons's murder and shook his head.

"Let this be a lesson to you Haley," he said, pointing to the hazy image of a decapitated body in the dark photo, "My former college girlfriend and Chief Operating Officer at the DCP Pharmacy seems to have lost her head while I was out of the country."

She leaned over, taking a gander at the stock company head shot that sat below the crime scene picture. "I remember her. She's the one you coerced into preparing the poisonous chemo cocktail for Dr. Rogers. Who killed her?"

"How would I know?" His face turned red. "It could have been anyone of my old crew at *The Health Club*."

Haley cast her eyes on the floor, averting his penetrating gaze. "I'm sure that you're right."

Mesmerized by the photo, he said, "Good ole' Lauren. She certainly tried her best. Well, I guess I can cross off her name on my hit list."

She grabbed his arm, walking toward the exit to the street. "Whatever happened to your wife?"

"She passed away. Her cancer won. To think, that I once gave her personal oncologist so many chances to save Alexis's life with our DCP drug *Zazotene*. Now, he's dead as well. He was a damn traitor. Tom Knowton may have been a great oncologist but he didn't deserve to live."

Connor hailed a taxi. "It feels good to be back in Michigan."

Hopping in the back seat with him, she innocently asked, "Is every member of *The Health Club* that I knew, except you and me, dead or in prison?"

"Not quite yet, my dear." He nibbled on her earlobe. "Not quite yet!"

***

Connor Lucas strolled out of the Human Resources corporate office at Sunview Pharmaceuticals. He thought back to a couple of scathing speeches he once delivered about crushing his chief competitor. *Shit! Now, I'm one of them.* While he was the DCP CEO, he was widely known as a ruthless leader who would do anything to maximize shareholder value. He forced an ear-to-ear grin as he passed by company co-workers. To him, his middle management sales position at Sunview was just a first step, but a beginning nonetheless toward reclaiming his former throne.

As he walked toward his new work area, he noticed a reflection of his new visage, the result of the loss of thirty-six pounds of flab, in one of the windows leading to another wing at Sunview. He looked down at his form fitted Armani dark blue suit. Pleased with what he saw, Connor's confidence remained unshaken, as always. Anxious to drive sales of Sunview cancer drugs among large physician groups in Michigan, he knew what he had to do.

As he neared his cubicle in the rear of the building, he noticed the small placard bearing his name on the outside wall facing the aisle. Connor sat down at his four by five-work space. *This is a long way from the corner office.* He logged into the Sunview system. His inbox carried an email from his boss, Bob Shepard. He eagerly read on. The email was Connor's introduction to the Company. Two hundred senior colleagues received the welcoming message. The note was full of superlatives, all pronouncing him as the ultimate team player with tremendous business and people skills---destined to be a future Sunview rock star.

Connor relished the days ahead. He leaned back on his standard fare office chair, resting his eyes. After a minute of enjoying the moment, he sat up erect and clicked on his next email. His supervisor had laid out dates and times for their weekly sales staff meetings and their bi-weekly one -on -one meeting. He lifted his legs onto the three-foot wide counter alongside his computer and organized his plan to influence the physicians in his area to prescribe the Sunview cancer products.

At the end of the first day on the job, after logging off, he marveled upon seeing his reflection bouncing off the computer screen. Clearly, returning to his former company as the boss was his goal. *Move over Sean Parker. I'm gunning for you.*

******

In his newly rented apartment in Grand Rapids, Connor went through his hit list. Crossing off Lauren's name, he prioritized his future targets--Dr. Rogers, Marissa, Sean Parker, Tim Carver, and William Peabody. As he went over the names for a second time, he figured that

Carver and Peabody would prove to be more difficult since they were both still in prison. *With Rogers and Marissa, it's personal. With Parker, it's strictly business. Nice chap!*

While enjoying her tongue licking his neck, he asked, "Haley, I need your help."

"Just name it baby."

"I hear from my sources, that Jonathan Rogers will be nosing around DCP trying to find out information about their next blockbuster." He stared down at the photo taken by the taxi driver who had dropped off Rogers earlier that day. There was the Surgeon General clutching the pink and white stripped DC Sports Club gym bag---Lauren's bag.

"What do you want me to do?"

"When I'm ready to ask you, I want you to pay him a surprise visit."

"I've flirted with him before---in hot tubs---in pools."

He could not contain a raucous hoot. "This time, I promise you that he'll really have a blast!"

"Sounds like fun."

Connor walked over to the window, still clutching his crumpled hit list. "The more I think about it, I need to keep Parker in place at DCP until I've built up my reputation at Sunview. I'm not ready to make any rash moves on him, as yet." He glanced down at his notes. "I think Marissa may even move ahead of the Surgeon General. The one thing that I absolutely hate is disloyalty."

Haley stood behind Connor, reaching with her long arms to stroke his genital area. "Do you think you could get the DCP Board to approve your nomination as CEO of DCP with Parker around?"

"Normally, that would be an impossible feat, even for me. But, my ace is Xavier Rudolf. He's an influential DCP Board member and a close friend of someone whom I've kept in close contact since the old days when I led *The Health Club*." Connor turned around and saw her face light up, expressing a touch of giddiness.

"He sounds important." She giggled. "Could I meet Mr. Rudolf?"

"Why?" Connor spun around. His breathing cycles dramatically increased.

She purred, "Don't get mad. I thought it would help you."

Making a tight fist, he shouted, "I've told you before that you ask too many damn questions. My advice is for you to stop that habit immediately. Remember, Marissa was once my former squeeze and now she's on a DOA list that you don't want to be on, my dear."

"It won't happen again."

He pointed to the closet. "Pack your bags."

"Why? I said that it won't happen---."

He cut her off. "Sunview wants me to take a flight to DC. I need to lobby a congresswoman who is the influential chair of the Health Sub-Committee of Ways and Means."

Haley waited for him to speak, afraid to say anything more.

"Our flight leaves from Ford International Airport tomorrow morning at nine 'o clock."

CHAPTER SIX

Jonathan Rogers looked down from ten thousand feet. His Boeing 747 had been circling Detroit for twenty minutes. The pilot had just publicly announced that Flight 904 couldn't land until the dense fog lifted. He craned his neck out the window but could see no trace of Ford International Airport. Checking his watch, he realized that he still had ninety minutes before he would show up unannounced for a meeting with CEO Sean Parker and Dr. Hussein Nasters, the top scientist at DCP.

He passed some of the time reflecting back on his past year. His career advancement from Commissioner of Health in Michigan to Surgeon General was solely due to the President's appointment of him as "top doc." Earlier this day, he had called Cassie at the Regional Medical Center. He was pleased to learn that her abdominal infection was clearing up. There was even better news. By the end of the week, the hospital would release Emma and her Mom.

Just before boarding at Reagan outside of DC, he heard on the cable news TV show that Congress had passed an emergency bill that authorized full health care coverage of any seriously injured victim of the nuclear blast who otherwise couldn't afford private health insurance. He pulled his shoulders back and held his head high, thankful and proud to be serving in the Williams administration.

***

Hours later, while getting his baggage at Ford International Airport in Michigan, Rogers spotted a woman that he knew all too well. *Hayley Tyler* She was holding hands with an athletic looking middle-aged man who seemed to be in a hurry to leave the area. Observant, as always, he noticed a sticker on the luggage of her escort. *Sun View Pharmaceuticals.*

He checked his watch—concerned that he was running behind time for his important meeting with Sean Parker. Sprinting toward an empty taxi, he hopped into the back seat—imploring the driver to get to his destination ASAP.

***

While sitting in the ostentatiously appointed corner office, the Surgeon General stared intently at the CEO. "Glad I made it on time." His briefcase lay on his lap.

Sean Parker said in a cold, almost painfully slow cadence. "Welcome to DCP. Your visit is quite a surprise. My assistant informed me that you were coming just a few hours ago."

Rogers looked across the huge maple wood desk at the CEO. "The last time that I recall seeing you, I was the Commissioner of Health of Michigan and we were both on the Prince America cruise ship. DCP was sponsoring a medical seminar for oncologists. You introduced Dr. Victor Carver to the oncologists after Dr. Knowton was murdered."

Parker anxiously tapped his fingers on the desk. "I don't believe that you and I actually met."

Rogers raised his right eyebrow. "That's true but I know that you worked closely with Zach Miller."

Seemingly taken aback by Rogers's comment, Parker spun his chair to face the huge plate glass windows that formed half of the room's wall space. He glared back at the Surgeon General out of the corner of his left eye, holding his tongue.

Rogers stiffened. "To be frank, Zach Miller hated my guts. And, I can assure you that the feeling was mutual."

The CEO centered his chair, now looking directly at his guest. "His Ferrari exploded while he was driving to the airport. It was literally blown to bits."

Rogers pointed at him with three bent fingers, a throwback from his memories of President John F. Kennedy and a direct imitation of what President Williams had also picked up as a habit. "That's what the police report stated."

Parker ignored his comment. "So, Dr. Rogers, are you having more fun as Surgeon General than you did being our Commissioner of Health? You certainly look a lot healthier."

He replied with a half-crooked smile, "Listen, can we get down to the reason why I came? I have a flight at two this afternoon back to Reagan."

Parker stood and motioned for Rogers to join him at the conference table. "Our chief scientist should be here any minute. We have coffee or water."

He moved over with his briefcase to take a seat at the table. "Water is fine."

The CEO picked up the pitcher and grabbed a glass from the tray. "So, how do you think our Michigan football team will do next week against State?"

"I don't follow college football that much. I'm more of a professional baseball and college basketball kind of guy." He placed his briefcase on the table just as he heard two sharp knocks on the door.

Parker had just finishing pouring the water into his glass when the door opened. He pushed the water across the glass tabletop toward

Rogers. Glancing up, he said, "Good morning Dr. Nasters. Please come in and meet Dr. Jonathan Rogers, the Surgeon General and our former Commissioner of Health."

Rogers rose and firmly shook hands with the DCP scientist before retaking his seat across from Parker. Dr. Nasters took a seat next to his colleague.

Pulling out a notepad from his briefcase, the Surgeon General held his pen at the ready. "In the interest of time, please permit me to be direct."

"Why am I not surprised?" he replied tersely. "Your reputation precedes you." The CEO slurped his coffee, keeping his eyes closely peeled on Rogers.

He frowned upon hearing the obvious dig. "So---I have many questions about the safety of *NeoBloc?*"

"Before we respond, I just want you to know that Dr. Nasters and I have already spoken with your boss. Secretary James, Dr. Nasters and I talked yesterday on a conference call."

"You spoke with the Secretary yesterday?"

"Yes. We spoke extensively about the vaccine's safety profile in our monkey-testing phase. As you know, the FDA has recently granted us a biologic license agreement to begin testing of our vaccine in human clinical trials. We expect to start within a week or so."

Rogers sipped his water. He scanned both faces. "Just so you know President Williams has empowered me to question the safety of *NeoBloc* until I'm fully satisfied. I want you to share with me the specific details on your clinical trial monkey data."

The Surgeon General glanced over to the scientist. He did a double take, suspending the movement of his water glass when it reached half way to his mouth. Naster's twisted mouth formed a frightening scowl.

"Doctor," Parker said, "I understand why you would want that data. And, to be honest, I would share it with you but, earlier this morning, I received an anonymous call. The caller claimed that you already had a confidential DCP report on that *NeoBloc* monkey research."

He slammed down his glass and raised his voice. "Who was this caller?"

"You look upset, doctor. Let's just say I believe the person who called would have a damn good reason to know the truth."

"Not upset, just curious." He put on his best altar boy face. His mind had already jumped to the checkmate question. *What do they know?* He picked up his water glass and took a large gulp.

He pursed his lips. "So, is it true? Do you already have the safety report?"

"No, I don't have any DCP confidential report," he coolly replied.

"But, have you seen it?" Parker persisted.

Parsing his words carefully, he said, "I have read no such report."

He swiveled his chair to face his scientist. "Doctor, please provide your perspective."

"As the lead clinical researcher for *NeoBloc*, I can verify that our testing on the monkeys has yielded fruitful results. Not one monkey treated with the vaccine and exposed to nuclear radiation has developed cancer."

I'm being played. "You're sidestepping the safety issue. Doctor, did any of the monkeys who were treated with *NeoBloc* die?"

"I already told you that not one monkey developed cancer." Nasters smiled. "All animals eventually die, doctor. All people ultimately die." His lips snarled. "Even *you* will one day die."

His eyes blazed. "That's not my point. Did any of the *NeoBloc* vaccinated monkeys die?"

The scientist bit his lower lip. He casually folded his hands on the table. "Why would you ask that?"

"Please answer my question." Rogers leaned forward. "Did any of the monkeys die after receiving an inoculation with *NeoBloc*? It's either a yes or a no?"

Nasters seemed to be counting to himself as his right index finger systematically touched each of his other digits. At the end of his diversionary drill, he categorically stated, "Mr. Parker, I'm sorry but I will not sit here and be insulted. In my country, we don't accept such rudeness."

He lightly touched the sleeve of the scientist. "I'm sure that he doesn't mean any harm. He's just doing his job."

Rogers held out both hands, palms up, in front of him. "Doctor, I'm sorry if you feel offended in any way but President Williams has asked me to fully evaluate *NeoBloc*. If the government is going to permit DCP to begin a fast track on human testing, I must be comfortable about the health of the monkeys who received your vaccine."

"Please rest assured that I will communicate all relevant facts concerning the safety of *NeoBloc*." Nasters looked down at his watch. "Mr. Parker, I must beg your indulgence but just prior to my coming to this meeting, I received word of a serious family problem back in Pakistan. I need to immediately plan a trip in order to attend to a grave matter back in my country." The scientist sprung quickly to his feet, followed in turn by his boss.

"Sorry for your troubles," Parker said compassionately while placing his hand on the shoulder of the scientist. "I do hope things will be all right. I'm sure that Dr. Virginia Washington can handle the workload until you return."

Both Nasters and Parker started walking toward the door. The scientist said sadly, "Sir, I want to thank you for your understanding.

My intent is to depart by tomorrow. I'll update you as soon as I get to Pakistan. I pray that my family is all right."

"Before you leave, please give the Surgeon General your card so he can follow up with you when you return."

Rogers stood and met up with the duo at the door. He reached out his right hand to accept it. "Thank you." He filed the card in his shirt pocket. "I'll call you."

Dr. Nasters shook hands with Parker but merely nodded at the Surgeon General before closing the door behind him.

"Standing with his hands resting on the top of his chair, he said, "My issue stands. I want DCP to produce documentation of the safety of *NeoBloc*."

Parker replied, "Let me ask you one more time." Rolling his eyes, he queried, "Have you ever seen the confidential DCP research?"

Frustrated with the same line of questioning, Rogers walked over to the conference table and picked up his briefcase before heading for the door. With his back to his host, he said in annoyed tone, "I told you that I've never read the report."

"So you have seen it."

Rogers grabbed the doorknob and looked back at the CEO. "I never said that." He yanked the door open. "I need to catch my flight back to DC. Thank you for your time. I'll follow up directly with Dr. Nasters." He stormed out, flinging the door shut behind him.

***

As he was leaving the DCP grounds, Rogers was convinced that Nasters toyed with him. He appeared to be ready to dodge the Surgeon General's questions. Any disgruntled colleague of Lauren Timmons could have called Parker and the scientist. One thing was clear to him. The CEO seemed to know far more than he was willing to share.

In the taxi ride to the airport, he jotted down some observations of his meeting. Not once during the time that he was at the company did the name of Lauren Timmons ever come up. Despite recent national headlines detailing the gruesome murder, senior management at DCP ignored any mention of her death.

Rogers thought back to that fateful night, to Hurleys, to his secretive discussion with Lauren. Waiting for his flight to board, he found himself asking questions for which he knew no answers. *Why did Lauren choose him to share her secret? Who killed her? Who was the oddly behaving man sitting across from him in the tavern?*

The Surgeon General was convinced of one point: The high-ranking scientist would be the key to getting inside the Company and more importantly the one who knew the most about *NeoBloc*. The loudspeaker blared. *Time to board.*

******

Late that afternoon, when he arrived back in his office in DC, Rogers clicked on the *Google* toolbar. He typed in the name of Dr. Hussein Nasters. Thirteen matches instantly appeared on the screen. Scrolling down, he noted that the DCP scientist had graduated Harvard Medical School in 1984, practiced internal medicine as a solo practitioner for five years in Boston, before leaving his practice to earn a doctorate in chemistry at MIT. After that, Nasters had worked for a pharmaceutical research company back in his native Pakistan. Five years ago, he returned to a small biotech firm in California before landing the top scientist position at DCP just eighteen months ago.

Rogers pulled out his business card and placed the call himself. On the second ring, Nasters picked up.

He answered in a gruff sounding tone, "Hello."

Smiling into the phone, the Surgeon General wanted to re-establish a positive direction between the two of them. "This is Dr. Jonathan Rogers. I'm glad I got a hold of you before you left for Pakistan."

Silence.

"Doctor, are you still there?"

"You don't hear a dial tone, do you?" The scientist paused a second or two, apparently to let his overt sarcasm set in. He continued, "I was supposed to be on my way. However, the airline cancelled my earlier flight to Pakistan. The news of civil unrest in my country is all over the cable channels. So I came back to my office to do some work in preparing for the *NeoBloc* human clinical trials."

"I'm sorry to hear the problems in your native country. Do you have family still living there?"

There was no immediate response. After an uncomfortable pause, the scientist said, "Thanks for your concern."

He persisted. "With your permission, I would like to set a date to visit your DCP labs."

"Six weeks from this Tuesday is the best I can do."

"I see. Hmm. Actually, I was hoping for an earlier date."

"As soon as I'm booked to fly, I'll be visiting my family for three weeks. When I return, I will need sufficient time to review the initial month Phase 1 human trial data from *NeoBloc*."

"I understand." Rogers reluctantly agreed to a definitive date in October. He bid the scientist a safe trip. While Nasters was gone, he thought of his interim options. Now, he calculated that he had plenty of time to involve Beth Murphy, his secret weapon friend with the dimpled smile and the dark brown pixie haircut.

******

Rogers's neck ached. Popping an Advil, his osteoarthritis was flaring up again. He was scheduled to give a speech at the 5th World

Cancer Vaccines Summit in three days. For the past few days, he had worked until late in the evening, researching, writing and re-writing his speech. At his laptop for hours on end, he wanted to strike an appropriate balance between hard -nosed reality and cautious optimism. His talk was entitled: 'The Clinical Effects of Radiation Exposure on a Population.' Secretary James had expected him to discuss the science around a vaccine that would minimize the cancer causing effects of radiation---essentially the scientific background for *NeoBloc.*

His conclusion after delving deeply into the subject was quite the opposite. His private research placed serious doubts in his mind. In his opinion, the scientific facts stood for themselves. It was highly unlikely that a vaccine could be developed, based on existing knowledge, which would possess a high enough safety margin in doing what this so called savior vaccine was supposed to do.

The leader of the Boston held Summit had already informed Rogers of his expectations. Almost all the oncologists would be most interested in hearing about the President's call for rapid human testing with the *NeoBloc* vaccine. While he carefully worded his talk to reflect the future possibility that the vaccine might one day protect Americans from radiation-induced cancer, the prophetic words from Lauren Timmons overshadowed his every strike of the keypad. Rogers found the decision be easy. He would simply tell the truth.

Rogers was fully aware of the public scrutiny of his every word to the Vaccine Summit physicians. He massaged his neck, trying to break up muscle spasms that had been building in recent days. While silently re-reading his speech, he picked up the intercom in his office.

"Dr. Rogers, Sean Parker is returning your call on line one."

"Thanks Sally." He put down his speech and quickly collected his thoughts. Pressing line one, he answered, "Good afternoon, Mr. Parker."

The response was brusque. "I'm returning your call despite your less than admirable behavior at my office. What's on your mind?"

"I wanted you to know that I called Dr. Nasters. He has agreed to permit me to visit the DCP labs to review the monkey data with *NeoBloc.*"

"Is that what he told you?"

"Yes. The only problem is that he set up a meeting six weeks from now. That's a long time, if the vaccine killed all the monkeys-----"

Parker's voice soared. "Please stop right there. Why do you keep saying that?"

"I have my reasons."

"Then tell me exactly why you believe that our vaccine is problematic."

"I'm not at liberty to say."

With a sharp edge to his voice, the CEO stated, "We don't have any evidence that the vaccine killed any monkey."

He quickly countered, "Bear with me. Can we just postulate that *NeoBloc* was responsible for the monkeys dying? That would change everything---right? The FDA wouldn't proceed with human clinical trials."

Parker scratched his forehead. "Why are you are bringing up a purely hypothetical situation with no basis? Furthermore, this is not even appropriate to discuss with me. I'm not the scientist."

"I grant you that. The purpose of my call is to ask you a favor. Would you be able to have me speak to another scientist at DCP while Dr. Nasters is in Pakistan?"

"I'm afraid that would be impossible. If I did that, Dr. Nasters would resign. He is a very proud man. Besides, he is an imminently well -respected scientist both at DCP and within the scientific research community. I'm sure you checked out his reputation. We don't want to lose him."

Rogers shifted gears. "Mr. Parker, if I may change the subject, I'm shocked that you never said a word about the brutal murder of your COO, Laura Timmons at our recent meeting."

The CEO cleared his throat several times before speaking. "It is our company policy not to comment on crimes perpetrated against our employees."

"You know, it sounds like you read that line from your company HR handbook."

Parker barked, "Spare me your cynicism."

"I'm sorry. My last comment was inappropriate." He waited a few moments for his apology to sink in. "My goal is to develop a good working relationship with you. But, for whatever reasons, I don't believe that we are headed in that direction."

"I'm trying to be responsive to the needs of our President by working with you."

"Off the record, why don't you tell me what you thought about Ms. Lauren Timmons?"

"Why is this woman any of your business? Did you know her?"

Rogers impatiently began tapping his foot. "My understanding is that she was involved in the *NeoBloc* project. Is that correct?"

"Ms.Timmons was someone whom I would call a disgruntled employee. For no scientific reason, she believed that *NeoBloc* was not as safe as our scientists continue to believe."

"Please go on."

"What else do you want me to say?"

"Just the facts," Rogers reflexively rattled off, slightly bemusing himself that he sounded like Sergeant Joe Friday from the 1960's TV show *Dragnet.*

"Dr. Nasters gave you the facts," Parker replied in a snarky tone.

"Do you believe everything your scientists tell you?"

"Excuse me but do you really believe that I would expose the entire American population to an unsafe vaccine just to improve our financial margins?" His voice took on a decidedly hostile edge. "Who would consider such an unspeakable act? A lunatic? A rogue terrorist?"

"I would tend to agree with you."

He sighed deeply. "Are you accusing DCP of being a terrorist organization?"

"Of course not." Rogers heard the loud exhale over the line. It was obvious that Parker was struggling to remain as calm as possible.

"To be candid, I resent your whole line of questioning."

He knew that he was pushing too hard but he would not relent. "In any event, in order for me to do my job, I must see the research data."

"I believe I already stated our Company's position on your request. You will see all the data when Dr. Nasters returns and not a moment before."

"The fact remains that the President has asked me to look into this matter with all deliberate haste." Rogers picked a rubber ball out of his desk drawer and squeezed it.

Parker paused several seconds this time before replying. "For the last time, I'm in charge of whatever happens at DCP. That's the best I can do for you."

He threw the ball against a barren section of mahogany paneled wall. "This is not about me. It's about our country."

"Good day, Dr. Rogers. I'll see you when Dr. Nasters returns."

The dial tone droned on in the Surgeon General's ear.

***

"Sally, please request a meeting with Secretary James for tomorrow."

"He should be back from his Michigan trip in time to see you. I checked your calendar. I'll schedule the two of you for a one forty- five afternoon meeting in his office."

Expressing a fair degree of surprise, he asked, "Michigan? It seems like our department racks up many frequent flier miles going to that State. Do you know exactly where in Michigan that the Secretary visited?"

"His assistant, Bev, usually doesn't tell me those details. But, I could try to find out if you would like."

He quickly replied, "No, that's fine Sally. Just get me fifteen minutes with the Secretary. I can always ask him myself where he went in Michigan."

***

Putting the final touches on his Cancer Vaccines Summit speech, he found himself preoccupied about *NeoBloc*. Frustrated in having to wait so long to see the safety data, he did not know what else to do except to speak with the Secretary of Health. Perhaps Christian James could use his influence to bypass the intentional hold up.

After a dab of minor changes to his speech, he closed his office lights for the evening. On the way out of his office, he thought of Lauren Timmons. He blamed himself one more time for letting her walk alone through Rock Creek Park. Her severed head had haunted him for weeks. When he closed his eyes at night, he could not blot out her lifeless eyeballs staring down at him from the heavens. Rogers prayed for strength to avenge her brutal death by solving the life and death issues surrounding this so-called savior vaccine.

******

Having surprisingly slept well, he awoke to a sunny day. Rogers passed Sally's desk on his way out of the Department. "Thanks for confirming my meeting with the Secretary. I think I'll have lunch at Roma. Their outdoor patio is right off the street. Actually, I could use some fresh air to clear my mind."

His assistant smiled. "I'll call you on your cell phone if there is any change in your schedule. Enjoy the warm October weather."

"Thanks to El Nino."

***

Rogers hopped a cab and arrived at the Italian Restaurant in less than five minutes. The temperature was sixty -nine degrees and the sky was cloudless. He chose an end table on the outdoor patio, separated from K Street by a three-foot high plastic white fence.

Ordering a Caesar's salad, an entrée of tortellini, and a diet cola, he noticed that patrons filled every outdoor table. Upset with himself for not remembering to bring his sunglasses, he squinted in the mid-day sun. Served his cold drink, he sipped it slowly while observing the DC lunch crowd walking by his table, just several feet from him. Not seeing anyone he knew, he thought about his upcoming meeting with Christian James. He would play up the President's directive to review the monkey safety data on *NeoBloc*. James would understand, he hoped.

He checked his watch. Rogers glanced up as a familiar looking woman strolled by his table. *It's Haley.* Leaping to his feet, he reached out for her arm. "Excuse me, miss."

The red head slowed her pace and giggled. "Have we met?"

He extended his hand.

She grabbed it. "My name is Daisy but I don't believe our paths have ever crossed."

Maintaining his grip of her hand, he began pulling her toward him. "Haley, stop the games. I saw you a few days ago at the airport. From the look on your face, it looked as though you recognized me as well."

The red headed young woman said, "If you don't release my hand, I'll start screaming for the police."

He instantly let go of her hand. "Got a few minutes to talk? I need to ask you a few questions."

"My mom once told me not to speak with strangers. Besides, I don't know if I have the time."

Rogers noticed she was carrying an expensive looking Coach handbag in her left hand. "Please stop it! You always used to show up when I was in any danger."

Haley blinked twice. "Now I remember you. You're a doctor--- right? My mom always told me that I should have married a doctor."

"I only want a few minutes of your time."

"OK." She looked away from his piercing gaze and walked back to the entrance of the patio. As she sauntered toward him, he thought how sexy she looked in her bikini the first time they had accidentally met in the hotel hot tub. Haley sat down directly across from him and dropped her pricey -looking handbag on the patio floor.

"I don't have much time. Make mine, a double Scotch on the rocks."

He called out her order to the passing server. Dressed in a bright coral business suit and low heels, Haley looked as professional as she appeared a year ago, when he was about to approach her on Pennsylvania Avenue, just moments before he was shot twice in the chest.

He leaned forward and wasted no time. "Are you stalking me again?"

Haley's eyes twinkled. "What if I said yes? After all, you're a good-looking guy. Compared to when I saw you last year, it looks like you dropped a few pounds. Can't a nice girl have a little fun? Maybe I have a crush on you. You know more than most that life can be so short."

"You know exactly what I mean." He downed half of his soda in one gulp. "I can't believe that you didn't get convicted like the rest of your pack of wolves." Rogers interrupted the server who was clearing another table. He pointed at her. She ordered a blueberry muffin.

"The jury must have liked my dimples," she replied coyly. "Anyway, the bottom line is that they found me not guilty. It's over."

"You were as guilty as sin. You would do anything Zach Miller told you to do when he was the leader of *The Health Club*."

"Drop it," she replied coldly. And, don't harass me or I'll file a police complaint against you."

Looking over her shoulder, he saw their server approaching with his salad and entrée and her drink and muffin. The server placed down their order. Rogers let his eyes wander. Several customers were already leaving.

Haley took a sip of her Scotch, keeping her eyes on him the entire time. "Strong Scotch—that's the way I like my men---strong."

He dug into his salad. "I have a lot of questions for you."

She pursed her lips and looked away. He followed her line of vision. A parked taxicab across the street seemed to be her visual object of interest. A newbie Redskins fan himself, he noted the football team logo on the rear door of the taxi.

"Don't ask me about the past." Haley smacked her lips after taking a huge bite out of the muffin. She drained the rest of her drink. "Look, I was minding my own business when you corralled me."

"Excuse my bluntness. But, why did you try to trick my wife last year into thinking that you were a private---?" She cut him off in mid-sentence.

"Listen, I just laid down the ground rules for our little impromptu get together. Can't we forget about all that past crap? Enjoy the moment, the weather."

Her cell rang. She pulled it out of her handbag, flipped it open but said nothing. Shrugging her shoulders, she said, "Wrong number."

"You look upset."

Clinging to her cell, Haley's eyes began to dance, moving rapidly in all directions. She fidgeted while glancing down at her watch.

"And you suddenly look very nervous."

Haley took a deep breath. She jumped to her feet. "Umm, can you please excuse me? I need to go to the rest room. I'll be right back."

"You don't look very well," he added, observing that her skin color was turning paler and pastier by the second.

"It's a woman thing. You know---." She turned to walk toward the entrance of the restaurant. Half way there, she pivoted and gave a friendly wave. "Dr. Rogers, enjoy your salad. Just give me a couple of minutes. See you soon."

As he watched her trot the remainder of the way to the front door, his own cell chimed. "Yes Sally."

"Dr. Rogers, I'm sorry to bother you but the Secretary needs to see you right away. He's meeting the President in thirty minutes. Mr. James wants you to come to his office immediately. I told him you were at lunch and that you had a later appointment with him. But, he insisted."

He jumped to his feet. "I'm on my way." Except for a few servers cleaning up, he was the sole customer remaining. Thinking she would return shortly, he paced around his table as another minute or two ticked off. Her classy Coach bag lying beneath their table caught his attention. He thought it odd for her to leave it behind while she went off to a rest room.

A server emerged from the restaurant with the check. Rogers paid the bill, adding a few extra dollars, requesting that the server keep an eye on Haley's bag.

The plastic fence stood between him and the street. In an athletic move, he hopped over it. He spotted an empty cab cruising down K Street, thirty yards down ahead of him. While sprinting down the middle of the street, he furiously waved his arms and shouted for the taxi to stop. Behind him, he heard what sounded like a compacted version of the fireworks finale on the Fourth of July. Before he had a chance to stop running and pivot, there were several seconds of utter silence.

Rogers looked back toward the Roma restaurant. The front glass window of the restaurant had been completely shattered. An elderly couple was lying on the street just next to where he and Haley had been sitting on the patio. Bloodied faces of the seniors stared back at him. The table that he just left was shattered to bits. His server lay motionless on the ground.

He took a few steps toward the disaster area. People on the street were dashing in all directions, screaming in sheer panic. Patrons and staff streamed out from the inside of the restaurant onto the street. Every outdoor table and chair seemed obliterated into millions of pieces strewn across the patio. Amid frightened yells for help, his mind went blank. He thought, *Roma's restaurant looked like ground zero.* Sirens erupted. He spotted flashing lights from police cars and an ambulance in the distance speeding down K Street in his direction. *Where is Haley?*

A sea of cabs sped toward him. He backed up onto the sidewalk. Just as he stumbled against the curb, he spotted Haley. Seated in the backseat of taxicab with the rear door Redskins logo, Haley tried to cover her face with one hand shading her eyes. *It's her!*

Rogers hailed one of the cabs. It skidded to a hard stop. He hopped in and headed back to the Department of Health and Human Services, praying for the innocent victims of what clearly was a major explosion.

******

Once back inside the Department hallways, Rogers literally ran toward the Secretary's office. *I'm really late.* He kept replaying what had just happened repeatedly in his head. Opening the door to his boss's office, he was dumbfounded at what he saw.

James was dozing in his chair. As Rogers approached him, the Secretary stirred and vigorously rubbed his eyes. "Hey Jonathan, what's up?"

In a hurried voice, he said, "Sally said to rush back. That you wanted to see me immediately." He took in two gulps of air and tried to slow his breathing cycles with a modicum of success. "Don't you have a meeting with the President," he asked while glancing at his watch, "in fifteen minutes."

James sat up straight. He yawned. "Then, I better get moving."

Out of breath, he managed to eke out a weak statement. "You moved up our meeting."

The Secretary appeared unflustered. He calmly started to gather up scattered papers on his desk and began putting them into his briefcase.

He blurted out, "Christian, I think someone just tried to kill me."

"What?" James stretched and stifled another yawn.

Rogers paced the floor. "Good thing that you called Sally when you did." He took another deep breath. "Otherwise, I'd be dead by now," he shouted. "Christian, you saved my life!"

James stood and put on his gray tweed suit jacket. "Glad to be of service. What happened?"

Pumping his hands to emphasize his ordeal, he said, "There was an explosion at Roma's restaurant."

"Could it have been a broken gas main?"

In an argumentative tone, he loudly exclaimed, "Don't think so."

"Look, you're making me nervous. Slow down and lower your voice."

"I'll try." He sat down, watching the Secretary straighten his tie. He began to feel his heart slowing. "Christian, you know my track record for the past year. This wouldn't be the first time someone tried to kill me."

The Secretary grabbed his briefcase. "Did you call the police?"

"I saw them coming. Someone must have called 911."

Did you talk with anyone besides the server at Roma's?" James began to trot out of his office, not even caring to wait for Rogers.

Leaping out of his seat, he sprinted and caught up with his boss. "Yes, I spoke with a woman I once knew."

At the end of the hallway, they approached the elevator bank. "Who is she?" James pressed the button. He dropped his briefcase to the floor and tucked in his shirt beneath his black belt. "Was she injured?"

Rogers hesitated. "She left just before the explosion."

James picked up his briefcase, looking at the Surgeon General with a worrisome expression. The elevator door opened and they jumped in, taking it to the ground floor. "Do you think she was involved? And, you still didn't tell me who she is." The Secretary stepped out of the elevator, not looking at Rogers, and began walking quickly down a long corridor. The Surgeon General's heart began racing. He was barely able to keep pace with James, who by now was almost running.

"This same woman always seems to pop up when my life is on the line."

James stopped dead in his tracks. "Who is she?"

"She's an old acquaintance."

The Secretary sent an annoyed look at Rogers and began walking toward an exit door. "Look, I'm meeting with the President in ten minutes. But I do want to hear about your trip to DCP and more about what happened at Roma's."

"Christian, could we talk in your limo ride to the White House?"

As the pace of their walk increased again, James shouted, "That won't work. I've got to read my notes to prepare for my meeting with the President."

He grabbed the Secretary's arm. "Listen to me. We're talking about my life."

James shook him off, pulling his arm away in one quick move. "Keep talking while we walk. I'm being picked up out back." He checked the time on the wall clock and began to sprint once again. "I'm really running late. The President doesn't tolerate such behavior."

He ran alongside his boss and changed the subject. "DCP refuses to let me see the *NeoBloc* safety data until Dr. Nasters returns in six weeks."

A back door leading to an outside private road blocked their journey. James flung it open. "I'll inform President Williams." A breeze blew his long wavy brown hair in several directions as they approached the waiting limo.

The driver popped out of his driver seat, opened the rear door, and waited for him to jump inside. Showing concern for the first time, the Secretary stood on a walkway next to limo and directly faced the Surgeon General.

His heart was pumping. He asked, "Should we recommend holding up Project Moon Shot for now?"

The Secretary glared back. "Definitely not!"

"Look, I know this woman who I met at Roma's restaurant. Her name is Haley."

"Tell me again why you were having lunch with this woman."

The driver tapped James on his shoulder. The Secretary nodded and jumped into the rear of the black limo with his briefcase in tow. The driver slammed the door shut and headed for the steering wheel. James powered down his window and stuck out his hand. .

"I had questions for her." He pressed his palm into James's ice-cold hand.

"What kind of questions? Give me specific examples." James checked his watch and pounded on the glass separating him and the driver. "Take off in thirty seconds," he ordered the driver before again meeting Rogers's gaze for the final time.

"I had questions about Haley's involvement in personal situations that affected me and my family."

"You're being very vague. I have no idea of what you mean." James looked at his watch. "I'll see if I can get you into DCP before Dr. Nasters returns." The window began to close. The Secretary winked at him just before the limo sped off for his Oval Office meeting.

Alone, he stood at the curb. Since the ordeal at Roma's, clouds had marched into the overhead skies. A late fall cool breeze blasted his body. Rogers ambled back into the building. As he thought about what had happened at the restaurant, he realized that he had no evidence that the explosion was a bomb—let alone a bomb meant for him. Not wanting to appear paranoid, he decided not to call the police. *It could have been a gas leak. I'm safe.*

Back at his office desk, he cleared out his inbox. While sorting papers, his mind drifted to the safety of his wife and daughter. His mind boomeranged back to NeoBloc---to Lauren Timmons---to the President---to the fate of innocent Americans---to the survival of America.

CHAPTER SEVEN

Connor paced furiously in the living room. "Haley, you screwed up----again. You knew the bomb in your pocketbook was set to go off exactly at one twenty five. When I called you, I told you to stay put with Rogers on the restaurant patio."

He stopped, threatening to slap her face. "My gut tells me as soon as you hung up from me, you freaked out and bolted. Couldn't you have stayed around just a little longer to pin him down to his damn seat?" Backpedaling away from her, he pounded the opposite wall with his fist.

Haley quickly lit her cigarette. She took a long drag, her hands trembling. "I was afraid to wait another second. I gave myself only two minutes to get away. I knew when the bomb would explode." She coughed the smoke out while watching Connor rapidly approaching her.

He backed her slowly against the wall. Yanking the cigarette from her mouth, he tossed it on the floor. After stomping on it, he crushed the tobacco into a thin layer on the hardwood floor, squishing it as he would a black widow spider in his bedroom. Now, against the wall, her head bumped against a *Thomas Kincaid* painting of a small town village. He blasted away. "Well, your target just called me."

"That's impossible! I never mentioned you, not even once. You must believe me."

"He said he spotted you at Ford International Airport by the baggage area." Connor thought back and remembered. "Was he the person that you were gawking at?"

"No. But how could Rogers find you?"

"He spotted a Sunview Pharmaceutical sticker on my luggage."

"How would that lead him to you?"

"He's the Surgeon General and he's far from stupid. He merely called Sunview and described me." His eyes bulged. "Shit, our bumbling operator tells him that his description matched me to a tee. Can you believe that our operator even gave Rogers my office phone number? So, this morning, I pick up my phone and it's him."

"I'm sorry. I'll kill him myself next time. What did he want?"

"Shut up! He said that you looked like an old acquaintance. My God Haley, he named you. And, he placed you at the scene of the restaurant explosion." He rubbed his right eye. "Look, I had to tell Rogers that you and I had already broken up ten days ago. He described you to a tee. I said I had no idea where you were. I had to lie through my teeth. I told him how shocked I was when he told me that he was almost killed by what he believes was a bomb."

Her voice shrieked, "Please forgive me. Give me another chance."

His head began to pound. "I warned you before," he hollered. Connor pulled a wad of hundred dollar bills from his wallet. He pulled her bra toward him and stuffed the bills into her cleavage.

"Get out of town. Don't ever mention my name to anyone. If I hear you say or do anything that connects you to me, I'll hunt you down and personally slice your throat. Then, I'll watch you bleed to death."

Haley pleaded, "It will never happen again."

Her comment enraged him. Connor hated people who always wanted a second chance. He knew how to survive and giving second chances to losers was not one of them. He yelled, "Don't move." He looked over at his desk and spotted a gold plated letter opener. His monogrammed initials on it stared him in his face. Seizing it in his right hand, he ran back to her.

She whimpered, "Please don't kill me."

Connor thrust the sharp edge against her neck. He pressed his body close to Haley. He felt her heart pounding against his chest. "Beg for your life."

She squeezed her eyes shut. Haley sobbed, "My neck. It hurts. Please stop."

A few drops of blood began to trickle down onto her blouse and onto his hand. Her body quivered. Connor fought to regain any semblance of self-control. He pulled the blade away from her throat, holding it at his side.

"Thank you---thank you. I thought you loved me."

He pulled at her red hair and threw her to the floor. "I said beg like a dog!"

She stumbled to her feet. Connor held the pointed letter opener over her head. "If I don't hear you begging by the count of three, I think I might have to do something that you'll regret. One---two---"

Haley raised her hands to her chest. Dropping her wrists, she looked like a longhaired puppy begging for a treat. She screamed, "I beg you. I beg you. I beg you!"

Connor swiped his hand across her mouth. "Lick your damn blood from my hand."

Feeling her tongue whipping across the palm of his hand, he felt a rush. "Just remember what I said. If I ever hear that you've implicated me in any way, you're dead meat."

For another ten seconds, he watched Haley continuing to pant and beg. "Go---get out of my life forever."

As she ran toward the door, he pushed her one more time. She slammed headfirst into the door, fumbling for the doorknob. Her body shook as though she was having a seizure. A moment later, she was finally able to open the door. He listened to her footsteps running wildly down the stairway.

He slammed the door shut and headed straight for his liquor cabinet. *Dammit, Rogers must be a cat in disguise. How many lives does he have?* After three shots of straight Scotch, he made up his mind to end the life of his long time nemesis, Dr. Jonathan Rogers.

******

Frustrated with multiple failures to nail Rogers for over a year, Connor fidgeted in the rear of his van. It was externally marked with advertisements for a cable TV truck. He previously covered the license plates with black masking tape just before he turned the corner onto the Surgeon General's block.

At any moment, his mark was due to arrive home. It had not been difficult to learn his schedule. Connor keyed into the robotic-like daily routine of the Surgeon General. On most days, Rogers and his wife ate dinner promptly at six. Before sitting down with Kim, he would customarily unwind with a beer in his study for ten minutes or so while catching up on some personal email. Connor laughed aloud, knowing that he had done his homework. This would finally be the night to end the life of the most annoying doctor.

Connor looked at his gold plated Rolex. It was 5:50PM. A speaker hung from one corner of the van. The wireless device picked up the same radio wave band on the listening device in the study of the Rogers home. He hummed along with Kim as she sang *Hey Jude* to herself. From the angle of the video bug planted on the desk, he could see her, typing away at their computer in the study. Soon, his most prized target would occupy the same room. He smacked his lips and savored the moment. *No more sending amateurs like Haley to do a man's job*, he thought.

Kim was dressed in a low cut dress pocked with large roses. Connor still felt attracted to her. He recalled the first time they had met, years earlier. At that time, she was a real estate agent and he had pretended to be an interested buyer of an estate that Kim's company had listed. Looking at her through his black and white monitor screen, he wondered. Seducing the wife of his number one enemy would have put a feather in his cap. *Once Rogers is out of the way, I'll meet with Kim. The old sparks will fly!*

Giving a thumb's up sign to his hit man, he fondled the silencer on the murder weapon—a Remington .308 rifle. "Hey, Jonesy, good job on planting the bug in the doc's front room study just before you stole the DCP research on *NeoBloc* last month."

"No problem man." Jonesy's right shoulder jerked upward a few times.

"Nervous tic?"

"Don't worry boss. I'm just getting loose. You know I was a top sharpshooter in the Army."

"If I didn't trust your ability, you wouldn't be ripping me off for ten grand to do the job."

Jonesy snickered. "So, where the hell is our mark? You said he's always on time. I'm starving---want to eat me a couple of platefuls of some grits."

Connor made a scrunched face, feigning disgust by any mention of the thick corn based porridge. "I thought you Southern gentlemen took life as it comes. What's your problem man? Have some patience."

"Give me back my stick man. Listen; boss, my mom was from Orleans but my dad was a Chicago man. He was a big city man. I don't have much patience. I just want to do the fuckin job and get my damn money."

Connor handed the Remington back to Jonesy. He peered down at his watch. Rogers was late. An uneasy sense that something was going to spoil his plan descended upon him. His mood rapidly turned foul.

"Jonesy, put one ear plug in now. It will blunt some of the noise when you pull the rifle trigger. Stick this earpiece in your other ear. Attach this microphone to your shirt. I'll be listening and watching the whole time. When the angle and the precise moment are right, I'll give you the order."

Jonesy planted a loud smacking kiss on the 308. "Whatever you say --boss."

Connor stared at the hit man's chin. "Whatever possessed you to get that ugly cross tattoo?"

Jonesy was about to flip Connor the bird but held back. "What's wrong with it? My woman thinks it's sexy."

Glancing on the bulge in Jonesy's belly, he sneered, "Your blubber must get in the way when you're in bed with her."

"She likes it rough."

Suddenly, Connor's eyes picked up movement coming down from the street. He held up his index finger over his mouth. He motioned for Jonesy to kick the safety latch off the rifle.

"There's his taxi pulling up."

"I have a clear shot. Let me plug him as he's walking up the stone steps to his apartment."

"Not yet." Connor wanted this moment to be a crown of thorns for his nemesis. "Hold your fire until I give the order. I want him and Kim to be together when it happens. He needs to suffer. And I want to see the look on her face when his final moment comes."

"Man, I ain't got all day."

Connor grabbed Jonesy's polo shirt. "For the last time, shut the hell up"

Jonesy swiped Connor's hand off his shirt as if it were a fly. "Sure, whatever man. Just make sure you fork over my pay after I do the job." Jonesy violently twitched his right shoulder again. "Hey man, I'm just getting loose."

Connor's eyes bulged. "If you say one more word, I'll kill you myself,"

"With what? I've got the stick."

Connor pulled out a Glock from his shoulder holster and moved close to Jonesy's face. "Don't mess with me." He opened the rear door of the van. "Just do what we planned."

The hired sharpshooter shrugged his shoulders, cursed under his breath but followed the directive. Ten seconds later, he replied, "Boss, I'm now sitting in the driver's seat."

Connor watched Rogers slip out of the cab. After paying his fare, he leaped up the twelve stone steps to his doorstep, two steps at a time. He whispered to himself. "He's trying to make up time. *He's so damn predictable. What an obsessive-compulsive doc*

***

Tonight is my night! Connor's eyes glued themselves to the monitor screen. He tracked the Surgeon General entering the front room study to drop his briefcase on the desk.

Rogers yelled out to Kim. 'Hi Honey, I'm home. I'll see you in a minute.'

Sitting at his desk, the target's face was in full view of the tiny camera planted in the flowerpot, sitting on the right side of his desk. Connor sneered, seeing that Rogers's face tied in knots. He studied his victim. Rogers's eyes twitched uncontrollably, waiting for his computer to boot up. *I don't like that look on his face. Something went down.* He listened carefully on the audio feed.

Rogers's voice barked, 'Kim, come here right away.'

Connor spotted Kim coming into view, holding a can. 'Jonathan, here's your beer. What's so important?' She stood behind her husband, massaging his shoulders.

Rogers grabbed the can and swallowed two gulps. 'I've got to tell you something. It can't wait.'

She kissed the top of his head. 'Now what?'

The Surgeon General stood and gave his wife a tight hug.

Connor felt a bulge by the zipper of his pants. His long awaiting moment had finally arrived. "It looks like a perfect shot. Jonesy, be ready for my order."

Jonesy muttered something unintelligible. Rogers looked up at Kim, about to speak.

But Connor heard her interrupt. 'Jonathan, I don't like that look in your eye.'

'Honey, I think someone tried to kill me today.'

She backed away from the embrace, covering her mouth. 'Now what happened?'

'Someone tried to blow me up a few hours ago.' He shut his eyes, rubbing his forehead. "I already called the FBI."

The monitor picked up the horror that appeared to be building on her face. 'Jonathan, start from the beginning.'

'Thank God that Sally called me back to the office to meet with Christian James. Another minute more and it would have been too late." He drew her back into his arms. "But, I have an idea of who may be behind all of this.'

'Who?'

'Haley Tyler. Do you remember her? She always showed up when something bad used to happen to the both of us."

'You mean the good looking private detective who I once went to see at the recommendation of Zach Miller.'

Rogers shook his head in the affirmative. "Listen, Kim, I wasn't going to call the authorities. I don't really trust them. But I changed my mind and gave them a lot of information about what happened at the restaurant. I also told them about other people whom I suspect as well. An FBI agent should be here any minute to take my full statement.'

Connor's heart began to race. *I hope the prick didn't already tell the FBI about me.*

Rogers sat down at his desk and furiously began punching keys on the keyboard. 'I need to type notes to summarize today's events in a timeline so I don't forget any details that might be important.'

'Why do you think Haley was involved?'

'I had lunch with her today.'

She recoiled from him, backing up, holding both hands on the sides of her head. 'Are you nuts?'

'I spotted her as she walked by Roma's restaurant. I was on the outside patio. It was all spontaneous.'

'And, you decided to invite her to have lunch with you. Have you lost your mind?'

'Listen to me. Recently, I saw her at the airport in the baggage area.'

Connor punched his fist into his other hand.

Rogers turned back to his computer. "I suspect that she left a bomb in her handbag—a bomb intended for me.'

'Oh my God!' Kim paced the study floor. 'This is too much Jonathan. You know that I can't take this stress anymore.' She pulled out a tissue from her pocket and swiped the moisture from her eyes.

'Remember the night that the arrow shattered the window behind us.'

Kim blew her nose. 'How could I forget?'

Rogers stood, taking slow strides toward the front window. Connor now saw him in plain view, standing sideways to the window. He was ready to give the order to Jonesy but a gut feeling told him to hold off a little longer. *Crap! He may have already mentioned my name to the FBI.* Becoming increasingly ambivalent by the second, he listened intently to their revealing conversation.

'There's more.'

She clenched her fist. 'Jonathan, with you, there's always more.'

'Earlier that night, I met with a top executive who worked at Doctor's Choice Products. She gave me evidence about a top secret vaccine project'

'This is all news to me. Every night you come home. You say nothing exciting ever happens at the Department.'

'Kim, I couldn't tell you. Only a few others besides me even know about the project.' The Surgeon General pivoted, now directly facing the window. 'It's a vaccine in a development phase. President Williams wants to use the vaccine on every American to prevent radiation induced cancer from the nuclear bombs the terrorists have been using against America.' The window was half way pulled up from the bottom. 'Shit, where is the damn FBI?' Rogers bent down and peered out.

Connor turned down a request by Jonesy to shoot him in the head. *Let him talk some more. This is good intel.* The Surgeon General suddenly ducked back inside the study, several steps away from the window.

Rogers visibly shook. 'Five minutes after I left the poor woman, I found her slaughtered.'

'Was that the woman who was found beheaded in the Park? Her voice began to tremble. 'I read about it in the *Post*. According to the article, it seemed as though she was executed—a contract hit.'

Rogers's reached out to hug her.

Kim backed away and spun around in a small circle. She stopped on a dime, looking straight at him. 'Stop right there! I've had enough! I want you to resign immediately as Surgeon General. If you love me, you'll get us away from all of this danger.'

'You know that I love you. Just trust me----trust me. I can't just walk away. That woman gave her life so I could carry on her cause to find out if the vaccine is safe or not."

Kim yelled, 'Her cause! What about us? What about our dream to see our daughter grow up, to see her get married, to see her have her own children?" After pausing and just staring at him for several seconds, she pleaded, 'Do you even care about *our* cause?'

'You and Ashley mean more to me than anything in the world. But the cause to save millions of lives is important as well. The President needs my help.'

Kim screamed, 'Look, I've had enough. This is killing me inside. I can't take it anymore. I will no longer allow you to put your life---our lives continually on the line—no matter how noble the cause.'

He gently placed his hands around both of her shoulders and looked into her eyes. 'Kim, please give me some more time to work this all out. I promise you that everything will be fine. Please----I promise.'

She took one-step back. 'No! We've got to get out of this--- whatever mess you've gotten us into---again.'

Rogers reached out to stroke her hair. "Millions of lives are at stake.'

'What about *our* lives?'

'The President is counting on me.'

'What about me? Who can I count on?'

'You know that I'll always do whatever I can to protect you and Ashley. And, I promise to be more careful than before."

Her eyes seemed to freeze in an expression of disbelief. 'What if you're wrong?'

'I'll never do anything to put you or Ashley in jeopardy. I promise you.'

Connor could barely contain himself, stifling a guffaw. *This is the best soap opera I've ever seen.* "Rogers has no clue that he's making promises that he can't possibly keep."

'Jonathan, what do you mean that millions of lives are at stake?'

'In this top secret project, there is a new vaccine that is supposed to save countless lives from radiation exposure. The vaccine is manufactured by DCP.'

Connor chuckled upon seeing her mouth gape wide open and her eyebrows oscillating.

'That's Zach Miller's old company.'

'That's right but he's no longer around.' Rogers pounded his fist into the palm of his other hand. 'By now, he should be burning in hell.'

Connor fanned himself, finding it hard not to laugh. *Actually, the night air is a little chilly, not hot in the least.*

Rogers again stared out the window, hoping to see the FBI pull up any second. *Kim is right. I need to protect my family. The FBI will have to shield us from any risk.* Kim drew closer to him, resting her face on his chest. 'Jonathan, you know that I love you more than anything. But why are you always putting us through these endless crusades of yours?'

This is his last crusade! Connor whispered into his microphone, "Jonesy, get ready. On my order,"

"Yep"

Rogers kissed Kim gently on her lips. 'Honey, everything will be all right. Don't worry. I spoke to one of the agents from the FBI. The agent now knows everything. I told them that I saw Haley with a man at the Michigan airport. His name is Connor Lucas. I called Lucas today at his workplace but he said he had already broken up with Haley weeks ago. But, I don't believe him. I told the FBI to follow him closely.'

Connor jaw clenched tight upon hearing Rogers divulge that he had already spoken to the FBI about him. *He fingered me. If I kill him now, I won't know who he spoke with—nor do I know exactly what he said about me.* He thought hard for several seconds. *I need to neutralize any agent he told about me. Wish the damn agent would pull up right now. Jonesey will take them all out. No witnesses.*

'Jonathan, I'm freaking out-- just listening to you. Your job description doesn't say that you must right every wrong in the country.' She tightly held him around his waist.

'Kim, it's who I am. I'm doing my best to protect our nation from getting a vaccine that could be deadly. Recently, someone gave me information about DCP. Sean Parker and Dr. Nasters are the ones who should be nervous, not us.'

'I know you really believe what you're saying but you promised me many times before that we would be safe. You swore that this craziness would be over with Zach Miller's death. But, this never seems to end.'

Rogers smiled warmly at Kim. 'Honey, any second, the FBI will be here. Soon, they will be all over Haley and Connor Lucas. Then, this tension will be over.' He hesitated and bit his lower lip. 'OK?'

'OK what?' she fired back. 'Are you going to do what I asked?'

'Yes. After this project is completed, I promise to resign as Surgeon General. I see what I'm doing to you. You're right. It's not fair. Above all, I love you and Ashley. We'll take a long vacation to figure out something that I can do to make a difference without always putting our lives on the line." He kissed her forehead. "For a while now, I've been thinking of volunteering for Doctors without Borders.'

Kim looked deeply into his eyes. 'Jonathan, I love you so much. Are you sure?'

'I'm sure.' His arms tightened around her.

Once we kill Rogers, the FBI will be all over me, asking questions. Dammit! Now furious, Connor stared at the tender scene that was playing out before his eyes.

Rogers released her from his embrace. Poking his head out the window again, he exclaimed in exasperation, 'Don't know why the FBI is taking so long. Something doesn't smell right. They should have been here by now'

Nervously, he began pacing the study floor. He looked over at Kim. She was sobbing uncontrollably. Rogers took two steps toward her. They were now standing no more than a foot apart, just to the left of his study desk. Kim's back was to the front window.

'Ashley called today. Good news! She did well on her exam.' Kim's face lit up. 'Just before she hung up, she said she loved me. It felt so good to hear those words once again.'

He nodded. 'Ashley and I both love you more than anything.'

She stroked his wavy hair and gazed into his eyes. Rogers held her hand, kissing it.

Connor gritted his teeth. He thought, *It's time to initiate Plan B*. He calculated the precise spot on the road. Jonesy needed direction in order to execute the new plan. *The FBI will be here any second! I've got to find and do away with the agent who Rogers told about me.*

"Jonesy, start the engine and drive slowly. Stop about ten feet past the center of the study window."

"Got it boss!"

Connor wished that he could personally pull the trigger. *Rogers did a great job of calming Kim down by swearing that he would resign. He must really love her to do that. I've never met such an idealist, always wanting to do what's right. It makes me sick!* He continued to gawk at the screen as the van moved along in stealth like fashion.

A moment later, the van came to a rolling stop. Lucas again scanned the street, anxiously looking for an unmarked car with an FBI agent. There was a blue mini-van and a silver coupe parked nearby. Yet, the street was deathly quiet. *There's no FBI coming tonight. Time to kill!*

"Jonesy, drop down the window and take a head shot."

The hit man followed orders and peered through his 10X scope. "I'm ready to squeeze off two shots into his forehead. Just give me the order to kill him."

Connor spotted the barrel of the rifle protruding a foot outside the front door window of the van. He stuck in one earplug and covered his hand over the other ear, on top of his earpiece. *Plan B—here it comes!* He shouted into his mouthpiece, "No! Re-direct the target."

"What the f---? You told me to shoot that Rogers dude."

Connor commanded, "Follow my order dammit!" Jonesy's befuddled look in the side rear view mirror of the van came into sharp focus.

In his Southern drawl, the hit man complained. "Shit boss. Don't bumfuzzle me. What the hell do you want me to do?"

"Hit the woman---two shots behind the ear---do it now!"

The 308 barked.

With a bird's eye view on the monitor, his eyes widened as Kim's head was propelled forward onto her husband's chest. Blood gushed from the back of her head as brain tissue flew into the air.

Connor relished seeing the Surgeon General blinking his wife's blood from his eyes and spitting it out of his mouth. Kim's head rolled back. Her body turned limp. The van speaker picked up a feeble moan. Rogers screamed out in agony.

"Jonesy, drop the rifle on the passenger seat and take off."

The van jerked forward. As they sped down the street, Connor pumped his fist. He loathed himself for not taping the precise moment of impact. Nevertheless, his instincts told him otherwise. *Leave no evidence.*

Rogers bawled, 'Oh my God. No—No---Kim, stay with me. Oh my God.' He gently cradled her head, lowering her body to the floor.

He ripped off his shirt and tied it around her head. He cried, 'Kim, I love you. Can you hear me? Don't leave me. I need you. Oh my God, what have I done to you?'

Connor watched Rogers fall helplessly upon the motionless body. Then, he abruptly sat up and arched back Kim's neck. He began CPR.

The former Zach Miller—Rogers's long time nemesis-- leaned back and lit his Cuban. Inhaling deeply, he blew rings around the inside of his van. *At last, Rogers will be ready to roll over and play dead. He'll not dare tell the FBI anything. He'll be shaking in his boots. I can finally work in peace. Actually, its better off that he's still alive. When the FBI calls on me, asking me about Haley and stuff, Rogers will be unharmed. At least, for now!*

Connor smirked upon hearing the trembling cadence of the Surgeon General's voice.

'911 operator'

Rogers shouted into his cell phone, 'My wife's been shot in the head. She's not breathing. She has no pulse. Oh my God!'

'Sir, please give me your name and address.'

'Jonathan Rogers. 493 Elm Street in DC.'

'The police and ambulance are on the way. Are you sure she has no pulse?'

Sobbing hysterically, he replied, 'Yes. I'm doing chest compressions. I've already done mouth-to-mouth breathing. Please dear God, help us. She's not responding.'

Connor clapped in his van. He yelled into his mouthpiece, "Good job Jonesy." The CEO took another puff as he listened closely to the audio feed.

Rogers's voice quivered. He begged the 911 operator, 'Get us help! Where's the ambulance? Dear God, please let her live. Please---.'

'The ambulance and the police should be there any minute. Continue your chest compressions until the squad arrives.'

Rogers pressed his face next to Kim's bloodied head. His final words were frantic. 'I love you. Stay with me." He shrieked out in anguish, "Please don't die. Oh my God what have I done to you?'

Connor took another puff of his Cuban. "Rogers, it's your fault. You should have listened to her and gone back into private practice. I guess he never heard of the expression—*No good deed goes unpunished.* "After tonight, he'll be impotent. Things will be different now with the Surgeon General off my back."

CHAPTER EIGHT

At the Oldwyck River Front cemetery, a black golf umbrella kept one-inch hailstones in the driving freezing rainstorm from pelting Rogers and his daughter. His swollen reddened eyes were mere slits. Heavily medicated with Xanax, he felt frozen in place—in time. While Kim's casket cranked lower into the open crypt, Ashley pressed her crestfallen face into his chest, unable to look.

Rogers's sight locked on the mahogany wood box. Yet, what he saw was not a box-- but Kim herself. The love of his life was inside that coffin. *I need to be with her.*

The priest had just concluded the service. Soon, the rain began to fall even harder—now blowing sideways directly into his face. Despite being in shock, he realized that no one was saying anything. The only sound he heard was Kim's casket hitting the bottom of the grave.

Out the blue, in his mind, their wedding song, *Follow me* was being sung by his wife's teenage niece. *This is my fault! I killed her!*

Ashley clung tightly to him. He scrunched his own face, barely able to look at the painful contortions on his daughter's visage. Now, Ashley was all that he had left. Still oblivious to the fact that fellow grievers had already begun to file away, he felt a gentle touch on his left shoulder. Casting a momentary sideways glance, he saw that it was Beth Murphy. All during the service, she had been holding the golf umbrella above him and Ashley. Subconsciously, he realized that this was the first time that anyone besides Kim or Ashley were able to creep into his awareness of what was transpiring on this dreadful day. He painfully acknowledged Beth's kindness with a brief nod.

Breaking up with emotion, he took one step toward the six-foot deep hole in the muddy ground. Before he could take another, Father Thomas put his arms around Rogers and helped him turn away. Ashley reached out for her father's hand. Amid the downpour, they shuffled in the mud, plodding up the rolling grassy hill toward the waiting limo. Beth Murphy closely followed, holding the umbrella, shielding them as best she could from the torrential downpour of hail.

With each sloshing step forward, the image of Kim's face seemed to appear in front of him. *How can I leave her here?* At the top of the hill, he motioned for Ashley and Beth to head for the shelter of the limo. His daughter reluctantly released his hand. A split second later, he turned on his heels. With each stride, the frigid rain whipped his mop of graying hair across his eyes. *Kim never liked the cold.*

Rogers ran as fast as he could---sprinting toward the gravesite. He heard no sounds, no voices shouting at him to stop his mad dash. As if time had stood still, he sensed Kim getting closer. He began to feel better. It was time for him to do whatever he could to comfort her.

A few feet from the edge of the gravesite, he skidded to a stop, dropping onto his knees. The burial workers were beginning to shovel the soaked cakes dirt onto the casket. Each throw of the sludge landed on the wooden box with a loud thud. He uttered a quiet command for them to stop but all he heard was the excruciating rhythmic cadence of mud hitting Kim's casket.

Kneeling in the muck, he peered down into the crevice—the final resting spot for the love of his life. From the just concluded Christian service, he picked up a rose petal that was lying on the ground. Rogers reached his hand toward Kim. He knew that she would find it. She always did. He dropped the rose into the dug- out fissure while praying to God to give him the strength to survive---- to survive for Ashley. He fought an impulse---to leap into the crevice---to be with Kim---to cover her body just one more time---to shelter her from the brutal cold. *You will always be with me. Your tender touch---your beautiful face. Ashley and I will never forget you. Kim, I love you so much.*

A moment later, an eerie sense that someone was standing over his shoulder came upon him. He bent his neck backwards, looking skyward. Without turning around to see who was helping him, he slowly regained his feet. The helping hand that gripped his numb fingers was warm and soft. He believed it was Ashley.

He turned slowly to hug his daughter for her caring—her empathy to try to lessen his suffering. But, he cringed upon seeing the woman's drenched red hair. He cried out, "No!"

Rogers took a step back from Haley, slipping somewhat in the soaked earth-- backwards toward the cavern behind him. Looking at her steely eyes, he now completely lost his precarious balance. His feet slid back much further this time, now a foot's length just over the edge of the grave, toward Kim's casket. He clawed the earth. The gravediggers surrounded him but inexplicably offered no assistance.

Haley reached out for him. She sat in the mud as a willing contender in a tug-a-war. Successful at grabbing his fore arms with her strong hands, she began to yank Rogers toward her in a series of methodical pulls. She was quickly able to move from her tenuous clutch on his slippery forearms to a firm grasp around his shoulders.

To help himself, he crawled forward on his knees, making some progress. He dug his shoes deeply into the drenched earth. One mighty leap forward propelled him toward her, causing him to fall on top of her chest. Her face, absent her usual make-up, was blotchy and red. It was as though he was lying on top of an iceberg. He shivered, feeling her pulsating heart pushing her breasts toward his chest.

"Dr. Rogers, please forgive me. I came here to tell you how sorry I am, for everything. I came to tell you the whole truth."

Grimacing, he quickly rolled off her and tumbled over in the bitter slush. With the back of his hand, he wiped a thick pack of clinging mud from his soiled eyes. He blinked wildly. Rogers struggled to regain his footing. He stumbled badly but soon was able to get his bearings.

Erect, he spotted Ashley, standing a few feet behind Haley. It all seemed like a bad dream. *I've got to help Kim. It's freezing out here.* The sadness that he felt in his heart was overwhelming. It was all too real.

He pointed at the redhead. "Get the hell away from us," he shouted. "How dare you come here?"

She covered her eyes with her left hand as if to block out the gravesite in front of her. Trembling, she said, "I'm so sorry. You--you need to know the truth. It's not all my fault."

At the top of his lungs, he thundered, "You tried to kill me. More than once-----Get away from us or I'll----." With his chest heaving, he sprinted toward Ashley, barely clinging onto his breath. Weakened, his feet gave way causing him to take a headlong fall into the icy slosh. With his mind racing, he stumbled to his feet and grabbed Ashley's hand, running toward the waiting limo. His mind focused on only one thing-----getting his daughter away from this maniacal killer. With each unsteady step forward, he could hear Haley's footsteps close behind both of them as they slowly advanced through the slop beneath their feet.

"Please listen to me," Haley screamed. "When I heard of your wife's murder, I came to confess—to tell you everything."

Her words finally registered. He stopped in his tracks. "Ashley, run ahead and get inside the limo. I'll be there soon."

"But daddy!"

His mind was spinning. "Honey, I promise---I'll be there in a minute. Please get in the limo."

"Daddy---"

"Run Ashley---please do it---do it for Mom."

His daughter dashed toward the limo. For a second, he wondered where Beth Murphy had gone. He pivoted to face Kim's grave. By now, Haley was only ten yards away and running straight right at him.

She cried out, "You need to know something."

"You're a murderer. Leave us alone. The FBI will be knocking on your door. This time, we'll nail you. The police found explosives embedded in shreds of your handbag."

A second later, Haley was standing in front of him. Her expression froze in place as if an arctic blast had suddenly enveloped her face. "Dr. Rogers, the truth is that Zach Miller---."

He shouted, "You worked for Zach Miller. He died last year. Didn't he?"

Abruptly, her eyes wildly flickered, staring at something over his left shoulder. He noticed that Haley's mouth had suddenly clamped shut. Her feet began to shuffle as if she were searching for a firm footing, as if she was prepared to run off, to get away from something that had frightened her out of her wits. Her eyes darted—as if a grizzly bear was about to pounce on her.

Rogers turned on his heels. Across the road, twenty yards away from where a parked limo lurked, he spotted Connor Lucas. He stood casually, clad in a long black topcoat, holding an open black umbrella above his head.

He looked back to Haley but she was already twenty yards away from him, running as fast as she could. In an all-out gallop, she fell forward. She slid head long in the mud. Clawing her way, she leaped to her feet and continued running without ever glancing behind her.

Connor began trotting straight toward him. Rogers heard Ashley shouting for him to get inside the limo. He dashed toward her. Just five feet from the town car, the uninvited visitor intercepted Rogers. He held out a monographed handkerchief. Connor's face was exceptionally calm, his hair bone dry under the huge golf sized umbrella that he held in his left hand. His face conveyed a smugness that the Surgeon General fiercely disliked. A heartbeat later, the steady right hand of Lucas drew closer to Rogers's face.

"Doctor, wipe the mud from your eyebrows and mouth," he said with a touch of sarcasm. He grinned. "Your appearance is just not becoming for the Surgeon General of the United States of America."

Rogers angrily wiped his hand away. He began angling himself toward the limo. Taking a quick glance, he saw the fright on Ashley's face as she peered out the limo side window. "Lucas, why did you come here with your girlfriend? You told me on the phone that you were finished with Haley."

"You mean Daisy. That is her name. I've never heard of anyone named Haley," he snapped back with a devilish glance. "I told you when you called me. Daisy and I are separated---forever."

"Stop the crap. Her name is Haley and you damn well know it. But, I don't care what alias she uses. She is the same woman who is always around me when trouble hits. Haley is a killer." He began inching his way toward the limo.

Feigning shock, he replied, "In America, we are all innocent until proven guilty. You know that Dr. Rogers."

"And, why the hell are you here?"

Connor's eyes glistened. "To warn you!"

"Who are you to advise me of anything?"

"If you only knew," Connor smirked.

By now, Rogers had one hand on the door of the limo. "The FBI will be after you. I promise you that, Mr. Lucas."

"Why would I worry about the FBI? I've done nothing wrong. You may look a little ragged but you're totally unharmed."

"Look, if I find out that you or Haley Tyler had anything to do with the murder of Kim, I'll personally strangle you to death with my bare hands."

He held up his hands as if preparing to defend himself against a sucker punch. "I'm sorry for your loss but there is no need for you to lash out at me. I didn't kill anyone." Connor looked away, in the direction Haley was running. "Look, doctor, there are sensitive things that you should leave alone! Just take care of Ashley."

Rogers's eyes popped. His neck veins pulsated. "How do you know my daughter's name?"

He firmly patted the shoulder of the Surgeon General. "You're under a lot of pressure. I really must be on my way," he said as his eyes focused on Haley's back, now more than a half football field away.

A second later, Ashley begged him to come to her side. "Daddy, let's go! Please Daddy!"

"Cutie, I'll be there in a few seconds."

Rogers forced himself to linger a few more moments. Turning toward Connor, the mud dripped off his hands like melting wax off a candle. He stared at two icy looking blue globes that did not move. He took a half step forward, invading the unwelcomed intruder's space. "Listen Mr. Lucas, just who the hell are you?"

Grinning, he replied, "I only came to pay my respects. I watched the entire burial service from the hill."

"Why?"

"Let me finish. Co-incidentally, my ex-girlfriend's car pulled into the cemetery ahead of me. I have no idea why she came. As you can see, her actions are quite bizarre. I'll have to demand that she will leave you alone. You can count on that. You'll never see her again."

Connor dropped his umbrella and began sprinting toward Haley. He shouted back, "Who would do such a nasty thing to Kim?"

Rogers practically dove into the backseat of the limo, slamming the door behind him. Hugging Ashley tightly, he looked out the window.

Connor galloped across the open cemetery field, gaining rapidly on Haley with each long stride. She was less than one hundred yards ahead of him when they both disappeared from his sight.

The limo driver turned on the key and slowly drove from the cemetery. Rogers feared for his daughter's safety. As he began to pray, his cell rang. It was his boss's administrative assistant. Secretary of Health, Christian James, had thoughtfully arranged for a move of their furniture from their townhouse to a two-bedroom apartment at the *Watergate*. Ashley would stay with him, at least for now.

As the limo pulled onto the main street, he could not blot out one reoccurring impulse---going back and throwing himself into the abyss---with Kim---with his best friend. He tightly held onto Ashley with his right arm. Using his left hand, he held his mother's old Irish lace handkerchief to soak up a torrent of tears from the both of them.

Memories of Kim's beautiful face—indelibly etched in his brain---never to be forgotten—stared hauntingly back at him.

CHAPTER NINE

Dr. Hussein Nasters kissed the ground. He knelt down on the tarmac at Kandahar Airport just minutes after exiting a Turkish Airlines Boeing 737-300 plane.

The scientist looked up at the blazing sun, praising Allah for ensuring his safe passage to a country adjacent to his homeland. He calculated the probable direction of Mecca, angling himself to face the holiest city. Going through his ritual, he pounded his chest with his right fist. The scorching heat penetrated every pore of his skin. Beads of sweat fell from his forehead as he tried in vain to blink away the moisture. He concluded his custom with the Moslem prayer of thanks, anxious to see his beloved father.

Picking up his briefcase, he rolled his luggage across the tarmac to the terminal. The cab ride to his father's apartment on the outskirts of Kandahar would take slightly more than an hour. His last conversation with his father two weeks earlier had been hopeful but worrisome. His father allowed no discussion of specifics. However, Ali Nasters did ask Hussein to come as quickly as he could, given the tense political atmosphere that seemed to be escalating every day along the Afghan-Pakistani border.

Thankfully, the security lines were short on this particular day. Within thirty minutes, he had picked up his one checked suitcase in the baggage department. He quickly exited the terminal.

On the bustling main avenue, waves of Afghans encircled him. He waved down a taxi and settled in for the long ride that would culminate in Hussein seeing his beloved father. Everything seemed so different.

Nasters recalled his childhood days growing up in an upper class Defence section of Karachi, Pakistan. His father had been a prosperous executive in a top tier bank while his mother had worked as an attorney for a prominent law firm in the capital. Well educated, life had been good for their family and especially for the youngest child, Hussein.

As the taxi wound its way through the narrow cobblestones streets, he pictured himself his youthful days when he looked out at the vast Arabian Sea in southeastern Pakistan, near the Indus River delta. He began to reminisce. Subconsciously, the tragic events of recent years broke through the happy memories of earlier days. His seventy-year-old father had always been mentally sharp and engaged on any matter of consequence. Two months earlier, Ali Hussein had relocated from Karachi to Kandahar. Therefore, when Hussein's weekly letters to his father were no longer answered within the past month, he began to think the worst, based upon what had previously happened to his family

Past nightmares came flooding back. In addition to his well-regarded standing in the business community, Hussein's father was an outspoken political leader. Three years earlier, Hussein's mother tried in vain to stop her husband from immersing himself in politics. She repeatedly warned him that it was only a matter of time before the government would force the bank to eliminate his position. Hussein had privately agreed with his mother but to no avail. His father was a Pakistani freedom-fighting warrior.

Hussein comforted himself that at least he had kept in regular contact with his father through the mail since his last visit to Karachi eighteen months earlier. Ali Nasters, during this period, publicly expressed tremendous pride in his son's well-known scientific accomplishments. In addition, he repeatedly assured Hussein that he was well pleased that his son was following what his heart dictated.

However, in the last two months, everything had changed. Widespread civil unrest in Karachi had clearly worsened according to the American media. By necessity, his father had relocated to Kandahar. During this transition time, Ali's letters had ceased to arrive. As tears welled in his eyes, the scientist harbored deep and rising concerns about the safety of his father.

Nasters's real life ordeal of two years earlier flashed before his eyes. One terrible night, an opposing religious fanatic slaughtered his mother and three brothers with a machete. The murderer apparently came to their home looking for his father. After the tragedy, Hussein returned to his homeland for the family funerals. What he learned from local authorities was devastating and deeply disturbing to him. It was something that had haunted him every single day---ever since his father first informed Hussein of the massacre of most of his immediate family. Since his last visit, Nasters held in his seething anger about this personal tragedy and confided in no one.

A high-ranking government official confirmed the massacre of most of his family. Yet the official story from the government was far different from what Ali had told Hussein. Local police maintained that the American CIA killed his family during their brutal hunt for his father on that fateful night. There were unsubstantiated charges that Ali had been a high-level spy for terrorist elements within the Pakistani Freedom Fighters against the United States. Yet, his father had always steadfastly refused to confirm to anyone—even Hussein---whether he was in fact, a secret agent. After the mass slayings of his family, several government officials accused Ali Nasters---but never convicted him---of infiltrating the American embassy to obtain strategic intelligence.

As Hussein discovered, his own father had survived the bloodbath purely on luck. Several days before the gruesome butchery wiped out his family, his heart failure worsened. The night of the attack, his admission into Aga Khan Hospital for treatment of severe congestive heart failure had saved his life. Yet, based on hospital records, his shortness of breath had miraculously begun to improve on the day of the actual bloodbath. In fact, his cardiologist was prepared to discharge him just hours before the carnage. However, his primary care doctor who would have sent Ali home that morning was himself involved in a fatal car accident. Therefore, discharge orders never came that day. The following morning, Ali received the heartbreaking news from a new cardiologist who then sent him home, just twelve hours after the carnage inflicted on his family.

On his last visit, Ali had confided in Hussein his version of what had transpired. In the year prior to the mass murders of his family, his father had formally asked the United States government, through his high-level contacts at the American embassy in Karachi, to intervene in getting his immediate family out of Pakistan so that they could join Hussein in America. Ali had diligently filed the appropriate papers to gain a visa through the US ambassador. Nevertheless, little did Ali know at the time that an Embassy clerk had simply forgotten to process the application. Despite multiple calls by Ali and even Hussein, the American Embassy did not act. Because of the lack of action to grant a visa by the US consultant, his entire family had been wiped out that fateful night—just by being in the wrong place at the wrong time. Hussein had heard his father's repeated rant since that dreadful day that retribution against the United States was not only justified but revenge was what Allah had demanded. Ali would never let Hussein believe for a moment that a single clerical error was responsible for the deaths of most of his immediate family. No---Ali shouted—what led to the mass execution of his loved ones was willful, inexcusable, and wanton neglect on the part of the United States.

With weeks after the multiple killings, the bank eliminated Ali Nasters's position. Within six months due to mounting mortgage payments and bills with no real income, his father fell on hard times. Moving from his comfortable home where he and his wife had reared their children, he found himself on the verge of bankruptcy, forced to relocate to a poor neighborhood in Kandahar, Afghanistan, where he had one close ally.

Even though Ali informed Hussein that members of a religious tribe had actually killed the family, his father still blamed the United States for not granting the visa that would have allowed all of them to leave Pakistan before harm came their way. Thus, Hussein developed an overwhelming hatred for the most powerful nation on earth. Working in

America for many years as a well-respected scientist, he had within the past year or so waged an internal struggle within himself to masquerade his deep resentment toward the United States.

He peered out the taxi window. Whizzing by, he caught glimpses of the rundown neighborhoods of Kandahar. An hour later, the taxi skidded to a halt in front of a decrepit looking apartment building next to a small rural railway station. He paid the driver sixty rupees and pulled his luggage from the back seat. Carrying his suitcase and briefcase to the splintered wooden door of the ground level apartment, red flags appeared from the start. *Number six.* The door was half-open. Upon entering the apartment, Nasters smelled gas. He dropped his load on the warped floorboards and shouted out to his father. *Silence.*

The living room was adjacent to the small entrance hallway. The smashed TV screen caught his eye. His head began to pound. Scattered huge gashes in the black woolen fabric of a couch came into view. A Death to the Infidels placard, in his father's own script, lay rumpled on the floor. The gas fumes grew stronger.

Hussein ran into the kitchen, covering his mouth and nose. He began to gasp for air. Two burners on the stove were blazing. A coffee stained towel that he found near the sink provided cover for his mouth and nose. He began coughing as his lungs felt increasingly heavy. A steak knife covered in dark red, dried blood was lying on a small wooden table. Unable to stop coughing, he cupped his hands under the faucet above the sink and swallowed hard. The metallic tasting water cleared his throat of some of the dust and fumes.

Hussein began to believe what he had feared all along. He whirled around. Sprinting toward his father's bedroom, he pushed the hanging multi-colored beads over the entrance to one side. He screamed. There his beloved father lay on the bed, motionless with eyes and mouth wide open. A crusty patch of dried blood circled his mouth and heavy beard. A fly rested on his pale cheekbone, seemingly ready to make another dive into the open orifice at any moment.

Hussein dropped to his knees and prayed to Allah for strength. His tear filled eyes latched onto a crumpled piece of paper lying on the floor next to the bed. He uncurled the paper. It was a note handwritten from his father. The date on the message was yesterday. *My dearest Hussein, I want you to know how much I have always loved you. Never blame yourself for what has happened to me or to your family. Your mother, your brothers, and I all know that you have tried your best to help us. I know that the infidels in America have not listened to your pleas for help. Today, I am very weak and wounded. I hope to last until you come to visit me. I pray that I'm not attacked again. Remember; Seek personal revenge for our family in the name of Allah. Your loving father, Ali.*

Nasters's tears flowed like a raging river. He cursed his father's enemy for what had happened. He vowed vengeance. From this day forward, this would be his destiny. His duty was now clear. It all made perfect sense.

There was the reason that Allah had enabled him to become the top scientist at DCP. Hussein possessed the authority and the credibility as a scientist to do what he needed to do. No lingering doubts would ever stop him again. *Americans must pay—every last one of them.*

He began to recite as he rubbed away the sorrow from his eyes and from memory repeated the Janazah prayer, the Salat-al-Janazah. Allah would help him in the difficult days that lay ahead. Struggling to regain his feet, he approached his father's body. A fresh jagged knife wound near his liver stood out—the final mortal blow.

The faithful son reverently washed the corpse after placing a white cloth, which he discovered in the bedroom cabinet, on his father's abdomen and genitals. A basin, found under the kitchen sink, filled with tap water and carefully poured over Ali's body.

Hussein completed the drying of the physically cleansed body and wrapped it in a clean white sheet found in a nearby chest of drawers. The cloth sheet, the kafan, conveyed dignity and respect. Hussein prayed, glued to his father's face.

Once darkness had fallen, he carried the shrouded body a hundred yards or so to the rear of a grassy field, near a large papal tree whose branches sprang out like a huge umbrella. Returning quickly to the apartment, he searched for a tool to dig a grave. The largest instrument he could find was a metal spatula. He resigned himself to what he needed to do, promptly returning to the field.

Under Islamic law, it was already past the time for an appropriate burial. He filled his lungs with the cool nighttime air and mentally prepared himself for the arduous task ahead. Hussein looked up at the stars. From his past learning, he visualized Mecca to be horizontal to the thickest bough of the papal tree. He methodically clawed at the dirt with the spatula, digging perpendicular to the Qibla, towards the Holy City of Mecca. On his knees, over a period of six hours, he dug with the four-inch spatula to a depth of four feet and a length of five feet. Near exhaustion, Hussein then carefully picked up the shrouded body and placed it into the grave. Ali's head faced Qibla.

He reached down for a handful of soil. With the first handful that he tossed onto the corpse, he recited a prayer. "We created you from it, and return you into it, and from it we will raise you a second time." He then threw a second and a third handful of dirt into the grave, each time quietly repeating the prayer that asked for forgiveness of the deceased and a reminder to the deceased of their profession of faith.

The quarter moon shed little light at the gravesite, a fact for which Hussein was grateful, not wanting to draw any attention from anyone in the row of apartments that lay a football length away. About to collapse from dehydration, he returned to his father's apartment. He poured himself a half dozen glasses of water from the sink and downed each of them in seemingly insatiable gulps.

He walked into Ali's bedroom and sat on the floor, facing the bed where he had found his beloved father. His muscles ached, especially his low back. After praying to Allah, he rested for an additional ten minutes before returning to the gravesite.

Painstakingly, he covered the body with the loose soil. When the dirt had reached the level of the ground, he stomped on it to compact it further. To gather more dirt, he walked behind the tree and dug with the now bent spatula. He pulled his shirt from his body and used it as a basin to hold a dozen scoops of soil. Each time his shirt was full, he returned the twenty yards to empty the dirt onto the gravesite. He stomped repeatedly until the earth grew to a height of six inches over his father's grave.

Hussein prayed again for eternal forgiveness of his father. For the first time since he had begun the burial, he noticed a dim light coming from the east. Dawn was only minutes away. Silently, he recited the Eid prayer that was by tradition recited at a time when the sun was three meters from the horizon. Tearfully, he bid Ali a farewell for now and promised aloud once again to carry out his father's wishes for retaliation.

The sky seemed to brighten exponentially with the passing of each minute. The dilapidated apartment buildings were now clearly in view. He summoned a spurt of adrenalin and sprinted across the field to Ali's place, quietly closing the door behind him. The tattered couch would be his resting spot. Exhausted, he fell into a profound sleep.

A loud series of honks from a car horn outside on the nearby road awakened him. Sunlight creased his eyes. Shielding his eyes, he stumbled to the kitchen. He guzzled down a half-filled glass of water before sitting on the tiled floor to pray to Allah for guidance.

For three consecutive nights, he would return to Ali's gravesite to mourn and pray throughout each night. Each day at the first sign of dawn, he would return to the apartment to sleep, drink water, and eat the apples, bananas, and dry cereal that filled his father's pantry.

Rarely during these dreadful days did he allow himself the luxury of thinking anything other than the death of his beloved father. The American Presidential demand for the mass deployment of *NeoBloc* found a pathway to his extremely disciplined mind. Bowing toward Mecca, Dr. Hussein Nasters could hardly wait to serve the American ignorance of the truth.

******

The day was humid and dusty. A high noon sunburned brightly in the cloudless sky. Nasters approached the abandoned storefront office with confidence in his step. His mourning period was over. It was time to act on his father's wishes. In recent days, he had remembered this location. It was the place where several political allies of his father met. Now, it was time to pay them a visit.

Hussein walked into the plain looking headquarters of the Pakistani Freedom Fighters, determined to seek retribution for his family. He believed that he would need their help in launching his jihad against the Americans. Looking around the Spartan like foyer, it was barren of any furniture. The outside windows had been white washed to prevent anyone from looking into this hideaway---a place where the Pakistani Freedom Fighters would occasionally congregate to plot strategies.

He noticed an opening in the back of the ten-foot square barren room. A brown tweed curtain hung, covering the entrance to what his father used to refer to as "The Clubhouse." Hussein waited patiently for ten minutes, hoping that someone would come out the infamous backroom. While praying to Allah, a soft-spoken voice rang out from behind a curtain. "May I help you?" An elderly man wearing a red turban approached the scientist.

"Good morning, my name is Hussein Nasters."

In a stern but subdued voice, he said, "Please show me your passport."

Nasters presented it and respectfully bowed his head. "For your consideration of allowing me membership in your organization," he said with as much humility as he could muster.

The Pakistani elder with a long white beard and a deep scar across his left cheek looked carefully at the United State passport. He raised his eyes, looking suspiciously at Nasters. "We will check you out. If you are acceptable to the PFF, someone will contact you. You will never hear directly from me again. Do not attempt to contact me. Do not contact the PFF. Understood?"

"Praise be to Allah. I will drop off a resume."

The response was swift and loud. "No! We do not need your help. We are in charge of everything. Is that clear?"

"I beg your indulgence. I pray that Allah sees the goodness in my soul. I'll await a call if I am deemed worthy."

The scientist left the storefront foyer quickly. Calling the airline reservations department, he confirmed his return flight to the States. He needed to give the PFF adequate time. Within three weeks, Hussein planned to leave Kandahar. If he didn't receive word by then, he would return to DCP. One fact was clear. *NeoBloc* was his savior to avenge the honor of his family. The American public would serve as his sacrificial lambs.

Hussein Nasters checked into a two star Kandahar hotel. He checked his email account three times each day, using the computer in the hotel's lobby. Sean Parker had asked several times how he was doing. Each time, he lied, saying that everything was fine with his family and that he was looking forward to returning to his work at DCP. Hussein was particularly annoyed when he read one specific email from his boss. It had alerted him to the fact that the Surgeon General had asked for an expedited visit to DCP to review all of the *NeoBloc* monkey vaccine data. Upon learning that the White House had agreed with the request of Dr. Rogers, he cringed. As the days passed uneventfully, his planned flight to America was fast approaching. Each day, he hoped that his PFF contact would reach out to him but his cell phone remained silent as one week quickly passed.

To maintain his sanity, Nasters had been keeping up with some of the major world newspapers. Enjoying a somewhat unusual hobby, he loved to scan the obituaries in the International Edition of the *Washington Post.* After seeing the easily recognized name among the dead, he flipped to the well-covered story of Kim Rogers's violent death in the main section of the paper. Though not particularly liking Dr Rogers's, today he felt tremendous sorrow for him. Nasters continued with the story. Local police had reported finding a miniature camera and speaker in the front room study of their townhome. The FBI reported that they had no suspects. He wondered what the repercussions of the loss of his wife would be on the Surgeon General's drive to investigate his savior vaccine. *Time will tell!*

On page three of the *Post*, he stumbled across another sign of what he believed to be American decadence. A young woman found dead in her hotel room from an apparent suicide due to an overdose of barbiturates grabbed his attention. The name of the woman was Haley Tyler.

Smack in the middle of his three-week isolation in Kandahar, his cell phone rang. He seized it, as if it was a life preserver and he was a non-swimmer in the middle of the Arabian Sea.

"Hello."

The voice was firm. "Be at eleven Dacca Bengal Road at six tonight."

Nasters heard the steady drone of the dial tone before he could respond.

******

The number eleven, on the tiny hut that appeared to be made of bamboo shoots tied together, had worn off, becoming unreadable. He checked the address on the hut next door. *Number thirteen.* Nasters returned to the first shanty and knocked on the door. No answer. He fiddled with the locked doorknob. Wondering again if he was at the wrong address, he trusted what he heard and decided to sit on the curb to wait. *Patience Hussein!* His father's advice rang in his ears.

The night grew darker. He prayed to Allah. His thoughts rambled between memories of his slain family, a salvo of curses toward America, and the personal revenge that he would achieve through *NeoBloc.* When a street light lamp down the street came on for the night, the door behind him screeched open.

He rose and walked toward the entrance. There was no one there. He heard footsteps running inside. He softly murmured, "Hello."

No response. He entered the ten by ten extremely barren space. An overhead light bulb hung from a wire that entered a space between the bamboo shoots in the center of the ceiling. A mosaic of cracked red marble stone comprised the uneven floor, stained with brown colored gravel in many sections. Directly in front of him, on the far wall, he saw a webcam and a small loudspeaker resting on top of a small-unpainted box made of bamboo.

As he walked toward the wall, the door slammed shut behind him. He did an about face and walked back to the door. Examining the lock, he spotted a wire running from a motor mounted near the door hinges. He followed the copper wire's course. Taped down into a tiny crevice that ran the length of the stone floor, the wire exited in a small hole near the base of the back wall next to the video camera that pointed at him. In the left corner of the room, there was a grimy looking wooden trap door with a rusty handle embedded in the stone floor. Nasters tried to pull it open. It would not budge.

The remainder of the room, stripped bare except for two other objects--a quart sized canter lying in the right corner and a razor blade taped to the wall directly in front of him, at eye level, threw him into a tizzy. Nasters sat down and shivered on the cold marble stones for the better part of the next hour. In meditation to Allah, he wasn't sure at first if he was hallucinating when he thought he heard an almost inaudible voice. Staring at the loudspeaker, he jumped back a step or two when it vibrated to life.

"Hussein Nasters, listen carefully."

He replied in a reverent tone. "I am your servant. Praise be to Allah!" He bowed at the source of the booming voice. "Allah is great!"

"Your fate is in your hands. If you fail, you will never contact us again. In order for us to accept you, Hussein, you will need to demonstrate your loyalty. I must say that we currently see you as a captain of a corrupt American industry. You are a scientist working at a high level with infidels. You rapaciously maximize the profits of your shareholders. Thus, you have much to prove to us. We will set the bar very high for you."

"My father, Ali Nasters, gave his life for the cause of Allah. America killed my entire family. I am not their agent. I am acting as a Trojan horse in order to destroy our common enemy. To me, the cause is intense—deeply personal."

"Words are easy to say. They mean nothing to us. We have already taken action related to your business."

"What action?"

"Do not question us. Never forget that we do not as yet trust you. You must first demonstrate your unwavering allegiance. We will test your commitment and we will consult with Allah."

Nasters lowered his head. "I humbly submit myself to Allah and to you."

"Enough talk. It is time."

Silence.

"You will stay here for two days. You will not eat. There is some clean water in the canter. However, we have prepared a few challenges for you. Your torture is about to begin."

"I will gladly bear it."

"Are you afraid?"

"Yes. I am human. I have many flaws. But, I submit myself to the will of Allah. God is great!"

"Good. Stand up and rip the razor blade from the wall. Then sit down on the floor and face the webcam. Place the razor on the floor in front of you."

Nasters complied and stared into the lens.

The voice grew more somber. "Remember, just as we are watching you now, we'll always be watching you---until you die."

"I understand."

"Rip apart your shirt at the buttons."

He inserted his fingers on both sides of his white button down collar dress shirt. Pulling each side back in one violent motion, he exposed his hairy chest to the camera. "As you say."

"Pick up the razor blade."

He took a deep breath. Thoughts of how much his father loved him paraded through his mind. Ali Nasters would be so proud of what he was about to do. Holding the single edge blade in his right hand, he closed his eyes. "Allah is our only savior!"

"Remember those words Hussein. I do not want to hear any more propaganda of your vaccine as the savior. It is Allah and Allah only who is our savior."

"It is my belief as well."

"Place the blade on your skin just above your belly button."

He did as commanded. After feeling a slight twinge, he looked down to see if there was any bleeding. He saw a solitary drop.

The speaker rang out, "Do not look!!" The deep-throated voice was stern and livid sounding.

"I'm sorry. I will do only as you say."

"Follow my commands but never look down again. Make a circle of blood appear; starting from your present point. If you cut deep enough, there will be blood. There is no need for you to confirm that by looking. The severity of inflicted pain will be your signal as to when to cease."

Nasters shut his eyes and imagined that this was all a dream. Enveloped as though he was in a deep trance, he envisioned that he was already in heaven----with his family. *Praise Allah!* He carried out the order by pressing harder on the blade. In creating a circle, he blocked out the piercing pain. Warm blood dripped onto his hand. Upon completion of this particular task, he flashed his eyes open. "I await your next order."

"Hussein, do not move until you hear my voice again. I shall return in twelve hours."

Nasters slammed his eyes tightly shut and tried to ignore the pool of blood that he felt flowing down his groin. His skin began to itch. He prayed to Allah and began drifting into a profound sleep so as not to be tempted to scratch.

***

Sunlight brightened the dungy looking bamboo room. Hussein toppled back and smacked his head on the stone floor. Feeling faint, he had no idea how long he had been sleeping. He twisted his body toward his right side and painfully regained his sitting position, staring at the webcam, wondering how much longer he would need to suffer. The muscle spasms in his back and legs grew in intensity but Nasters persevered and remained a stone figure. His father's overarching command of seeking revenge on America kept him going. A series of ripples of searing pain shot down his back yet he bore his fate—his destiny. *I will not fail.*

The loudspeaker blared a split second later. "Hussein, you may now stand. Take one mouthful of water from the canter and pour the remaining contents from the canter on your abdominal wound but be certain to save the bottom twenty percent of water."

Nasters tried to rise but tumbled onto his side. His legs felt paralyzed. They felt numb. Slapping his muscles to bring them back to life, he was gradually able to move them. He massaged the blood through his muscular tissues. The pins and needles sensation came and went until he felt some strength returning. Agonizing pain with each movement was his reward for moving closer to what he needed to achieve to carry out his mission.

Unsteady, he wobbled to his feet but quickly fell to one knee. Using his arms to prop himself upright, he stood but stumbled awkwardly toward the right corner of the room. He leaned against the wall. He forced his mind to focus on this task. Minutes later, he struggled to move toward the canter but eventually he was able to grasp it in his weakened grip. The water jug appeared to be made of tin—rusty tin.

He took a few sips. His parched throat ached as the initial few drops of metallic tasting water passed through his food pipe.

Nasters looked down at the caked mass of dried blood on his abdomen and poured most of the canter contents on the wound as previously directed. It was counterintuitive to pour most of the water from the canter on his wound—more than his allotment to drink—but he followed the harsh command. *Do not question!* Nasters thanked Allah for any mercy. Bowing toward the webcam, the scientist gently placed the canter back on the stone floor as the last drop evaporated.

"Resume your position in front of me and remove your shirt. Use your garment to wipe your bloody circle. Then you will utilize your shirt as a pen. Use your blood to write the first letters of our organization on the wall to your left. If you complete all three letters, you may drink the remaining water in the canter as you wish. If the blood is still dry and you cannot write the first letters of the Pakistani Freedom Fighters, you will have to use whatever water remains in the canter to provide needed moisture to the dried blood. If you fail to complete the task of writing all three letters, you will be abandoned by us, forever."

Nasters wrote the P and the F letters without much difficulty. But the bloody shirt had run dry. The last F was impossible to trace on the wall. He returned to the right corner. His tongue felt as though desert sand caked every crevice. Using half of the remaining water left in the canter, he was barely able to draw the final F on the wall. After completing his order, he swirled the last mouthful of water around his gums and teeth before celebrating with a hard swallow. He returned to the webcam, awaiting further orders.

"So far, you have done well. Sit down again. This time you will face the door. When you see sunlight below the doorstep, you may rise. You may then go outside the door. Search in the weeds on the left side of the hut. You will find a small pistol. Bring it back with you into the room. We will then contact you with your last duty. Your membership in the PFF will depend on how well you execute our final order."

Nasters sat and fixated on the darkness beneath the door. *At least only hours remain.*

✳✳✳

The morning sun blinded him as he opened the door. He would have to use his sense of touch in the thorny weeds to find the gun. Fighting off the pain of the cuts from the bristles of the dense weeds, Nasters soon returned to the room with the pistol.

The pistol reminded him of the cheap one used on the streets by gangs—"a Saturday night special." He flipped open the chamber to see the contents. He found just one bullet. Nasters faced the webcam while holding the gun at his side. Fatigued by the exhaustive two days in the hut, he felt himself nodding off just when the familiar voice rang out.

"Hold the pistol to your temple. Spin the cylinder. To complete this task properly, you must squeeze the trigger twice without re-spinning. If Allah wants you to join the PFF, he will protect you. If not, you will die. This is your final reminder that we are all here to do his bidding. Allah will decide!"

Nasters felt his heart exploding with each beat. His chest ached. Sweat oozed from his hand. His grip on the weapon became slippery. Taking a final gulp of air, he pictured his mother and father in paradise. He prayed for forgiveness before closing his eyes. He squeezed the trigger. Opening his eyes, he saw the wall. Without hesitation, he again held the pistol against his right temple. Without a second thought, he pulled the trigger again. The hammer clicked for the second time. Heaving a huge sigh, the wall remained in view. *Thank Allah!*

The speaker rang out in a cheerful tone. "Hussein, you have done well, my son. Your father is proud of you. You are now free to leave. You will be contacted after you are back in America."

Nasters quickly left the hut. Exhilarated, he found himself almost leaping down the mountain. After reaching the main road, he hailed a taxi back to his hotel. Asking the cabbie to wait, he went upstairs for several rupees and a desperate move to down two glasses of water. He returned to the street to pay his fare before kneeling down to kiss the slimy cobblestones. Pointing to the heavens, he promised to seek revenge on America for their willful neglect of his loving family. *My jihad will be magnificent!*

CHAPTER TEN

Rogers clicked off the snooze alarm. He had experienced two weeks of extreme loneliness and depression since Kim's funeral. In a robotic manner, he methodically put on his dark blue shorts, a pullover gray sweatshirt, and dirty sneakers into his gym bag before grabbing his suit and dress shoes. Just before closing the door to his new apartment at the *Watergate*, he shuffled over to the second bedroom. Quietly, he opened the door. Ashley did not stir. Seeing her curled up under her pink down feathered quilt brought back a flood of happy reminiscences.

His daughter had always been a godsend—a joy in his life. Now, more than ever, her presence gave him some reason to go on. Back on anti-depressant medication since Kim's death, he knew in his soul that it was his love for their daughter, which prevented him from slipping into an even deeper melancholy mood.

Partly as an opportunity to spend more time with her, last week he had suggested that they both learn martial arts. Ashley embraced the idea. The twice a week class that he shared with her was something to look forward to doing. From the time since she was a baby, he recalled the times when he would sit next to her crib and just stare at her angelic face---a true miracle from God.

Kim would be so proud if she were standing alongside him today. She would be the first to agree that their love for one another had created a caring, intelligent, and beautiful human being. He smiled down at his only remaining connection with Kim. *Nothing will ever happen to Ashley. I will sacrifice my life for her life.*

Slowly backpedaling toward the door, it sprang to mind that his daughter had a special gift. People trusted and respected her. Mature for her age, her emotional quotient surpassed her superior intelligence—at least in his opinion—even if biased.

When Ashley was only twelve, she once told him that she wanted to dedicate her life to help people live healthier lives---just as he did during his career as a practicing physician, a Commissioner of Health, and now as Surgeon General. After Kim's death, she had taken some time off from medical school at the University of Michigan. In addition to spending private time with her father at martial arts class or just enjoying a long walk together in the park, she was also beginning to be somewhat of a regular visitor to his office at the Department of Health and Human Services. In short, Ashley had become his closest and most trusted confidant.

Rogers closed the door to her room and locked the apartment door. He hopped into the elevator and rode it down to the gym on the third floor of the well-known capitol complex.

In the locker room, he looked in the mirror. He slammed his eyes shut. It was so obvious—embarrassing to be so out of shape. After nodding to some of the early morning gym rats, he pumped the elliptical at a ten-minute mile pace. He tried not to think about his mounting problems, but it was to no avail. When he hit the three-mile mark, he jumped off the machine. Rogers headed for a quick shower before taking his usual subway commute to the Department of Health and Human Services.

***

Today would be a special day. Rogers was meeting with President Williams and Secretary James in the Oval Office to discuss the safety of *NeoBloc*. In a taxi ride over to the White House, he scribbled down his main talking points on a yellow legal pad.

The cab stopped at the outside gate and dropped him off. Rogers flashed his personal ID. The initial guard cleared him to report to the second security gatehouse. At the latter checkpoint, he received his White House identification badge for the day. Snaking through the winding corridors leading to the Oval Office, he arrived at the waiting room just outside of the President's office. There he spotted Christian James. The Secretary's head was hanging low, pacing the floor.

James glanced up at Rogers. He beamed a smile that revealed more than half of his full set of pearly white teeth. "Good morning. I'm truly sorry for your loss."

"Thank you."

The Secretary patted him on the shoulder. He pointed to a pair of wingback chairs. "Let's sit down and just talk."

"Glad to be back to work. At home, I feel so guilty about Kim."

"It must be rough. How is your daughter handling this?"

"Last night, Ashley and I had a long talk."

"I can only imagine what the last several weeks have been for the both of you."

"It's been really rough for both of us." Rogers's voice cracked. "I told Ashley that it's not fair to her for me to expect a twenty-something to baby sit her Dad. I convinced her to move back to her own apartment later this week."

James stood and Rogers followed suit. His boss gave him a half-hug. "Again, let me know if there is anything that I can do. You and Ashley are in my daily thoughts and prayers."

"I really appreciate your concern."

The Secretary glanced at his Rolex. "Madison told me that the President is running a few minutes behind. We have time to talk about what we're going to say to her. Jonathan, since you requested this meeting, what's your agenda?"

"I sent the President's chief of staff an email yesterday stating that I wanted to talk about my concern about the DCP monkey safety data. I copied you."

"I don't recall seeing anything more specific than you wanted to meet to discuss your worries about *NeoBloc*."

"That sounds about right."

"Why would you not email me with more details of this meeting with the President? After all, you and I are a team."

"It must have slipped my mind." Rogers rubbed his chin. "While I was out on bereavement leave, I got to thinking. I remembered that I never told you something that is very important."

"Tell me now."

"When Lauren Timmons met me in a Georgetown pub the night she was murdered, she gave me what the CIA would call a high value asset."

"What high value asset?" James's eyes narrowed to mere slits. His face turned crimson red. In a measured low cadence, the Secretary spoke. "All I knew was that you were going through the Park in a taxi and you heard a scream. You got out of the taxi and found her decapitated." He grimaced. "Look, if you're going to work for me, you just can't hold back any information."

"I have been under tremendous pressure."

"I know you've been through a lot." He smiled broadly. "OK. It's forgotten. So, exactly what did Lauren tell you and what did she give you?"

"She gave me confidential information-- on the safety research of *NeoBloc*. Lauren said the vaccine was not safe."

James's face became taut. "Where is this research?"

"It's been stolen from my town home."

James eyebrows knitted in a deep crease above his Roman like nose. "So, what else haven't you told me?"

"That's it."

"Are you absolutely sure?"

Rogers nodded. He felt good, having this all come out before meeting with the President. "Christian, I'm worried about that woman who I told you about after our last meeting. I think she's the one who tried to blow me up at Roma's."

"You still haven't told me who she is."

He hesitated. Rogers stroked his hair, locking on the Secretary's darting eyes. "I've met her several times in the last year. Her first name is Haley. Bad things usually followed when she comes on a scene."

"Like what?"

The Surgeon General heard the doorknob to the Oval Office turning. He pointed to the door flinging open.

James persisted, "Like---"

"The President is ready for the meeting." Madison walked over to escort them into the Oval Office. Rogers marched in step behind Secretary James.

Bypassing the Secretary, Jane Williams approached the Surgeon General with an empathetic smile. "Please accept my deepest sympathies on your loss. I pray for you and your daughter each night."

"Your prayers are greatly appreciated, Madame President."

She waved in the direction of the seating arrangement in the center of the room. "Gentlemen, please have a seat."

A collective coordinated reply ensued. "Thank you."

Rogers sat at the far end of the couch. He remembered it to be the same location on the same Oval Office couch that the former chief of staff of the previous President had taken when Rogers had initially interviewed last year for the Surgeon General position. However, that was at another time and another administration. *This President wants to do what's right.* James took a seat at the near end of the couch, closest to the President.

Williams set her eyes directly on Rogers. "My chief of staff told me that you want to discuss your concerns about Project Moon Shot."

He spoke with conviction. "I have good reason to be concerned that the vaccine *NeoBloc* is dangerous."

"Is that so?" She cast a shocked side -ways glance at James. "Do you have specific evidence to back up your claim?"

"I'm still connecting the dots." With his head cocked to one side, he looked warily over at James. "I have strong suspicions, especially after my meeting with the DCP CEO Sean Parker and his top scientist, Dr. Hussein Nasters."

Williams shot James a puzzled look. The Secretary shrugged his shoulders and bit his lower lip. The President refocused. "Dr. Rogers, I need much more than your reservations."

"I understand." Her face was now pensive and unsettled. By her changed expression, she appeared clearly annoyed. "I've been invited back to DCP in a couple of weeks to review the preliminary results of the early human testing and to drill down much deeper on their final monkey safety data."

"So, why would you want to share your reservations with me on the human clinical trials before you have any proof?"

"If *NeoBloc* did in fact kill every monkey in the animal trials, it would most likely do the same in the human clinical trials. Therefore, I believe these trials should not commence until I review the monkey data.

It is my hope that you could put a moratorium on the human trials. That would save lives if the vaccine is actually lethal."

Williams sat back in her chair. "I'm sure that you understand the importance of *NeoBloc* for the future of our country. We are at war with terrorists. This vaccine could save many lives. Therefore, I will not commit to delaying the human trials based solely on your doubts—no matter how strongly you may feel."

"I understand that you need to do what is right for our entire nation." Rogers leaned forward, adding, "As a physician who is pro-life, every life is precious."

The President gave a half smile. "You're my official physician advisor. I believe that you are acting appropriately to question the safety of the vaccine."

James turned to Rogers, passing his index finger across his neck. He replied to Williams, "Madame President, the DCP top scientist is on vacation in Pakistan. I happen to know for a fact that their CEO wants him to be there when Dr. Rogers reviews all the data." James sent a sideways glare, followed by a quick wink in the direction of the Surgeon General. "To me, it only seems right that clinical people talk with fellow scientists."

Williams stood. "Well let me inform both of you gentlemen that I'll be meeting with Congressional leaders in the coming weeks to ask for appropriate funding to "fast track" the DCP human trials." She extended her hand to the Surgeon General. "Doctor, please keep the Secretary and myself informed of your evaluation of the safety data, both human and monkey trials. But, let me be clear, we're moving forward with the human trials on the vaccine unless you bring us compelling evidence to the contrary."

James replied, "Thank you for your time, Madame President."

While walking alongside, she whispered, "Dr. Rogers, you can contact me at any time, if you discover anything about *NeoBloc*"

"Certainly," he replied, catching a glimpse of James heading toward the door.

Standing in the doorway, James looked unnerved. Rogers sensed that a confrontation was about to begin. Once outside the Oval Office, he felt confident that his instincts proved to be correct. After closing the door, his boss sauntered up and poked a finger into his chest.

"Listen, this is the last time that I want you bothering the President with your paranoia. Next time, you'll give me the evidence on *NeoBloc*. I'll decide if it's compelling or not."

Rogers covered his heart with his right hand. "Promise to keep you in the loop."

"I'm glad that we see eye to eye on the chain of command. And, we still need to finish our conversation about Lauren Timmons and Haley

Tyler. But, not now! I need to run to a cabinet meeting. Have Sally call Bev to get on my schedule."

Recalling the Secretary's words, Rogers felt a sudden chill zooming down his spine. "What did you just say?"

"Have Sally call---"

The Surgeon General interrupted. "No. You mentioned the name of Haley Tyler."

James was stone---faced. "What?"

"I never mentioned Haley's last name to you."

James broke out into a slight grin. "Relax, it's a coincidence. I remembered reading a blurb about a woman named Haley Tyler in the *Post.*"

"Why was Haley Tyler's name mentioned in the newspaper?"

"Suicide, I believe an overdose."

Rogers felt a sinking feeling in the pit of his stomach. He said nothing.

"Look, Jonathan, don't change the subject to this woman who I don't even know."

"Excuse me, you mentioned her name first." Rogers took a step back. "On the issue that we're discussing, you just heard the President direct me to tell her if I have any safety concerns with the vaccine. After I brief you on my findings of my upcoming meeting with Dr. Nasters, I intend to speak to her about what I find."

"The hell you will." James pressed his chest into the Surgeon General. "That's my job. Your job is to provide me with medical information and judgment that either I don't understand or don't possess." He paused a second and then raised his voice. "Is that clear?"

Rogers held his ground. "With all due respect, I know what I'm supposed to do. There's no need to remind me."

James waved his index finger at the Surgeon General. "Just don't ever forget that you serve at the pleasure of the President." After taking a few more steps backing away, he said, "And you serve at my pleasure as well."

Rogers did not blink. "I'll do my best."

"Not good enough. You'll follow my lead or else." James continued to backpedal. "I hope this is the last time we have this conversation."

A frigid silence hung between them until the Surgeon General crisply responded, "By the way, I still find it interesting that you brought up Haley's name. Have a good day, Mr. Secretary."

"Stay out of trouble doc." He winked. "A bit of advice for you, stop looking for it."

******

Rogers's stomach felt twisted in knots. Since the recent confrontation outside the Oval Office, tension had escalated between him and Christian James. One point was clear. The President rightfully demanded proof of his allegations on *NeoBloc*. Feeling like he had let the Commander-in-Chief down by not bringing actual evidence to substantiate his suspicions, he looked at his calendar. His meeting with Nasters was only a week away. He flipped through his Rolodex and dialed Beth Murphy's number.

On the first ring, she picked up. "Hello Jonathan."

"Beth, it's so good to hear your voice. It's been a while."

Her voice was soft and empathetic. "How are you doing? I haven't called you since---well I wanted you and Ashley to have some time together."

"It's been tough. The nights are much harder than the days. Last week, I partially snapped out of my funk and spoke frankly with Ashley. I felt that it was time for her to get on with her life. He winced. *I say the words but I don't really believe them.* So, this past weekend, Ashley moved back to her own apartment off the medical school campus."

An uncomfortable silence held a couple of seconds before she chimed in, changing the subject. "Umm, so how are the challenges of being the "top doc" in America?"

He replied decisively, "Actually, that's why I called you. Next week, I have a meeting with Dr. Nasters to review the monkey trial data on their so-called "savior" cancer vaccine. I would like you to come with me. Another clinical set of eyes from an experienced nurse like you will really help."

"You're much more skilled in interpreting medical data than I am."

"Well, you have a Masters degree in Public Health besides your R.N. You know the score. But, more importantly, outside of Ashley, I trust you more than anyone else."

Beth fell silent.

Rogers exclaimed, "I need you."

Her response came as quick as a lightning bolt from a stormy sky. "Jonathan, I'll be there. What day is the meeting?"

"It's Tuesday at eight in the morning."

"How about meeting at the diner? You know the place—the one that is a mile down the highway from DCP headquarters."

Rogers smiled into the phone. "I feel better now. I'll need someone to play the good cop when we meet with Nasters. That will be you."

"My stepfather would have approved of that role. Sam Murphy always thought that one of my best skills was sprinkling honey on simmering coals."

"This means a lot to me." He pulled the phone away from his face and cleared his throat. "Your professional input will make a big difference."

Without pausing, she replied, "I hope that you know that you can always count on me------for anything."

"Thank you." He looked over at the picture of Kim, hanging in the living room. "And, I'm also planning on inviting my daughter. She wants to learn more about clinical trial data interpretation."

"I'm sure that you feel better just having Ashley around."

"After what happened, I can't let anything happen to her---I won't let anyone hurt her. If anyone else has to die, let it be me. I'll take the bullet next time."

"Hey, I need to run. I'll see you at the diner."

***

After two knocks, Sally opened his office door. "Dr. Rogers, you have a visitor from the FBI. Special Agent Susan Masters wants to see you. She apologized for showing up without an appointment. Ms. Masters says it's extremely important."

Upon hearing her name, he flinched. Over one year ago, she was the lead FBI agent investigating his own shooting on Pennsylvania Avenue, a near death experience that had befallen him just moments after meeting with the previous President. Yet Masters seemed much more interested in protecting the political interests of the corrupt predecessor to President Jane Williams than in seeking out those who were responsible for his near fatal assassination attempt.

"Show her in." He stood behind his desk, using it as a barricade between them.

Masters pranced through the doorway, wearing a solemn face. Her eyes scampered about his office. Marching toward him, she stopped a yard in front of his desk. Her cadence was rapid. "Dr. Rogers, let me get right to my point."

"Why would I expect anything other than that from you?" he asked in an acerbic tone, so usually uncharacteristic for him, except when he felt the other party deserved a cold shoulder.

"After our extensive investigations, we believe that your wife took two bullets that were really meant for you."

He stepped out to the side of his desk. "Why would you say that?" Rogers took a half- step closer to her.

"We listened to a taped conversation between you and your wife just before she was shot."

His voice soared. "You were listening to our private conversation? Who gave you that right?"

Masters began to blink repeatedly. "I'm sorry to be the one to tell you but we've been wire tapping your townhouse for weeks. We received word from someone on the inside---information that you're working for the President on a major project that impacts national security."

He launched an angry question. "Under whose damn orders did you plant the wiretap?"

"That's confidential information," she replied evenly.

"So, you just broke into my home to plant a bug?"

"Please, Dr. Rogers; I know you're under a lot of stress. We're only trying to help."

He shouted, "You are really pissing me off!" He sucked in a long breath and took several steps away from her. After pacing for several moments, he pivoted to face her. "All right, so tell me why my wife was mistakenly shot instead of me."

"Ok. Then promise me that you will hear me out." The agent held up her hand in front of his face. "We listened to two men eavesdropping on your conversation with Kim in the front room study of your townhouse the night she was shot."

"What two men? What did they say?"

"Please let me finish." She narrowed her eyes and raised her hand close to his face. "Local DC police found a miniature microphone and camera in your study---but it wasn't one of our FBI devices."

"So, where did it come from?"

"We don't know for sure!"

Rogers returned to stand behind his desk. "Were these men making threats towards me?"

She commanded, "Please slow down."

"How dare you tell me to slow down?" He pounded his fist on the desk. "Why didn't you stop these men before they shot Kim?"

"We didn't know exactly where they were. We were close by but our efforts failed at triangulating their location. Besides, we had a report that the FBI was on their way to meet with you. They were supposed to be at your home at any minute."

"Let me get this straight. You were near enough to our townhouse the night Kim was shot and you chose to do nothing." His nostrils flared, his stomach growled.

"We thought we had time before the man would actually do what he was---." She caught herself before saying another word.

Rogers marched up to the Special Agent. He was a fist space away from her. "Finish your sentence. Before the man would do what he was---told?"

"Look, we were just conducting surveillance." She backpedaled, taking two steps away from him. We thought the FBI agent that you spoke with earlier would arrive before anything happened."

"So because you miscalculated the time of when these men would shoot Kim, my wife is dead."

"That's a harsh statement."

"Tell me exactly what the man said!" he shouted.

"That is highly classified."

Rogers moved forward and accidentally bumped her chest. She stepped to his left.

"You were about to say that you thought you had time before the man murdered Kim." He pursued her as she quickly walked to the door. "Isn't that the truth, Agent Masters?"

She stopped in mid-stride and faced him. "Look, for the last time, an FBI agent was on his way to help you. He was expected to arrive any minute."

"Obviously, none of you were soon enough to prevent the shooting." Rogers glared at her. "I thought I read in the papers that the FBI reported having no suspects in Kim's murder. Now you tell me two men were involved." He scratched his nose and fired off a series of queries. "Did the FBI check the microphone and camera for fingerprints?" His voice grew louder with each question. "Can you tell where these items were bought? Was it at a specialty camera store? How many shops like that could there be in the area? Did you visit the stores and inquire about receipts, payments of credit cards?" He slapped his hands together, punching his right fist into his left palm. "In so many words, what the hell have you been doing to find my wife's killer?"

Masters met his twisted gaze, tilting her head. "We've been trying to piece this all together."

"Well, you're doing a damn lousy job, Lieutenant." His eyes flashed. "Dammit!" He leaned on a radiator cover by the far window and hung his head.

"We're doing the best we can. We ran the voices of the two men through our voice analysis unit. But, their voices did not match with anyone in our system. But, I can tell you that we heard one man order the other guy called Jonesy to redirect his shot from the man to the woman." Masters walked over to him. "We suspected that it may have had something to do with what you said about your conversation with the FBI that made the killer change his mind as to the final target."

He walked back to sit in his chair. Covering his face with both hands, he uttered, "So, you're saying that I'm responsible for the shooter killing Kim."

Masters said delicately, "For some reason, the shooter held off taking you out at this time."

Rogers rubbed his forehead, one stroke at a time. "Last year, you arrested Zach Miller and his evil colleagues. Does this have anything to do with the Health Club?"

"After Mr. Miller died in the car crash, the wicked Health Club was led for a while by Dylan Matthews. In the last year, they have maintained a low profile."

He persisted. "Answer my question! Can you tell me if The Health Club had anything to do with the killing of Kim?"

"Analysis of what you said to your wife on our surveillance tape before she was shot leads us to believe that the person identified as the boss believes that he needed to pick the right time to eliminate you. The bottom line is that your wife was murdered as a warning for you to back off."

"Back off what?"

"Dr. Rogers, I think you know the answer to your own question."

He felt the blood drain from his face. "It has to be the Health Club." He shook his head from side to side. "Kim's shooting must be connected to whoever tried to blow me up at the restaurant plus every other attempt on my life in the past year. What about Haley Tyler?"

"As you probably have read in the papers, she is dead from an apparent suicide."

"That's what I heard from Secretary James."

"Until her death, she was our main lead into the whereabouts of the Health Club."

"What about her boyfriend, Connor Lucas?"

"We checked him out. His record is spotless. He is former CIA. Lucas has one of the highest security clearances. We couldn't even find a traffic ticket attached to his name. He works at Sunview Pharmaceuticals."

"Hold on." Rogers leaped to his feet. "What's a former CIA agent doing as a salesman at a drug company?"

"Agents burn out. They find new careers."

"That's absurd!" Frowning at Masters, he asked, "By the way, what about the bomb that almost killed me at the Roma restaurant? Where was it made?"

"Home grown. Witnesses saw nothing that helps us."

"So, let's go back. How did these murderers get into my townhouse?"

"We don't know. And, there were no signs of forced entry."

Rogers's thoughts drifted to his daughter. "Have you swept my new place at Watergate?"

"Clean." Masters stared at the floor for a second and then looked up, meeting his livid gaze. "Be assured that something will turn up." The

Special Agent looked at her watch. "And, we checked out your daughter's apartment. We know that she just moved out of yours."

"What about her place?"

"Her apartment is clean."

His eyes popped wide. "So, what else have you found out?"

"Confidentially, Governor Adam Timmons is currently being considered to lead The Health Club. But we don't think he'll be chosen." Masters held out her arms in front of her, anticipating his reaction.

"Why not?"

"I'm not at liberty to say why."

"Screw that crap! We're talking about my wife, dammit. Find her killer!"

"We're doing the best---."

"Not good enough." He sucked in a deep breath through his nose and exhaled forcefully. "If you can't flush them out and bring the bastards who killed my wife to justice, then I will."

Masters walked to the door and yanked it open. She turned sharply on her heels, facing him. "I would strongly advise you to let the FBI resolve this."

"I'm not counting on it." He spun away from her. Walking toward his window on the far side of his office, all he could think of was --- *Kim is dead because of me!*

******

Dr. Rogers stood tall behind the podium. The physicians attending the 4th World Cancer Vaccines Summit in Boston sat in rapt attention. He glanced down at his prepared remarks before looking out on hundreds of oncologists and primary care physicians. He spotted his daughter in the first row. Ashley was beaming. The Surgeon General lowered his line of sight to scan the photographers sitting on the floor in front of the stage. One barrage of flashes caused him to see stars.

He blinked several times before beginning. "Good morning." He heard them reply in unison. As the flash from the cameras wore off, the clarity of their faces returned to sight. "As a former practicing physician, I can relate to what each of you is going through. On behalf of President Williams and Secretary of Health James, please accept our sincere gratitude for your dedicated service in tending to the dramatic rise in the number of cancer patients since the nuclear attacks."

He paused and took a prolonged sip from his water glass while surveying the audience. Their faces appeared dejected. Yet, in her lap, Ashley cradled a thumbs-up sign.

"Historically, from the fallout of radiation on human beings after Hiroshima and Nagasaki, our medical community has learned many important lessons. It is now time to revisit those findings." He paused and locked on the face of one doctor in the front row who was staring down, rather sadly, at the hardwood floor.

Rogers's eyes danced around the auditorium. "From past data, leukemia appeared to have peaked after three years in those who survived the initial blast. Yet, almost seven decades later, the overall likelihood of developing leukemia is still higher than the baseline prevalence in areas not exposed directly to the radiation. For solid malignant tumors, the burden of this disease rose until it dropped off after three decades of much pain and suffering."

Pausing to take a drink, he looked down at his notes. "Therefore, Americans exposed to the terrorist dirty bombs and uranium bomb will likely experience a similar fate unless we find a way to alter the radiation induced biological response leading to these cancers."

He looked up to survey the reactions. Ashley's jaw squared off and her lips pursed. She craned her neck, scanning the audience in the rows behind her. The physicians seemed anxious, frequently shifting positions in their seats. He believed they were expecting solutions, or at least a plan to resolve the problems, not a mere recitation of history of what happened in Japan decades ago.

"Much to my disappointment, governmental regulators have known that millions of gallons of radioactive water have leaked from nuclear power plants since the 1970's. There are 65 nuclear power sites in our nation and now the regulators are admitting that nearly all of them have leaked cancer causing tritium into our ground water drinking supply."

He straightened his tie. "Let's put this nuclear radiation into context." What can we do about all this exposure? Can science help us? Well, for several years, physicians have been using a vaccine to prevent cervical cancer caused by an infectious agent. Now, we are dealing with an equally, if not a much more complicated agent, radiation. As you know from her statements to the press, our President remains firmly committed toward supporting research and eventual deployment of a vaccine to prevent such radiation induced neoplasms."

Acting on his gut, he decided to skip any direct reference to *NeoBloc*. He folded his notes and stuffed them in the inside pocket of his suit jacket despite knowing that there would be personal fallout from Secretary James for his failure to mention more information on the vaccine that the President had openly championed. *I will not raise expectation on what I believe to be a deadly vaccine.*

For the next fifteen minutes, he spoke from memory about the several potential cellular mechanisms to prevent radiation-induced tumors. Rogers modeled his hypotheses after the vaccine already available to prevent viral induced cervical growths in women. He began winding down his talk by announcing a National Institute of Health sponsored Cancer Summit, to be held in Washington DC at a date to be announced later, for practicing oncologists and Chief Medical Officers of private insurance companies. All cancer treatments including the latest cancer preventing vaccines would be on the agenda.

The physicians' faces brightened upon hearing the news that the Centers for Medicare and Medicaid Services (CMS) had recently lifted all utilization management hurdles on all eligible patients for physician ordered cancer treatments. He explained that the purpose of the Summit was to try to convince the private payors to follow the lead of CMS.

"We must find a cure for all radiation induced cancers. It is my fervent hope that we can do it. But, we must do it safely."

The physicians clapped politely, nodding toward each other.

"Thank you for your attention. Are there any questions?"

An elderly man with a full beard and a balding head stood. "My name is Dr. Anthony Gregg. Is there a reason why you have not discussed the widely talked about vaccine called *NeoBloc?*"

"Thank you for your question." Rogers glanced down at Ashley. Her face tightened. He replied with an air of confidence, "I believe we need to know whether that vaccine is safe before we approve it. So, we are still evaluating the safety evidence on *NeoBloc.*"

Dr. Gregg persisted. "Do you have reason to suspect that the vaccine is not safe?"

"Let me just say that until we resolve further scientific issues, I don't want to raise false hopes nor communicate any final decisions."

The physician's voice grew somber. "I hear you saying that there are scientific issues to be resolved. Yet, we have not heard that in the enthusiastic public announcements by President Williams." Gregg took his seat.

While he pondered on how to respond, another question was shouted out from the back of the auditorium. "Is *NeoBloc* in jeopardy of not being approved by the FDA?"

"It's too early to say based on current information."

Gregg raised his hand. "I apologize for monopolizing the time of my colleagues. I have one final question. Are you aware that there is another firm working on a similar vaccine as *NeoBloc?*"

"I am aware of additional ongoing research." Rogers smiled. "It is my promise to you that I will promptly report to the American Cancer Society and to this Summit if the current research on *NeoBloc* proves that we have a vaccine that is both effective and safe. Good day to all." Amid a round of respectful applause, he hoped that he had struck the right chord in his speech.

Ashley jumped up the side stairs, onto the stage, toward him. She gave him a warm hug.

"Dad, I thought your speech was terrific."

"It wasn't exactly what they wanted to hear."

She lowered her voice. "You're too honest to say things you don't believe."

"I'll be checking out the data on *NeoBloc* this coming week. Beth Murphy is meeting me at DCP. Can you join us?"

"What do you think?" She sent a look that left no doubt in his mind.

"You're a real healthcare warrior. I can't wait to see you graduate with your medical degree."

"We need to talk about that. I've been missing classes, spending time with you at the Department of Health. I'm thinking of dropping out, just for a semester."

"Have you---?"

She replied firmly, cutting him off, "Dad, it's *my* life."

"Honey, I just want what's best for you."

"What's best for me is that nothing bad happens to you." Her eyes began to well up. "You're all I have."

He turned away and pretended that he was about to sneeze. He swiftly brushed away a tear. Looking back at Ashley, he said, "How about you and I go grab a couple of vanilla milk shakes?"

"You're on."

CHAPTER ELEVEN

Connor reclined on an ergonomically customized chair in his cubicle, holding his gold plated wooden plaque high above his head. Selected sales representative of the month for Sunview, he knew that it was well worth the effort for him to achieve his final goals. *An important steppingstone for an early promotion* he thought.

No longer needing to worry about Haley, he set his sights on several former scores to settle. He drew a rough caricature of each future victim on a three by two inch plain white sheet of paper. After admiring his drawing skill, he pasted the images to one side of a partial deck of playing cards. He shuffled the deck after he removed the cards for Rogers and Sean Parker--only for the moment. *Time is not yet right!*

Still in the potential victim deck was Dr. Tim Carver, the lead power broker of *The Health Club*, who had intentionally been given the reins to lead the wicked group after Zach Miller alias Connor Lucas purposely stepped down to lower his profile and escape capture by the authorities. Also, in the running was former Michigan Governor Bill Peabody who testified in court that Zach Miller was the prior leader of *The Health Club*.

Connor took pleasure in looking at the drawing of his former girlfriend, Marissa Jones. It had come to his attention that she had recently hooked up with the present Governor of Michigan, Adam Timmons, after she dumped the former chief of sales at DCP, Dylan Matthews—the initial successor to Dr. Carver as leader of *The Health Club*. Rumor had it that Timmons was in serious contention to take the lead if Dylan slipped. And, curiously Lauren Timmons, just recently divorced from Adam Timmons was found beheaded. *At the right time, I'll convince Governor Timmons to let me re -take the lead as head of The Health Club. Only I can make it purr!*

For good measure, he pasted the picture of Dylan on one card and Adam Timmons on the other. Connor cut the deck and reshuffled it one more time. He dealt one card: Marissa. Pulling a Cuban from his top drawer, he sucked on one end. *Payback time!*

***

Two blocks down from his office, Connor walked into O' Malley's tavern. He sat down at a table near the back and straightened his dark sunglasses. Ordering a diet cola, he waited for Jonesy to appear.

On his second refill, he looked up just as the hit man wandered in from the downtown streets of DuPont looking rather like a typical college student. He was wearing gold horn rimmed glasses, dressed in dark blue khakis pants, a powder blue sweatshirt bearing the name of North Carolina, and brown sandals.

Jonesy sat down across from him and whispered, "My one ear still hurts from the rifle blast when I shot that lady." He pushed up his eyeglasses so that they rested on his forehead. "So boss, do you have another job for me?"

Connor's eyes twinkled. "Someone has to keep food on your table." He placed the picture card of Marissa face up on the table. "Her long neck would easily accommodate a rope. Don't you think?"

Jonesy flipped down his glasses to stare at the photo. "So, where does this broad hang out?"

"Every evening, she works out at *The Sports Club*, over on Oakhurst. Wait for her in the parking lot. Use your favorite Saturday night special to get her into your car. Carry a thirty-foot rope with you. Drive her into the dense woods past Oldwyck Pond. Give her an opportunity to try to escape. Let her run a few yards and then lasso her around the neck. Flip one end of the rope over a thick tree branch. Pull with all your might and hang the little devil."

"Ten thousand," Jonesy demanded.

Without even giving it a second thought, Connor smirked. He replied crisply, "Happy eating!"

"Your money buys me a lot of booze, steaks and grits. Plus I'm saving up for my retirement. My generation can't count on Social Security so I do what I can for number one."

Connor chuckled. "Don't forget today's already scheduled job. I'll wait for you outside. You can follow me in your car. I'll need your special talents for even more important jobs after you take care of the current responsibilities on your plate."

Strolling out of O' Malley's, he checked the directions to Hatfield on his Blackberry. As he headed toward his car, Connor felt strangely uncomfortable. There were still too many loose ends. *Zach never would have tolerated what I've been doing these days.* He waited for Jonesy to get into his car before he drove himself to the theatre. *I need closure! No more witnesses!*

******

Connor had rented out the entire theatre for the entire afternoon. Attending a private showing of an early *James Bond* flick, he grabbed a small bag of popcorn from a scantily clad woman in the lobby. *See you later honey in the balcony.* The prostitute blew him a kiss. She would be the only one in the vacant Virginia theatre except for his one invited guest. The tall, perfectly proportioned young woman parted from him and walked up a steep stairway leading to the projection room.

Meanwhile, he headed straight to the balcony. *I like controlling my fantasies.*

The CEO reached the top of the stairs and selected a seat in the last row by the wall. He plopped down and quickly immersed himself in the opening scene of the movie. An exciting boat chase on the big screen held his interest.

Christian James appeared at the bottom of the center aisle, diverting his attention. After grabbing another handful of popcorn, he watched James leap up the aisle -two or three steps at a time.

The Secretary sat down alongside him. Connor asked, "Do you have the package?"

James handed over the confidential DCP file on *NeoBloc* monkey research. "Better to give it to you than to Dr. Rogers."

Connor thumbed through a few pages. "Looks like a lot of scientific mumbo-jumbo. Is it the conclusion of all this verbiage that the vaccine is safe and actually works? "

The Secretary responded while keeping his eyes glued on Bond's latest bedroom escapade. "Yes."

"Are you absolutely sure the vaccine is safe?"

"Count on it."

Connor squinted in sending a harsh glare towards James. "By the way, how are you doing with managing the expectations of the President?"

"Without her knowledge, I followed her when she met with the CEO's. After I eavesdropped on her meeting in the Green Room, I was convinced that she was committed to the vaccine. Now, after a recent meeting with the Surgeon General and me, she sounds like she is leaning toward believing whatever Rogers says about *NeoBloc.* "

He stuffed a handful of popcorn in his mouth. Talking while crunching the kernels, he muttered, "Keep that idealistic prick away from her as much as possible."

"I'll work with the Chief of Staff to make it happen."

"Do it yourself. You're his boss." He cast a threatening gaze at James. "So, can Parker handle the heat that will be coming his way?"

"Not sure. A lot depends on Nasters. We'll need him to keep a lid on any minor side effect problems once the human clinical trials with *NeoBloc* begin. Plus, Rogers is hot to trot on finding problems with the monkey data as well."

"You said you would keep him under wraps, working with Mac."

"I will," James replied with conviction.

Connor sniffed in a full chest of air and then forcefully expelled it. "Can we trust Nasters?"

"I think his DCP stock options will keep him in check. But, there seems to be something else driving him. I just can't put my finger on it."

"Maybe, he just wants his fifteen minutes of fame." Connor launched his feet on top of the seat in front of him. "I'm glad to hear that he doesn't seem to be a bleeding heart zealot like Rogers." He grabbed a handful of popcorn and shoved it into his mouth. Mumbling while chewing, he said, "The assholes that always give me the most heartburn are those who are driven by what they believe and not by what they can put into their pockets."

James reached into Connor's bag and stole a handful of popcorn. "Let me know when you want me to release that incriminating tape on Sean Parker."

Connor tossed a few kernels of popcorn into the air and caught them with his tongue. "Not yet. I'll know when the time is right." He gulped hard and tossed a few more kernels into the air. All of them landed in the precise target zone inside his mouth. "Bet you can't do this!"

The Secretary nodded. "When do you think you'll be a credible candidate for his position as CEO of DCP?"

"It will take a couple of months." Connor's eyes locked on the silver screen. While being mesmerized by a steamy scene of James Bond making love to his latest squeeze, his hand slipped to his genital area.

"OK. I see that you're busy." The Secretary rose. "Enjoy the movie. By the way, did anyone ever tell you that you have more lives than Bond?"

Connor reached out. He grabbed his wrist. "Just don't get any ideas. I can smell a rat a mile away---even those who don't wear your easily recognized brand of musk cologne."

"Don't worry. You're the real leader of *The Health Club*. I know that you once intentionally gave it to Dr. Victor Carver just to save your own ass."

He sighed. "That reminds me." He pointed to the seat. "Sit down." The Secretary plunked down again. Connor leaned toward James.

"Talk to me about the rumors."

"About what?"

Connor pursed his lips. "I've been hearing gossip that Adam Timmons may be trying to lead *The Health Club.*"

"Who told you that?"

"That would be none of your business." Raising his voice, he asked, "Is it true?"

"Don't think so. Dylan Matthews seemed to have control of the Club for a while. However, the job was more than he could handle. When the members heard that you were back in town, they dumped Dylan and are ready to support you for another term."

"What about Adam Timmons?"

"The Governor?" James looked straight ahead without blinking an eyelash. "I only know what I already told you. Don't know about Timmons."

"Is that so? And, what about the chairman of the DCP board, Xavier Rudolf?"

The Secretary shrugged his shoulders.

Connor flipped the bag of popcorn onto the floor and punched his right fist into his left palm. "Wish you had told me what is going on with the *Health Club* before I had to ask."

"I guess---I didn't think you wanted to know."

"Then why did you bring it up?" Connor sneered. "People in this business who lie or forget important stuff usually end up dead." He stretched his hands above his head, watching James Bond coming to a climax. "You know. It's too bad Kim Rogers had to go. Both of us once had real possibilities. I met her a few years ago when she tried to sell me a lake house. That was after Rogers survived his first shooting after meeting with the former President. My nephew just missed a fatal shot to his heart. Anyway, while he was recuperating, Kim and I were beginning to hit it off. But in the end, she loved Rogers. God knows why!"

"She was a fine looking lady." James began to fidget, his eyes anxiously darting from Connor to the movie.

"It was just infatuation on her part with me—an innocent flirtatious fling that went nowhere. In all seriousness, Rogers and Kim were truly two peas in a pod."

While confessing, Connor watched his colleague's eyes. He did not like what he saw. "Actually, ole Jonathan is a decent chap. Kim never would have left him. But, he's been a major pain in the ass for me. One day, it will be his turn."

"Why wait?"

In a sinister tone, he replied, "Don't ever ask me that again!" Connor turned back to the movie.

"I'm sorry. Don't want to offend you." For the second time, James stood up and faced the big screen.

With his eyes focused on Bond diving to the ground after the building behind him had just exploded, he jutted his jaw forward. "Next time, tell me something I don't already know."

The Secretary walked down the stairs, muttering under his breath, "Don't worry about me. You can always trust me."

"I heard that. If you have to say it, it makes me wonder how loyal you really are to me." Connor leaped to his feet. "Don't mess with me James."

After throwing his hands above his head as if to surrender, James soon disappeared out the side exit.

Connor checked his watch and sat down. The logical choice for being the incoming leader of *The Health Club* inhaled, recognizing the sensual blend of lilies, roses, and marigolds. The scent of her perfume arrived moments before she did. His late afternoon treat was perfectly on time. He relished every moment while she slinked up the center aisle of the balcony toward him.

Her high heels, furry boots adorning her legs, her long and shapely legs made him hard. Red hot pants and a pink scarf were all she wore. He changed seats and plopped down on the love seat in line with the center of the theatre. Exhaling forcefully, he rested his head on the back wall. After spreading his legs, he loosened his belt buckle. Connor felt hungry but in a far different way that any bag of popcorn could possibly have helped.

She would satisfy his needs. Her scent was now on top of him. Today was not the first time that she would work her magic on him but it would be the last.

Five minutes later, she was gone. He flipped open his cell and punched in the number. "Jonesy, just as we planned. She'll be out the front door in a minute. Take her to a secluded spot. Make it short and quick. I don't want her to suffer."

"It's no skin off my back if you feel that way, but I'm curious. Why do you want me to kill her?"

"Listen, I'll tell you for the last time. The least amount of witnesses who can identify me, the safer it will be for me. And, I'm not done yet!"

"You're the boss."

"And don't you ever forget that."

CHAPTER TWELVE

In his locked office at DCP, Hussein Nasters knelt down to pray. Per his daily ritual, he began by giving thanks to Allah. The first few days of the human clinical trials with *NeoBloc* had passed uneventfully. *It did take the monkeys a year to die after getting NeoBloc. So far, I have everyone believing that it was a virus that wiped them out.* Ever since he passed his loyalty test with the PFF, he began to relish the thought that they would soon call him to support his biologic jihad. America would then be toast.

The doorknob jiggle interrupted his prayer time. Nasters pushed himself off the floor. He released the lock and yanked open his door. It was his chief assistant scientist, Dr. Virginia Washington. The African-American middle-aged woman was dressed in her long white lab coat. The conjunctiva surrounding her brown eyes looked blood shot. She clutched a manila folder closely against her chest.

He waved her into his office with a friendly smile. "Good to see you again. It's nice to be back in the United States. Hope you weren't too swamped with work on our *NeoBloc* project in my absence."

She ignored his greeting and rushed past him to the other side of his office, not saying a word, and not offering even a casual wave.

"You look upset." He pointed toward his desk. "Please have a seat. What's on your mind?" She slowly eased herself into a chair in front of his desk. He took his usual seat. No sooner had they sat down when she tossed the manila folder on his desk.

In a grim tone, she stated, "While you were gone, I've thoroughly reviewed the monkey safety data. I'm no longer convinced of our previous hypothesis that all the *NeoBloc* monkeys died due to a virus."

He chose to ignore looking at the folder, concentrating on her.

"Look at it!" Washington pushed the folder closer toward Nasters. "Couldn't their deaths be due to a delayed response to the vaccine?"

"Now, you're starting to sound like Lauren Timmons. Doctor, please give me one hard fact that leads you to believe that is even scientifically possible."

She pulled out a folded sheet of white computer paper from her lab coat pocket. "These are my notes." Washington laid them on the table and pointed to a series of scientific terms connected by arrows. "OK. Let's get into this discussion. As scientists, we both know that *NeoBloc* ramps up the immune system to increase production of nitriloside by a thousand fold. Moreover, the latter compound is most likely the active ingredient in preventing radiation induced cancer. Moreover, this information about nitriloside is almost a hundred years old. Almost every medical student is aware of it."

"Please get to your point." His knees began to vibrate, faster and faster as her face took on a disbelieving distrustful look that he had never previously seen.

She held up the paper and began reading. "In my research, I looked for other compounds in the enzymatic cycle that provide our bodies with energy. I reached my hypothesis. To put it bluntly, I believe that *NeoBloc* can kill."

Nasters bolted to his feet. He snatched the paper from her and silently finished reading the first paragraph. "Who gave you permission to delve into this matter?"

"I don't need anyone's approval to search for legitimacy. And, I double checked the data."

Nasters walked behind her and hovered above his assistant scientist. He held her notepaper at his side. "And, you believe that you have found your so- called truth?"

She turned toward him and yanked back the sheet from him. Craning her neck upward to look at him, she said, "Actually, there was one finding which would be significant if it is duplicated in our human clinical trials. Upon reviewing the monkey data of those who received *NeoBloc*, the super high levels of nitriloside seem to have blocked a critical life sustaining enzyme, acetyl coenzyme A in all the monkeys who died."

Nasters returned to his former position, standing behind his desk. "You are partially correct. It's a scientific fact that both monkeys and humans need that particular enzyme to live," he conceded. "But, how do you know that a virus didn't block the enzyme? Why blame *NeoBloc*?"

"The burden of proof is upon us to prove that NeoBloc is safe. How do you know that it wasn't the vaccine? It could have been the nitriloside. Let me turn the tables and ask you what proof do you have that it was a random virus that killed all the monkeys?"

"Ha. Can you prove that I'm wrong?"

"With all due respect, we could go back and forth all day. However, this issue is much too important to base our decision on speculation. We need to find out if humans would be deprived of this life-sustaining enzyme after they receive *NeoBloc*. So, my recommendation is to place an immediate moratorium on the recently started human trials. We should redo a whole new set of monkey clinical trials, measuring blood levels of acetyl coenzyme A from baseline to monthly intervals after they receive the vaccine."

Closing his eyes for several seconds, Nasters sensed that he needed a fresh approach. *Appeal to her scientific sense----of absolute accuracy.*

He rolled over his leather high back chair and sat down next to her, positioning to face her directly.

He smiled before putting on his game face. "Dr. Washington, as dedicated scientists, let's review what we know. The monkeys didn't die for at least a year after receiving the vaccine."

"Yes, they died sometime between the twelfth and thirteenth month after getting the vaccine."

"So, even if you're correct that NeoBloc stops production of the life sustaining acetyl coenzyme A, why did it take that long to block the enzyme? It would have been highly likely that your proposed enzyme blockade would have occurred much sooner than twelve months."

"Not necessarily." Her head was half cocked to the left when she asked, "What peer reviewed scientific journal proves what you just said?"

Nasters's face tightened. "I think it's intuitive."

Washington shook her head. "We need scientific data, not opinion."

He looked up at the ceiling for several seconds as if deep in thought. "Since all the monkeys died within a month after the twelve month mark of getting the vaccine, something most likely happened to all of them during that one month period."

"It appears that way."

"You're saying that *NeoBloc* may be the culprit." He held out his hands, palms facing upward, as a sign of openness. "It is my scientific conclusion based on my two decades of experience that a virus would much more likely be the cause given the fact that they all died in a cluster---within one month's time."

She leaned forward. "We each have our scientific position. Either is possible. The right thing to do is to repeat the clinical trials with the monkeys to find out which of us is correct. If the acetyl coenzyme A levels remain normal and the monkeys live past the 13th month, then you are right. But if---"

Nasters interrupted, "I do see your point." He scratched his head. "You're right." He softened his face. "We do need to know for sure. There is no question that we should rule out the vaccine as a cause of the monkey deaths."

Her face brightened. "And, we must be rigorous in our science."

They both stood at the same time.

She asked, "Can you just imagine what would happen if every American would receive a killer vaccine? You and I would feel that we were personally responsible."

Coughing, he replied, "That would indeed be a tragedy." He cleared his throat. "I think that we need to carefully measure the acetyl coenzyme A in our human trials. But, we need to do it correctly. It may take many months. Then, we can summarize our data."

She shook her head. "I disagree. I'm against moving ahead with the human trials. I want to repeat the monkey trials. In that case, at least no humans will be killed if we do discover that *NeoBloc* does actually kill the monkeys by blocking the life sustaining acetyl coenzyme A."

"I admire your scientific integrity but I do not need to remind you that the *NeoBloc* project on humans is a high priority for President Williams. Waiting another thirteen months to re-do the entire monkey trials is a non-starter. If you're wrong, we've wasted a year where we could have saved many lives if more terrorist attacks should occur on our homeland."

"I'm talking science. If you're wrong, you'll kill every American who takes *NeoBloc.*"

"That's where you're being too zealous. Be reasonable. Listen, I'm talking about saving human life from radiation induced cancers."

"I only want to ensure that we won't do more harm than good."

He rubbed his nose. "Listen, I have a compromise. Why don't we collect the enzyme data on humans for up to twelve months? That will be before we submit *NeoBloc* to the FDA. After all, nothing happened to the monkeys for a whole twelve months. At least, we would be testing your theory by measuring the acetyl coenzyme A the entire time people are actually getting *NeoBloc.*"

Washington crossed her arms over her chest. "But, what if human subjects are more sensitive to *NeoBloc* than the monkeys and what if people actually die during the clinical trials? There is simply no evidence that people will react the same way as monkeys to the vaccine."

Nasters held his hands together in front of his face as if he was suddenly praying. He spoke in a measured cadence, careful to avoid any emotion. "President Williams, in consultation with her health expects at the Department of Health and at the FDA, made a decision to continue the human trials. We must respect our chosen leader. She speaks for the American people."

She shot back. "Political leaders have been known to be wrong. We are the scientists, not them. In addition, one of their medical experts is Surgeon General Jonathan Rogers. I would like to see what he thinks after seeing our monkey data."

Nasters noted a hive like rash breaking out on her chest and neck. Thinking about his slain family back in Pakistan, he replied swiftly, "Let me speak with Sean Parker." He extended his hand. "And, Dr. Rogers will be here in a few days."

"As a scientist, I just want to ensure that we are correct."
Washington firmly shook his hand.

He gently put his hand on her shoulder. "Your concern for our great land is to be commended. Science will triumph in the end. It is best to sleep on our collective thinking. Perhaps, things will be clearer after we give this important matter more thought."

She walked toward the door and turned around to face him. "I hope you understand where I'm coming from. Please don't take me for an obstructionist."

"Of course not. I respect your scientific approach. That's why I hired you."

"I'm glad we spoke."

"Thank you for taking the initiative."

"I just didn't want to surprise you with my new thinking in front of the Surgeon General. But to be clear, my position is that it's far preferable to retest the monkeys than to risk human life. I have spent a good amount of time reflecting upon this before I came to you today. And, I don't believe a good night's sleep will change my mind."

He replied with an edge to his voice. "Our Commander in Chief will decide whether to risk one life in a clinical trial to save many American lives."

"Every life is precious. But if *NeoBloc* becomes FDA approved and actually is deadly, we could wipe out the entire population of America."

Nasters could feel his heart beating. He knew that he needed to move off the scientific point and counterpoint. He replied sternly, "We are at war! Americans are dying every day of radiation-induced cancer from nuclear explosions. I thank you for your concerns. But President Williams has galvanized American opinion around what we should all do to support the homeland. Her words say it all. '*NeoBloc* is the savior of America.' Dr. Washington, I agree with her. That is my final answer to you."

"Then we are at a stalemate." She grabbed the doorknob, opening the door before quietly closing it behind her.

CHAPTER THIRTEEN

The trio joined up at a DuPont diner, a ten-minute trip from DCP. In their taxi ride over to meet Dr. Nasters, the Surgeon General led the group in reviewing their game plan to uncover the real story of *NeoBloc*. Each of them knew their precise role before arriving at the six story stone faced building. Their mission was to do whatever it would take to expose any cover up of the truth on the vaccine's safety.

Pulling up to the vaccine manufacturer's main building, they hopped out of the cab upon reaching the security checkpoint that marked the entrance to DCP. "Good morning, I'm Dr. Rogers. This is my assistant, Beth Murphy and my daughter Ashley Rogers. We're here for our appointment with Dr. Hussein Nasters."

A security guard with a nametag of Hopkins checked her list. "He is expecting all of you."

After pinning his security badge on his lapel, he watched the two women do the same. The guard pressed a button to unlock the steel gate that spanned ten feet from the floor to the ceiling. Rogers walked in front, Tey were escorted through the opening into the closely guarded research lab area of the Doctor's Choice Products pharmaceutical company.

***

Walking past the reinforced see- through plate glass of the research laboratories, Rogers noticed at least a dozen scientists walking around the laboratory amid a sea of flasks, Bunsen burners and glass tubing. The scene reminded him of his organic chemistry class in college. He deeply appreciated the tremendous value of many pharmaceuticals, developed to save lives and prevent suffering.

The security guard brought them to the end of a long corridor. Hopkins knocked on the steel door three times. Rogers noticed a Glock semi-automatic strapped to his leather belt. He pushed the door open and motioned for them to enter. The DCP chief scientist was standing just inside the doorway. Nasters was dour faced, arms folded across his chest.

"Surgeon General Rogers, we meet again. I'm so glad that you and your guests have safely arrived."

"It's nice to see you again." Rogers extended his hand. Nasters weakly clasped his hand. The Surgeon General noted that the scientist's eyes seemed oddly focused --mainly on Ashley.

"I'm sorry that I've been out of the country for so long. As you know, I had family business to attend to back in Pakistan."

"I hope everything went well."

Nasters stood perfectly still. His blank expression was totally fixed, without a trace of emotion, on the Surgeon General.

"Well, let me say that we really appreciate this opportunity." Rogers turned toward Beth and Ashley. "Doctor Nasters, I would like to introduce my clinical advisor, Beth Murphy. She is a registered nurse in one of the hospitals in the area. And this is my daughter who is a medical student at the University."

"Ms. Murphy and Ms. Rogers, I'm glad to make your acquaintance." He motioned toward a middle-aged African-American woman wearing a white lab coat. "I would like to introduce my chief assistant, Dr. Virginia Washington."

Rogers took a quick look around the room. Massive ledgers, at least six inches thick, spread out on a half- dozen tables. Nasters's arms now hung at his side. Clad in his knee -high white lab coat, he looked professional indeed. His assistant's eyes flickered about the room, settling on the face of the lead DCP scientist.

The host pointed at the tables. "Doctor, I know that you wanted to see the monkey safety data on *NeoBloc*. Well, I have prepared a feast of data for you to consume."

"This is all very impressive."

"It's our pleasure. Dr. Washington and I have cleared our calendars. Where would you like to begin?"

Rogers could not help but wonder why his host was being so accommodative. "Well, Dr. Nasters, since we are fortunate to have clinical advisors with each of us today, I propose that we split up. Ashley and I will stay with you and Ms. Murphy can work with Dr. Washington. If we work separately, we can ensure that we go through all the data that you have so painstakingly prepared."

Nasters shot a concerned look at his assistant. Furrowing his brow, he replied, "Perhaps, it would be better if we all work together since Dr. Washington may be more familiar with some data than I am. And, none of us wants any of the data misinterpreted."

Beth interjected a comment. "Our visit is just a formality. I'm sure the data is all here. If we break into groups, we can finish in two hours and then reconvene for a working lunch with the entire group to discuss our findings." She smiled broadly. "Maybe you can show us your preliminary human clinical trial data this afternoon."

"Unfortunately, the human trial data is not yet ready for your review."

Washington commented, "I think Dr. Rogers is right. In order to be thorough, we should split up so we can go carefully through all of the monkey data."

Nasters glared at his assistant. He held his chin in his hand. After a few moments of silence, he replied, "We can accommodate your wishes."

Beth put out her hands in front of her. "Dr. Washington, you and I can work in the adjoining room. I'll help carry one of these ledgers. Pass me the heavy looking one."

Rogers smiled inwardly. His plan appeared to be working. But, he knew that he would have to wait until his ride back with Beth and Ashley to the airport to know for sure whether or not it had succeeded.

******

Beth dropped the ledger that she was carrying onto a circular conference table in the adjoining room. She closed the door that separated them from the adjacent room where Rogers and Ashley would be working with Nasters. The assistant scientist lowered the ledger she was lugging and placed it on top of the other one.

"Dr. Washington, I see that you take your job very seriously. It is an admirable trait."

The scientist's face softened with the compliment. "Ms. Murphy, I'm only interested in pursuing the truth." Washington sat down in front of the closed data ledgers.

Beth sat down next to her. "Please take the lead."

Opening the top ledger, the scientist said, "Let's start on this executive summary. And, during our review, please feel free to ask me anything about the monkey data."

"Our journey begins."

***

"Dr. Washington, I need a break. Can we pick up some lunch? If I look at one more Excel spreadsheet of data, I think I'll collapse."

"We can go to the DCP cafeteria and get something."

Beth shook her head. "Actually, I need to get some fresh air. I must confess that I suffer from claustrophobia if I feel cooped up too long inside. Can we go somewhere off site to eat?"

"Sure. We'll take my car. I'll drive to the diner. It's really close to here."

Beth patted the scientist on the wrist. "I can use the exercise. Let's walk."

"Ok." Washington happily replied. "Shouldn't we invite the others?"

She pretended to be considering the suggestion. "Hmm." She frowned. "Actually, Dr. Rogers doesn't like to be interrupted when he's working. Let's just go without them."

"We can leave by this private exit that will take us to the main corridor."

Walking side by side on the winding sidewalk from DCP to their destination, Beth struck up some small talk. "DuPont seems to have many diners. On the way here, we stopped at Lugar's, just off the main highway."

Washington laughed. "I've been there. Not bad."

"What's the name of the place where we're going?"

"The Jackson Diner."

"Wonder if the locals ever call it ole Hickory?"

The scientist laughed. "A lot of executives at DCP stop by for a quick bite. I wouldn't be surprised if a few squabbles among our corporate leadership were resolved over a turkey club sandwich. As you might expect, we do have a difference of opinion even on scientific matters.

"I'll bet you do. It happens everywhere."

Washington pointed. "There it is—a block ahead on the right."

***

Digging into her grilled chicken salad, Beth asked Washington, "So, how long have you worked at DCP?"

"Six years." The scientist sipped her tall glass of ice tea. "Actually, I came here before Dr. Nasters. But, he is my supervisor as he is much more experienced than me."

"Don't be so modest. I'm greatly impressed with your knowledge."

Washington picked up her burger in two hands. "Actually, Dr. Nasters is a genius at what he does. In the field of vaccines, he enjoys a world- wide reputation as an expert."

"You're both such dedicated scientists."

She seemed taken aback by Beth's compliment. Her face flushed. "Dr. Nasters reports to the CEO, Sean Parker. It is my belief that it's hard to be a scientist and a business leader at the same time."

"Maybe one day, you'll be the top scientist here." Beth speared a piece of chicken with her fork.

Washington wiped a dab of ketchup from her mouth after biting into her hamburger. "I just want to do a good job. I'm not interested in playing corporate politics."

Beth wrinkled her forehead. "I'm not sure that I know exactly what you mean."

"To be frank, as I said on our walk over here, scientists don't always agree."

She scooped up a mouthful of lettuce sprinkled with Italian vinaigrette dressing. She hoped Washington would elaborate further. A few seconds later, her wish bore fruit.

"Dr. Nasters has pressures put on him by senior management to always increase our profit margins. I would never put myself in that position. I'm here to do pure science. If our products are safe and effective to make people well, I'm pleased."

She gulped her diet cola. "You know, I like your perspective. There's something to be said about not being the boss. At my hospital, the chief of nursing always seems to be disgruntled about something." She forked up another mouthful of lettuce and green peppers. "I like spending a lot of time with my patients."

Washington changed the subject. "You seem to be enjoying your salad."

"I guess I was a lot hungrier than I thought." Beth rubbed her temple. She felt a migraine coming on but she wanted the bonding to continue." She glanced down at Dr. Washington's feet. "By the way, I love your beige shoes. I noticed them while we were walking over here. They look very stylish"

"Thank you. Reasonably priced, they are very comfortable. Shoes are my one vice."

"You'll have to tell me where you bought them. Like you, I'm on my feet a lot, especially when I do a double nursing shift."

"I can relate." She patted Beth's hand. "You know, I'm so glad that we're getting a chance to know each other. I'm so busy at work. I have so little time for socializing,"

As her headache intensified, Beth shielded her eyes from the overhead lighting. Biting her lower lip, she began to see flickering spots of light in front of her. The right side of her head began to pound. She dropped her fork onto her plate and closed her eyes.

"Ms. Murphy, are you all right?"

"Doctor, I think I'm having a full blown migraine. It's been coming on since the last ten minutes or so when we were working with the *NeoBloc* data."

"We should call it a day."

"I'm sorry. I know you had the day planned to work with us. I'm afraid that I'll have to take a rain check. And, by the way, please call me Beth"

"If you feel up to it in a couple of days, we can resume our review of the data."

"Give me your business card and I'll call you."

Washington pulled a card from her lab coat pocket. "Beth, I'm also writing my private home number on the back of the card. Feel free to call me at any time. Maybe, we can go shopping for shoes."

She stuffed the card into her purse. "Deal."

The scientist stood and walked to the cashier. Beth followed close behind as a wave of nausea swept over her. Washington paid the bill.

"Thanks for lunch. Next time, I'll reciprocate. Again, I'm so sorry to have spoiled your day. I just need to lie down in a dark room. I'll be fine. Listen, we need a taxi."

The scientist asked the cashier to make the call. "Don't think anything of it. And, please call me Virginia."

Grimacing, Beth added, "Please express my apologies to Drs. Rogers and Nasters and also to Ashley. The taxi can drop you off at DCP and then take me back to my apartment."

The cashier announced that the taxi was less than a block away.

"I hope you'll be able to call me soon. I do want to share with you some thoughts of mine on the *NeoBloc* data."

"I'll do that." A moment later, Beth spotted the taxi pulling up in front of the Jackson Diner. "There's our ride."

"I'll explain to the group that you weren't feeling well." Washington steadied Beth by holding onto her arm as they walked down the stairs to the parking lot.

"I do hope that we can be friends," Beth added as she hopped into the back seat of the cab, alongside Virginia.

"Absolutely."

******

When Dr. Washington returned without Beth with her excuse for the absence in hand, the Surgeon General prayed that she had spent enough time with the scientist to gain her trust.

As the group continued to pour over the monkey data, Rogers admitted to himself that Hussein Nasters was a pro. The data looked clean---too clean. *Why would Lauren have lied?*

Ever since Washington had returned from lunch, it was increasingly obvious that she wanted to say something. But, each time she tried to interject, Nasters spoke up to make a point in defense of the data and cut her off.

While they were on the last page of data, he asked with a touch of arrogance, "So Dr. Rogers are you now convinced that the monkey data proves that *NeoBloc* is safe?"

Intently studying the faces of each scientist, he paused. He picked up a twitch in Washington's eyebrows. Rogers looked over at Ashley. His daughter's face was noncommittal. He glanced back at Nasters and held his gaze on him. The DCP doctor's mouth seemed to tighten with each passing moment.

"Everything does seem in order but---."

Nasters repeated his question, raising his voice an octave.

Rogers rubbed his eyes. He replied pensively, "Being a physician, I'm always skeptical. I'm just not sure. Actually, I would like to see the results of the initial phase of your human clinical trials."

Nasters looked sternly at his assistant. "We weren't planning on looking at the human data. And, I'm not sure when my schedule would permit us to do that."

Ashley intervened. "Why don't we all check our calendars now?"

Rogers curtly responded, "I can't commit to a date at this time. I'm headed back to DC this evening. I'll have to call in a few days."

The scientist was apologetic. "I wish I could accommodate you today while you are here in Michigan but I'm afraid that it's impossible."

"Understood. We'll do it the next time that I can get away from DC and when you are available."

Rogers shook hands firmly with each and then followed the DCP security escort to the door.

******

An hour later, he and his daughter met up with Beth at her apartment. By now, her migraine had subsided somewhat.

The Surgeon General was pleased to hear Beth's report that she appeared to have gained the confidence of Dr. Washington—not much more. He hugged Beth and Ashley and headed off to the airport. Rogers knew that his visit to DCP would eventually prove to have been worthwhile if the assistant scientist would fess up to her new friend on the *NeoBloc* data.

In the taxi, one thought clobbered him. The entire day he had kept trying to recall what about the data he saw today was different from what he had seen before. Now, he remembered what it was. Today, there was no signature at the bottom of the pages of monkey data A distant memory of his brief scan of the monkey research report before he closed it the night that Kim had entered the study triggered just enough neurons to recall this critical fact. *Nasters showed me a forgery.*

******

Nasters's cell phone rang. The executive summary report on the early human trial data slipped through his fingers onto his desk. He checked the caller ID. Seeing a blocked number appear on the screen, he responded warily. "Hello."

"Hussein?"

Picking up quickly on the Pakistani accent, he replied more enthusiastically, "Hussein Nasters at your service."

"I'm your contact in America."

"Praise be to Allah!"

"You will come to Oldwyck Park at ten o clock tonight."

"As you say."

"I'll see you there."

"Where in the park do I meet you?"

"Never ask questions. Hussein, I'll always find you whenever I want."

"I beg your indulgence. I'll be there as you command." There was no further response as a dial tone replaced conversation. Nasters dropped to his knees and prayed to Allah.

CHAPTER FOURTEEN

The Surgeon General sat down in front of her desk in the Oval Office, wondering if he should have told the Secretary of Health of the surprise invitation by the President.

"Dr. Rogers, I'll be meeting with Congressional leaders this afternoon. I wanted to hear your clinical insights from your review of the DCP monkey data?"

"Thank you for this second opportunity to discuss the safety of *NeoBloc*." Preparing for this meeting, he had thought about whether he would claim the data that he was shown was not the original report—the report with the signature of Dr. Nasters at the bottom of each page. But, he had decided his recollection was not enough without actually having the actual original data report. *If I make that claim without evidence, a chain of events will be set into motion.* President Williams would then feel a need to inform Secretary James so the Department of HHS would make a formal inquiry. And with potential advance notice by a mole, DCP could simply add a signature to each page before showing the monkey data again. *Hold your tongue Rogers.*

"Madame President, I've discovered no direct evidence to back up my concerns on the vaccine. But, I believe my earlier contact with an executive within DCP was telling the truth. She believed *NeoBloc* was dangerous."

"I would like to speak with your contact."

Rogers shot a blank stare at Williams. "My contact is dead."

"Oh."

"She was found in the park--beheaded!"

Williams shot Rogers a knowing glance. "Actually, I do remember reading in the *Post* about a woman that was brutally murdered. I believe her name was Lauren Timmons. If my memory serves me, the story said she was attacked while jogging in the park just after dusk."

"Not exactly, Madame President."

"Then please tell me what you know."

"Lauren Timmons gave me internal DCP reports that supposedly showed that every monkey that was given *NeoBloc* died within a year."

The President raised her voice, clearly annoyed. "Supposedly?"

"I never actually read the report."

"That makes no sense doctor. Why not?"

"Before I had a chance to read it, it was stolen from my home!"

"How long did you have it in your possession before it disappeared from your sight?" Williams leaned back in her chair.

"Maybe two hours or so."

"Certainly enough time to read it," she retorted.

Do I have to explain why I didn't want Kim to know? Rogers said in a matter of fact tone, "I was planning on doing so after relaxing with my wife. It had been a long day. I'm sure you can understand."

"I see." The President leaned forward. "Why are you so sure that your contact was telling the truth?"

"Something else happened the same night the report was stolen. An arrow was shot at me."

"Did you tell the police?"

"No." He closed his eyes for several seconds, recalling the message on the arrow. "This is not the first time that I've been a target in this city."

"I'm well aware of your history. Do you suppose that it may have been one of your enemies from *The Health Club?*"

"You know about them?"

The President grinned. "Don't forget, Dr. Rogers, I know everything about you. Otherwise, I never would have appointed you to be my Surgeon General."

He nodded. "Madame President, I trusted what Lauren said to me--- before she was so brutally murdered."

The President looked away. He noted the back of a picture frame on her desk. Her focus was on it for several seconds until she sneezed loudly. Williams looked up at him. Blinking several times, her steely eyes bore into him. "With all due respect, I can't stop all human clinical trial research on a vaccine that might save America from a full blown economic depression based on your hunch."

"I'm trying to get evidence for you."

"Look, you're my top doctor. I trust you. But, the fact remains that the Secretary of Health and my Chief of Staff fully support Project Moon Shot." She crossed her arms across her chest. "Just do what you have to do to uncover the truth."

"I'll do whatever it takes."

"Dr. Rogers, one last point. Be careful! I don't want to lose my Surgeon General the way you lost your wife. Don't be a hero Doctor." She lowered her eyes to a corner of her desk.

"Madame President, I'm only doing my job."

Rogers took a step to the side of the President's desk. He leaned forward to see the photo on the picture frame that held the President's rapt attention.

"It's my sister Maryann. She died in the Minneapolis nuclear attack."

It's personal for her. The Surgeon General replied crisply, "Madame President, I'm sure you will make the right decision for our country."

"Pray that I will. Pray that I will."

******

Rogers sat at his computer and gawked at his screen saver. Shining as the screensaver was their wedding picture. Each night, he found himself just staring at Kim, talking to her, asking for forgiveness, wanting desperately for her to come back to him and knowing that would never happen. He needed someone to talk to, someone he could trust. Feeling all alone, he picked up his desk phone and dialed.

"Hello."

In a somber voice, he began. "It's Jonathan."

In an upbeat singsong manner, she asked, "Hey, how's it going?"

"Not so good Beth. I can't sleep at night. I wake up and Kim's not here. I blame myself for everything that has happened."

There was a momentary pause on her end. She asked, "What's the latest from the FBI?"

"Special Agent Masters just told me that their only lead had recently committed suicide." Rogers shook. "It was Haley Tyler. When she showed up at Kim's funeral, I had a bad feeling that something was going to happen."

"From my car, I saw Haley running away across the cemetery field and that guy was chasing her."

"The FBI told me that the bullet that killed Kim was meant for me. It's my fault. Kim never wanted me in politics. Why didn't I listen to her? Dammit, she would be alive today."

"Don't do this to yourself. She loved you for who you are---you're just doing your job."

He pulled the phone from his ear and pinched his nose where it met both eyebrows. Sitting back on his kitchen chair, he gritted his teeth. "It's results that count, not just effort. I've got to do more to find Kim's killer."

"You're doing what you can."

"I feel like crap." He paused. "I'm sorry I said that. This is my problem, not yours. I shouldn't be unloading on you. It's not fair to you. Again, I'm sorry."

"Listen; do you want me to come over? I'll pick up an espresso from Starbucks. We can talk as much as you want."

He hesitated for a moment. "It's late. I'm tired."

"Just remember, I'm here for you if you need me."

"Let's talk about something else." He stretched his back. "Have you contacted Dr. Washington about reviewing the data on the *NeoBloc* human trials?"

"I called and left a message. I haven't heard back as yet. But, I believe she is a decent person and an honest scientist. If there are any problems with the vaccine, I think that she'll let me know."

"If she goes counter to Dr Nasters, she'll be taking a huge chance with her career."

"That's for sure. Being a whistleblower is risky business. My own stepfather found that out—the hard way."

His mind flashed back to Kim and Sam Murphy. He blinked away the gathering moisture around his weary eyes. "We've both lost someone we love."

"Let's be positive. You know that you can always count on me."

He thought of how Beth had always come through for him in the past. He stared blankly at the computer screen saver. "I've been thinking. Maybe I should start making a list of everyone who ever considered me an enemy."

"I'm not so sure that would help.'

"I do."

"Well, at least you don't have to worry about Zach Miller."

Hearing his name, a shiver sped down his spine. "You know that they never found his body after his Ferrari exploded. I've been thinking about talking with Peabody and Carver who are at the Milan Federal Prison in Michigan."

"I would hold off on talking to them. I'd bet that they're still connected to the inner circles of *The Health Club*. Don't forget, they were part of a master plot that tried to kill you."

He added wistfully, "Kim would be alive today if they could have pulled it off. Sometimes, I wish they had succeeded."

"Stop it!" she shouted. Pausing several seconds, she added, "Jonathan, I'm really worried about you. Look, do you want me to stay with you this weekend? You have two bedrooms. From the way you're talking, I think you can use a real friend."

He tried rubbing the spasm from his neck muscles. "No, I need to work through this on my own. I checked my schedule and called Nasters. I'm returning to DCP in ten days to review the early human trial data."

"Jonathan, I'm hoping Virginia Washington will be our mole within DCP."

His voice grew stern. "Just make sure she doesn't put herself in any personal jeopardy. And, that goes for you as well."

"Jonathan, call again if you need me. Good night."

***

Rogers had never before owned a gun. He felt uneasy standing before the sales clerk while he held a Browning 9mm semi-automatic in his right hand.

"Sir, how would you like to pay for it? Cash or credit?"

Rogers felt his lungs growing tight. Fear cycled through his brain. He blurted out, "Cash." Watching the gun storeowner ring up the sale, he wondered whether he was doing the right thing. *I'll need to take some lessons at the shooting range. With my loathing of guns, I hope I don't shoot myself.*

CHAPTER FIFTEEN

Connor laid down the latest *NeoBloc* research report on his bed. Not fully understanding the complex statistics of the many subgroups within the early human trial data, he had believed Dr. Nasters's story that the two deaths during the first week of the trial were due to other unrelated causes and not directly to the vaccine. However, he was convinced that it was time to take control of DCP before Parker and Nasters would somehow make fatal mistakes to ruin the FDA approval and launch of the vaccine. He puffed his chest. The President stood behind the vaccine. She publicly referred to *NeoBloc* as The Savior Vaccine.

He dialed the cell phone of the Secretary of Health.

James replied on the third ring. "Yes Connor."

Bypassing any social convention that even came close to standard etiquette; he got to his point immediately. "I've decided that DCP needs a professional to run the business. Call your contacts to begin undermining Sean Parker. I need to take over this company within a month."

"Isn't that awfully quick?"

Connor was not amused with the question. He made a tight fist. "Look, I'm not asking for your godamm opinion. You wouldn't be where you are today without my help. Got it?"

James reacted instantly, "I'm sorry. I'll make the calls."

"Get back to me within the week. No excuses."

Throwing his cell against the wall, Connor promised himself that he would never again depend on anyone. As he looked at himself in the bedroom mirror, he winked at the only one in the whole world who he knew could be trusted.

CHAPTER SIXTEEN

President Williams let her eyes wander the quaint ambiance in the Senate Majority Leader's office. She tuned out the Senator's mini-filibuster with the House Speaker and admired the antique furnishings. Williams focused on a row of photographs of the Leader with the past six Presidents that lined the wall behind his enormous teak wood desk.

She glanced over to the Speaker, Charlie Jackson. He seemed frustrated, seemingly not able to get in a single word, as the Leader's booming voice echoed in his chamber. While Senator Richard Yarborough droned on explaining to the Speaker of the House a few choice political positions, she finally tuned into his boisterous rant.

Yarborough proclaimed, "So, Charlie, as far as the new healthcare reform law, I'm determined to lead the fight to repeal it."

The Speaker shook his head in violent opposition. "The hell you will."

The Leader of the Senate grunted something unintelligible and leaned back in his seat.

Jackson chimed in, "In deference to the President, let's move on to the main reason why we are here."

Yarborough sighed. "Madam President, in the three months since you declared war on cancer, your Office of Management and Budget has reported that our Gross National Product has fallen 9.8% for the fourth quarter." The Leader put up his feet on his desk. "Our country's GDP has not declined that much since the Great Depression of the 1930's when the GDP declined eleven percent. We are a hairs breath away from our first full-blown depression in nearly eight decades. What the hell are we going to do?"

The President's demeanor was calm. "Senator Yarborough, I'm well aware of the facts. The nuclear attacks have shaken the confidence of the American public. Polls show that two-thirds of Americans believe they will die of radiation poisoning within the next ten years. You and I know that skyrocketing healthcare costs have blown a hole larger than the Grand Canyon in our budget. The bottom line is simple. We just can't tolerate any more cancer related costs from another nuclear attack and we need to restore public confidence that not everyone is going to get cancer. Fear is overtaking America."

"You're playing defense, Madame President. I suggest that we blow the terrorists, who are gradually nuking us to death, off the face of the earth."

Williams tersely replied, "Be realistic Richard. We can't just indiscriminatingly drop bombs on whole populations of innocent civilians. We would need targeted surgical strikes on the terrorist camps—if we could find them."

The Senator raised his voice. "I say, kill them all before they pull the trigger again."

"You sound just like my predecessor."

"With all due respect to you, at least he did what had to be done against these extremists."

The President addressed the third person in the order of Presidential succession. "Charlie, what are your thoughts?"

Charlie Jackson plucked an unlit cigar from his mouth. "Madame President, before I explain my position, I have a question for you." He cleared his raspy voice. "Can you give us an update on how the human clinical trials with *NeoBloc* are progressing?"

"I have been kept well informed by Secretary James and Surgeon General Rogers. So far, so good."

"Well, if things are progressing so well, why can't we start the vaccinations before we land in a full scale depression during the upcoming quarter? God forbid, if we suffer another nuclear attack, the cancer rate will continue to escalate exponentially. We simply can't afford the continued costs of this precipitous rise in cancer among our citizens." He carefully laid his cigar on the edge of the Majority Leader's desk. "And you said before---the media has eighty percent of the country in a total panic that they're going to develop cancer. Even our healthy citizens can't be productive at work. All they think about is getting cancer."

Williams replied, "The FDA wants more data."

Jackson scratched his bulbous nose. "So, if we have an effective and safe vaccine that can prevent these cancers, why not deploy *NeoBloc* now? The FDA just wants more data as a CYA maneuver."

"Charlie, we must be certain that the vaccine is safe before I will mandate its use for every citizen. To be clear, the vaccine needs testing on at least two thousand volunteers in clinical trials before the FDA will consider its approval. That takes time. The National Quality Board is also reviewing the data. They are doing the best they can to ensure the vaccine works and is safe." She paused to let her words sink in and then added as an afterthought, "The Secretary of Health agrees with my position."

Senator Richard Yarborough leaned forward in his seat. "All I know is that Rome burned while Nero fiddled. My patience is ebbing away. The mid-term elections are fast approaching."

Williams paused. She held back what she really wanted to say. "Rest assured that no one wants to save American lives more than I do."

She stood and paced in front of Yarborough's desk. Williams squared up to face the leaders. Her voice tightened. "What I'm going to say to you must not be repeated outside this room. The Surgeon General has some unsubstantiated information that *NeoBloc* might not be safe."

Yarborough raised his eyebrows. "Unsubstantiated? On what basis?"

"This is strictly confidential. Dr. Rogers is working on getting the facts that we need. He's returning to DCP next week to review the results of the early human clinical trial data. I trust him."

Jackson stood. At five feet seven, his eyes were three inches below those of the President. "With unemployment at fifteen percent, in my thirty two years in Congress, I've never seen the country so riled up as it is today. Each day, it is getting much worse out there. I hear it all the time from my constituents. Madame President, just remember that it's your neck that will be chopped off first if you're wrong."

For a moment or two, Williams looked stone faced at the Congressional leaders before heading toward the door. She heard them whispering. After a couple of paces, the President stopped her march to turn around.

The Senate Leader sent her a piercing stare. Yarborough said softly, "Good day, Madam President. It's your---our last chance."

***

The President sipped a couple of mouthfuls of her favorite Brazilian coffee. "Dr. Rogers, I've been thinking of what you told me at our last private meeting. By the way, I did not share the fact that we met with Secretary James." She put her oversized coffee cup on her desk and swiveled her chair to look out at the Rose Garden. "I kept thinking of that woman."

"Lauren Timmons?"

The President briefly glanced back at him, looking over her shoulder. "You said it last time. Why would she lie about the safety of the vaccine?" Williams then resumed her gaze out the Oval Office windows.

"That's been my dilemma all along. By stepping forward to give me the monkey vaccine data, she knew that she was, at the very least, putting her career on the line."

Williams stood, still facing the windows. "I wonder if she ever thought that she might be risking much more than just her career."

"Thinking back to the night when she requested meeting me in the Georgetown tavern, I never should have let her go through the Park---- alone."

The President spun around to face him. "It's not your fault."

"I should have insisted that she come with me in my taxi. I could have dropped her off at the subway stop."

Williams waited for more details.

"Lauren said she was meeting someone who agreed with her on the vaccine—an ally. She stormed out of the tavern where we met—walked straight into the park."

"Did anyone follow her out of the tavern?"

The lumberjack sitting next to us? "Not that I saw."

"So, she met with someone in the Park."

"The person who killed her probably thought she had the monkey data with her. Someone had to see her taking it out of the DCP building and into that tavern to meet with me. But why would someone who agreed that the vaccine was dangerous want to kill Lauren?"

The President returned to her chair. "Are you sure that no one knew that Timmons gave you the data in the tavern?"

Mikey? "I can't say with absolute certitude." The Surgeon General projected a vacant stare, thinking of the beheaded woman and other random thoughts. *Who was the man next to me in the tavern that was text messaging?*

"Dr. Rogers, I believe in you. Always remember that. Just be careful when you return to DCP. Be very careful."

******

President Williams had been looking forward to hosting the formal dinner of chosen business CEO's. Given the worsening economic and political conditions, she believed that the dinner would be a good opportunity to mend fences and build bridges.

Divorced for an almost a dozen years, she had long since assumed additional roles usually delegated to the First Lady. It was at her insistence that the executive chef would report directly to her. After her election and during the transition of administrations, she had interviewed and retained Chef Ernesto, who had been in charge of food preparation at the White House since the 90's. Two weeks earlier, she had signed off on the menu for this evening. Williams had also approved of the horseshoe configuration of the three oak wood dinner tables. The hardest decision was who to invite. But she had always prided herself in her critical thinking skills. After reviewing her final selections, the President was pleased with her influential guest list.

Wearing an ankle length black wool dinner dress, Williams entered the State Dining Room promptly at eight o clock. She spotted the vacant Queen Anne-style chair at the head of the table. While walking toward her seat, she returned several polite good wishes from her invited guests with brief greetings. All eyes followed her as she took her place of honor at the head of the table.

Williams stood behind her classically carved oak chair. Three Secret Service agents as well as a grinning Ernesto stood next to the Corinthian columns in the far corner of the room. After nodding to them, she sat down.

Behind her chair, the heat from the roaring blaze of the fireplace felt soothing on this bitter wintry night. Before the President unfolded her linen napkin, her eyes roamed across the smiling faces of those seated around her. She warmed up when she met the handsome gaze of David Keeting, CEO of General Security Technology. Seated to her right at the traditional place of honor for a guest, it was not by chance that she had arranged for him to sit there. She twisted her torso to face him, whispering in his ear. "David, I'll need your support tonight." His warm smile gave her courage.

The President picked up her glass of Napa Valley Merlot. Williams paused until each of her twenty guests followed her lead. She then stood, feeling anxious. Since her meeting several hours earlier with the Surgeon General, she had made a difficult decision. *If NeoBloc was indeed deadly and Lauren Timmons had given her life for it, how can I condone continuing to give it to healthy volunteers who do not know the information that I possess.* She predicted that most of her guests would disagree with her gut wrenching decision to place a moratorium on the human testing of the vaccine, *NeoBloc*. She raised her glass as high as possible. She toasted, "To America."

She lowered her glass after taking a sip but remained standing. "Thank you all for coming tonight. Please take your seats. Before, we enjoy the feast that Ernesto has prepared for us; I would like to read a passage that means a lot to me. The words came from a letter written by John Adams on his second night living in the White House."

The President turned sharply on her heels to face the fireplace. Reading from the words carved into the stone mantel above the blazing fire, she read Adam's immortal words. "I pray Heaven to Bestow the Best of Blessings on THIS HOUSE and on All that shall hereafter inhabit it. May none but honest and wise Men ever rule under this roof."

Keeting softly replied, "Amen." He pulled out her chair and helped Williams take her seat.

The President watched as Ernesto's steward and two assistants appeared with plates of his well-known winter salad of pears, walnuts, almonds, and Maytag blue cheese. While Keeting was chatting with his wife, Williams turned toward Victor Grasso, seated to her immediate left.

His face looked like a mass of knots, almost as if his muscles were in spasms. Grasso began, "Madam President, who would have thought that one of our Founding Fathers could have made such a blunder?"

"Sir?"

He pointed toward the mantel. "He should have said wise persons, not wise men."

She gave a half-smile. "Victor, I'm sure that Adams was only reflecting on the mores of his times."

"No question about that point. Suffice it to say that if Adams were here tonight, he would probably stress the word wise and leave it at that." The skin around his eyes grew taut. "The gender is irrelevant but all of us do want a wise leader during times like these."

She replied crisply, "I hope to be up to Adam's standards."

Grasso shook his head in obvious agreement.

She continued to make small talk to those within earshot. Several times, she would raise her voice for a good cheer shout out. "I hope everyone is enjoying themselves." While listening to Keeting commenting on the salad, she slowly chewed a mouth full, savoring the taste.

Williams remarked, "The salad seems to be overpowered by the almonds."

The CEO smiled. "My sense of smell is poor. I suffer from chronic sinusitis. He shrugged his shoulders. "But my salad is delicious."

"Glad you're enjoying it." The President took another mouthful of wine and washed it down with a swig of water. She began to collect her thoughts. Williams glanced at the place cards in front of her guests. Their titles carried weight across the spectrum of business in the country. *I'll need their support.* She rose slowly. Her guests quickly took notice of her stance. Williams began when she had the undivided spotlight.

"Before our main course, I would like to share with you an important decision that I've made. It was not an easy one and I wanted to inform you personally before you hear about it on the news tomorrow." She presented a half-smile. "I have been briefed by our Surgeon General on the status of *NeoBloc*. Dr. Rogers and I have reason to be concerned about the safety of the vaccine. To this point, I've confided my decision only with my Chief of Staff. I have not yet spoken to the press and have chosen you to hear it first. Because of the probability that *NeoBloc* could be unsafe for American citizens in the clinical trials, I've decided to put a moratorium on current human testing. I will not take a chance that innocent volunteers participating in these clinical trials might die. My position, as you know, is that all life is indeed precious."

Some of their faces froze, expressionless and dumfounded. Keeting looked somewhat quizzical. The mouths of several of her guests gaped open. Complete shock at her decision was clearly the prevailing emotion.

Williams heaved a huge breath and continued. "Under the powers granted to me under martial law, I intend to sign an executive order that DCP shall return to the testing of *NeoBloc* on monkeys. Once we are assured that the vaccine is safe on the animal population, I'll lift my moratorium on the human testing phase".

She saw Grasso's raised hand from the corner of her eye. She ignored him for the moment. "Secretary Christian James will be working closely with our FDA chief. Whereas, we need *NeoBloc* as part of our national security plan, our government needs to absolutely ensure the safety of this vaccine."

By now, Grasso appeared ready to leap to his feet as he continued to wave his hand. Reluctantly, she pointed in his direction. "Madam President, with all due respect, may I ask if you have definite proof that *NeoBloc* is dangerous in monkeys or humans?"

"I can assure you that my staff is doing everything they can to protect the American people. Red flags about the safety of the vaccine have been raised."

He narrowed his eyes. "I sincerely hope this is a wise decision." He turned his face toward the fireplace. "Adams would want it to be so."

Keeting raised his hand. Once acknowledged, he surveyed each face and then spoke. "Madam President, there is no doubt in my mind that you fully understand how desperate we are to deploy a vaccine to stop the precipitous rise in cancer due to the nuclear fallout. However, we must not use a vaccine that could make matters even worse. Therefore, I fully support your decision."

The President nodded. "Are there any further comments?" She spotted the CEO of American Food and Beverage trying to get her attention. "Yes, Ms. Wolfe."

"I must say in all honesty that I am completely taken aback by your choice of how to proceed. Perhaps, Dr. Rogers and I could discuss his concerns in private. I also wonder whether the Surgeon General's concern is shared by Secretary James and others at Health and Human Services."

"I'm sure that he will be pleased to respond to any questions that you may have."

As another business CEO was about to raise her hand, the chefs appeared with the main entrée in hand. "Since dinner is now here, let's enjoy our meal. In the next day or two, I will make my medical team from HHS available to speak with any of you. Please call my assistant to schedule a mutually convenient time."

She pointed at her Chief of Staff, MacKenzie Pitnar. He was standing in the rear of the room. Mac walked quickly toward her. Williams whispered in his ear, "Please contact Dr. Rogers immediately. Ask if he could come to the White House to meet with Ms. Sandra Wolfe within the half hour."

"I will call him now."

President Williams gave a thumbs-up sign to Sandra Wolfe. The CEO nodded her approval.

Keeting picked up his fork. "Madame President, I'll follow up with you tomorrow. I have some questions that I would like to discuss in private."

While looking down at her plate, her stomach began to cramp. She corralled a few almonds with her fork. A wave of nausea struck her. She wiped a bead of sweat from her right eyebrow.

Nerves? She was pleased that she had made her announcement. At least, she would be able to say that Fortune 500 business leaders were briefed when she would publicly announce her decision on *NeoBloc* at tomorrow's TV press conference. Williams chewed a few almonds. As time passed, she began to feel better. Her anxiety appeared to be abating.

Ernesto was now walking toward her with a platter in one hand. She was looking forward to consuming her crab and shrimp. She leaned toward Keeting to permit the chef from over her left shoulder to place her entrée on her plate

"Madame President," Ernesto said, "I've added a touch of garlic as you prefer."

Keeting interrupted the chef. "If I wasn't allergic to shellfish, I would have chosen the shrimp. It looks great, Madam President."

"David thanks again for your support of my difficult decision." Picking up her fork, she speared a hefty chunk of shrimp. The President continued making pleasant small talk with her guests. Thirty minutes after dinner began; she began feeling her stomach kicking up again. *Relax, it's over.* She tried to ingratiate herself even to her strongest doubters, asking Grasso about his braised pork tenderloin with onions and avocado salsa.

He replied, "The pork is great." Leaning closer to her, Grasso lowered his voice. "I'll be calling Madison in the morning for a time when we can talk in private. I'll be up front with you. I totally disagree with your decision."

Williams put on her game face. She grinned. "I'm looking forward to it." Seconds later, the pains in her stomach intensified. *I can't let him get me upset.* Williams took several mouthfuls of the Merlot. Strangely, her mouth felt increasingly sore with each gulp. Her head began to ache. Checking her watch, she had looked forward to dessert all evening. Now, even thinking about the warm brie with spiced pecan topping caused her to shudder.

Keeting shot a worried look. "Are you all right?"

"Just a little upset stomach."

She scanned the room looking for Agent Henry. He was nowhere in sight. The room was spinning. The faces of her guests appeared fuzzy.

The room seemed to have gone silent. A sharp abdominal cramp struck a second later. Williams then spotted her chef. Ernesto was walking slowly toward her. Strangely, it was like he was walking in slow motion. By the time he arrived at her side, she felt herself about to retch. The President sprang to her feet and began running toward the exit door.

In the corridor outside the dining room, she turned her head around to see a female agent following her in close pursuit to the rest room. A moment later, she was looking up to see Agent Genevieve cradling her head. The abdominal cramps were incredibly intense. As if a rack of spotlights from a Broadway show bounced off her eyes, she felt blinded by a white light that seemed to grow brighter by the second. The President gasped for air but a moment or two later, she felt nothing.

CHAPTER SEVENTEEN

Dr. Rogers arrived at the outer gate of the White House grounds. Summoned from his apartment at the *Watergate* only ten minutes earlier, he had promptly responded to an urgent phone call from Mackenzie Pitnar. Sandra Wolfe, CEO of American Food and Beverage, he was told, wanted to meet with him right away at the White House to discuss *NeoBloc*. While waiting for the guard to confirm his credentials, out of the bone chilling darkness, he heard the footsteps of a woman wearing a black business suit sprinting toward him.

"I'm Agent Henry," she shouted. Puffing heavily, she took two deep breaths. "Dr. Rogers, we need your help right away. President Williams has collapsed. She is in the medical unit. The White House doctor is on his way."

The guard returned the ID and waved him through the security gate. As Rogers ran alongside the agent, Henry provided him with what the Surgeon General thought to be sketchy details. Just after entering a side entrance to the White House, an agent quickly escorted him to the medical unit, located off a side corridor that led to the Oval Office.

At the door, the Surgeon General another FBI agent greeted him. "I'm Agent Genevieve. President Williams is not doing---."

Interrupting her, he held up his hand upon spotting the President. She was lying motionless on a gurney. He side stepped Agent Genevieve and ran toward the Commander in Chief. His initial observation was that her skin took on an unusual pinkish hue. He took in the frantic scene. A nurse had just finished inserting an intravenous line. A bottle of normal saline was slowly dripping into the President's veins. Rogers smelled a pungent whiff of garlic as he neared her face.

Her glassy looking eyes were drooping. Williams seemed unable to focus clearly. A U-shaped scar covered her throat area. A remnant from probable thyroid surgery, it resembled a large smile upon his closer inspection. Her chest was heaving in a faster than normal rhythmic respiratory rate in the thirties and her nostrils were flaring as she tried to suck in more oxygen with each breath.

He patted her cheek several times, trying to get her to focus. "Madam President, talk to me."

She mumbled, "My hands feel like pins and needle." Her eyes intermittently rolled back so that he could occasionally only see the white part of her eyeball. "I can't catch my breath," she uttered as a grimace crossed her face.

"Nurse, strap on a nasal cannula. Turn up the oxygen to 2 liters/minute." A moment later, he caught wind of a strong fecal odor just before seeing a soiled towel on the floor. A nurse had just strapped a blood pressure cuff around the President's upper right arm and pumped up the cuff, temporarily blocking blood flow to the brachial artery.

He glanced up an anxiously looking Agent Henry. "Did anyone else get sick tonight?"

"No. Only the President became ill."

"What did she eat? Did anyone else have the same entrée?"

"The President had baked shrimp stuffed with crab. Several others at the dinner also ate the same entrée."

"Did she eat anything that contained garlic?"

"I believe that everyone with the shrimp entrée had a dash or two of garlic sprinkled on it."

Rogers gently lifted the stethoscope from the nurse's neck. He listened at the President's elbow for the standard Korotkoff sounds while slowly releasing air from the cuff. "Her blood pressure is very low. Eighty over fifty. Speed up the flow of fluids into the line to one hundred and fifty cc's an hour." The nurse reacted instantly to his order.

Out of the corner of his eye, he spotted the President's attending physician rushing toward them. He checked the nametag on the house physician's white coat just as he arrived at bedside. "Dr. Hopkinson, I think we may be dealing with arsenic poisoning."

The White House physician looked perplexed. "Why do you suspect that diagnosis?"

"She has classic neurological and gastrointestinal signs. Also, the smell of garlic on her breath was another clue. As you know, it's pretty rare. But, when I was in private practice, I once saw a case just like this."

Hopkinson put the earpieces of his stethoscope into his ears and pumped up the blood pressure cuff. He watched the rapid flow of saline drops entering the intravenous line. Releasing the cuff pressure, he listened while pressing the head of his stethoscope into the President's antecubital fossa. "Ninety over sixty."

Rogers shouted out an order. "Nurse, get me a large bore rubber gastric suction tube. I'm going to flush out her stomach just in case that I'm right about arsenic."

"If there is arsenic, we can suck out most of it before it's absorbed into her blood stream," Hopkinson added.

Rogers pulled up the patient's eyelid. Her eyes were rolling in their sockets like doll's eyes. He pinched the President's forearm. She moaned, but her eyes remained closed. *Getting worse.* Snatching the gastric tube from the hands of a breathless nurse who had just returned from the stockroom next to the medical unit, he bent down so that his mouth was next to the President's ear. "Stay with me. I'm going to pass a tube into the back of your mouth. Keep breathing slowly and deeply through your nose. Swallow when I say so."

Though appearing very groggy, Williams attempted following his commands. Her mouth slowly opened. She gagged as the tube touched the soft palate in the back of her mouth as he passed the gastric tube past her uvula, ready to enter the esophagus.

"Take deep breaths through your nose. Just focus on your breathing." The gagging stopped after several seconds. He barked out the next order, "Swallow----again---swallow hard."

The tube passed the epiglottis into the esophagus. "Good, very good." Threading the tube further into the back of her mouth, he asked her to keep breathing slowly and deeply through her nose. "You're doing great."

After insertion of the tube at fifty centimeters, he looked over at the nurse. Holding the end of the rubber tube, he ordered, "Hook this end to a suction unit."

"Yes, Dr. Rogers."

The Surgeon General held the garden hose like apparatus in place around the President's mouth. He pinched her forearm again. She winced though her eyes remained closed. He raised his voice. "Stay with me."

The nurse flipped the switch to the suction unit. Instantly, brown and green colored thick fluids began filling up the jar.

Dr Hopkinson read out her latest blood pressure reading. "One hundred over seventy. Her color is returning. I'm slowing down the IV to 100 cc an hour."

Her eyes popped open. He carefully observed the President's eye movements. Her eyes and eyebrows were flickering in a series of irregular sequences, like Morse code. For a second or two, he believed that she was actually trying to connect with him using intentional eye movements. He spoke softly into her ear. "I'll take this tube out in a minute. Just continue to breathe slowly through your nose." Williams followed his orders. "You're doing great."

While watching the contents of her stomach fill up the suction jar, Rogers counted down another minute by staring at the wall clock. About to pull the stomach tube, he felt a tap on his left shoulder. He glanced over and recognized the President's Chief of Staff. Pitnar yanked on the arm of the Surgeon General, taking him a few steps away from the gurney.

"Doctor, what do you think? Will she be OK?"

"It's too early to say. I think its arsenic. And, Dr. Hopkinson appears to agree with my working diagnosis."

"How the hell could she have been poisoned with arsenic?"

Rogers looked back at Williams. Her eyes were wildly darting around the ceiling. "Please excuse me." He took two steps back to the gurney, directing the nurse to send a sample of the suction jar brown liquid over to the lab for a general toxicology screen. "Check specifically for arsenic."

Hopkinson began to take charge. "Someone, hand me a pair of scissors. I want to clip off a sample of her hair."

The nurse quickly scouted up a pair and handed them to the White House physician. He dropped a few strands of hair into a gauze pad, which he then handed to the nurse. "Have the lab check her hair for arsenic."

He was about to check the President's pulse when Pitnar began moving between the Surgeon General and the patient. "Hey doc, you didn't answer my question. I said, how could she have gotten arsenic?" The Chief of Staff grabbed his arm for the second time.

Shaking off the grip on his forearm as he would if a fly landed on him, Rogers curtly replied, "I heard you the first time. It had to be something she ate within the last hour."

Dr. Hopkinson nodded in agreement.

He asked, "Who prepared the meal and served it to the President?"

"Chef Ernesto," Pitnar replied.

"Where is he now?"

"He's serving dessert to the President's guests."

Rogers motioned for Pitnar to back away. "Speak with Agent Henry. The Secret Service needs to immediately question the chef."

"Why do you suspect arsenic?" Pitnar asked again, this time in a pompous tone.

"Her breath smelled like garlic. It's a classic odor with arsenic poisoning."

Pitnar snapped back, "Her entrée contained garlic. Of course, it would be on her breath."

Rogers tapped his right foot several times. "Look, she also had neurological symptoms that were characteristic. And, she favorably responded clinically to the removal of the garlic smelling substance from her stomach."

"I'm no doctor but---."

The Surgeon General glared at him. "You're right about that Mac. You're *not* a doctor."

He directed his attention back to his patient. The suction jar was already three fourths filled when he slowly began to withdraw the tube from her stomach. "Breathe slowly. It's almost out." He quickly pulled out the last ten centimeters of the tube. "Good job, Madame President." Williams gagged and coughed several times. "Clear your throat and breathe slowly. It's over."

Amid a fit of coughing, the President mumbled a weak thank you.

Hopkinson spoke up. "She'll still need medication to remove any additional arsenic from her bloodstream. Some was probably already absorbed before we pumped her stomach."

Pitnar persisted. "Doctor, I need to know what is going on here."

Rogers twisted his neck to look back at the Chief of Staff. "What do you want to know? " He exclaimed, clearly annoyed.

"If you're right about the diagnosis, could there be any serious long term effects on the President?"

The Surgeon General walked away from the gurney. Out of earshot of the President, he murmured, "Too soon to say. For now, we'll just monitor her vital signs."

"Did I just hear you say that it's too soon to say whether there will be long term consequences?" He scrunched his face. "Doctor, we're talking about the President. What exactly does that mean?"

"Confidentially, it's not common but on some occasions arsenic poisoning has been found to lead to the development of cancer."

Pitnar did a double take, his eyes bulging. He blurted out, "Cancer?"

"It's happened before."

The Chief of Staff's face surprisingly brightened. "This is just one more reason why we need to move ahead on human testing with *NeoBloc.*"

"You're talking apples and oranges." He held up his hands. "Stop right there. The *NeoBloc* vaccine doesn't prevent cancer due to arsenic. It may work against cancer caused by radiation, although we still don't know if it's safe."

"The President believes in the vaccine." Pitnar turned away to walk toward Agent Henry. Without looking back to Rogers, he said in a loud voice, "Let me know when I can take you to Ms. Wolfe."

The Surgeon General observed Dr. Hopkinson performing a neurological exam on the President. Concluding his exam, the house physician ordered a nurse to request several bottles of EDTA, an intravenous medication that latches onto arsenic to remove it safely from her body, from the George Washington Medical Center. "Call me when the EDTA arrives and I'll administer it."

Rogers stepped back a few paces. Moments later, a technician took an electrocardiogram on the President. Another tech drew several vials of blood. William's eyes were now fully open and steady. She clearly focused on her house physician's face.

"Madame President," Hopkinson said, "How are you feeling?"

She hesitated. "Better---much better. The stomach cramps are gone."

The White House physician looked over at Rogers. "She was able to execute during my exam. I'm pleased at her rapid progress. I'll start her on a high sulfur diet to help remove any of the potential arsenic that the EDTA doesn't clear out."

"Doc, you're in charge."

"I've ordered a full drug screen, electrolytes and a chemistry panel." Hopkinson grabbed the electrocardiogram print out from the tech. "Normal sinus rhythm. No acute changes. And, the nasal oxygen should further assist in cellular oxygenation. "

Rogers rubbed his eyes. "Thanks again for your help."

He was about to search for Pitnar when he heard his name being whispered by the President. Drawing near her face, he was pleased to see her gaze so focused.

"Madam President, how are you doing?"

"I'm alive."

"You should be fine now."

Williams reached out for his hand. "I heard Dr. Hopkinson say that your quick diagnosis and treatment probably saved my life."

Rogers let her hand touch his for a few moments. "We're both trained to deal with medical emergencies. What counts most is that both your personal doctor and I believe that you should have a full recovery."

Williams gave him a half smile. "Just before I came down ill, I announced my suspension of human testing of *NeoBloc*. My soul would not permit me to let innocent people volunteer to take the vaccine in light of what we both know about Lauren Timmons. It's not fair to these clinical trial subjects unless we fully disclose our safety concerns. If we did that, no one would volunteer. So, I placed a moratorium on the vaccine until all issues with the monkey data have been cleared up."

A warm feeling began to pulsate through his veins. "Madame President, I believe you made the right decision."

"Doctor, you and I may be the only ones to think so."

"Let's just focus on getting you back to health. We can talk in a few days about the vaccine after your strength returns." He looked to his left and nodded. "I just got a wave of the hand from Pitnar. He will be taking me to Ms. Wolfe so I can answer her questions about *NeoBloc*."

"I want to warn you, she can be a barracuda but it's better to convince one killer fish at a time that we need your scientific guidance on the vaccine."

"There is one caveat Madame President which we haven't previously discussed. I don't know why but Secretary James dismissed it when I first raised the issue."

"Oh?"

"In the *NeoBloc* monkey trials, these animals were given twenty five times the dose that is being given to humans in their trials."

"What would that mean in scientific terms?"

"It's impossible to compare the monkey and the human clinical trials because of the dose differences."

"So, it's possible at lower doses the vaccine is safe in humans whereas it might have been deadly for the monkeys since they received massive doses?"

Rogers nodded sheepishly. "It's theoretically possible but highly unlikely in my opinion."

"But I stopped the human clinical trials under my understanding that we need to first ensure that the monkeys are safe with *NeoBloc*."

"That is true. However, comparing animal data with human data is always subject to some variance because of the much higher doses typically used in animal trials."

A deep frown crossed her brow. "Why haven't you or Secretary James told me this before?"

"I did inform the Secretary previously on this point just as I told you. To my dismay, he chose to ignore this critical issue."

Williams groaned. "Dr. Rogers, I need your help."

"This is not a good time to be discussing this. You need your rest."

She raised her voice, "Look, I need to know the truth—the whole truth."

Rogers noticed a few nurses eavesdropping on their conversation. He shot them a hard look. After they moved away, he softly continued, "Christian James and I have talked about the different doses used for animal and human trials. We discussed that there could be differences comparing the two sets of data. But, he believes the monkey's died from a virus and not from *NeoBloc*."

"What is his evidence for believing that?"

"Nothing at all except that Dr. Nasters and Sean Parker told him that's their hypothesis."

The President's face flushed a crimson red. "I expect my Secretary of Health to deal in science and not conjecture. And, I expect my Surgeon General to ensure that science prevails."

"You have made a wise decision. I fully support it. But, I really think you need your rest. You have just been through a lot."

Williams stared at him for ten long seconds before speaking. Her jaw tightened. "Now, I'm more ambivalent than ever about *NeoBloc*."

He peered into her darting eyes. "Science is not perfect. Nothing is."

"I am obviously not a physician or a scientist. I depend on the professionals to tell me the truth."

"I always have."

"Then the others are misleading me."

"Madame President, as you know, the forces of malice are all around us. They killed my wife. I'm almost certain it was because of my opposition to the vaccine. Now, you were a target."

"I'm holding you accountable to do what is right for the American people."

******

Rogers sipped his morning coffee. His prior night's conversation with Sandra Wolfe in a White House office had gone reasonably well. Yet, she had displayed her well-known characteristic testiness during their private talk about *NeoBloc*. Ms. Wolfe had eventually accepted the rationale for the President's decision. The CEO also stated she would hold Williams accountable if her decision flopped. A not so subtle threat to fund her opponent in the next Presidential election became the elephant in the room.

After stretching his arms high above his head and unhurriedly twisting his back to relax his taut muscles, Rogers picked up *The Washington Post* from his kitchen table. He gaped at the two-column headline. There was front-page coverage of an apparent murder-suicide of the President's chef, Ernesto, and his roommate, Joseph. According to the article, both men, reported as violently arguing with each other at a local bar, did so several hours after the President became ill. As he continued reading, he noted that an unnamed friend, who was with both of them at the bar, had called Ernesto the following morning. Getting no response after repeated attempts, the mutual friend went to their apartment and found thier door unlocked. He entered, found the bodies and called the police.

According to article in *the Post*, the police found Ernesto and Joseph holding.38 caliber revolvers in their hands. According to the official report, it concluded the double homicide to be secondary to a lovers' quarrel. *I had better not miss any more classes at the shooting range.*

******

While winding through the corridors leading to the waiting area outside the Oval Office, Secretary James spoke bluntly, "Listen, I'll take the lead on handling any questions about *NeoBloc*."

Rogers's face was quizzical. "I was surprised to get your call to come here. Who called for this urgent meeting with the President?"

"Mackenzie Pitnar and the President have an important matter that they want to discuss with us."

"What's the goal of the meeting?"

James began to trot ahead. Sprinting ahead, he took the lead by ten steps. He shouted back, "We're late."

Rogers ran to catch up. "I was right about my diagnosis. Dr. Hopkinson called me today. The analysis of the President's hair strand showed that it contained arsenic."

The Secretary shouted over his shoulder as he dashed down the hallway, "At least, you haven't forgotten your basic medicine. That's a good thing if you ever need to support yourself by going back into private practice." James suddenly slowed down to a power walk pace and stared menacingly at him.

Now, walking alongside him, the Surgeon General asked, "What are you telling me?"

James slapped him across the back. "I'm just kidding. Don't take everything so serious."

Rogers grabbed the right shoulder of the Secretary, forcing him to come to a dead stop. "For the record, I was pleased the President decided to suspend human trials with *NeoBloc*."

He brushed Rogers hand off his shoulder. He continued walking without saying a word. They arrived at a stairwell. James began scaling the steps, two at a time. The stairwell led to the hallway outside the Oval Office. Reaching the hallway door together, James flung it open and fired himself ahead of Rogers into the waiting room. Madison was at her desk and looked up when she heard their fast approaching footsteps.

The Secretary asked, "Is the President ready for us?"

"I'll check." The administrative assistant rose and knocked twice on the Oval Office door before opening it. Madison peeked inside and then looked back over her shoulder. "Gentlemen, the President and the Chief of Staff will see you now."

James turned to Rogers. "Let's get in there and--- watch your step."

***

The President was standing behind her desk. She was chatting quietly with her Chief of Staff. Rogers saw her glance over at him. She sent a crooked smile in his direction.

As they both walked steadily toward her, Williams abruptly dropped her conversation with Pitnar. She greeted them with a friendly wave and pointed to the two couches in the center of the room. "Good morning, gentlemen. Let's take a seat."

Rogers waited until the President and Pitnar sat on the pale blue couch. He took a spot on the beige colored couch alongside his boss and across from the Chief of Staff. A sturdy looking wood coffee table with four glasses of water occupied the center of their group seating.

The Surgeon General spoke up first. "Madam President. Before we begin, I'm glad that you're looking so well."

Williams half saluted the Surgeon General.

"It was arsenic."

"You were right Dr. Rogers. You did save my life."

"I'm glad that I was able to help. It was a team effort. Dr Hopkinson did a terrific job."

"Excuse me." The Chief of Staff raised his index finger. "The President called for this meeting to discuss the recent moratorium on the human clinical testing trials with *NeoBloc*."

Rogers craned his neck toward James. *Thanks for the lack of a heads-up boss.* The Secretary's jaw jutted forward. He squirmed in his seat while focusing his gaze squarely on Pitnar.

Pitnar continued, "Madame President, it is my understanding that you made your decision to suspend testing after you reached out to the Surgeon General."

Williams glanced over at Rogers. "That is correct. I asked the Surgeon General to come to me, to all of us, with hard evidence on the vaccine's safety. Clearly, I am not an expert on these matters. I depend on my scientific advisors."

Pitnar looked at each of them before delicately asking, "Has anyone seen such hard evidence?

Williams waved in the direction of the Surgeon General. "Dr. Rogers is working to obtain evidence. So far, we have none."

"I have a question," Pitnar interjected, "for the Secretary of Health. What are your thoughts on the moratorium?"

"I'm by no means the clinical expert but I come here today not driven by personal opinions but armed with facts. To begin, I've been reassured by the leaders of DCP, Sean Parker and Dr. Hussein Nasters, that their vaccine is safe. Moreover, I have personally seen the monkey clinical trial data. It appears that their summary findings are all positive as far as efficacy and safety. I have also spoken with Dr. Ulrich who is the chairperson of the National Quality Board that oversees the DCP human clinical trials on *NeoBloc*. The Board met yesterday. " James paused to take a sip of water, staring at Pitnar.

I see where this meeting is going, Rogers mused inwardly.

James glanced over at Williams. "Please excuse me if I'm speaking too long."

The President replied, "Not at all."

The Chief of Staff broke out into a wide smile. "Don't keep us hanging Christian," Pitnar chuckled, "What exactly did Dr. Peter Ulrich tell you."

"Dr. Ulrich told me that the Quality Board previously deemed the monkey trials with *NeoBloc* to be safe and they have not changed their minds."

The President looked over to Rogers. "Were you aware of yesterday's meeting of the National Quality Board?"

He bolted to an upright posture. "No, this is the first time that I'm hearing this."

James lurched toward Rogers, landing his hand on the couch, a few feet from where the Surgeon General sat. "I'm sorry Jonathan. It was at the top of my list to discuss with you. But then this urgent meeting was called."

Rogers's face turned beat red. He ignored the Secretary and looked directly at the President. "I have noticed something about the monkey data that perhaps the Board overlooked." He then fired off a quick sideways glare at James. "Madame President, I know someone who sits on that Board and she didn't tell me anything about any recent Board meeting discussing *NeoBloc*. This needs to be---"

The Chief of Staff interrupted, "If I may----. He looked over at the President. "The National Quality Board meeting was called on an urgent basis in view of your recent change in *NeoBloc* human testing policy. A quorum of the Board voted that human testing of the vaccine could always be halted, at a later date, if any significant safety issues emerged."

Pitnar took a sip of water and locked his line of sight with Secretary James. He added, "Of course, the Board is only an advisory group. I leave it to your expertise, Mr. Secretary."

Rogers was about to erupt when James took complete control. "Madame President, I believe that Mr. Pitnar makes an excellent point. I understand your sincere concern for the American volunteers taking the vaccine in the clinical trials but there is a greater good principle involved."

Williams nodded. "Christian, go on."

"If *NeoBloc* works and is fully deployed for every citizen, we could save millions of American lives." He glanced out the Oval Office windows. "We cannot forget the fact that we live in a dangerous world." He gestured toward the Surgeon General. "Thanks to his personal feelings on the vaccine, we have been alerted to his opinion that *NeoBloc* may cause problems. But with no disrespect intended, his beliefs are not backed up with facts." James looked back at the President. "It is my strong recommendation that you immediately lift the moratorium. Now, if you agree with me, we'll be closely monitoring the human trials. If anyone becomes ill, we can always halt the trials at that time."

Eyebrows raised, Williams locked on the Surgeon General. "It seems that everyone except you is convinced the monkey trial data showed the vaccine to be safe."

"There is a well accepted principle in medicine going back thousands of years that states: first do no harm. I firmly hold to my considered position that the monkey trials need to be repeated to absolutely prove that *NeoBloc* is safe for human testing."

Williams rose slowly. "Mr. Secretary, I do appreciate your larger point that clinical trials are always risky for anyone involved. And, tens of thousands have already died in the terrorist war on our nation." She walked over to the window behind her desk. Motionless for almost a minute, she was obviously deep in thought.

To his consternation, Rogers was now convinced that the President was at the tipping point of rethinking her decision to place a moratorium Project Moon Shot. *This was a set up.* He was ready to break the silence when Secretary James turned toward him and caught his attention. His boss placed his right forefinger against his own lips. *He's telling me to keep my mouth shut.* Looking over to the Chief of Staff, Rogers picked up a nasty scowl. "Madame President, may I say something?"

A moment later, Williams turned toward all of them. She strode quickly back to her seat, carrying her shoulders high. Her step was sure footed. "Dr. Rogers, it is my turn to speak." Blinking repeatedly, she said ruefully, "Gentlemen, I've thought long and hard about reconsidering my recent decision based on the National Quality Board's advice"

Rogers spoke up. "Madame President---"

Williams held out her right hand in front of her. "Please let me finish."

He held his tongue and picked up a slight smirk curling the lips of the Chief of Staff.

"A couple of weeks ago, the Surgeon General and I visited a hospital in Minneapolis. We met two young victims of the nuclear attacks. Both were suffering from radiation sickness and both will be at a high risk for developing radiation-induced cancer at some point in their lives. From the experience of previous victims of nuclear attacks in Japan, leukemia could develop within the next year. Well, on that day, I promised Cassie that I would do everything possible to save her and her daughter, Emma."

Rogers saw her expression suddenly turning more somber. The President looked directly at the Surgeon General and asked, "Final thoughts?"

He did not flinch. Used to having to fight for what was right, this time there was no margin for error. "I strongly supported your decision to place a moratorium on the human trials and re-start the monkey trials. As you have always maintained, every life is precious. Are you willing to take a chance on thousand people needlessly and immorally dying? Scientifically speaking, there is no question in my mind that we must re-test the vaccine on the monkeys to prove its safety."

Secretary James stood and looked down at Rogers. "I vehemently disagree. You have no facts to support your position. You are purely speculating." He wagged his index finger at Rogers and looked back at the President. "For the sake of the entire country, we need to re-start Project Moon Shot immediately."

The Surgeon General quickly countered. "The fact of the matter is that a high ranking executive of DCP was beheaded just minutes after telling me that *NeoBloc* was deadly. She had no motive to risk her life to make up a story that the vaccine was unsafe."

The Secretary sat down. He spoke slowly but with passion. "Doctor, with all due respect, that was purely her personal opinion." James focused his eyes on the President. "Madame President, what about the opinions of other well respected physicians? Shall we simply disregard what both Dr. Peter Ulrich and Dr. Hussein Nasters believe?" He then pointed at Rogers. "What I don't understand is why the Surgeon General regards Ms. Lauren Timmon's perspective higher than these two well informed physicians as well as other ranking members of the National Quality Board!"

Rogers knitted his eyebrows and kept his focus on the President. "Because Ms. Timmons gave up her life to support something in which she believed. I don't know many people who would do that. And, she gave me the monkey data that proves *NeoBloc* is dangerous."

The Secretary of Health spoke in a quiet tone. "Show us this monkey data. Where is it?"

"It's been stolen."

James rolled his eyes. "Look, Ms Timmons was killed while walking alone through the metropolitan park at night. It was a random act of violence. It happens all the time in cities like Washington! It's a tragedy. We all feel bad for what happened to her. But what I don't understand is why do you ascribe a sinister motive to her death that is somehow connected to *NeoBloc*?" He paused a moment. "The bottom line is that you simply have no evidence to back up your beliefs."

The President cleared her voice. "Mr. Secretary, I heard from Dr. Rogers that there is a possibility that even if the monkeys died from *Neobloc,* that it's still possible that it won't affect humans since the dose for people is so much lower. Is that your understanding?"

James shook his head in agreement. "Yes, Madame President, that is a fair point, although not conclusive."

Pitnar coughed twice. The assembly took notice. When all eyes were upon him, he said, "Madame President, in view of the compelling information presented by the Secretary of Health, I would strongly recommend that you rescind your order to suspend *NeoBloc* testing on humans."

Someone is coercing the President into changing her decision. Rogers's mind flashed back to the severed head of Lauren Timmons. He glowered at James. The Secretary did not meet his gaze. The Surgeon General looked back at the President.

She spoke powerfully, "I'm not a scientist. You are my advisors. Based on the totality of feedback, I've reconsidered. It is my decision to order the immediate restarting of human testing with *NeoBloc*."

The Chief of Staff chimed in, "Thank you Madame President. It takes a strong leader to be willing to do what is right. I will immediately communicate your decision to the appropriate people at the FDA, DCP, and the Press."

The President turned to the Surgeon General. "Dr. Rogers, I want you to continue to stay on top of the human clinical trials and report back anything you find to the group."

Rogers stiffened. It was understandable why the President had reversed her decision. *It's my fault the monkey data on NeoBloc was stolen.* "I will do so Madame President."

James put his hand over his heart. "Today's headline about Pakistan threatening India with a nuclear attack puts a sharp point on the need for the number one superpower in the world to have savior vaccines like *NeoBloc*."

Williams stood. The trio quickly rose in unison. The President walked back to her desk. James and Pitnar strolled toward the exit door. Intentionally trailing them, Rogers heard the President shout out, "Doctor, we'll talk again. Thanks again for all of your help."

It was now all out in the open. Rogers was all alone in championing his beliefs on the risks of *NeoBloc*. *I could be fired in a heartbeat and NeoBloc will move forward, conceivably killing millions.* His mind shifted to Beth. He needed confirmation about the so-called urgent National Quality Board meeting. It was obvious that it would be up to Beth, Ashley, and him to find out the truth before the *NeoBloc* clinical trial human participants might meet the same deadly fate as the monkeys had experienced.

Rogers dashed to the rest room. He splashed his face with cold water and looked up at the mirror. With his mind unsettled, he imagined that he saw Lauren's bloodless face propped up alongside a stone in the park's grass. Staring at the bags below his bloodshot eyes, he wondered whether his own head would be the next to roll. *I need to maintain my job as Surgeon General so I can be a voice of reason among these political animals.*

******

Rogers gawked at the month's calendar, taped to his refrigerator door. Tomorrow was circled in red. He paced his apartment, certain of his next move regarding *NeoBloc*. Flicking on the TV, he mindlessly surfed every channel. After settling on one station, a regular season NBA basketball game bored him. He picked up the phone from the corner table next to the couch in his living room.

On the second ring, she picked up. "Hi Beth. It's Jonathan. I have a question for you. Was there an urgent meeting of the Board yesterday?"

"Not to my knowledge."

He wrinkled his forehead. "Is that so? Today, Secretary James revealed that the Board met and recommended that the *NeoBloc* human trials move forward based on proven safety of the monkey trials."

She hesitated. "Under Board rules, Dr. Ulrich might have convened a quorum that made that recommendation. It only takes seven members. They wouldn't have necessarily needed me."

"Can you find out for me?"

"I'll do my best." Her voice tightened. "I heard this evening that the President reversed her decision to suspend human trial testing. I can't believe that the clinical trials have re-started."

"The decision of the National Quality Board was a major factor in the President changing her mind. James and Pitnar are probably doing an end zone celebration right now."

"Don't they know they are pawns falling into DCP's game plan?"

He thought about replying to her question but changed his mind. "Beth, I'm walking a tightrope. James could axe me any day. He could make up something and charge me with insubordination. I have already stuck my neck out pretty far."

In an upbeat tone, she replied, "Tomorrow we'll uncover something."

"I don't believe Sean Parker or Dr. Nasters will ever tell us the truth. Have you spoken to the other scientist recently?"

"Virginia Washington and I are having an early breakfast. It will be two hours before our meeting tomorrow at DCP."

"Why didn't you call to tell me?"

"I don't know. I guess I didn't want to raise your expectations in case Dr. Washington doesn't spill the real beans on *NeoBloc*."

"Who set up the breakfast?"

"It was her idea. She wasn't specific on why she wanted to meet. I didn't want to push. I don't want her to think that I'm using our relationship to gather corporate intelligence."

"Right now, she's our main lead. Tomorrow, I'll wait for you in the lobby of DCP. Be there by nine fifty five. Now that the human trials have re-started, we've got to review the first few weeks of data."

Silence

"Beth, are you still there?"

She paused a second or two. "So on a personal note, how are you doing Jonathan?"

"I'm keeping busy at work."

"You know that's not what I mean."

Rogers looked over at his wedding photo sitting on the opposite end table. He cursed himself for the thousandth time for what happened. "Good night Beth." He pressed the off button on the phone and hung his head.

CHAPTER EIGTHTEEN

Beth slurped dry her third cup of coffee. Dressed in a smart looking business suit, she sat at a table in the back of the busiest restaurant in town, the DuPont Diner. Virginia Washington had specifically chosen this one, bypassing the Jackson Diner that was much closer to DCP headquarters.

She glanced down at her watch. It was fifteen minutes past the time that Virginia had set for their breakfast meeting. She fidgeted with her empty cup. It felt good that Jonathan was depending on her but she was feeling the pressure placed on her to succeed in gaining trust and information from Dr. Washington.

Preoccupied with looking out the windows to scan the parking lot for any sign of Virginia, a light tap on her shoulder startled her. She jerked her head around and looked up. There stood a young woman wearing an oversized hooded Lehigh University sweatshirt and expensive looking dark tinted sunglasses. The brown hood completely covered the sides of her face.

The tall attractive looking woman with scattered freckles whispered, "My name is Marissa. Virginia Washington didn't want to come into the diner so she sent me to get you."

"Who are you?"

"Virginia and I are close friends. In fact, we are roommates."

"Where is she?"

"Outside-- in the parking lot."

Something is not right. Why would Virginia not want to be seen when it was her who set up the meeting place? She asked with a sharp edge to her voice, "Why didn't she come in---?"

Marissa replied with an ear-to-ear smile, "She has a really bad cold and wanted to stay in her car. Come on. I'll take you to her."

Hesitating just for a moment or two, she rose. After paying for her coffee, she followed the woman out the door to the parking lot. Oddly, she *thought*, that Marissa was taking such long strides, always a step or two ahead. She skipped over a foot high stone curb that separated the diner parking area from the adjacent parking lot of a furniture store. Beth followed close behind like a puppy dog

"Where is Virginia," Beth asked while stepping over the low barricade. "Where are we going?"

Marissa said nothing. She actually speeded up her walk, moving further from public view of the street and the diner parking lot with each stride.

Beth sensed that they were heading toward a parked van, fifty yards away in the rear of a junkyard lot, adjacent to the diner. "Stop! I'm not taking another step unless you tell me what's going on."

Marissa pivoted on a dime. An instant later, Beth was staring down the barrel of a small .380 auto pistol pointed at her head. Instinctively, she scanned the rear of the parking lot. They were alone. Her heart began to race.

Nervously, she said, "Look, if you want money, I can get you whatever you need." Her stomach felt like it was sloshing around inside a washing machine.

Marissa ripped off her sunglasses with her left hand. "Shut the hell up and walk toward the van."

She complied; walking toward her left side. The van was now just ten feet away. Marissa flipped her hood down on her shoulders and slipped the 380 under her sweatshirt. Beth could still see the gun pointing outward at the level of the right hip of her kidnapper.

Upon reaching the van, Marissa commanded, "Open the rear door."

She kept her eyes peeled on the pistol and took cautious steps toward the rear of the van. "OK, OK." Yanking on the right side handle, she lugged the rear door open. Instantly, a gagged man tied around the chest and abdomen with a thick rope against the back of the front passenger seat came into view. The blue and red tattoo cross on the lightly bearded man's chin drew her attention. A friendly acting Border collie roamed around the van, panting. The dog's leash was tied the man's leg.

"Get in!" Marissa yelled, sticking her left finger into Beth's chest. While maintaining a firm grip on the pistol in her other hand, she put her sunglasses on, pushing them to the top of her head.

Fearing for the worst, Beth held her ground. Marissa pushed her forward, causing her to strike her kneecap on the rear bumper.

"Ouch, my knee!" She massaged her injured joint. "Look, I'm not getting in there with that crazy looking guy."

Her captor responded with an expressionless stare. "Don't you want to see Virginia?"

Stay in control. "Hold on. If you didn't need me for some reason, you wouldn't have come into the diner to invite me out here. So, you're not going to shoot me. And, just exactly who are you besides a so-called friend of Dr Washington?"

"Virginia and I have a history. And, it's none of your business. Look, as a favor to Ginny, I'm asking you to cooperate." Her arm holding the gun dropped to her side, her face softening a tad.

"If this was a robbery, you wouldn't have exposed yourself in a public place."

Marissa smirked. "You think you're so smart."

"Not at all. Drop the gun and let's talk."

"Ginny said that you were clever. Get in the van."

"No," she quietly replied, still keeping her eyes focused on the 380 at Marissa's side. "Look, in another second, I'm going to start screaming." Beth pointed, looking toward the street. "See those men walking over there. After they hear me holler, they'll be here in a few seconds."

Marissa shoved her pistol under her belt. She held out her empty hands. "OK, you want to talk then let's talk. Listen lady, I'm not losing my life just because of your friend Rogers."

Her mouth dropped. Upon hearing his name, she shuddered. She tried to cover up and asked innocently, "Who is Rogers?"

Marissa's face exploded with rage. "You know damn well who he is!" A second later, she pointed the pistol at Beth. Her hand began to shake as she took a step closer to her captive. "You're starting to really piss me off."

She took a step back, forcing a half-smile. "I'm sorry." She glanced into the rear of the van. "So, how do you know Jonathan Rogers?"

"I'll tell what went down. My former boyfriend tried to kill Rogers several times. But, I've long since moved on with my life." Her face brightened. "I went back to school. I worked hard to get a life of my own. I'm proud to be a practicing pharmacist—helping people."

Beth listened intently.

"Let me tell you who I have in the van," she bristled. "Last night, in the parking lot outside the *Sports Club,* this guy jumps me from behind. A heartbeat later, I pulled my 380 from my purse and suddenly he's my unwanted catch of the day."

"What does all this have to do with me?"

"Look, I ask this guy to toss his wallet on the ground. So, I pick it up and look inside. I find two pictures. One is a photo of this guy and a blond woman. It's inscribed: To Jonesy, Love Betty."

A police siren interrupted their conversation. Beth looked over her shoulder, praying that someone was aware of what was happening in this parking lot. Her eyes wandered to the junk yard, fifty feet to her left.

Marissa shouted, "Hey lady, are you listening to me?"

Seconds later, the siren's blare faded. "Of course, the guy in your van is Jonesy. So, did you call the police to arrest him?"

"I would have if I didn't fear for my life."

She rubbed her forehead. "I don't get it. If you had a gun on this creep, why wouldn't you just call the authorities?"

"I told you there were two photos."

"I'm listening."

"The second one was a half photo. My picture was on one side. The other side was ripped away from this photo." She used her index finger to point toward her head. "But I recall the location where it took place and a lot more."

"Where was it taken?"

"I remember the day it was snapped. My clue was the clothes I wore that day. It was my favorite outfit. We were in front of the Capitol Building in DC. "

"Who was with you that day? Is there some connection with him and Jonesy?'

Marissa shook her head. "You don't understand. The picture of the man torn from this photo is someone capable of killing anyone, especially me. It's my old boyfriend. Trust me, he would figure a way to corrupt a police officer or two. He knows how to find people and have someone else kill them."

She saw Marissa's hand tightening around the stock of the gun. It remained pointed at her. "I still don't know how any of this has anything to do with me---with Virginia Washington."

"Look, I panicked and called Ginny. I told you that she's my roommate."

She began to worry as a twitch in Marissa's left eye appeared. "Let me speak with her."

Her eyes darted from side to side. "She told me to call the police but I can't." Her facial tic spread to her mouth. It seemed to jerk to the left every few seconds. "He'll kill me."

"Who are you afraid of? Who is this guy that was torn from the photo?"

She hesitated and then blurted out. "It's Zach Miller."

Beth's eyes widened. "I know about him. He's dead."

"That's what the police reported but they never found his body."

"His Ferrari blew up. I assumed that he was torn into a million pieces."

"Ha." Marissa lowered her pistol a foot or two.

She glanced at her watch. By now, Jonathan would be at DCP, waiting for her. "So, what do you want from me?"

"I want to know if Rogers has any clue that Zach is actually alive and if so, where he might be."

"How would he?"

"Missy, knowing Zach like I do, I'm sure that he's back and settling old scores. It's only a matter of time before he gets to Rogers."

"Marissa, this is crazy."

The woman's eyes zagged around the parking lot. "Didn't Kim Rogers just get killed?"

"You think---."

"No doubt in my mind."

"Now I know why you're acting this way."

"What's nuts is that I'm convinced that Zach wanted Jonesy to hang me. And, a week ago, when I heard that Haley Tyler was found dead, I knew it had to be him."

"So, why did you bring me out here? What do you want from me?"

"I want you to take me to Rogers."

Beth squinted. "If you're right about Zach and he is alive, how do I know this is not a set up? How do I know that you and Jonesy won't try to hurt----I mean kill Dr. Rogers and even me?"

"Trust me; I don't want to hurt Rogers." Marissa pushed the pistol back under her belt. "Look, a couple of years ago, I double crossed Zach. I was there when his car blew up. Even though the police never found his body, I'm almost certain that he's still alive. All this time, I've been worried that he would come after me. That's why I bought this handgun."

"All right, I can see why you're freaking out. But unless you get Dr. Washington on the phone, I'm leaving."

"Why won't you take me to Rogers?"

"I don't trust you." She placed her hands on both hips. "I also have news for you. Dr. Rogers is expecting me. If I don't show up at DCP in thirty minutes, he'll get suspicious that something happened to me. He's like that. Rogers will call the police. He knows that I was at the diner this morning. He'll track down Dr. Washington and find us.

Marissa chewed a wad of gum that she had popped into her mouth. "Nicotine gum. I'm trying to quit smoking." Her foot tapped repeatedly against the pavement while the twitch in her left eye returned. "Give me a minute to think."

Beth swiped her hand through her hair. "I'm leaving." She turned toward the street.

"Wait, I'll get Ginny on my cell." Marissa dialed a number. "It's ringing."

She reached out for the cell. She recognized Dr. Washington's voice.

"Marissa, what's going on?" The doctor's voice sounded shaky and frightened.

"Hello Virginia. This is Beth. Your roommate pulled a gun on me."

"Oh My God! There was a pause of several seconds. Washington's tone was contrite. "I'm so sorry that all this is happening. I was going to give you a folder with my original *NeoBloc* monkey data at breakfast today. But, I made the mistake of telling Marissa that I was meeting you. And, when she came home during the early morning hours with that wild looking guy who attacked her, she stumbled upon my DCP folder that I had carelessly left on my desk."

Beth twisted away from Marissa and whispered, "She's wound tighter than a drum."

"She's scared, afraid for her life. Marissa remembered hearing about you last year when her boyfriend Zach Miller had it out for Dr. Rogers. She thought that you might know who sent the hit man to hang her."

She glanced back at Marissa. "Virginia, where is the *NeoBloc* folder?"

"Marissa took it. I'm so sorry."

"I know that. I understand. Let's focus on what we're going to do to get out of this mess."

"It's my fault. I told her I was meeting you this morning for breakfast. She's been driving around all night with that tattooed contract killer guy, planning on meeting you at the diner."

Marissa grabbed the cell phone. "We've done enough talking. Get in the damn van now!"

Beth shook her head. "First, I want to see that you have the *NeoBloc* research." *Anything to get my hands on the real monkey data*

"It's on the front seat of the van. I'll get it," she replied uneasily.

Marissa walked to the front door and reached through the open window. She then held up the plastic covered bound report as she advanced toward Beth.

"Let me look at it. I want to read it with my own eyes." Her mind was whirling. She had been calculating what she would do once she had the actual file in her own hands.

Marissa handed over the original NeoBloc monkey file.

"Give me a minute to read the summary." She scanned the first paragraph. *All monkeys died within a year of getting NeoBloc. Deaths could be due to a virus or could be due to a delayed lethal side effect of the vaccine. Each page was personally signed at the bottom by Dr. Hussein Nasters.* Beth turned her back on Marissa and spotted a young couple walking from the diner toward their car in the parking lot, about one hundred feet away.

She began screaming, "Help, help!" Clutching the DCP research report to her chest, she began sprinting toward the couple. Behind her, she heard the van door slam and the engine start a few seconds later. She then heard the van's motor gunning. The couple froze in their tracks. A look of horror appeared on their faces. Beth glanced over her shoulder. The van was coming directly at her.

The man shouted, "Watch out." She darted to her left and then made another sharp left. Falling to the pavement, she watched as the van sped directly out of the lot to the street before vanishing seconds later.

CHAPTER NINETEEN

Rogers paced the huge glass paneled lobby of DCP. Beth was already ten minutes late. It was so unlike her not to even call. One of the security guards at the front desk had already tried to escort him back to his scheduled meeting with Dr. Nasters but he had stalled, expecting her to show any minute.

After another five minutes had passed, he left a note for Beth with the other guard at the front desk. Escorted through the security checkpoints, from his memory of his last visit, the clearance process was now tighter. After going through the final electronic gate, he was free to proceed on his own to the DCP conference room twenty yards ahead.

Through the frosted glass, he saw images of Sean Parker and Dr. Nasters huddled together at a conference table. He spotted two leather open bound ledgers on the long table. As he turned the doorknob to enter the room, he felt determined to peel back the onion of the ongoing mystique surrounding *NeoBloc*.

Parker and Nasters rose to their feet. The CEO spoke first. "Good morning, Dr. Rogers. I'm extremely sorry to hear about your wife."

"Thank you," he curtly replied.

Nasters asked, "Where is your data partner, Beth Murphy?"

Reaching out to shake hands with each of the DCP duo, he replied, "Should be here any minute." He asked Nasters if Dr. Washington would be joining them.

"She will not." The scientist blinked several times but fixed his eyes on the two ledgers lying on the table. "Dr. Rogers, we have prepared an executive summary of the first two weeks of human trial data with *NeoBloc*. Please sit next to me."

The Surgeon General settled into his appointed chair and warily glanced out of the corner of his eye at the scientist. Looking across the conference table, Parker wore a slight smirk.

Nasters angled himself toward Rogers and flipped the first page. "If I may, I will lead our discussion through this first ledger."

"Sure, but may I ask if Dr. Washington is still involved with the project?"

Parker's face tightened. "Dr. Rogers, you're asking about confidential DCP information."

Nasters grimaced.

On a dime, Parker softened his eyes. "Before we begin, how are you feeling? You look like you've lost a lot of weight since our last meeting."

Not feeling like sharing what he was going through, he replied smartly, "I'm just working out harder at the gym." He tapped Nasters on his wrist. "Please lead us through the data."

The scientist jerked his arm away, shooting a scornful look at Rogers. "As you can see by the executive summary, so far, two hundred and thirty two people received the *NeoBloc* vaccine. There have been no serious reactions. Mild stuffiness of the nose, a few sore throats, and three cases of constipation have been the only side effects that we have seen." Nasters turned the page so that they could view the first set of raw data.

Rogers tracked along, not saying a word. It was already obvious that the numbers before him all spelled out a picture that *NeoBloc* was completely fine. Changing gears, he asked, "Can I see the original vaccine monkey data?"

Parker interjected. "May I ask why? You saw the monkey data last time. The human data is more important."

"Not really. The human data is too new. I recall that no monkey died until a year after the vaccine. What if it takes a year or so for significant side effects to appear in people after receiving *NeoBloc?*"

Nasters scratched his forehead. "Unless you have scientific proof of your preposterous theory that this vaccine is dangerous, I would suggest that we avoid that subject for the remainder of our meeting. We're here today to show you the human data."

Rogers elevated his eyebrows. "Excuse me for being blunt. But, I think that the monkey data you showed me last time was altered." The Surgeon General raised his voice. "In fact, I want to see the exact same monkey data that Lauren Timmons saw."

The scientist rose, walked around the table and stood behind Parker. "Any blasphemous charge that the monkey data was changed in any way is totally false." The scientist reached over the conference table to the ledger and slammed it shut. "The trouble with you Americans is that you think the whole world revolves around you. You think you can insult us and then say you didn't mean to do so. In my country, such behavior results in punishment. Is it any wonder that---?" Nasters caught himself and stopped speaking when Parker loudly cleared his throat.

The CEO interjected, "I don't really believe that the Surgeon General is trying to insult anyone." He shrugged his shoulders. "He is simply misinformed and misguided in his beliefs."

Rogers clenched his jaw. "No personal insult was intended but my charge is well founded."

The DCP scientist circled back and sat next to Rogers. He sighed loudly. "I will give you one more chance. Let's return to our review of the human data."

He pounded his fist on the table. "Don't patronize me. You know damn well that all the monkeys died after getting *NeoBloc*."

"That's a bold faced lie," Nasters shouted. He gritted his teeth. Inhaling a deep breath, he forcefully exhaled through his nose as if he were a spitting fire dragon.

Parker interrupted. "Doctors, please, let's lower our voices. This is just a legitimate disagreement on the scientific interpretation of the data. Reasonable men can disagree."

An instant later, the door opened. Rogers looked up and saw a familiar face. Beth Murphy wore a confident smile. She held a thick manila folder in her left hand. As she strolled toward them, the men stood to greet her.

Parker held out his hand and shook hers in a friendly manner. "Ms. Murphy, we've been expecting you."

"Sorry that I'm late. You just never know whom you might meet at breakfast these days. I ran into an old friend of Dr. Rogers and couldn't get away."

The Surgeon General scratched his right temple. "Who was that?"

Murphy laughed. "Jonathan, we'll talk later."

Nasters piped up. "Can we get down to business? I would like to show Ms. Murphy the human data. Perhaps she will be more professional."

Rogers tightened his fists but said nothing. Parker tried to force a smile. It came across as a sneer.

By now, Beth had taken a seat next to Rogers and plopped her file on the conference table, midway between both of them. She leaned over and whispered in his ear. "Jonathan, I've got it."

He looked back at her with a puzzled glance.

Parker broke the tension. "Ms. Murphy, we'd like to get your reaction to the *NeoBloc* human clinical trial data."

"I think I'll pass on your numbers game." Beth opened up her own unbound two-inch thick file. Rogers noted that she had earmarked a half -dozen pages. "It's now my turn to show some real data."

He strained his eyes, looking at Beth's open file resting on the conference table. He saw the executive summary title page. *Different than what Nasters just showed.* Her file looked identical to the one Lauren had given him—the one that he once viewed for several moments in his study. One point caught his eye. Nasters signature was at the bottom of the page.

Beth fired off a disdainful look at the scientist. "I have in front of us a copy, and I emphasize the word copy, of the original DCP *NeoBloc* monkey data. To be sure, I made many copies of this original and true data."

The scientist reached across the table and grabbed the file. Quickly, scanning the documents, he bellowed, "These are all forgeries." He threw the file on the table. The pages flew apart and landed haphazardly across the conference table.

She blasted, "Dr. Nasters, stop your charade. Just admit that this data proves that every single monkey receiving *NeoBloc* died within a year of the administration of the vaccine."

Parker slapped his hand on the table. "I've had enough. Ms. Murphy is turning this meeting into a circus."

Beth picked up one of the scattered pages. "If this is a fake, why is Dr. Hussein Nasters's signature at the bottom of each page of this data?" she asked.

Parker began shuffling through the scattered document. He looked at each of the signatures, page by page. He glanced up from time to time to direct his look of shock at Beth. "There must be some mistake here. Someone obviously forged his name."

She shook her head. "Nice try Mr. Parker." Gathering the pages, she stacked them into one pile. "You can keep this copy of the document. I've already filed the original and several other copies."

Nasters was boiling—his nostrils flared. He shouted, "You Americans are all so damn arrogant."

Rogers leaped to his feet. The others quickly rose. Taking a step toward the scientist, the Surgeon General stuck his face no more than six inches from Nasters's heaving chest. "I thought you were a citizen of America. Does that make you arrogant as well?"

"I am a loyal citizen of the United States."

"I think your actions tell us where your loyalties lie. Rogers then backpedaled from the scientist and straightened his suit jacket.

Nasters strutted toward his boss. Mocking Rogers by pouting, he proclaimed, "No one will ever believe you. We have our bases covered. Checkmate doctor!"

Rogers joined Beth at the door. Before exiting, he said, "Just remember, gentlemen, I'll be chatting with President Williams about this real monkey data well before your evil hearts even begin their pathetic attempts to slow down."

CHAPTER TWENTY

While seated in his new mid-sized office at Sunview, Connor dialed the Secretary of Health for a progress report. James picked up just after the first ring. "Christian, so what's the latest?'

"I called Xavier Rudolf per your instruction. He's quite an interesting fellow."

"Did you identify yourself and your position within our organization?"

"Yes, I told him that I was a close friend of Zach Miller. As soon as I mentioned that name, Xavier asked me all sorts of questions." He paused. "It was though he was testing me-- to see if I was telling the truth."

"What did he ask?"

"Strange questions like who was the chief legal counsel for Zach when he was CEO at DCP?"

"I once gave you a notebook of confidential information. I hope you remembered the name of the legal counsel who was killed in a highway accident after a contentious DCP Board meeting."

"After I named Liz Harmon, he asked me how she died. I remembered. Pleased at my quick reply, he seemed to loosen up a bit. But, he did ask one more question."

"What?"

"He wanted to know if I knew where your old squeeze, Marissa Jones, was living these days."

Connor chortled, "Hopefully, she's in a ditch with a broken neck."

"I told him that I didn't know. Anyway, he seemed satisfied. So, how did you meet Rudolf?"

Connor rolled his eyes. "Knock off the questions. Remember, I pulled strings to get you appointed Secretary of Health. Don't make me regret that." Increasingly intolerant of seemingly everything about James, he felt his blood pressure rising. "By the way, you're starting to sound like a diarrhea of the mouth bureaucrat."

He fired back, "Boss, I'm just doing my job. And I have good news. Xavier has agreed to confidentially plant some rumors throughout DCP and to members of their Board about Sean Parker."

"Did you--?"

James cut him off. "I made up some lies that couldn't be traced back to any of us."

Connor nodded. "And?"

"I let on to Xavier that Zach Miller introduced me to a well respected businessman named Connor Lucas."

He puffed his chest. He sketched out the principal players in the DCP organization chart on a yellow legal pad. "We'll need Xavier to push my candidacy for the top position at DCP after I dispose of Sean Parker." He drew a large X over the current CEO's name.

"I'm sure he will."

On another page in the pad, Connor wrote Xavier's name in ink at the top of a yellow legal pad. On the second row, he penciled in the names of Dylan Mathews and Adam Timmons. He added, "I'm pleased that Pitnar and you successfully convinced the President that the *NeoBloc* human trials needed to be re-started. But that idealistic chap needs to pay for almost succeeding. After he saved her life, President Williams would almost believe anything Rogers says."

"Not without solid evidence."

Connor drew a caricature of a middle-aged man with an extra bowling ball of fat in his gut. "Rogers is dead meat." He stuck his pen into the drawing----straight at the heart.

"You already killed his wife. Now what?"

Connor took out a red marker and drew a bulls-eye on his drawing. "After I hang up, get on your laptop and *Google* his name. I've had contacts put some pretty ugly blogs out there on the Surgeon General. One blog quoted Dr. Rogers as saying that he didn't believe a vaccine could ever be developed that would safely prevent radiation-induced cancer. My contacts who know well- regarded scientists have persuaded these medical leaders to blog, supporting these planted lies, falsely attributed to the Surgeon General. These geeks will soon make Rogers sound like he is the only person in the country against the President's Project Moon Shot."

"Good work. So far, I've kept him at bay. I believe that he is convinced that I might fire him for insubordination if he doesn't follow my lead. But, I have a hunch that he thinks he can out- fox me."

"Never underestimate him."

In a cocksure manner, the Secretary replied, "He desperately wants to keep his Surgeon General position and continue to exert his influence with the President. He is so predictable that I can almost read his mind."

"Keep him quiet." Meanwhile, Connor was drawing a stick man in his hangman game. He scribbled the words, 'The Secretary' below the dangling feet.

"I'm doing my best"

"Effort is assumed. Results are demanded."

James paused. "So, how are you doing in working your way up the corporate ladder at Sunview?"

Penciling in a noose, he drew it around the Secretary's neck. "I'm now the assistant to the senior VP for sales." Connor pulled out a dart game out of his desk drawer and began to thumb tack it to the wall. "By the way, are you sure Nasters is doing whatever it takes to convince Rogers to cease and desist from spreading the nonsense that the vaccine is deadly? I'd be really pissed off if he ever gets the President to torpedo the *NeoBloc* launch."

"Don't worry."

"Look, he's smart but I think that he is misinterpreting the monkey trial data just because Lauren Timmons told him the vaccine was dangerous. And, of course, he has always been distrustful of anything that DCP does."

"I'll check with Parker. He'll know the latest."

"Like I said-----I'd be really pissed off."

"Oh shit! I just noticed the time. Need to meet the President's Chief of Staff in five minutes."

Connor beamed. "For your information, Pitnar is my protégé."

"Is there anyone that you don't know Connor?"

"Hey, when I used to be known as Zach, I had a half dozen Rolodex wheels chock full of pawns. I've narrowed it down to one. But, you know, its better this way."

"Why do you say that?"

"Don't you get it?" Connor threw a plastic play dart at a bulls-eye board that he had just hung up in his new office. It bounced off. He stood to retrieve the rubber tipped missile from the floor. Holding up his legal pad, he stuck the dart in the eye of the stick man with the noose around his neck. "I want as few people as possible knowing that I was once Zach Miller."

"I would hate to be on your list of enemies. I'm glad that I'm on your team."

"Just do your job." Connor plucked out the dart from the eye of the stick man and plunged it into the caricature of the Secretary's heart. "And, you're late for your meeting with Pitnar."

"I'll be in touch."

"Just make it happen!"

CHAPTER TWENTY-ONE

Rogers opened the file cabinet in his Department of Health office. He stashed Dr. Virginia Washington's copy of the *NeoBloc* original monkey safety data. On last night's flight back to the Capitol, he had poured over the data. Lauren was right! All monkeys receiving *NeoBloc* were dead within one year.

He locked the cabinet drawer and headed toward the office of the Secretary of Health. Thinking about leaking the monkey safety data anonymously to the *Washington Post*, he decided to keep that option open for now. *If the report were ever traced back to me, I'd be fired for insubordination. Then I'd have no further access to the President.*

He strolled into the Secretary's office. His boss seemed preoccupied looking through a cluster of papers that were strewn all about his desk. The Surgeon General dropped a folder containing a copy of the original monkey data on a corner of the desk. The bundle of data landed with a thud.

Rogers said in a terse voice. "Good morning Christian."

Seated behind his desk, the Secretary did not look up. James kept his eyes down, shuffling his documents. Almost under his breath, he muttered, "So, how was your trip to DCP?"

The Surgeon General deadpanned, "Uneventful!"

"Hardly dull, from what I've heard!" he snapped. He leaned back, looking at Rogers. "So, what's in the folder? Did you enclose a personal plan for you to one day go back into practice?"

"You like surprises. Take a peek."

James scoffed and pushed the folder away from him. He peered over his bifocals. "Sean Parker called me late last night. He told me you stole the monkey data from DCP by twisting the arm of one of their key scientists. He's seriously thinking of calling the police." The Secretary twisted his mouth in an eerie way. "I might need to fire you if this story ever hits the mass media."

Rogers folded his arms across his chest. He forced himself to count to ten before speaking. "I didn't steal it or force anyone to hand it over."

James shook his head and unloaded a look of disgust toward Rogers. "Take a look at what I've been reading on the Internet." He turned the computer monitor toward the Surgeon General and then keyed in Dr. Jonathan Rogers into the *Google* search bar. "It's all about you."

"What do you mean-----about me?" He scanned the monitor screen. After clicking and perusing through a few links, his heart began to pound. "These blogs are all lies. This is sheer nonsense. I'm certainly not against saving America from radiation sickness."

"Other scientists appear swayed against you." James stood to walk toward Rogers. "With your reputation being challenged by the Americans for Fair Play Coalition, do you think the President will find credible the monkey data report that Parker is alleging that you stole from DCP?"

Stay calm! He kept his tone non-confrontational. "I told you that I did not steal it."

"Well technically speaking your accomplice, Ms Murphy, did."

"As a point of fact, it was given to her. Beth has an extremely reliable source."

James fired a piercing stare. "Listen to me. You are being very naïve about this. Some well-respected scientists believe that you have already lost your scientific objectivity. Therefore, given all that I know, I would advise you to throw that stolen data in the garbage. It's the human trial data that President Williams cares about, not some old monkey data."

His eyes narrowed. "What exactly do you mean when you say 'given all that you know?'"

Standing toe to toe, James's did not change his expression. "It's your call. Either you discard this phony monkey data or you'll risk throwing away your position as Surgeon General."

"Are you threatening me?"

He lowered his voice to just above a whisper. "I'm just doing my job."

Rogers held his boss's stern gaze. He said curtly, "I've got some work to do," before picking up the monkey data folder from the desk and walking out the door. He knew what he had to do. A call to the President in the morning would be his priority.

******

Rogers waited patiently. Almost sixty minutes of staring at his office phone did not produce his desired effect. Madison had promised him that the President would call back on his private line within a half hour. Anxious, he rose to pace. All the while, his eyes kept drifting back to his silent desk phone. He circled the perimeter of his office five times, thinking about what he would tell Williams.

Ten minutes later, he sat down again and tried to concentrate on a public health research proposal from several state Medicaid plans. When he turned past page nine, a restricted phone number appeared on his caller ID screen.

Pressing intercom button number three, he answered, "Dr. Rogers."

The President's southern accent was unmistakable. "Madison told me that it was important. I only have two minutes. I'm sorry that I couldn't accommodate your request for a face-to-face meeting. I'm meeting with the Prime Minister of England in a short while."

"I'm calling you about the original DCP safety report on the monkey trials. I've obtained the original signed research." He sucked in a short but deep breath. "Lauren Timmons was telling the truth."

"How did you get this report?"

"From a mole within DCP."

"Did you share it with Secretary James?"

"He knows about it." Pausing a moment, he asked, "Didn't he tell you about it?"

"I was at a meeting with him earlier today on federal funding for Medicare. But, we had no conversation on *NeoBloc* at all."

"Madame President, I need to share with you an Internet rumor about me which is taking on a life of its own. Several well-known scientists are blogging against me on the Internet. It is all lies. They are saying that I'm completely opposed to any vaccine to stop radiation induced cancer."

"Why would they single you out?"

"It's complicated."

"I see. So what does your newly found data show?"

He spoke with conviction. "All monkeys exposed to *Neobloc* died within the year after getting inoculated."

There was a long pause.

"Madame President, are you still---"

The President's voice sounded strained. "If the Secretary is aware of this data, he should have told me."

"I don't want to speculate." He rubbed his chin. "I know you have to leave any second. When can I show you the actual data?"

"We can meet tomorrow. Call Madison for a time. And, if this data is accurate, I will stop the human testing trials while we find independent minded credible scientists to confirm what you are telling me. And, Dr Rogers---"

"Yes."

"This time, don't let the data out of your sight."

******

"Christian, play back the President's conversation with our troublesome boy"

The Secretary of Health set the recorder on rewind and replayed the tape. They listened closely, throwing in a few choice expletives along the way.

"This sucks." Connor's nostrils flared.

James said, "I'm going to fire Rogers for insubordination."

Connor blasted, "That would be a stupid move. That would blow your cover and he would still be free to talk to the press about the monkey data."

"I see your point."

He pounded his fist against the wall. "Who is this DCP whistleblower?"

"Parker didn't do it. I'm more convinced than ever after calling him earlier today."

"What about that scientist?" Connor squared up to James, standing a foot away from him.

"There's no reason to suspect Nasters."

"Why not?" He poked his finger into the Secretary's chest. "Look, what exactly do we know about him?"

"He is very well respected at DCP and in the scientific community at large. But, emotionally, he can be a wild card. My intelligence tells me that he went ballistic when Rogers and his sidekick, Beth Murphy, pulled out the actual monkey data."

"Is that the late Sam Murphy--the whistleblower's step daughter?"

He nodded. "Tell you what—she's a spunky lady."

Connor grabbed a fistful of his own wavy hair. "You promised me that the President would not find out anything that could jeopardize *NeoBloc*. And, you promised me that you were managing Parker and Nasters so confidential information would not get out. Now you tell me Rogers, Murphy, and the President each has evidence that could all destroy our mega-blockbuster vaccine."

James sheepishly replied, "I trusted Parker when he said the vaccine was safe."

He growled, "You trusted Parker, the man who I want to replace as CEO of DCP!" Connor paced away from the Secretary, made a tight fist, and slammed in with full force into the wall. "If Pitnar had not wire tapped the President's Oval Office phone, we would not even know that Rogers is spilling the beans."

"I'm sorry," James pleaded. "Don't worry. I'll make it right for us."

"Shut up!" He began pacing the room. "I need to take over the Company." He slapped his hands together. "No more waiting. I need to take over as CEO—now!"

"You're right. Only you can run this Company. And I bet you'll have fun doing it."

Connor smiled sardonically. "It will not be fun for all of us my friend. Not for all of us."

******

Rogers tossed restlessly in bed. He had just awoken in a cold sweat. He glanced at the glowing scarlet digits on his nightstand clock. Still fighting his demons, he thought that the color reminded him of the bright red blood trickling out of Lauren's severed neck. It was a little past two-thirty in the middle of the night.

As he turned over to face the window, the room darkening blue shades were fully drawn. An aura of moonlight streamed in around the edges. He closed his eyes tightly. His life -long habit of preferring total darkness in trying to fall asleep reared itself. Flipping onto his stomach, he tried letting his mind go blank. Yet, all he could think about was his fast approaching appointment with the President at eight the following morning. Rogers focused on his breathing. He slowed his cycles. It had usually worked. But, the mounting lies about him on the web kept peace a far distance away.

He sat up in bed, now fully awake, thinking about getting up to mindlessly watch some TV. A motorcycle whizzed by outside his window. He thought, *Washington is a very noisy place*. Seconds later, he thought he heard a banging sound from the hallway outside his bedroom. He grabbed his 9 mm semi-automatic Browning from underneath his bed and listened carefully.

He released the safety latch on the Browning. It was fully loaded. He waited a minute or two, his hand firmly gripping the stock. *Nothing*. Owning a gun for the first time in his life, he felt particularly uncomfortable holding it. After another minute or two passed of relative quiet, he put back the safety latch and lowered the semi-automatic to the floor, shoving it under his bed.

An eerie sense of silence took hold. It appeared that the streets were suddenly empty of life as the usual sounds of city life had suddenly ceased. It was so surreal that Rogers even imagined that he could hear his own heart beating. He concluded the earlier noise that he heard outside his bedroom was just a random creak of the building. Exhausted by everything that was going on, he passed off the random noise as a part of living at the *Watergate Towers*. He soon drifted off.

Awakened by a violent dream, Rogers reached out for Kim's pillow for comfort. He rested his head on it. This past week he had washed her pillowcase for the first time since her murder. Despite the absence of her scent, he let his mind wander to think about the happy times. The day they were married---the day Ashley was born---the day that he was appointed Surgeon General, his lifelong dream achieved.

He flipped over toward his own pillow, feeling the pressure in his bladder building. The clock read two fifty-five. He stood to stretch, fully naked. Groping his way in the dark, he traced with his hand the common wall separating his bedroom from the adjacent kitchen.

A sliver of the full moon peeking around the shades helped to guide him. After a dozen or so shuffles, he reached the bathroom door. It was already open. He took three small steps forward and flicked on the small nightlight over the sink. For no apparent reason, he closed the door behind him. In the full-length mirror that he now faced, shadows of his craggy looking face stared back at him. Not wanting his visual neurons to be aroused any further, he flicked off the nightlight and sat down on the toilet. His mind wandered back again to how much he missed Kim. *Why couldn't it have been me instead of her!*

A half minute later, Rogers reached behind his back to flush the toilet. Strangely, he caught an odd smelling whiff of leather. He stumbled slightly in standing. *Not as awake as I thought.* After opening the bathroom door, his tired eyes picked up a glint of light from the window streaming toward him. The smell of leather intensified.

With his first step forward, he felt something covering his mouth. *What the hell?* He grabbed for whatever it was and groped around in a furious manner. It felt like a human hand. He latched onto a finger and violently forced it backwards. A stifled scream followed the cracking sound. *No dream!*

Before he could turn around, he received a hard kick to his back just above his right kidney. A sharp cutting pain in his low back stunned him. While trying to catch his breath, he felt a hairy muscular forearm around his neck, choking him. Instinctively, he elbowed his assailant in his ribs. The grip around his neck loosened just enough for him to break free with just enough time to lunge and flick on the light switch.

His right rib cage absorbed a hard punch. A knee upper cut sliced into his groin, causing him to let out a scream. Rogers stumbled backwards, reeling back toward the shower curtain. One foot landed squarely in the bathtub. He reached out for the hanging plastic curtain to prevent himself from falling. He caught his balance and glanced up to see his attacker standing tall. A shiny blade flashed in front of him, catching a glint from the nightlight.

Searing pain over his ribs and kidney intensified. Yanking the shower curtains down off the rod, he wrapped his hands inside the vinyl material. *Take the offense.* He rushed his opponent using the shower curtain covered hands as boxing gloves. Rogers tripped over the three-foot wall of the tub, causing him to lunge awkwardly into his assailant. The force of his charge forward triggered a toppling backward of the hit man. A dull thud made by the striking of his assailant's head striking the bathroom tiles was a welcome sound.

Rogers found himself sitting on top of the assassin. He kept furiously punching straight ahead, landing several blows to the rib cage. His vinyl covered hands throbbed with pain with each further clout. The would-be killer reached up and squeezed Rogers's neck. The grip was so strong that the Surgeon General felt his strength ebbing quickly. No matter how much he tried, he could not pry apart the powerful chokehold. Forcing his quads to push him to a vertical position, creating some degree of separation from the killer, Rogers used his knee to whip it repeatedly into the attacker's genital area. The killer's screams were deafening.

But the grip on his neck tightened. The room began to spin around as oxygen deprivation to his brain increased. No longer able to muster enough energy to continue using his knees as a battering ram, Rogers tried to pry loose the assailant's hands. He changed tactics and began punching as hard as he could at the assailant's facial bones. He heard another crack and soon smelled the odor of fresh blood.

Mounting no defense of his own, Rogers took a hard shot to his own chin from a blow by his attacker. Nausea and powerful feelings of faintness were now almost overwhelming. He felt for his assailant's hand and was able to yank a pinkie finger back as viciously as he could. The snapping sound followed another agonizing grunt and a sudden release of the chokehold around his neck.

Rogers sucked in two quick breaths. He catapulted himself backwards onto his backside and used his legs to push off the killer's feet. His bare buttocks slid on the bathroom tile floor until his back was now flush with the outside cold porcelain of the bathtub. Spotting a shimmering object on the floor, he grabbed it. He felt one end. It was almost razor sharp. He pressed the butt of the knife onto his chest so that the point faced outward. An instant later, his assailant's chest pummeled him against the wall of the tub. A frightening scream rang out.

An uncontrollable rage took hold of his mind. Rogers felt his heart racing. He jammed the knife further into the body of the hit man. He caught a glimpse. The blade had penetrated about three inches into the abdominal wall, just below the right rib cage. *Hit the liver and intestines.* Rogers ferociously twisted the knife, rotating the handle to do maximal damage to as much internal body tissue as possible. Another cry of agony rang out.

Again, the assailant squeezed Rogers's neck. Out of his mind in fear, he thrust the knife into the contract killer's abdomen repeatedly; each time pulling out an inch or two before lunging forward again. The grip around his neck began to weaken. He was able to gulp in a breath of air that was now mixed with a stream of warm liquid coming from his would be killer's mouth. Spitting out the foul smelling liquid, he pulled the hands from his neck.

His chest ached while he gasped for much needed oxygen. Mindlessly, he continued to plunge the knife deeper and deeper into the dead weight, fully draped over him. Somehow, Rogers summoned enough willpower to push the bloodied body off him. The dead weight flopped backwards. The head of his assailant bounced with a loud thud off the base of the porcelain toilet bowl.

Rogers looked down at the knife in his hand. Blinking wildly, he spat blood from his mouth. He reached behind him, finding the edge of the tub before pushing himself upward to a sitting position on the ledge. Despite the searing pain in his ribs and low back, he forced his thighs to thrust upward, enabling him to lurch to his feet.

The bloodied body at his feet did not move. Rogers stepped warily over the legs to reach the sink. He looked up into the mirror. Aghast at his bloodied image, he turned on the cold-water faucet and cupped a few handfuls to splash on his face.

He turned, not able to escape seeing his heaving blood splattered chest in the full-length mirror behind the door. It reminded him of an animal like crazed murderer in a vampire movie. His heart felt ready to explode out of his chest as if he just drank twenty cups of steaming Espresso.

Dazed, Rogers staggered toward the kitchen. While leaning against the countertop next to the stove, he lunged for the receiver and dialed 911. He mumbled something to the operator. Unable to stand any longer, he fell to the kitchen floor, somehow keeping his head from striking the Italian tiles a split second before he passed out.

CHAPTER TWENTY-TWO

The *Washington Post* headline screamed Connor's worst fear. He punched a hole in the front section of the newspaper. After reading that the police chalked the entire Rogers *Watergate* incident up to a routine burglary, he threw down the paper on the floor. Enraged, he stomped on it as if it were a poisonous rattlesnake. Continuing his frenzy, he flipped over his captain's chair, kicking it several times around his kitchen. He shouted to himself, "That lucky SOB survives a knife attack in the middle of the night. He kills the hit man in self-defense. Now, he's a bigger hero than ever."

***

Connor punched in the private number on his cell. He murmured, "No more chances. No more." He paced his living room, dropkicking a throw pillow. Sent flying, the pillow knocked over a lamp on the end table. The bulb burst on striking the floor. *Damnit!* After four rings went unanswered, he shouted into the cell, "Pick up the phone."

About to heave it against the wall, a low-pitched voice echoed. "I know. I know. I read the papers just like you."

Connor bellowed, "What the hell is wrong with you? Can't you hire someone who can kill the target?"

James whispered, "My hit man was a pro."

Connor screeched at the top of his lungs. "A pro--at what---tiddlywinks?"

The Secretary of Health hesitated a few seconds. He meekly said, "How would I know that Rogers could survive a professional hit? He's like a cat."

"I don't care if you have to use a submachine gun or a bazooka next time." He banged his cell on the coffee table twice and then re-started his rant into the receiver. "I'm so pissed. I want you to kill Rogers and I don't give a shit if you die in getting it done. No more chances James. Also, set up a meeting with Nasters. You had better keep him in line. Do your damn job---or else."

Connor flung the cell against the wall. He ran toward it, stomped on it, cracking it open. *Never again will I trust anyone!*

CHAPTER TWENTY-THREE

Nasters sped down the empty DCP corridor as if he were on roller skates, simmering like a volcano. With each shout of an anti-American curse, curds of saliva spouted from his mouth. He stormed into Sean Parker's corner office.

The CEO, sitting behind his desk, held his hands in front of him, palms facing outward. "Back off."

"Now, what the hell are we going to do?"

Parker motioned to a seat on the other side of his expansive teak wood desk. "Calm down. Let's try to analyze this in a reasonable way. First of all, there are few at DCP who have access to the actual *NeoBloc* monkey data. Besides you, Virginia Washington, and associate researcher Tom Smathers, no one else had access to all the original data. Isn't that correct?"

Nasters remaining on his feet took one-step closer to the CEO. He thundered, "What about you?"

Parker stood up from his swivel chair. "You think I'm the mole?"

"As much as you think that I might be the one." Nasters lightly brushed up against Parker's chest.

The CEO said softly, "Hold on doctor. I'm not accusing you." Parker took two steps back. "Have you spoken to Washington and Smathers?"

Nasters shook his head. "Both just happened to be out sick today."

"Let's sit down and take a deep breath." Parker led the way, plopping down hard on his high back executive style leather chair.

Nasters hissed before taking his seat. "When I called Virginia's apartment, her roommate told me she was suffering from the flu and could not even come to the phone. I don't believe it."

Parker sighed deeply and closed his eyes, saying nothing. After a few seconds, he leaped to his feet and walked over to his closet, grabbing his wool coat. He looked back at Nasters who remained seated, still facing Parker's empty seat.

"The good news is that the *Washington Post* has refused to print the monkey data story that Rogers finally ended up giving them," the CEO said. "Their editor called me earlier today to verify his story. I told them it's all hogwash. It's obvious that the blogs we planted on the web have had their desired effect on the Surgeon General's credibility"

Nasters rose slowly, facing Parker. He flexed his fingers. His blood shot eyes appeared to want to pop out of their sockets. "I don't trust the

American press. Eventually, they'll print anything just to sell newspapers. By now, Rogers has most likely blabbed our whole scheme to President Williams."

He pointed to the door. "Calm down before you have a stroke. Let's go have some lunch. We'll formulate a plan after we get some food in our stomachs at *Christys*. We can talk on the way."

Nasters followed his boss out of the office. "What if the President believes Rogers?"

The CEO headed for the elevator. Twisting his head back, he shot the scientist an exasperated look. "I know the problem. Think of solutions."

After exiting the building, Parker took long and quick strides, head focused down on the pavement. In almost a half trot, Nasters struggled to keep pace. A block from the restaurant, the scientist's attention was drawn to a cable truck barreling down Willard Street in their direction.

He continued to walk with his head down. With the truck now fifty feet away, Nasters heard the tires squeal as they tried to grip the road. A heavily bearded driver of the truck wore a *Tigers* baseball cap.

The scientist's eyes wandered upward from the truck's cab to a tall crane, connected to a basket, where a technician would typically stand to fix the phone lines. He thought it odd that the crane was fully extended while the truck was moving so rapidly. Ten yards from Parker, the truck came to a dead halt. Nasters watched the operator back up the truck to park it alongside the curb.

"What are the solutions?" Parker raised his voice and repeated his question, all the while maintaining his steely-eyed gaze on the sidewalk. "Did you hear me?"

The scientist sprinted forward. "I don't have a solution. You're the business guy. Why don't you figure a way out of this mess?" Nasters folded his arms across his chest and stopped in mid-stride. "Rogers has our actual data signed off by me showing the deaths of all the monkeys within the first year."

He stopped on a dime, pivoted on his heels and squared up to the scientist. "You once told me the monkeys died from a virus."

"That still remains my scientific opinion. But, the Americans won't believe me once Rogers convinces the President to stop the human trials."

Parker threw his hands skyward and began walking again. Nasters could see the sign for *Christy's* a quarter of a block away. His stomach growled. He glanced at the empty basket at the end of the crane. As he caught up once again to him, the steel basket seemed to be hovering directly above their heads. He looked into the cab of the truck. The operator had just pulled back a lever. The scientist's mind clouded over, his anger at the situation rising with each passing second.

Nasters yelled out, "All I know is that we're screwed. And, what are you going do about it, Mr. CEO?"

Parker did not respond to his question but slowed his pace.

The scientist stood in place. While Nasters cursed under his breath, he caught another glimpse of the cable basket. This time, it was swaying back and forth. He now trailed Parker by several feet. Out the corner of his eye, he noticed that the operator in the cab was maneuvering the crane. Despite their trek getting closer to the restaurant, the basket was still above their heads.

Nasters felt a hard sneeze coming on. He bent over and covered his mouth and nose. After a series of loud roars, everything seemed blurry to him.

Parker yelled back, "God bless you."

Nasters grabbed a handkerchief from his pocket and blew his nose. As his vision cleared, he looked upward but couldn't get the words out quick enough. The basket was already in free fall. Quickly, his eyes shot to Parker, directly below the mass of steel. Instantaneously, the scientist heard a thunderous bang. A second later, the basket tumbled over on its side off the crumpled bloodied pulp of a lifeless body.

Nasters covered his mouth. Sean Parker lay motionless on the sidewalk. His face was a mass of crushed bone protruding through a river of blood. Looking away for a moment, the scientist's eyes rested on the truck cab. The operator with the *Tigers* baseball cap was gone.

******

With Parker so brutally smashed to death, Dr. Nasters felt completely unnerved. Outside his office door back at DCP, he fumbled with his keys. After several attempts, he unlocked the door.

A letter rested on his desk. The return address was a post office box in Afghanistan. Postmarked from Detroit, he locked the door and tore open the letter. His eyes darted across the Arabic symbols. A smile came to him. He dropped to his knees and prayed to Allah.

***

Nasters sat quietly, reading the *Koran.* The holy book seemed to be getting heavier in his hands. His written instructions from the PFF were for him to come to this first floor spot. He had arrived just shortly after the mall opened. A scattered few Monday morning shoppers passed within view. The deep economic recession had driven down store traffic to a fifty year low. Waiting on a long wooden bench without a back to lean against, he sat patiently at the crossroads of several anchor stores located inside the DuPont mall.

The DCP scientist put down the *Koran* next to him and rubbed his eyes. He stretched out a spasm in his lower back. Sitting rigidly upright, the ache in his unsupported lower back intensified. He scanned his surroundings. The two escalators leading to the second floor were barren of any customers. He looked up at the second floor balcony above him. Except for two well-dressed Arabic men leaning against the railing and engrossed in a lively but inaudible conversation, the mall appeared sparsely populated.

Using strong will power and patient determination, he blocked out the shooting pains that pinged his lower back muscles and picked up his reading once again. Immersed in prayer, he did not immediately sense the presence of the same two Arabic men, who stood above him only minutes ago, sitting down alongside him. An older unshaven man flanked his right while the younger clean cut young man had taken a seat to his left. Neither man looked at Nasters, focusing their eyes up at the second floor landing, exactly where they were previously standing.

Disturbed, he dropped his head and tried to distract himself by reading more prayers from the *Koran*. With the palpable tension now existing, the words seemed jumbled. Each page became a complete blur. He glanced at the two men sitting motionless alongside him. *Something is up.* Looking up again to the second floor landing, Nasters now saw three despondent looking men dressed in their traditional Arabic garb. His eyes darted back to the men sitting alongside him. No one was meeting his gaze. *I will stay put and ask no questions.*

Time slowly passed. After fifteen minutes had ticked by, nothing was happening. His eyes wandered to the mall clock on the overhanging arch. He prayed to Allah for endurance. His neck muscles grew tense. Massaging them, he craned his neck once again to the second floor, his eyes landing twenty feet to his right. Three tall bearded Arabic looking men were staring back at him. Jerking his head to the left, he saw three balding Arabic looking men leaning over the railing. Scanning the full balcony, all nine pairs of eyes joined to his.

The back of his head began to pound. He imagined the heat from their collective vision piercing his skull. He turned his body toward the older man on his right. His bench mate twisted his head toward Nasters. The tenth pair of Arabic eyes now locked into his. Nasters turned to the young man on his left. He was not surprised that the eleventh pair of eyes were linked to his sight. Nasters felt a chill run up his spine as he realized that he was now the singular focus of eleven Arabic men.

He prayed to Allah for understanding. Darting his head from side to side, he noted that the two men alongside him had withdrawn their gaze. Subconsciously, he subtracted their energy from the total pair of eyes. He looked up. The nine men continued to stare down at him. He squirmed in his seat. His fellow bench sitters were again looking at him. *Nine plus two more.* He glanced back and forth several times, each time confirming his suspicions of the presumed code they were giving him. Nasters mumbled the words quietly, *Nine Eleven.*

A sense of warmth descended upon him. He relaxed his facial muscles and believed that his father and mother were smiling down at him. His destiny was at hand.

Several moments later, the elder unshaven man spoke calmly. "Good morning, Brother Hussein. My faith leads me to believe that you have understood our message. Is that so?"

Nasters nodded repeatedly. "Yes, another day for America to pay is at hand." He felt the tap of the young man on his left shoulder. The scientist angled his body to face him.

The young Arabic man whispered, "We know about *NeoBloc*. But, this is our jihad, not yours."

Nasters bowed and thanked Allah again for his greatness.

The elder man murmured, "Minneapolis was first. Atlanta is next. Remember my son, the word MAD. Atlanta is where the dirty birds play. After the A city, there will be a third American city that will be destroyed."

The scientist replied respectfully, "It is the will of Allah!" His father's life long teachings rang loudly in his brain. He repeated to himself a well-known story about the prophet Mohammad that his father would often relate to him. Peace was finally at hand. He closed his eyes to savor the moment. Opening his eyes, after silently reciting another prayer, he looked around. All eleven men had vanished.

CHAPTER TWENTY-FOUR

Rogers dragged his achy body into the Oval Office carrying a folder with the *NeoBloc* monkey research. The President sat in her customary chair opposite the couch. He noticed a copy of the *Washington Post* on her lap.

A worried look creased her brow. "Dr. Rogers, thank God you survived. I was just reading how you fought off your assailant. You're truly an amazing man."

"I was lucky." He stretched a back spasm. "My pain meds have thrown me for a loop. I feel very groggy."

"Please sit down."

He gently lowered himself onto the couch, careful not to lean fully back lest he might irritate the superficial knife wound above his right kidney. Rogers grimaced.

"I'm so sorry that you went through such an attack on your life. Thank you for having the fortitude to make this appointment, given your condition."

"Please forgive me for my unshaven appearance. I'm still very shaken up over what happened." He paused. "The ER doc told me before he discharged me two hours ago that I'll heal from my physical wounds and bruises. But to be honest, I'm emotionally distraught."

"I think you need to take off for a few weeks to heal."

"Madame President, I'm not sure that I will ever be fully healed. I've never killed anyone before. It's taken a heavy toll on my psyche."

Williams shook her head and reached over to rest her hand on his. "It was self defense. I don't want you to dwell a second longer on what happened at your apartment. If you can, I need you focused. Dr. Rogers, the fact of the matter is that I need you now more than ever."

The President withdrew her hand and leaned back in her chair. "Let me see the evidence that you spoke to me about yesterday."

He opened the manila folder and gingerly handed her the original monkey data that Beth Murphy had received from Dr. Virginia Washington.

Williams scanned the first two pages for approximately a minute. "I'm certainly no expert on interpretation of clinical trial data but the concluding paragraphs clearly points to what you've been saying all along."

"You will note that Dr. Nasters, the chief scientist at DCP personally signed the bottom of each page."

"I saw that." She shot him a worried glance. "I bet the press would have a field day with this story. But, I know you would never embarrass this administration by going public with this controversy."

"Excuse me." Rogers looked down at his shoes for several seconds before meeting her irritated gaze. "I have already showed this data to the editor of *The Post.*"

She countered with a sharp edge to her voice. "Why would you do that before speaking with me?"

He locked into her fixed angry looking stare. "The editor refused to print it, citing my recent loss of credibility due to the negative Internet blogs about me."

A heartbeat later, Williams frowned. "You will be shocked to hear this but I have another monkey trial safety report. And, it's nothing like yours." She picked up a folder that was lying on her lap. "This morning, Secretary James gave me this report. His name is on the cover."

His eyes flashed. "May I see it?"

She handed him the James file. He quickly scanned the three page executive report and read the complete opposite conclusion on the last page. "Madame President, this is altered data. It's a forgery. The bottom of each page does not bear the signature of Dr. Nasters. I can assure you that it is DCP standard practice for every page in an authentic report to be signed by the principal investigator in charge of the research. And, this is not even the data that Beth Murphy was shown by Dr Virginia Washington when we made our trip to DCP."

"So, you're saying that the Secretary of Health and the top scientist at DCP are not telling the whole story."

"Correct." His face grew grim. "More to the point, they are blatantly lying."

Her eyes narrowed. She abruptly rose to her feet. He strained to rise from the couch. Once on his feet, he walked slowly, each step causing shooting pains to erupt on his torso. Halfway to the Oval Office door, she pivoted sharply to face him. "You once saved my life but I can't guarantee that I'll be able to save yours. In your service to our country as Surgeon General, you've made enemies who appear that they will stop at nothing to keep you from finding the truth about *NeoBloc.*"

"Thank you for showing me the fake report. I know what I need to do. I'll be in touch as soon as I can."

"Please be careful."

"I have a lot of experience at trying to do that."

"Do you need Secret Service protection?"

He began backing up. "No thank you. I bought my own protection. I just hope that I don't have to use it." He turned, grabbed for the doorknob, and opened the door. He looked back to Williams; a quizzical look plastered on her face. "Please don't ask. Thank you Madame President."

******

Rogers sat motionless in his office chair and stared blankly out the back windows. Even before his meeting with the President, he had abandoned an impulse to call one of the television networks. *I have final sign off on the safety of NeoBloc only as long as I'm the Surgeon General. And I'm the SG only as long as I'm alive.*

Rogers swung his leather chair around to pick up today's *Wall Street Journal* that Sally had placed in his inbox. With the Dow down over thirty-seven percent in the last year, he read story after story of home foreclosures and personal bankruptcies. Saudi Arabia and China were drastically reducing their purchase of US Treasury Bonds. Interest rates in America were soaring, much worse than the stagflation days of the early eighties. The expectation of the price of gold was soaring. Two thousand dollars an ounce was the consensus target price.

He flipped toward the op-ed page. The lead opinion column was unbelievable. The piece detailed a scientifically compelling case for an immediate FDA approval and inoculation of every American with *Neobloc*. Dr. Hussein Nasters wrote the op-ed piece.

Hearing his intercom buzz, he dropped the *Journal* down on his desk.

"There is a Dr. Robert Woodhall on the line. He is the CEO and Executive Medical Director of Weston and Weston Pharmaceuticals."

Rogers went through his mental Rolodex. "I don't know him. What does he want?"

"He told me he wanted to talk to you about a vaccine that his Company is developing to prevent cancer from nuclear radiation."

He winced. "I'll take the call." Pressing the blinking incoming call button, he answered, "Hello, this is Dr. Rogers."

'Good afternoon. Thank you for speaking with me. My company-- W &W is testing a compound that our scientists believe can substantially reduce the incidence of radiation-induced cancer. I wanted to make you aware of this based upon what I have been reading in the newspapers and the blogosphere."

Not another killer vaccine! Rogers felt his stomach churning. "Have you been in contact with the FDA?"

"Of course, we have spoken several times to them. We filed our new drug application with them late last year. We are currently testing our compound on monkeys."

Rogers's interest was piqued. "I'm sure that you're aware that you have competition in this space."

"Well aware. As CEO, that's my job. I've been reading in the trade journals about the Phase Three human trials with *NeoBloc.*"

"Then I'm sure you've read that DCP is trying to fast track their trials. I anticipate that they are closer than we would think to final data submission to the FDA."

"At W &W, we now have a corporate culture that insists on absolute consumer safety at all times. Prior to my arrival, our Company was once heavily fined by the FDA for a safety violation in conducting our clinical trials a few years ago."

The Surgeon General rose and stretched his back. "I vaguely recall reading something about that."

"Since that costly incident, our Board has given senior management strict guidance not to rush any of our pipeline compounds through the approval process."

"I'm pleased to hear of your concern for drug safety. As Surgeon General, as you probably know, I've been publicly speaking on that critical subject since I was appointed by President Williams."

"That's why I contacted you. I want to extend a standing invitation for you and your staff to visit W & W without any prior notice. Please feel free to examine our data."

The Surgeon General paused a moment. He rubbed his chin. "I think that I will take you up on your invitation. I'll be in touch."

Rogers clicked off the call. He wished that the late Sean Parker had been as transparent as Dr Woodhull seemed to be implying. Thinking of what he had said earlier that day to the President about Secretary James and Dr. Nasters, he wondered why his phone was not already ringing off the hook.

He turned on his portable TV set and tuned into CNN. After watching the headlines, he was upset that the President had not yet publicly issued an order to stop Project Moon Shot given the monumental evidence that he had just presented to her on *NeoBloc.*

Sitting down behind his desk, he covered his face in his hands. *No more excuses for not packing my Browning 9 mm.*

CHAPTER TWENTY-FIVE

A few days later, there was an announcement of Connor's promotion at the regularly scheduled Board meeting at Sunview. All the Department chiefs were invited. Along with Board members, all senior management sat around the huge forty-foot long glass top conference table. Harrison Pelo, CEO of Sunview, stood behind the podium and used the microphone to broadcast the value that the promotion of Connor added to the Company. "Please come up on the dais and be welcomed to our family."

The fast rising star rose amid the enthusiastic applause of his peers. While strolling confidently toward the top man, he briefly reflected on what he viewed to be his good fortune. Just last week, the police discovered that Bob Shepard, the former SVP of Sales was dead, apparently of an unexpected heart attack. Within twenty-four hours, he Board offered the vacancy to Connor.

He covered his heart with his right hand and began. "Thank you Mr. Pelo and the Board of Sunview for your confidence in me." He paused, feigning overwhelming grief. "I'm sorry." He acted with far more sincerity than he ever actually possessed. "I'm deeply saddened by the unfortunate tragedy that led to my promotion. Bob Shepard was my mentor and a dear friend. I will do my best to try to fill his shoes by executing on the strategy that he so brilliantly developed to advance Sunview products."

The CEO began the round of clapping that instantly spread throughout the room. He pointed toward Connor and dished off a quick wink. Everyone in the room stood as Pelo commented. "Thank you for your kind words. We do have full confidence that you will take Sunview to the next level."

Connor felt an orgasmic rush coming on. Shouldering Pelo partially away from his position at the podium, the new chief shielded his unexpected bulge by remaining squarely behind the stand. "I'm looking forward to providing sales leadership for many years at Sunview. My principal goal will be to out sell our chief competitor, DCP."

The Sunview CEO realized that he had assumed full command of the podium. Pelo moved over several feet to the side. Without a podium microphone, the CEO realized that he needed to speak louder. He glanced over at the newly crowned leader and didn't miss a beat. "Although you've been here at Sunview for only four months, you've made an impressive footprint on our business. Based on what you have so far achieved, it is my high privilege to ask you to take your seat on our senior management team as our Senior Vice President of Sales."

Using the podium as a power prop, Connor spoke to those seated in front of the dais, essentially ignoring Pelo. "Board members and senior management, thank you for your faith in me. I promise never to disappoint you."

Without even acknowledging Pelo after he had spoken, he held his head high while walking away from the podium. He sat down alongside the Chief Operating Officer and quietly pulled out of his inner jacket pocket a copy of his upcoming daylong interview schedule for the vacant CEO position at DCP. Concealing it from view below the level of the conference table, he fantasized that his first act after he got the top position at DCP would be to have a six foot high portrait of himself hung in the Board Room. Connor could not prevent a broad smile from breaking out as he pretended to listen to the latest Sunview quarterly financial report given by the Chief Financial Officer. *I'll bury this bozo.*

******

Connor had already ensured through his contacts that Nasters would be part of the selection committee for the top job at DCP. Xavier Rudolf had convinced the lawyers at the Company that it was critical to have a physician from the Medical Affairs department to gain a clinical perspective in evaluating all the candidates. As the top DCP scientist, Nasters was the obvious choice.

On the day of his interview, Connor approached the scientist's office with a swagger. Presenting a firm handshake, he said warmly, "It is my honor to meet you Dr. Nasters."

The scientist replied in a matter of fact tone. "Mr. Lucas, please have a seat. Thank you for coming in today."

"Before we begin, please permit me to say that you're to be highly commended on your pioneering work with *Neobloc*"

"Well, thank you Mr. Lucas." Nasters leaned back and carefully studied Connor's face.

"In my opinion, all Americans need to be inoculated with our vaccine as soon as possible. If I were to be so fortunate to be chosen as CEO of DCP, I would do everything in my power to work with you on the FDA approval and rapid distribution of this life saving vaccine."

I love his passion. The DCP scientist broke out into an expansive smile. "Mr. Lucas, I like the way you present yourself. In addition, I'm pleased that you've done your homework on our flagship pipeline product. Let me ask you a hypothetical but yet a very serious question"

"Fire away doctor."

Furrowing his brow, the scientist pointedly asked, "If the consensus of scientists is that *NeoBloc* is safe but there were one or two physicians either within DCP or in a high ranking government regulator position who still had safety concerns with the vaccine, what would be your response as CEO of DCP?"

"Doctor, you and I will be a team. I know the business end and you are the expert on the science. Our relationship will center on our mutual trust of each other's capabilities. We will collaborate with all relevant stakeholders to produce the best vaccine possible and we should not let a minority viewpoint stand in our way."

Nasters's face softened. "I see that you've listed Xavier Rudolph as one of your references."

He shook his head in the affirmative. "I know that he is an extremely influential Board member at DCP. It is my understanding that he wields tremendous power within the Company."

"Mr. Rudolf was instrumental in my coming to DCP." Nasters stood. "Mr. Lucas, I've read about your accomplishments. You are a very impressive candidate." Connor rose and followed the scientist to the door. "You'll be hearing from the selection committee in a few days."

After shaking hands, he gave a slight bow. "Dr. Nasters, nothing would please me more than for you to be nominated for the Nobel Peace Prize for developing *NeoBloc*. Everyone would hail you as the savior of America. If I were to be so fortunate to be selected as your CEO, one of my priorities would be to do whatever is needed to be done to ensure your nomination."

******

Connor had just hung up the phone on Xavier Rudolf. He pumped his fist into the air and shrieked with joy at the top of his lungs. His Sunview administrative assistant ran in his office when she heard the commotion. Sharing his good news with Andrea, she instantly accepted his offer to join him as his executive administrative assistant at DCP. While laughing heartily, he typed out his resignation email to Harrison Pelo.

Dear Harrison. I've enjoyed my five days of being your SVP of Sales at Sunview. Effective immediately, I'm tendering my resignation. I am now the CEO of Doctor's Choice Products. Starting Monday, you and I will be fierce competitors. Check out the stock price of DCP today and again in a month. Perhaps you should consider a severance agreement before its too late. Sincerely, Connor.

The newly appointed CEO of DCP whisked Andrea down the corridor at Sunview to the gawking eyes of his ex-colleagues. He kissed her hard on her mouth just outside the elevator, opening his eyes for just a few seconds for a gratuitous wink at the curious group that encircled them.

The door opened and Connor walked hand in hand with Andrea into the elevator. *Nobody does it better! Time to celebrate!*

CHAPTER TWENTY-SIX

The President jumped in her seat upon hearing two booming bangs on the Oval Office door. The door flew open. Mackenzie Pitnar barged in without saying a word. He stormed past her without saying a word while she sat stunned behind her desk.

The Chief of Staff flicked on the flat screen TV mounted on the far west wall. The President saw *Breaking News* flash across the screen. Williams leaped to her feet and walked quickly toward the spot where Pitnar was gawking. Her jaw dropped upon seeing a CNN news captions screaming across the bottom of the screen. *America attacked—again!*

Pitnar reflexively reached out for his boss, lightly touching her hand. Williams gaped at her Chief of Staff. His face looked ashen. The frightened glassy look in his eyes coupled with scenes of what she was seeing on the screen---people profusely bleeding and screaming as they scattered triggered her shout. "What the hell happened?"

"Madam President, word from our Homeland Security Secretary came in a minute ago. A uranium nuclear bomb exploded a couple of minutes ago outside a baseball stadium in Atlanta. The Braves were hosting the Cubs."

Immersed in the unfolding events, she covered her mouth with both hands. Williams steadied her pelvis against the couch. Her mind raced to what the Government could do to help the victims. With her eyes glued to the leveled northern and western sides of the domed stadium, she began demanding answers. "Mac, have our emergency plans been put into motion?"

"Yes. Homeland Security, CIA, FBI, and the Joint Chiefs are all on their way to the secured situation room. F-22's have scrambled over all major cities. We have gone to code red. The entire country has been placed on full scale alert."

Pitnar did not take his eyes off the screen. A close up shot of the debris showed scattered bones from human remains mixed with concrete fragments. His body shivered. "Madame President, we must evacuate you as soon as possible. Marine One will be flying you to Andrews. We'll be in the air on Air Force One well within the hour."

Even before he finished speaking, she heard a stampede of footsteps galloping toward the Oval Office. The President spotted special agents Henry and Genevieve rushing forward. Her attention lingered on the chaos, playing out on CNN. She felt the hands of one of the agents tugging on her forearm. She pulled her arm away from the agent's grip. The caption on the screen: *America suffers another nuclear attack.*

Cameras were now scanning the still standing southern and eastern sections of the stadium. As they zoomed in, the President could barely look. The skin on some bloodied victims appeared peeled back; revealing white areas Williams presumed was exposed bone. Motionless bodies were lying everywhere.

The Commander in Chief felt a firm tap on her shoulder. Agent Genevieve said in an authoritative tone, "Madam President, we're evacuating you immediately. Marine One is ready to take us to Andrews."

Agent Henry led the way out of the Oval Office, down the corridor to the side door. Williams ran in the middle of the pack of agents. Out of the corner of her eye, she saw her administrative assistance, Madison, crying hysterically as she was being ushered away by a Secret Service agent.

On her getaway out of the White House to the waiting helicopter, the President thought of her sister Maryann. She stumbled on a downward slope of the south lawn. Instantly, someone helped her regain her balance. Her guardian angel, her Chief of Staff, who was trotting alongside assisted her. Marine One was fifty yards ahead. She remembered him mumbling something. There were murmurs that the White House was a target. Pitnar urged her to run faster.

Her heart raced. She realized how out of shape she had let herself become. The rotor wash created by the cambered airfoils of the helicopter blew strands of her blonde medium length locks onto her face. Trying to catch her breath, she eked out, "Where is Vice President Stockard?"

"He's at a public appearance in Chicago. We have notified him. The Secret Service is currently taking him to a secure location." As they got closer to the blades of the helicopter, her Chief of Staff yelled out, "Madame President, duck your head."

The whirling rotor blades of Marine One were at flight idle speed. Plowing through the thick grass cropping up on the south lawn, she attempted to center her mind on strategic next steps. Ten feet from the staircase, she noticed the conspicuous absence of a Marine guard. It had always been customary for a Marine to be posted at the stairway.

Agent Henry reached out for her hand. She felt herself almost flying up the three steps as he yanked her upward. Once aboard Marine One, she craned her head to check her surroundings. It was her Chief of Staff. He was breathing down her neck. Pitnar held onto her arm as they made their way down the corridor to the on board situation room.

Just a few seconds after she sat down and buckled herself into her seat at the head of a small conference table, she felt the helicopter rising into the air. Williams blankly stared at her Chief of Staff. Still in a state of shock that she realized was only beginning to take hold, she was absorbed watching him buckling himself into his seat, to her right.

Scanning the twelve-foot square room, she noted four Secret Service agents secured in their seats around the perimeter. A black speakerphone lay on the table directly in front of her. Williams closed her eyes and silently said a short prayer for the survival of her beloved country.

"The phone is live Madame President," Pitnar announced abruptly, interrupting the end of her plea to God. "We're all ready when you are."

Collecting her thoughts, she began with a steady voice, "This is President Williams."

A baritone like voice replied immediately. "Madam President, this is Homeland Security Secretary Justin Lenz."

"Give us your assessment."

Lenz replied in his deep baritone voice, "I'm in the National Security Defense room along with four of the Joint Chiefs, Secretary of Defense Bill Stapleton and Secretary of State Marcia David. Also, we have assembled the Directors from CIA, FBI, and the National Security Defense senior staff. Vice-President Chester Stockard is on the line."

Williams zeroed in on the Defense Secretary. "Who did this to us?"

"Madam President, we have unconfirmed intelligence from the CIA that a rogue cell calling itself the Pakistani Freedom Fighters is responsible."

As he was speaking, a passing nightmarish recollection of the Minneapolis attack, several months earlier, distracted her. *More victims that are innocent like my sister Maryann, the mother I met in the Minneapolis hospital Cassie and her daughter, Emma.* Sighing deeply, she fought to re-center her full attention back on the intercom in front of her.

"The President asked the Secretary of State, "Marcia, any word yet from the Pakistani ambassador?"

"Not yet. But, I have placed the highest priority call. I expect to hear shortly."

Williams spoke forcefully. "Justin, what is the current status of the situation on the ground in Atlanta?"

"The National Guard has been mobilized and is maintaining as much order as possible, given the immense chaos. From the damage appraisal, our experts calculated that the bomb was approximately a five-ton uranium enriched weapon. The detonation appeared to have occurred at street level close to home plate of the Georgia Dome. The bomb leveled half of the stadium to the ground. The explosion spared the center field area but nuclear radiation levels are high throughout the entire complex and neighboring streets. Winds are not a factor at this moment so there is minimal scatter of radioactive particles beyond immediate ground zero."

The President interrupted, "Have we spoken to any of the people who survived the attack?"

"Survivors who had walked by the home plate area on route to the center field bleachers only ten minutes earlier recalled seeing a large moving van parked outside the main gate. They reported a verbal scuffle between the drivers of the van and two policewomen from the Atlanta force."

Williams massaged her temple as a migraine began pounding. "What was done about the suspicious van?"

Lenz hesitated. He cleared his throat. "A short time later, sometime during the third inning of an Atlanta Braves-Chicago Cubs baseball game, the bomb exploded. It's too early to estimate the number of casualties but there were forty thousand fans at the game."

The Vice President's strident voice entered the discussion. "From what I'm hearing, this appears to be the same terrorist group that hit us in Minneapolis. Madame President, I would like to hear from the Generals. I want to know if they would recommend striking back at Pakistan."

Williams felt her lungs growing tight. "Mr. Vice-President, I want to hear more discussion from our security team before I ask the Joint Chiefs to weigh in." She glanced at her Chief of Staff. Pitnar nodded in agreement. *The Generals are here to execute policy, not to make policy.* Her thoughts shifted to her VP. *Stockard would be President today were it not for the Surgeon General and my White House physician who both saved me from arsenic poisoning.*

Williams rubbed her forehead, asking the Secretary of State, "Marcia, have we heard anything from our allies?"

"Yes, the Israeli Prime Minister was the first to call. An emergency session of the Knesset will begin within the hour. Shalom Nussbaum is certain that the Israeli government will strongly support an immediate strike on a major high value target in Pakistan. As is their long standing rapid retaliation policy on such matters, they are fully prepared to launch their nuclear weapons on your order."

Williams pressed her further. "What about the British, the French, the Germans, the Chinese, the Japanese?"

In a sober voice, the Secretary of State replied, "Nothing yet."

The Vice President chimed in. His tone was angry. "My gut tells me we're on our own. Jane, I repeat my request to hear from the Generals."

"Chester, hold on. Bill, what do you guys at Defense know?"

"Madam President, as you ask me that question, I've just received a note. Please give me a second to read it." Stapleton paused. He read it aloud. "The message is from an FBI field agent based in Atlanta.

Apparently, the FBI had this same Atlanta based PFF terrorist cell under surveillance ever since Minneapolis. They have just arrested a member of the cell. No further information is available at this time."

"Keep me informed the moment you find out anything further."

"I will."

The Secretary of State chimed in. "I've just heard from the English Prime Minister. England is calling for full pursuit of diplomatic channels. They are worried if we strike Pakistan that their government will use this opportunity to attack India and other allies like Israel with their own nuclear warheads." Marcia David nervously added, "That would be the start of World War Three."

A disquieting feeling forced her to pause, for several seconds. As she weighed her options, Williams downed a full glass of water. In her mind, she began drawing strategic lines between the dots presented by her chief advisors. *Don't act out of anger.*

"Ladies and Gentlemen, let's take a step back for a moment. We do not yet know for sure that it was the Pakistani Freedom Fighters. However, even if we confirm that it is, do we have any intelligence to say that the governments of Afghanistan or Pakistan are supporting them?"

"Marcia again, it's unclear whether the governments are sympathetic to the PFF. In the past, many elements of their government, as we now know, were accommodative to the Taliban and Al-Kaida. But, we have no direct knowledge that this particular rogue cell is under the control of anyone in the region. The cell may be acting independently."

The President looked out the window. Marine One was fifty feet above the landing area. Williams glanced over at her Chief of Staff. As he began to open his mouth, she put her hand on his forearm and then called upon General Titus. Pitnar leaned back and mumbled a few unrecognizable words under his breath.

"General, can you summarize the thoughts of the Joint Chiefs?"

Titus replied crisply, "We all agree that this second nuclear attack already brings us to the brink of World War Three. If we strike at them, Russia would most likely intercede, as will the Chinese. The Middle East will explode. In addition, as you well know, our troops are already stretched beyond capacity for any ground additional offensives. However, we stand at the ready to execute your orders."

Williams felt a slight jolt as the landing gear touched down on the tarmac. She pointed at Pitnar. He had already unbuckled himself and was simply waiting for the pilot to give the order to disembark.

The Chief of Staff leaned into the intercom. "We just landed at Andrews. We will resume our meeting in ten minutes once the President is aboard Air Force One." Pitnar disconnected the call.

******

After Air Force One had leveled off, she thanked Pitnar for his assistance. In the last few minutes, she read a half-dozen telegrams faxed from several allies. All were calling for restraint, especially Russia. Williams said a quick prayer before pushing the intercom to resume the senior advisor conference call.

"What have we learned since we last spoke?"

"This is Bill Stapleton. I have new information. After persuasive interrogation of the PFF cell member that we captured, the twenty-five year old Pakistani woman confessed that it was her terrorist group that set off the nuke."

"How do we know if she was telling the truth?"

"We found a note in her pocket. We saw the word "Mad" written around the edges. In the center was a riddle, inscribed in Arabic. We've already translated it."

"What does it say?" Williams anxiously asked.

"The dirty birds will fly the coop after a blast that will not be the last."

Williams looked over at her Chief of Staff. Pitnar shrugged his shoulders. The President asked, "Bill, what does that mean?"

Stapleton replied, "With the help of our decoding experts, we believe we know. In Atlanta, the football Falcons local code name is the dirty birds. The Braves baseball team is currently sharing the Georgia Dome football stadium while their new baseball complex is completed. So, the note correctly confirmed the location of the attack and the football Falcons need to fly the coop to play elsewhere."

Williams barely heard anything after the riddle. Certain key words clanged around every corner of her troubled brain. *A blast that will not be the last.* She addressed Homeland Security Secretary Lenz. "It sounds like we have credible information that there will be another attack. We will need to secure all major cities. Please coordinate with the FBI and the National Guard."

Lenz responded sharply, "Madam President, we will immediately initiate our plan."

"Thank you Justin. One more point. Has anyone come up with the significance of the word MAD on the note?"

The Defense Secretary replied, "Well, the note said there will be another attack. That would be the third on this recent offensive. MAD has three letters. The first city nuked was Minneapolis and now Atlanta. Maybe the third city begins with the letter D?"

She saw the glint in Mac's eyes. The Chief of Staff replied, "It makes sense. We know these damn terrorists are always using symbolism."

The President added, "It could mean anything but the acronym might relate to cities that have been attacked. So, where is next? Dallas?"

Detroit? Denver? Secretary Lenz, prepare for me a list of all major cities beginning with the letter D. We'll prioritize our defense on these cities."

"Yes, Madam President."

Williams sat back and briefly reflected on what General Titus has predicted if she launched a strike against Pakistan. The possibilities were terrifying. Then, as though she crossed a railroad track without looking, fear clobbered the President faster than a runaway locomotive bearing down on her. Leaning forward into the intercom, she stated firmly, "Please return to your posts. We will reconvene in two hours. Thank you."

******

Landing at a secure spot in Omaha, the President parked herself in a well-padded leather covered chair surrounded by the ten by ten foot steel reinforced security block. Williams read one email after another sent to her from world leaders. Informed that her top-level security team was closely monitoring the horrific situation, she prayed.

A knock on the door startled her. The Secret Service agent in the cellblock with her looked at the TV camera and determined that it was safe to open the concrete door.

It was Pitnar. He was scowling. He said curtly, "Madam President, your team is assembled. We will take the call in the main bunker conference room."

Williams rose to her feet. "You look upset."

"I'm fine," he replied. "We need to move fast," the Chief of Staff added while trotting ahead of her down the long corridor.

She found herself needing to power walk just to keep up with him. Surrounded by eight by eight stone blocks and located one hundred and fifty feet below the surface, Williams felt the chill blowing through her bones from the national security situation as much as she felt the frosty attitude that her Chief of Staff had recently adopted toward her. *Something happened.*

The President entered the conference room. Several advisors sat before her. Except for several computers at one end of the glass conference table, a large screen TV on the far wall, and one conference phone in the middle of the table, the thirty-foot square cellblock was barren. The President took her seat at the head of the table and nodded at Chester Stockard and Marcia David.

Mac remained standing. He seemed unusually fidgety. She motioned for him to take a seat next to her. With a vacant expression plastered on his face, he complied without saying a word.

She swiveled her chair toward him and whispered, "Are you all right?"

He did not return her gaze but just pointed to the phone. "Madame President, your team is awaiting your decision to begin the meeting."

Williams gaped at him suspiciously. She pressed the intercom. "Who is on the line?"

Justin Lenz, Bill Stapelton, and General Titus each identified themselves. Williams fixed her eyes on the phone. "Team, what have we learned in the last few hours?"

She cringed when the first voice who spoke up was that of the Vice President, sitting at the far end of the conference table.

Stockard took up where he had left off. He thundered, "We must not let Pakistan use us for a punching bag. We must retaliate. Otherwise, they will view America as a paper tiger."

The President set her jaw. "Chester, I'm certainly not prepared to go that far at present." Stockard hardened his face. Williams looked over at her Secretary of State. "Marcia, have we made diplomatic contact with the Prime Ministers of these countries?"

"Yes, both vehemently deny any involvement. But, one PM did add an ominous comment to our tense conversation."

Williams pursed her lips, furrowing her brow. "What exactly did he say?"

"Pakistani intelligence picked up information that Israel was preparing to launch a nuclear weapon on your order. President Sharma said if America allows such an act of war against his country, he will unleash forces against America and Israel that are beyond our imagination."

The VP's husky voice chimed in, "Just my point. We cannot sit back and be threatened like this. You need to face reality. It's us or them."

"We are not attacking anyone based on current information." The President sharpened her gaze on the VP. "I want to hear from the others."

A deep voice from the conference phone barked. "Madam President, this is Justin Lenz. Information gathered from my Homeland Security Department reveals an early causality report of at least nine thousand killed by the direct force of the blast and another twenty thousand directly exposed to the radiation. At least, six thousand have been hospitalized so far in hospitals in Atlanta and surrounding counties."

Williams slammed her eyes shut. She said a silent short prayer.

Lenz continued, "I have prepared a list of cities starting with the letter D for your review. We can secure the larger cities to a greater degree."

The President's eyes gaped open, landing on her VP, seated directly across from her at the far end of the conference table.

Stockard looked antsy. "What are we doing?" he asked. "This is like trying to play prevent defense in football. It never works. Any good quarterback can pick apart this kind of defense. It's time we take the offense to protect our homeland."

Williams had heard enough from her VP. Against her better judgment, she joined his argument. "Mr. Vice-President, with all due respect, you are doing your best to dominate this discussion. I am asking you to let others have their say. I fully understand your position." Her voice was strong, her cadence quick. "You have made your point repeatedly all day."

Stockard's chiseled facial features did not move. He returned the President's glare without batting an eye, holding his tongue.

She inhaled deeply. Her eyes shifted to her Secretary of State. "Marcia, contact Israeli Prime Minister Nussbaum. Convey my message that I do not want any Israeli attack on any country without my direct order. Also, convey to him that I would greatly appreciate a lowering of Israeli rhetoric."

"I'll take care of it." She paused before asking the question of the day. "Madam President, may I also assure President Sharma that there will be no imminent attack on Pakistan?"

"Definitely! They are an ally of America." The President took a sip of water. "So, at this point, our strategy will be to exhaust diplomatic channels while trying to defend our major cities starting with the letter D. Clearly, we are not going to war at this time with any country over this latest attack until we conclusively know that a state government is responsible."

Secretary of State Marcia David pursed her lips. Secretary of Defense Stapelton spoke loudly through the conference phone. "Understood."

Williams fired off a volley at the phone. "Justin, has your department discovered any fresh leads from the FBI or CIA?"

"Only the Atlanta cell member that we captured with the note with the word MAD. These rogue cells could be anywhere. It's like finding a needle in a haystack."

In a disgruntled tone, Stockard intervened. "Madam President, may I remind---?"

"Please, Mr. Vice-President." She inhaled deeply. "Ladies and Gentlemen, America is at a crossroads. We can no longer be the sole policeman of the world," she stated, her voice rising in pitch with each spoken word. "We need to start building bridges to our allies as well as to countries that we would consider to be our enemies. We will defend America the best we know how." Casting scowl at her VP, she added, "However, if we conclusively identify a high value military target responsible for these nuclear attacks, we will strike back with the full force of our military. Thank you for your input today. This meeting is adjourned."

Williams pressed the intercom button, extinguishing the red light. She asked Mac, Marcia, and Chester if they would give her a few minutes of solitude. The VP and Secretary of State filed out in silence. Pitnar remained seated, his eyes fixed on the President. Abruptly, he sprung to his feet and headed toward the door.

"Mac," she called out. "We will get through this."

He wheeled around to face the President. Pitnar looked unnerved. "Madame President, the VP is making sense."

"I disagree. The American people did not elect a cowboy."

"You're right. The people want a leader who will do whatever it takes to protect them."

She fired back, "I'm the President. Support my policies or resign."

Pinar opened the door and gently closed it behind him.

CHAPTER TWENTY-SEVEN

The Secretary of Health approached Rogers's desk in a deliberate manner, head held high, chest fully puffed. "Jonathan, I've had a serious conversation with the President." James handed the Surgeon General a signed note. "It's about you."

Glancing down at the message, Rogers's pulse quickened. He peered over his bifocals at his boss. "You want me to take a few days off."

"Not at all," Secretary James replied. Tapping his foot on the floorboards, he stated, "I'm ordering you to take off a full two weeks to go on a vacation."

"I have important work to do---on *NeoBloc.*"

"It can wait. Maybe with a little perspective you'll change your mind. You're obsessed with *NeoBloc.*" James's eyes narrowed. "Permit me to be blunt. Well regarded scientists are speaking out against you in blogs on the web and op-ed pieces in the *Washington Post* and the *New York Times* are hurting not only your professional reputation but also that of the Williams administration."

"Christian, those scientists have a conflict of interest. Most of them take honoraria from DCP. *NeoBloc* is deadly. Don't you see that?"

"No."

Rogers catapulted to his feet. "Deep down, I'm convinced that the President agrees with me."

"We'll deal with the vaccine issue when you return. Right now, you need balance in your life. Maybe you should try to connect with old friends with whom you may have lost contact. Besides, the President is focusing on the latest terrorist attack. She can't be distracted by your inclinations to dramatize the vaccine issue."

"Distracted!" Suddenly, Rogers's mind was on fire. He shouted, "Are you firing me? If you are, then I'll be on every TV talk show in America warning about *NeoBloc.*"

The Secretary walked toward Rogers and put his hand gently on the Surgeon General's shoulder. "Jonathan, I'm talking just two weeks. You're not being let go. The President expressed to me her utmost confidence in you. She wants you to remain as her "top doc." The President even gave you final sign off on *NeoBloc.* What more do you want?"

Rogers brushed the Secretary's hand off his shoulder. "Why did you send the President a forgery of made up monkey safety data?"

The Secretary inched closer to the Surgeon General, his taut face now no more than a foot away. "Stop it. Stop your philosophic arguments," James screeched. "Two weeks Jonathan, effective immediately."

Rogers took his seat and slumped in his leather chair. He thought of picking up the phone and immediately calling the President. *As Surgeon General, I have veto power over distribution of the deadly vaccine.* He craned his neck upward, nodding at James. "Ok, two weeks."

"Get some rest Jonathan. You've been through a lot."

Rogers's thoughts jumped to Kim. He angrily looked at James, saying nothing.

******

Rogers sat in his living room chair flipping through a creaky Rolodex that he cradled on his lap. He wondered if anyone else besides him still used these relics anymore. When he came across the one name that he had been searching for, a broad smile crossed his face. *Dante Joseph Panzzanini*

He remembered his childhood days. While growing up in Brooklyn, his click loved to play stickball in the streets. If anyone hit a Spaulding rubber ball on the highest roof of one of the stores lining Fort Hamilton Parkway, a few boys would just climb up after it. To retrieve the twenty-five cent rubber ball, you needed to jump over a four-foot wide alley, a mere two stories above the alley concrete pavement below.

He laughed aloud. Anytime he would tell Ashley of this escapade, he would always smile when she asked if he ever worried that he might have slipped and fallen after taking a running start and doing his version of an Olympic broad jump. His answer was always the same; he never even gave it a thought. At ten years old, all that mattered to any of his friends was retrieving the Spaulding. It was their prize. Without that scuffed up ball, their stickball game---their fun for the day---would come to a halt. *Mom wouldn't shell out another quarter for a replacement ball without putting me through a grilling. Heck, it was easier to find the damn ball.* Memories of his friends' facial expressions each time after they successfully jumped the alleyway always made him chuckle. It was like each one of them had just scaled the summit of Mount Everest. *To us, it was!*

He laid down the plastic Rolodex and tried to remember when he had last spoken with Joey Panini, or more importantly, why they had lost touch. *He was my best man at my wedding.* He picked up the phone and dialed. On the third ring, a jovial voice mail chimed in.

'Yo, you've reached Joey Panini. Leave a message or I won't call you back.' Beep

'Panini, this is your ole buddy Jonathan Rogers. You're probably saying why the hell is he calling after all these years. It's a great question. I take full responsibility for not keeping in touch after our last fishing trip. I think that was twenty years ago. Look, I'd like to speak with you. Drop me an email JRogersa@gov.org. or call my private cell line 517-100-0001'

******

Jonathan tossed in bed, unable to accept his forced exile. His mind kept coming back to the original data signed off by Dr. Nasters confirming that all the monkeys died after receiving *NeoBloc*. He silently cursed James for sending the President inaccurate data. He blamed Nasters for altering the facts. Closing his eyes, he tried to think things through. *Some relaxation!*

His cell phone on the nightstand rang. Reflexively, he looked over at his Browning, lying on the nightstand. He checked his clock. It was almost midnight.

'Who would be calling at this time of night?'

"Hello"

The voice was somber and muffled. Punctuated by a second or so delay, each word leaked out. "Is this Jonathan Rogers?"

Instincts aroused, he sat up in bed. His first thought shot to the whereabouts of Ashley. "Who is this?"

No response was forthcoming. Yet he heard music.

Rogers listened carefully. He thought he heard a familiar theme song playing in the background. He tried to make out the words. A heartbeat later, the volume soared to a deafening pitch. Yanking the phone away from his ear, he heard the refrain. *'Glory Days'* "Who the hell is this?"

In classic Brooklynese, a deep voice replied, "Hey. You called me old pal. What's up with you?"

In a flash, it came to him. He laughed. "Panini. It's you. Even after all of these years, I can still remember your accent."

"Well, excuse me Doctor Jonathan Rogers. I can see that being a big shot doctor has taken away yours."

"I may have lost my accent but I'm still a Brooklyn kid at heart."

Panini snorted. "I'm just messing with you. So Johnny Boy, how did you track me down? Bet you saw my good looking mug on one of those Internet social networking sites."

He grinned, thinking of how all the years in Michigan and Washington DC had stomped out his New York accent. He responded with a twinge of frivolity. "I don't see you as the Facebook type."

"You got that right Johnny Boy."

"All kidding aside, how are things my good friend?"

"Well, since the last time you called me after our fishing trip together, I got married and then divorced. I have three young grandchildren. I've been hospitalized twice with an infection in a broken hip after being smacked in a hit and run accident. I've had colon cancer, which is in remission. And, I'm now retired from the AFL-CIO union with a bad back. Recently, I've been a private detective."

"I see."

"At least, I'm alive. You on the other hand, I've been reading about in the papers. To tell the truth, I'm shocked that you're still alive. Rogers, my ole friend, I can't believe you ain't dead yet."

"Since you were once a seminarian, please pray for me." He changed the receiver to the other ear and rubbed his chin.

"Ex-seminarian."

"Listen, Panini, where are you living these days?

"Motown."

"I'm living in DC but I'm back in Michigan for a---for a short vacation. I'm staying at a hotel outside the town where I used to live— Oldwyck."

"You're a crazy dude. Why aren't you in Bermuda, Venice or somewhere nice? Why come back to Oldwyck, Michigan for a vacation? Are you nuts?"

"Well, this is where Kim and I lived during my days in private practice. It's been home for me."

"I see." Panini lowered his voice. "I'm very sorry for what happened to your wife. When I saw the story in the paper, I couldn't believe it. I still can't." He paused a few seconds. "I'm so sorry that I didn't reach out to you after it happened."

"No worries. I understand."

"You're a good man Jonathan. You've always been a straight shooter."

"Look, if I came to Detroit, would you grab a beer with me?"

Emphasizing his accent, Panini replied, "Gee, I never drank with an almost ghost before."

"I'm still kicking. Let's do it this week. Does that work for you?"

"How about dropping by on Tuesday? Stop over at three in the afternoon. I'm at 199 East Shady Court."

Rogers mind jumped from story to story of those earlier carefree days. "Can't wait to see you and talk about our adventures growing up in the City."

"Hey, do you remember when Freddie threw the carbon dioxide cylinder into the fire?"

"Holy Shit! Do I? The damn cylinder blew up and went right through Frankie's calf. He was right next to me. It could have been me."

Panini's voice turned serious. "Johnny, old boy, you used to be so lucky. What happened? It seems as though you have a huge bulls-eye on your back."

Rogers rolled his eyes. "You don't know the half of it. See you at your place on Tuesday at three."

CHAPTER TWENTY-EIGHT

"I owe you for supporting me." Connor firmly shook Dr. Nasters's hand. "Just so you know, it's usually not in my nature to state that I'm in debt to anyone."

The scientist beamed. "After I interviewed you for Sean Parker's position, it was an easy choice. You and I are both passionate about getting *NeoBloc* through the human clinical trials so we can realize the President's policy of inoculating every American. With the recent nuclear attack on Atlanta, who knows where the terrorists will strike next?"

Connor leaned back on his suede leather executive style chair and scanned his expansive office. It felt great to be back in charge at DCP. In the years since he was out of the country, Sean Parker had removed the wet bar and the board game that Connor had installed during the days when he previously strode around the classy digs as Zach Miller.

Nasters dropped the latest human trial report on the CEO's desk and took a seat. "The side effects of the vaccine on humans have been minimal."

He raised his hand. "Let's back up a little. Talk to me about the fact that Beth Murphy and Jonathan Rogers stumbled upon DCP data that showed that every monkey died after getting the vaccine."

The scientist exhaled forcefully, smiling inwardly. "Three points need to be made. Not all the monkeys died, some monkeys could have died from a viral illness or another cause to be determined, and finally and most importantly, monkeys are not humans. You must trust me as a scientist to interpret the data."

I trust no one but myself! "But the data showing that all the monkeys died was signed by you. Rogers has your damn signature on every page of that DCP research."

Dr. Nasters held his stern gaze. "Rest assured that the data that Dr. Rogers has in his possession with my signature are a forgery."

Connor twitched his mouth from side to side. He grunted, casting a suspicious look at Nasters. "Why would Rogers make this up? Give the devil his due. He's a stand up kind of guy."

"Perhaps Lauren Timmons or some other disgruntled employee altered the data on pages signed by me." Nasters shrugged his shoulders and sat down directly in front of Connor. "I just believe that Dr. Rogers is so brainwashed that Lauren was an honest whistleblower that he has fully bought into her story. He simply believes that martyr's don't lie."

"It's a possibility." He leaned back. "Is there anyone else that you suspect?"

"I'm beginning to worry about Dr. Virginia Washington. Obviously, I'll need proof." Nasters abruptly stood. He began to pace around the room, avoiding any direct contact with his new boss. "I'm deeply worried that any delay in getting *NeoBloc* approved by the FDA will jeopardize millions of American lives."

He slapped his hands together. "These damn terrorists just wiped out a chunk of Atlanta. Who will they hit next?"

"Since no one knows; we must *get NeoBloc* out as soon as possible. It will prevent the radiation induced sickness that has killed so many of our fellow countrymen."

"That won't help the thousands of Americans who are actually at ground zero."

Nasters stopped and squinted at the CEO. "That's true." He then walked toward the door, his back to Connor.

"You are making me very uncomfortable." He pointed to the chair that Nasters had vacated a minute earlier. "Please sit down."

Nasters promptly complied.

"Look, I have contacts in high places. And, I've learned from privileged sources that the President will soon publicly announce that the vaccine will not be deployed without a final sign off from Dr. Rogers."

Nasters angrily pumped his right fist in the air. "He'll never support *NeoBloc*."

He snapped his fingers. "Relax. I'll take care of the Surgeon General."

"There is no doubt in my mind about that." The scientist inhaled slowly as he collected his emotions. "I'm so glad that you're the boss."

"Don't ever forget that doctor." Connor put his feet up on the antique maple wood desk and pulled out a cigar from the inside pocket of his blue suit jacket. "I'll smoke this Cuban the day *NeoBloc* hits the streets."

Nasters winked. "I consider that goal my sole reason for living."

Connor shot a disdainful glance. "That sounds a little over the top. It's like you're leading a crusade."

"I am certainly filled with passion."

Pretending to blow rings of cigar smoke, he said quietly, "Just remember that many crusaders died horrific deaths."

***

Connor pressed the intercom. "Andrea, get me our VP of Public Relations and also Dr. Peter Ulrich from the National Quality Board."

Andrea replied, "I'll buzz you in a few minutes."

Pulling out his self-made deck of cards, he lined up the new faces as well as the old face cards. He pasted new pictures of Beth Murphy and Xavier Rudolph onto two blank cards. Connor spread the deck on his desk. He pulled out the faces of William Peabody and Victor Carver, both recently killed by guards while trying to escape from the federal prison. He ripped their faces to shreds and reshuffled the deck. He turned the cards over face down. As he was about to pick his next victim, his admin buzzed.

He hit the speaker button. "Yes"

"Penelope Woods, our PR Vice-President is on the line."

"Put her through." He flipped one of the cards face up before greeting Ms. Woods. Laughing mischievously, he barely eked out a weak, "Hello."

"Mr. Lucas, Good morning! I was just putting the final touches on the press release announcing your appointment as our CEO when Andrea called and said you wanted to speak with me."

He looked out the window. A black sparrow flew by. His face turned grim. "I've been thinking. Since I left Sunview so abruptly, I don't want to hurt DCP's reputation in any way by calling undue attention to myself. After all, I was their SVP of Sales for only a week. To me, it would look a bit strange that I left so soon after my promotion. So, I don't want any public announcements, at least not at this time."

"I see. She hesitated a few seconds before speaking again. "You should be so proud of your accomplishment. Don't you want your family and friends to read about it in the newspaper?"

The other intercom light was blinking. "Listen, Penelope, I need to go. There will be no public announcements about me. It's not open for further discussion." Before she could respond, he pressed Andrea's button. He waited for her to pick up. On the next ring, she answered, "I just got Dr. Ulrich on line 3."

"Great." He searched for the appropriate line, pressing the flashing button. "Good morning, Dr. Ulrich."

"Good morning Mr. Lucas. Congratulations on your appointment as CEO."

"Thank you so much. Doctor, I sincerely hope that we will become the best of colleagues."

"As the chairman of the National Quality Oversight Board, I look forward to working with you to ensure that your compounds receive a fair scientific evaluation. As you may know, our Board has already started our preliminary review of your pipeline vaccine *NeoBloc*. In fact, I recently called an urgent meeting of the Board that met quorum. I am pleased to report that we have already recommended to the FDA that the human clinical trials with *NeoBloc* should continue."

"I was already aware of that. Your input was critical to the President reversing her earlier inclination to place a moratorium on the human clinical trials. After she spoke with Dr. Rogers, she subsequently spoke with several scientists at the FDA. They all agreed with your Board's conclusion. But, even though she is continuing the clinical trials, she is giving the Surgeon General final sign off to ensure that there are no safety issues before deployment of the vaccine."

Ulrich paused several seconds.

Connor cocked his head. "Are you still there doc?"

"From my sources, I believe that that could be a challenge."

"Facts are facts. Rogers will eventually concede."

Ulrich uttered a brief humming sound. "So, how do you propose convincing him?"

"That's your job—you're the scientist." He picked up his chosen playing card. The Surgeon General's face stared back at him. Connor ripped it to pieces. "I know that you work with Beth Murphy." He threw the shreds of the Rogers playing card over his back.

"She's a tough cookie. But, her late stepfather was even worse. He used to give me heartburn. Sam Murphy would question everything during his time on the Board."

"I remember Sam. Very tenacious and frequently won his battles. I admire that in a man."

"Yes, he certainly was all of that. Getting back to Ms. Murphy, for some reason, we could not find her to attend our recent urgent meeting. But, I must say that she does take after her stepfather."

"Her behavior has come to my attention. As a personal favor, I want you to keep me informed of anything that she says or does regarding *NeoBloc*."

Ulrich hesitated in his response.

Connor rolled his eyes. "Did you hear me?"

Clearing his throat, the physician leader replied, "I will do my best, Mr. Lucas. By the way, our next regularly scheduled National Quality oversight board meeting comes up in three months, just before the FDA decides on whether to approve the vaccine."

He pretended to be puffing on his Cuban. Ulrich was the second person in recent days to promise him that they would do their best. *People usually disappoint me.*

"Doctor, you need to be aware that I have informed the FDA that DCP will be establishing clinical trial sites in Beijing, China. It's much cheaper to run part of our phase three studies in that country. It's also easier to get participants to volunteer to be paid subjects for these studies."

"Really?" Ulrich's voice now took on a commanding tone. "I would be remiss if I did not point out something to you. The quality of the data and the ethical standards of performing these clinical trials abroad on *NeoBloc* may not be as transparent as clinical trials performed in the United States."

"Is that so? Just stay close to me Dr. Ulrich. Stay very close."

"I carefully follow the data. I'm a scientist. My read of the *NeoBloc* data is that the vaccine is absolutely safe."

"Glad to hear your recommendation doctor."

CHAPTER TWENTY-NINE

President Williams took her seat at the end of the conference table. Under the table, she flexed her fingers while scanning her advisors, seated around her.

From his customary seat at the far end from her, Vice-President Chester Stockard raised his hand high in the air. "Madame President, what is your backup plan if a 3rd city is nuked?

His words echoed loudly. Williams cast a steely-eyed glance in his direction. "Chester, let's get an update from the rest of the team before I answer your question. Marcia, what's the latest on your diplomatic initiatives?"

"Madame President, the governments of Pakistan, India, Israel, Russia, and China are extremely edgy."

Williams nodded, expressionless. "Bill what's the latest from Defense?"

"Justin and I are coordinating Homeland Security efforts with our activities at the Pentagon. We've redeployed National Guard troops to Dallas, Denver, and Detroit. The FBI and CIA have discovered no new intelligence."

The President looked down the conference room table at her Chief of Staff. "Mac, you've been very quiet lately. It's not like you."

Pitnar dropped his eyes to the floor. Williams knew that he didn't like the spotlight. A moment later, he glanced over at Stockard. Her Chief of Staff responded, "Madame President, I believe the Vice President's question needs to be answered. I believe that it does make sense that America cannot suffer another attack by playing defense alone."

It's time! Williams stood, walking toward the Vice President. "I understand your anger and frustration. Chester, I know you want to bomb Karachi but what would that accomplish?" She held up her hands in front of her, wanting to thwart an immediate response from him to her question. "The report from The Tank said it would lead toward World War Three. The Joint Chiefs were unanimous in their conclusion."

The President shook her head from side to side. "We have no evidence that the governments of Pakistan or Afghanistan are even involved. Our best intelligence still points to a Pakistani Freedom Fighter rogue cell."

Williams looked over to Pitnar. He squirmed in his seat. By now, Stockard had again raised his hand.

"Chester---"

"Madame President, if I may. Mac is dead on. Who would honestly believe that a few terrorists in a rogue cell would have the capabilities to deploy not just one but two nuclear weapons? We have only one viable option. We need to hit Pakistan."

Williams turned her back on Stockard, hardening her face while she walked back to her seat and sat down. She cocked her head and spoke in a firm tone, eyes locked on the VP. "Please show me just one iota of evidence that the governments of Pakistan or Afghanistan are involved and I'll take action. Until you do that, we're not going to do something crazy like bombing any country."

Emphasizing the first word of his reply, the Vice-President said, "*You* are the Commander-in-Chief." Stockard bit his lower lip. "However, Madame President, I recommend you go before a televised joint session of Congress. You need to talk to our fellow Americans. They deserve to hear from you."

"That was my plan all along. I'm so glad that you agree with me." She looked at her Chief of Staff, "Mac, please arrange for this sometime within the next week."

Williams's face grew increasingly somber. She looked at each of her national security advisors. "In the meantime, let's find out who is doing this to America and how we can stop them. The future of our planet hangs in the balance."

CHAPTER THIRTY

Rogers knocked on the front door at 199 East Shady Court. It was a one-story wooden frame home, sorely in need of a fresh coat of white paint. Looking around, he noted the need for a fair amount of re-seeding of the grass on the ten-foot wide front lawn that abutted the badly cracked sidewalk. With another week off before Secretary James was willing to let him resume his duties as Surgeon General; he was excited to be connecting with his old friend Joey Panini currently living in Detroit.

Just after ringing the doorbell, the weathered dark brown painted wooden front door swung open. He looked down a dark hallway. Not seeing anyone, Rogers hollered, "Is that you Panini?"

Silence.

"Is anyone home?"

Silence.

Rogers turned around. The street was empty except for a hunched over woman who was walking her Golden Retriever across the street. He waved to the woman. She returned the gesture.

He closed the front door. Ringing the doorbell again, the door sprang open just as before. Feeling strangely uncomfortable, he thought twice about entering. He yelled out again, "Panini."

Silence.

Rogers pulled his cell phone from his pants pocket. He dialed his friend's number. After eight rings, he got Panini's voice message. *I come all the way to Detroit and he's not even home.* He sat down on the top concrete step of the stoop and counted five American made and twenty five foreign made cars whizz by, all stampeding over the posted twenty five mile an hour speed limit. He checked his watch. Growing impatient, he stood and looked again down the long narrow corridor beyond the open door. "Panini?" He checked the name on the inside mailbox. *Panzzanini*

A friendly sounding bark followed a voice from the sidewalk. The middle-aged woman with a cute Golden retriever asked, "Who are you looking for?

"Joey Panini," Rogers replied.

In an accusatory tone, she asked, "You a cop?"

"No. I'm his friend. Do you know him?"

The woman chuckled. She bent over to pet her dog. "Who doesn't know Joey Panini?"

"We were supposed to meet here but he's not at home." Rogers walked over and petted the retriever. "What's his name?"

"Sampson."

He shook a paw of the ninety-pound mass of good nature. Rogers pointed to the open front door. "No one is home."

"That can't be." She pointed toward the street. "There's his black Ford Ranger pick- up truck. He never goes anywhere without it."

"He doesn't answer his doorbell. And, I just called his house phone and got his voice mail."

The woman scratched her head. "Come to think of it, the Ranger hasn't moved from that spot in days." Sampson began yanking on his leash. The woman struggled but the dog was determined to pull her away. "And, I haven't seen Mr. Panini in a while"

"I hope he's all right."

"Gotta go." The retriever pulled the woman a few more yards down the street. "More to the point, Sampson wants to leave. He must be getting bored with you."

"That's OK with me. I can use more boredom—some down time. My life is way too exciting."

The dog barked again and continued pulling his owner further away. Rogers shrugged his shoulders, walked up the steps, and peered inside the door. "Is anyone home?"

Silence.

He didn't know why but he felt anxious in entering the building. The musty odor of the hallway caused him a brief spate of a dry cough. His heart felt as if it was going to burst from his chest as it began to beat faster and faster.

Fifteen feet down the hallway, he paused to flick on a light switch. The hallway ceiling bulb showered a dim light on the black painted walls. Squinting, he suddenly felt something falling on top of him. In a flash, he caught a glimpse of a modified two-piece hula-hoop strung together with one-inch nylon rope wrapped around his body. "What the hell!"

A section of plastic blue colored hoop alternated with a rope and then another hoop piece connected to another section of rope, forming a collapsible circle that enveloped him below his armpits. He cast his eyes upward and spotted a pulley bolted into the ceiling. Rogers followed the rope from the pulley to one of the side doors. He could feel sections of the hula-hoop and rope tightening around his mid-section. Stricken by waves of ever intensifying fear, his thoughts gathered quicker than fast approaching rain clouds during a mid-summer thunderstorm.

He tried to escape but the rope was taut, creating a virtual cage that progressively circled his chest and waist areas. The cage began to lift him upward. "What the---?" He looked down to see his feet dangling two feet or so above the wooden floorboards. "Help," he screamed. *Where is Panini?*

A door on the right side of the hallway creaked open. A rotund figure, head covered in a dark black hood, and wearing a long blue toga walked slowly toward him. Slits in the head covering corresponded to the usual orifices of the face. The arms were muscular. A tattoo of a sexy looking woman graced the left upper arm. The person's stature was short, no more than five foot seven. As the figure approached, he noticed that he was letting slack out in the ropes. Gradually, he felt himself lowered until he felt his shoes once again touching the floor.

The Surgeon General's voice cracked. "Who are you? Wha---What do you want?"

A hoarse voice crackled in a foreign accent. "I want to kill you." The hooded man stopped dead in his tracks. "You deserve a cruel death for what you have done."

The accent sounded familiar but he couldn't quite place it. He struggled to loosen the ropes. His hands and left foot squirmed out but his right foot became entangled in the ropes. Expecting the worst, he made up his mind on a plan.

Rogers screamed, "I don't even know you. Why are you doing this?"

"Why not," the man replied in a devilish tone while taking one-step closer. "You're a trespasser in my home. I'll tell the cops that I was just defending myself. This won't be the first time I knocked off an attempted break-in."

Rogers wiped away a few beads of sweat that had begun to trickle into his eyes. "I wasn't breaking in. I'm just looking for Joey Panini"

The man smirked. "You're not the first. Everybody wants a piece of him. Are you the repo man?" The hooded man began to shuffle his feet, producing an eerie sound. He was now four away.

"No, I'm Panini's friend from the old days in New York."

"You don't look like his type." The man took one-step closer, dragging his left leg as though suddenly paralyzed.

"We once threw a CO2 capsule into a backyard fire. It exploded and shot like a missile through the calf of Ernie Boy."

"What's your name mister? I better like it or I'll have to hang you on the spot"

"Jonathan Rogers."

"Panini once told me stories of the old days. He never would have been caught dead hanging out with preppy boys like you."

"I'm the Surgeon General."

The man scoffed. "I think I may need to do a little surgery on you, general doctor."

"Where's Panini?"

The hoarseness increased. "Let's just say that he's tied up at the moment. He's my next victim after you. He laughed as if imitating Count Dracula. You're dead meat mister."

Rogers stared into the eye slits. The peering dark brown eyes did not flinch. A moment later, he felt the ropes tightening again. "What are you doing?"

"Prepare yourself to die. I hope you know some short prayers that will get through. God is a busy man, especially these days." The hooded man outstretched his arms in front of him before dropping his right arm to his side. He then reached behind his back. From his belt area, a shiny pair of scissors appeared in his right hand. The man opened and closed the blades and erratically waved them in a half-arc in front of him.

He steadied his entrapped right foot, planting it firmly on the floorboards. His left leg was free, at the ready to strike an uppercut.

"I think I'll cut off one ear at a time before I get down to serious business."

I've got one shot at kicking the scissors from his hand, Rogers thought.

Taking a step closer, he pointed the open scissors at the Surgeon General's head. Rogers peered into the slits in the hood. His eyes were like glaciers, frozen and cold.

Rogers was ready to strike. It was time. He would strike on the count of three. *One, two...*

An instant later, the man screamed out in a jocular voice, "Hi, Johnny Boy. Need a haircut." He ripped off his hood and broke down in belly busting laughter.

He shouted, "Panini, you fat little bastard. You had me scared out of my wits. Another second and I would have kicked those scissors from your hand before picking them up to stab you straight through the heart."

Panini doubled over with laughter. "Now that would have made the ten o clock local news. Didn't think you doctor generals were so vicious."

He grabbed him by the shoulders and vigorously shook him. Pretending that he was going to smack him in the face, he said, "I can't believe you did this to me." He grabbed Panini's head in a headlock and rubbed his knuckles into his scalp. "You're going to pay with a nuggie."

Panini slipped out of the headlock and massaged his scalp. "You were starting to press in a little too hard my friend." He kept poking his wagging finger at Rogers, unable to stop a cascade of uncontrollable belly laughs. "Johnny Boy, you should have seen the look in your eyes. Man, they were twitching faster than our hips when we used to dance the twist back in the '60's. Shit, you were freakin scared out of your bird."

Rogers gave way to a reluctant chuckle. He tore away at the ropes. "Get this damn cage off of me." Once untangled, he gave his Motown host a potential rib-cracking bear hug. "You're still the same zany prankster that you were back in the City. You haven't changed a bit."

Panini grew pensive, studying his face, taking in every detail. "But you have, Johnny boy. You're so much more serious than I remember you. I guess being a doctor general made you a whole new man."

"My values haven't changed. Deep down, I'm still the same street kid that grew up with you on the streets of Brooklyn."

"I'm talking appearances man. Your face needs some fun, some joviality. You're a mass of wrinkles."

If he only knew. "The last year or two has probably aged me twenty years. But, I'm a survivor.' He punched Panini lightly on the shoulder. "Listen, you little weasel, you owe me a beer."

His friend pointed to the side door. "Step into my penthouse apartment."

Rogers put his arm around his childhood friend. "I've really missed you. I miss those days when we fearlessly jumped across the roof alleyways. To think that we risked our lives trying to find a twenty five cent Spaulding rubber ball that landed up on the roof."

"The alley was only four feet across---no big deal."

"And thirty feet straight down to the concrete pavement if we slipped. Talk about sudden death."

Panini sniggered. "Hey, when we were kids who the hell thought of dying; we just wanted to find our Spaulding to finish our damn stickball game." He pushed open the door to his place. "How much time do you have? We have a lot to catch up."

"Lead the way. I have nowhere to go, my friend. Nowhere."

Once inside the one bedroom flat, Panini pulled out two beers from the refrigerator and plunked them down on the kitchen table. "By the way, do you remember Cathy Parker?"

He unscrewed the cap and took a swig. He frowned. "I haven't thought of her for years."

"You know, she always had a thing for you.

Rogers stiffened. "It's been over for many years."

"Loosen up Johnny Boy----can't wait to get you drunk tonight----just like the old days----maybe I'll invite Cathy to stop over."

Though his interest was piqued, he hid his curiosity. "No, I'd rather just hang out with you." Rogers grabbed his right arm, preventing him from chugging the rest of the bottle. He wrinkled his forehead and narrowed his eyes. "But, now that you mentioned her, where does she live?"

"Would you believe next door?"

"You're not serious."

"You want me to knock on the wall. Crap, she can probably hear your voice through this thin plasterboard."

He let his mind go blank, not wanting to dredge up old memories of Cathy, not now. He took a long guzzle. "I hope you have lots of beer, my friend."

"Your old girlfriend could put it away with the best of them."

Rogers wanted to change the subject but found himself drawn in by the mention of her name and her close proximity to where he was now sitting. "The last I heard, she was in pharmaceutical sales."

Panini scrunched his face. "She's fallen on hard times—a tragedy in the family."

"Sorry to hear that." He took another swig but his mind began to wander. He refocused on the present moment and cackled, "Glad I'm here. I really needed this time away from the pressures of DC."

"The night is young. We've got a lot of fun ahead of us----a lot of fun."

Rogers gave Panini a high five. "Pass me another beer."

CHAPTER THIRTY-ONE

Nasters felt pensive. He could not stop the twitch of his right eyebrow as he studied a two-foot long spreadsheet listing of reported serious effects suffered by the Beijing subjects in the overseas *NeoBloc* human clinical trial. His cell phone rang out and he snatched it off the conference table on the first ring, angrily replying, "Hello."

"Brother Nasters." The voice on the other end of the line was deep, foreboding, and tense. He recognized the caller's heavy Pakistani accent

His heart raced. Before he could reply, the caller spoke. The voice dropped several octaves, almost to a whisper. "Do you recall what we told you in the mall?"

The scientist's mind flashed back-- as though he was once again in front of the eleven elders. He hesitated a moment, thinking of potential implications before speaking. "Yes. Remember the word 'MAD."

"Listen carefully. This is your last chance to save yourself."

Nasters shoved the spreadsheet away from him. He pushed off the cleared edge of the conference table and unsteadily rose to his feet.

"You must leave DuPont this week. No further warnings will be issued."

He held back his scientific proclivity to ask questions. "I will comply."

"We are pleased that you understand the grave danger that is about to strike."

His mind unscrambled the puzzle. *The D in MAD has to be Detroit.* He plopped back down in his chair, tightly holding his throbbing temples. *A nuclear detonation just forty miles away.* He coughed nervously. Clearing his throat, he asked, "May I ask whether we can meet before the coming event?"

Silence.

Nasters heard muffled sounds on the phone. A distant sounding voice seemed to be mumbling. He began to repeat his question. "Brother, can we---?"

"I heard you the first time." The voice hissed. "For what specific purpose do you want to meet with us?"

"I want to share my scientific work with you. I have a foolproof plan to kill all of the Americans. Our ends are the same."

The reply was curt. "We have been aware of your so called mass murder vaccine for some time now."

"Then you know that there is no doubt about the final outcome with *NeoBloc*"

"Brother Nasters, by past actions you have proven yourself worthy. We will meet at Turkey Hill Park at four tomorrow afternoon."

"Allah is great. We will meet as you say."

"Make sure that you come alone." A dial tone ended the conversation.

Nasters catapulted to his feet. *If the PFF nukes Detroit, the downwind spread of radiation will reach DuPont---our NeoBloc manufacturing plant. My jihad will be destroyed. I need to stop these terrorists.*

******

Nasters took off to the corner office in a semi-trot. The door was open. The boss looked up with a worried expression painted on his face.

"Connor, we need to talk."

Lucas cast a sideways looking glare. "Doctor, I see that you've developed a tic in your right eye. Upset about something?"

"Not enough sleep." He vigorously rubbed both eyes with his knuckles. "I just want to discuss getting *NeoBloc* deployed sooner than originally planned." The scientist walked to the conference table where his boss was sitting. He took a seat directly opposite the CEO.

"Before you launch into your crusade, I want you to know that I've already spoken to Dr. Ulrich, the chairman of the Independent Quality Review Board. I informed him that I decided to outsource much of our *NeoBloc* human clinical trial work to China."

Nasters held up both hands in front of him. "I must interrupt. I have critical news that you must hear."

His eyes crisscrossed. Gritting his teeth, he did not appreciate his colleague's abrupt interruption. *This better be good! I don't like surprises.*

"I have come upon top secret facts that could jeopardize our *NeoBloc* project."

The CEO stared into the scientist's intense brown eyes. "Doc, go ahead--unload your bombshell." His jaw tightened. "But what could possibly stop *NeoBloc*? We're in the process of neutralizing any and all opposition."

"I'm afraid that you are seriously mistaken. You do not know your real opposition."

"Don't ever talk to me like that. Look, you're really pissing me off."

Nasters sucked in a deep breath and exhaled slowly. "Permit me to explain." A deep frown now creased his forehead. "Let's just say that I have friends who could be problematic. I believe they will try to destroy *NeoBloc*."

"Hold on," Connor demanded. "You come in here and brazenly tell me that your friends want to hurt our launch of *NeoBloc*."

Nasters began to stutter. "They---they are not exactly friends."

Connor flailed both arms. "What the hell does that supposed to mean?" The boss scoffed, "Just give me their damn names."

"It won't be so easy, to defeat them."

Raising his voice, he hollered, "Never underestimate me." Connor sat up straight and tightened his necktie. "Never!!"

"Boss, I am as proud to be an American as you are. I would do anything for our country." Nasters puffed his chest. "But, hear me clearly. These people are extremely powerful and dangerous. You must understand what I am saying to you and fully accept it."

Connor bristled. "Spit it out. Who are these assholes?"

"In some parts of the world my so called friends would be hailed as Freedom Fighters."

"Fighting for what?"

"Their goal is the end of America, as we know it."

The CEO's face twisted in a bed of knots. Nasters locked his gaze onto Connor's bulging eyeballs.

"In fact, they are our mortal enemies. They are Pakistani Freedom Fighters. I befriended them to eliminate them. You must trust me."

"Don't parse words with me." He curled his lower lip. "You used the term friends to initially describe them."

"You are aware of the well known expression, "Stay close to your friends and even closer to your enemies."

"Do you expect me to just believe anything you say?" he blasted.

"I told you what I know. If you choose not to believe me, it's your choice." Waiting for a response, there was silence. He continued, "We have an opportunity to meet with the PFF tomorrow at four at Turkey Hill Park."

Connor rose and walked back to his desk, picking a rubber ball out of his top drawer. Squeezing the ball several times, he replied with a snarl, "OK, I'll play along with you. Game on doc. But, I'll be bringing along some added protection."

The scientist walked toward the door before sharply pivoting. "I almost forget to tell you." Nasters paused. "I was told to go alone."

Taking a seat, he replied, "Of course you will. Then your friends will meet a surprise party."

"You must not upset them. This rogue cell will tell their powerful leaders. They can have me killed if they know I am leading them into an ambush. You must trust me on this. Their superiors will find out whatever happens in the Park."

"Dr. Nasters, relax. Life is short." Connor guffawed, "Anyone can have you knocked off. Don't ever forget that." The CEO mischievously grinned. "And, I want to correct what you said earlier"

The scientist hung his head for a moment. Nasters then returned the hard stare of Connor. "Excuse me."

"It is you, Dr Nasters, who must trust me." He telegraphed a furtive look. "And, don't worry. Most of your friends will not leave the Park in an unhappy mood."

"Mr. Lucas, I do not want to be viewed by the PFF as disloyal."

"Unless I have your loyalty, you have nothing! Are we clear?"

"I understand."

Connor squinted. "I still sense that you're holding something back. Tell me now. Exactly what are your friends trying to do?"

His right sided facial tic reappeared. Uneasily, he replied, "The PFF has confided in me. I could be killed if anyone found I am revealing their secret plans."

"I will find out one way or another---and you know what I mean."

Nasters trembled and spoke so low that Connor had to strain to hear. He blurted out the secret. "The PFF has a plan to detonate a nuclear bomb somewhere in Detroit?"

"Is that so?" He spun his chair to face the side window, breaking eye contact. "And, how do you know about this nuclear bomb?"

"I have sources that must be unnamed."

"I'll just bet that you do."

"The PFF must be stopped."

"I admire your patriotism," he added with an extra helping of sarcasm.

"*NeoBloc* must reach every American. It will be the Savior of America!"

"I'll do anything to make that happen. Anything! Count on it!"

Nasters gave a half-smile. "I feel that I can trust you on getting *NeoBloc* to every American."

Connor pointed his finger at the scientist. "Just don't ever mess with me. For the record, I trust no one except myself. Is that clear Dr. Nasters?"

"It is clear!"

"See you at the Park, tomorrow at four."

******

Nasters, driving alone, pulled off the main road onto a dusty winding country path that led into Turkey Knoll Park. It was ten minutes before the scheduled meeting time. He drove down to the 3rd parking lot, located in the center of the Park. There, he would wait for a signal from his brother members of this particular rogue PFF cell. *They are misguided. Their approach will kill hundreds of thousands. My vaccine NeoBloc will kill two hundred million Americans. Allah will be much more pleased with my plan. It is far superior. After my talk with their leaders, the PFF will realize that I am right. They will turn to me and abandon their counterproductive nuclear plan.*

He recalled arguing vehemently with his boss against bringing any weapons to his meeting with his Brothers. But, he was hardly surprised that he had lost that debate.

The DCP security team would arrive an hour earlier. Yet, he was not told that his boss planned on hiding in the forest close to the Park meadow with his hand-picked team of two vicious mercenaries, just back from Iraq where they fought for Blackwater.

Nasters had his choice of parking spots in the empty lot. He parked, facing the spot where he would wait for the PFF. Donning his Detroit Tiger's baseball cap, he flipped up the collar of his blue woolen overcoat and buttoned the top button.

After he exited his Honda Civic, he walked over to a nearby cement bench located at the entrance to the Park, hoping that the Pakistani Freedom Fighters would soon present themselves.

Staring out at the Park's meadow, the eerie quiet was palpable. The stiff frigid winds were bone chilling. At any moment, snowflakes appeared ready to drop from the sky. The scientist lingered his sight at the line of swaying spruce trees that lined the rolling open meadow.

There was a glaze over the grass from last night's freezing rainstorm. For sure, there would be no soccer game today and no Frisbee throwing in the frost covered fields. Nasters pulled out a note from his inside jacket pocket. He silently reviewed his talking points, personally handwritten by himself just before he left to drive to the Park.

He checked his watch. It was now twenty-three minutes past four. He began walking across the meadow, deeper into the Park, away from the parking lot. Lost in melancholy thoughts about the recent slaughter of his own father, Nasters jerked around in one whirling motion when he felt a tap on his shoulder. Three turban wearing and heavily bearded men stood no more than three feet away. All of them were wearing black woolen shawls.

The man in the center took a full step toward him. "Brother Hussein Nasters, my name is Mugandi. I am the leader of this cell. You have requested to speak with us. We have traveled some distance to meet with you."

Nasters bowed. "The PFF and I are one. I have a plan that will accomplish your goals."

"Let us sit and we will listen," Mugandi added.

The DCP scientist uneasily sat down on the frozen earth. He faced the heavily wooded side of the forest. The members of the PFF sat directly across from him. Nasters tossed his baseball cap aside and kissed the ground before beginning. "One day, my brothers, this land will be ours. Our compatriots will inhabit these fields. Every American infidel will be dead."

Mugandi replied, "It is our dream as well. Have you abandoned your prior plan?"

"I am the chief scientist at a major pharmaceutical company----"

Interrupting, the leader said softly, "We know all of this. But, I assumed that you had more to your plan than just using your vaccine *NeoBloc*."

The younger looking brother at the far right spoke loudly, "You must destroy *NeoBloc*. It will save many Americans. We heard President Williams say so."

Nasters felt a chill rocketing down his spine. He wondered where his boss and the DCP security force were hiding. "It's not true. *NeoBloc is* a killer vaccine." Nervously, he craned his neck in all directions, searching for Connor.

"You do not look at peace, my brother," Mugandi retorted. "I hope you have kept your word and have come here alone."

Nasters's eyes fixated at the leader's dark brown globes. "In our monkey trials, every animal died within one year after receiving the compound. In the human trials underway in China, the initial people who took the vaccine have died."

The last of the brothers held up his right hand. "What you say makes no sense. Your government would never approve a vaccine that would kill all of the American people."

"That is where you are mistaken. Their clinical trial approval process is sometimes sloppy and controlled largely by the American political process and unfettered rapacious capitalism. Negative studies on many pharmaceutical products are submerged and never see the light of day."

Nasters tucked his hands under his legs to keep them from the biting frigid wind. "And, I have good news to share with you. My company has infiltrated the FDA process. We control some of their leaders. On our command, we delayed the human clinical trials in America. We have expedited the foreign trials. The data the FDA receives from the trials conducted in China will be rigged to show safety where none exists. I must repeat again, many paid enrollees in these countries have already died after receiving the *NeoBloc*."

Mugandi raised his right eyebrow. "Are you certain that no one knows about these deaths in the human trials in China?"

"Only I know the truth."

"I see." The PFF leader folded his arms across his chest. "But, what if this information leaks out?"

"Do not trouble yourselves. It will remain a secret," Nasters replied with a cocksure tone of voice.

"Ha! Eventually, many secrets are revealed---by someone."

Nasters smiled. "My plan will be kept under wraps until every American has been inoculated. By then, it will be too late. What I do know is clear. Americans will start dying over a period of nine to twelve months. The sickest, the immuno-compromised will be the first to die. Once the biologic process from the vaccine starts, nothing can stop it. All Americans will eventually die. There is no antidote." Nasters searched the suspicious faces of his PFF brothers.

Mugandi shook his head. "I'm afraid that we cannot trust your plan. Something could go wrong. Our plan is much simpler. We have weapons grade uranium." The PFF leader motioned for the others to stand.

After rising, Mugandi walked toward Nasters, stopping a foot from his face. "Your plan is flawed. We cannot trust the FDA to approve *NeoBloc*. Lastly, you must leave this area. We have previously explained the danger. The swirling winds will sweep this field with deadly radiation. You have seven days." The leader placed his hand on the scientist's shoulder, pressing down firmly. "Are my words clear, my brother?"

Nasters heaved his chest. "The political pressure to approve *NeoBloc* is unprecedented. It will be approved."

Mugandi's face tightened. "We heard the President say on television that the Surgeon General will need to sign off on the safety of the vaccine. Is Dr. Rogers on your payroll as well?"

"Dr. Rogers will not be allowed to interfere. You must trust me."

The PFF leader shot a look of disgust. "I trust only Allah! My decision is final." He began to breathe heavily. "My brother, drop to both knees."

The scientist complied without a moment of hesitation. He looked up at the leader's crimson face. Mugandi cocked his right fist and raised it high above his head.

"Please forgive me for trying to convince you to change your plan."

"It is not I who needs to forgive. The will of Allah is stronger than what any of us humans want. You are not trusting in Allah. Instead, you want us to trust you in your *NeoBloc* plan." Mugandi began backpedaling away from the scientist. "Only the will of Allah is important. It is my decision to cut off all ties to you brother Hussein Nasters. If you speak any further of this, your heartbeats will be numbered. We won't be deterred. What Allah wants will prevail."

Catching a hint of movement, Nasters's eyes drifted to the forest. He spotted Connor, in full gallop running towards them. Flanked on each side by two heavily armed bodyguards, his boss charged forward.

The fast closing trio was sprinting toward them, now merely thirty yards away from their pack. Amazingly quiet in their stealth like approach across the grassy meadow, Connor hand signaled to Nasters not to give away their advantage. The scientist's eyes shifted and remained glued on Mugandi.

Nasters replied, "As you wish. I hate the Americans as much as you do."

The PFF leader rested his hand on the top of the scientist's head. "It is too late. Speak no more. You have broken our trust in you. We will leave now. Do not attempt to contact us—ever again."

Nasters looked up.

"Don't move," Connors shouted.

The two lower ranking Pakistani's reached inside their coats. But, before they were able to face Connor and his men; the bodyguards fired a salvo of bullets. Three seconds later, only the PFF leader was unharmed. Red blood gushed out the mouth of one Pakistani. The shells blew away the face of the younger man. A minute later, they were both dead.

Mugandi raised his hands high in the air, glaring menacingly at the DCP scientist. "My instincts about you were correct. You set up this trap. You will pay dearly for your deception. Our plan will occur as planned, even without my presence."

The scientist trembled as his boss approached. Nasters saw the revengeful look in Mugandi's eyes. *It's over for me.*

Connor lowered his voice. "Guess what doc? I heard your whole conversation." He pointed to the inside pocket on the scientist's jacket.

Finding the microphone embedded in his right inside pocket, Nasters fearfully said, "Everything is not always as it appears."

"Is that so?"

"Do not go by what you may have heard. You do not know the context of my remarks."

"You said that *NeoBloc* will destroy America. You said that you hate Americans. That says it all!"

Nasters murmured to Connor, hand covering his mouth, "Those words were part of my ploy." He stammered, "But, before I explain, why did you----why did you shoot these men?"

"These pricks were going to nuke Detroit." Connor motioned for his bodyguards to tie the hands of the Pakistani leader before looking back at the scientist. "Did you expect a tea party? I did what had to be done. Now, Mugandi is my hostage." He motioned for one of his bodyguard to march the hostage toward the parking lot.

With Mugandi out of earshot, he pleaded, "Listen to me. I tried to fool them into believing that they could achieve their ends to kill

Americans by supporting *NeoBloc*. Don't you get it? I was lying just to get them to stop their plan to blow up Detroit."

"Bull shit!" He spat at the ground. "I warned you before about underestimating me."

Nasters cringed upon seeing the second bodyguard, on Connor's order; fire a few more rounds at the heads of the two dead Freedom Fighters. Suddenly, he felt as though a lightning bolt would emerge from the sky any second to strike him down. The hairs on the back of his neck bristled. *My fate is sealed. I am a dead man. Allah will never forgive what I have done.*

CHAPTER THIRTY-TWO

President Williams peered out at the gathered assembly in the House of Representatives Capitol Building Chambers. Three strategically placed nationally televised cameras were focused on her every move. The President glanced down at her Timex. Williams looked up, staring directly into the center camera. The countdown began. Seconds later, she received the start signal with a hand wave by the camera operator. After holding an unwavering furrowed brow gaze for three seconds, she cocked her head and began reading from the teleprompter to her right.

"Good evening my fellow Americans, Mr. Speaker and Mr. Vice-President. I've called together this special joint session of Congress so that I can communicate to you a critical message." Williams looked down for a second or two before meeting the center camera lens head-on. "We are all deeply saddened by the tragedies in Minneapolis and Atlanta. Our prayers go out to the families of those who have passed away and to those who are still suffering."

She angled herself to face the left teleprompter. "As Commander-in-Chief, I take full responsibility to keep America safe." Her eyes narrowed. "Let the cowardly terrorists hear me loud and clear. We will find you and we will eliminate you from the face of the earth."

Williams took a sip of water and looked into the center camera. "Ladies and Gentlemen, our intelligence community has uncovered our attackers. Once we get our hands on these terrorists, we will make them pay dearly for what they have done to our great nation."

Williams scanned the room. She turned on her heels to clear her throat with a forced cough. She instantly locked eyes with the Vice-President. Stockard was stone faced. Williams quickly shifted her sight. The Speaker of the House gave her a somber nod. The President turned back around to face the camera and members of Congress. Many representatives covered their mouths with their hands, whispering to each other.

Williams looked steadfast at the center camera. "Our scientists are well along in the clinical trials of *NeoBloc*. Many of my medical experts assure me that this vaccine will prevent tens of millions of future cancers that would have otherwise been caused by exposure of our citizens to high doses of nuclear radiation from the terrorist attacks."

This time, a round of louder clapping broke out in some pockets of the historic chamber. She began again before there was complete silence. "It is my intention to mobilize the private and public health communities to begin mandatory inoculations of every American with this vaccine. Mass vaccinations will begin as soon as human testing has been completed and *NeoBloc* has been safely approved by the FDA."

The clapping began again—now throughout the chamber. She looked at the center camera lens, mustering the passion to deliver the key lines of her speech. "American scientists have been working around the clock to develop this vaccine—a vaccine that will truly save millions of lives and hundreds of billions in resources." She took a quick breath and raised her voice. "Let me be clear. America will survive."

The entire assembly now rose to their feet. The applause was much louder and lasted twice as long as the first round. Williams gathered strength from the response. She searched for a particular face. The President gave a pointed wave to Senator Yarborough, who gave her a thumb's up sign.

"My fellow Americans, I've charged both my Surgeon General and the Secretary of Health and Human Services with ensuring that the vaccine is both effective and safe. Specifically, I will ask Dr. Jonathan Rogers to provide final sign off on the safety of *NeoBloc* before we begin mandatory mass inoculations of the American public."

Williams spotted Secretary James. His face had broken out into a broad smile. The President alternated with her side Teleprompters, changing from the left to the right during the further deliverance of her remarks. "Our Secretary of State has made great progress in building alliances with our allies and in opening up a constructive dialogue with countries that have not previously been in agreement with our anti-terrorist policy. France, Germany, Japan, and Italy have joined Israel and England to support our just cause."

Congress rose, adding a few loud cheers to punctuate the applause from both sides of the aisle. Williams raised her right arm and patted them down to silence.

"As a result of these initiatives, I promise you that we will get through this ordeal. We will get our economy back on track." Her voice suddenly soared. "Our country will be safe. We will prosper once again. Good night and God Bless America."

The roar from Congress rose to a deafening pitch. Turning around, she shook the hands of the Speaker of the House and the Vice-President. As she pivoted for one final wave to Congress, Williams felt a sense of calmness that she had not experienced in many months. *America is back! They trust me again!*

Williams reached into her inner suit pocket. She pulled out the neatly folded paper that Pitnar gave her just prior to her address. She glanced at it for the first time. The words TOP SECRET caught her eye. She quickly read the English translation of the bolded words that the FBI and CIA had decoded. These were the exact words spoken by the

Pakistani cell member arrested after the Atlanta bombing. *The bengal and the motors shall merge.* A chill hit her like a runaway locomotive. She looked up and met the watchful eye of a familiar Secret Service agent. Williams stuffed the confidential paper into her inner pocket and followed the agent down the steps to meet the newly upbeat members of Congress.

CHAPTER THIRTY-THREE

Driving his blue 2006 Chevy sedan, Rogers pulled out from a parking spot on the street near his daughter's apartment. Ashley had made a last minute decision to join him.

He was looking forward to meeting with Dr. Robert Woodhull of Weston & Weston. On his prior phone call, the CEO had impressed him with his sincerity. On a spur of the moment, just an hour earlier, he had made up his mind to take up the CEO's offer to come unannounced.

He glanced over at his daughter. She pulled down the vanity mirror and dabbed on a fresh coat of pale pink lipstick. Suddenly, he heard a series of loud clanging noises below his car's floorboards. He looked at the side rear mirror. Behind the Chevy, a gust of wind was blowing several beer cans down the barren street. Rogers took a long sigh. *Get a grip!*

After flipping up the vanity mirror, Ashley sat calmly. For now, she appeared unaware of the anxiety that raged inside of her father. "Dad, thanks for asking me to go with you today. Your invitation to join you sounded much more interesting than attending another elective class in radiology."

"Glad you could come. This should be an excellent learning experience for you." As soon as his words came out, he thought about what he just said. He hastened to add, "Are you sure that you can afford to miss today's class?"

"I'm sure."

Rogers accelerated down Main Street. "I hope that W&W's data is as good as Dr. Woodhull believes it to be." He looked over at Ashley, letting his gaze on her dwell for several seconds.

She shouted, "Dad, watch out."

He spotted the red light just in time. He slammed on the brakes, catapulting both of them forward against their shoulder restraints and stopping just a few feet in front of the overhanging light.

"Dad, I'm worried about you." She placed her hand on his shoulder. "I didn't want to mention it earlier. But, you seem so preoccupied---so intense."

Rogers stared at the red light, almost mesmerized. "Just a little," he finally admitted after the light turned green.

She patted his shoulder. "You must be feeling the pressure from what the President expects from you in taking the lead to uncover the truth about *NeoBloc.*"

Honk! Honk! He looked in the rearview mirror. The driver behind him was giving him the finger. He looked up at the swaying vertical traffic light. From the angry look on the face of the man driving behind him, the light was most likely green for several seconds. Quickly, he pounded the pedal. The Chevy burned rubber, leaving the pick- up truck far behind.

Ashley's hand lingered on his right shoulder. He reached over and patted her hand. "The Secretary of Health seems to be playing mind games with President Williams. It appears as though my boss has already convinced the FDA scientists and key opinion leading oncologists of the safety of *NeoBloc.* Many of them have already gone on record as saying that even if the monkeys died from the vaccine, it doesn't necessarily mean that the vaccine will kill humans. Now, they are saying there could be species differences in the way the vaccine is metabolized." He paused and shook his head. "That's an unbelievably naive statement."

"But, at least, President Williams trusts you."

He ignored her comment. "I fear that many of these so-called scientists are paid consultants for DCP. Ashley, the medical-industrial complex is out in full force to preserve the status quo of rapacious capitalism."

"You will make a difference."

He gawked at a passing motorcyclist who had roared between the two lanes of traffic, cutting in and out. "That guy is going to get someone killed. With my track record, it will be me."

"Will you please listen to me? The President believes in you."

He looked right at his daughter, now totally focused. "But she has many key advisors giving her misinformation. Somehow, I would bet that DCP has a role in these unscrupulous shenanigans. "

Ashley withdrew her hand from his shoulder. "What's the National Quality Board going to do?"

"Good question. I'm going to call Beth Murphy to find out the exact time of her next meeting. You and I both need to be there, to listen."

"Let's not forget one important point. In her speech to Congress, the President granted you final sign off on the safety of the vaccine."

He gave her a squinting sideways glance. *If I'm still alive.*

"Dad, what if you refuse to agree that the vaccine is safe? Will your objection hold up?"

Rogers winced, shielding his eyes from a bolt of sunlight that struck him square in his eyes. *Good question Ashley. Good question.* "Let's not get ahead of the process." He turned the wheel and drove up the driveway of W&W.

"I searched the W&W web site. Their compound is a monoclonal antibody that is very similar in chemical structure to *NeoBloc*."

"I've already checked with the FDA. Their monkey data is clean. But it could be another twelve months before they complete their human trials. They just started a month ago. My initial impression from my background check on them is that they're doing extremely careful research but they're not anywhere near as well funded as DCP."

***

Rogers stopped at the gatehouse and powered down his window.

The portly guard asked, "Can I help you?"

"Yes, I'm Dr. Jonathan Rogers and this is my daughter Ashley Rogers."

He studied his clipboard. "You're not on today's list of appointments."

"I was told that I don't need an appointment."

He flipped a page and looked up a few seconds later. "Sir, you are correct. You are on Dr. Woodhull's priority list. Drive up to the Weston C Building. You can park in the adjacent lot. Go through the main doors. A security officer will then escort you and your daughter to Dr. Woodhull's office. Meanwhile, I will let his assistant know that you're on your way."

******

A tall slender silver haired man in a dark blue blazer, gray slacks and a white buttoned down collar shirt greeted Dr. Rogers and Ashley just inside his corner office. Stern faced, he spoke in a rapid cadence. "I'm glad you took me up on my offer. We will accommodate you in any way we can."

Woodhull glanced over at Ashley, "I understand that this young lady is your daughter."

Rogers gushed, "My daughter is studying to be a physician. She's in the top ten percent of her medical school senior class at the University of Michigan."

"Glad you didn't do what so many physicians do when their children express an interest in going to med school."

"She clearly makes up her own mind."

The host grinned at Rogers. "Terrific. Welcome again to W&W." The CEO pointed to two seats in front of his desk. Woodhull sat down on his plush executive style chair and opened up a three-inch blue binder. "Here is our safety data on Compound 45962. It includes three years of animal data, with trials on both rats and monkeys."

He reached over and began skimming the first page. "I notice that the very bottom page is signed by a physician."

"It's a W&W standard safety precaution." Woodhull donned a pair of silver plated horn rimmed bifocals. He glanced at the bottom of the page. "I insist that our scientists provide me with a signed copy of the latest data. This binder is updated daily by our Chief Scientist and brought to my office by eight AM."

Rogers wrinkled his forehead. He slid the binder closer to Ashley so they could both read the report. He silently read the first paragraph of the executive summary before glancing up at Woodhull. "I see that you have started the human trials."

"We completed the animal testing six months ago. We're almost through Phase 1 of our human clinical trials."

Rogers kept on reading.

"As I told you on the phone, we are very safety conscious at this Company."

The Surgeon General shot a sideways glance at Woodhull. "I applaud your concern for safety. As you know, DCP has been fast tracking *NeoBloc*."

Woodhull peered over his bifocals at Rogers. "I must ask you something that's been on my mind for some time now. Rumor on the street has it that all monkeys who received their vaccine died. Are you at liberty to discuss whether it's true?"

The Surgeon General kept his eyes peeled on the binder. "I cannot confirm or deny that statement as that would be a breach of confidentiality." He paused a few moments, absentmindedly turning a few pages, no longer reading. He then looked up at Woodhull. "But, I'm very interested in your compound."

The CEO scratched his nose. "After you and your daughter finish scanning the data, you're welcome to walk around. When the security guard at the gate let you through, he notified my office. Just before I met the two of you, I sent out word to my staff to answer any questions that you and your daughter may have about our compound."

He winked at his daughter. "We'll certainly be asking a lot of questions."

Ashley leaned into the conversation. "Dr. Woodhull, I'd like to return to your earlier statement. Beyond it being just gossip or an industry rumor, do you have good reason to believe that *NeoBloc* is deadly?"

"It's a complicated subject. But in my opinion the short answer to your question is yes."

Rogers closed his eyes and remained silent. *And the Secretary of Health believes NeoBloc is the savior of all Americans. Worse yet, he has the President believing it as well.*

"Dad, I've been thinking."

"Bet I can guess about what."

Rogers flicked on the white set of lights wrapped around their five foot Douglas Fir. Near the top, he spotted the ornament that Kim had given him the previous Christmas. It was a figurine of a doctor in a white coat with a stethoscope hanging around his neck. *Kim was always hinting for me to go back into private practice.*

Ashley put her arm around his waist. Her eyes welled up. "I really miss Mom."

He kissed his daughter on her forehead. "That makes two of us." Turning away from her, he pretended to sneeze. He pulled a tissue from the box on the glass-topped coffee table. Swiping his nose and moistened eyes, he plopped down on the couch. "My allergies are acting up again."

Ashley sat down next to him and rested her head on his shoulder. Her voice cracked as she spoke. "I think I want to go into public health."

He frowned.

She cleared her throat. "Like you."

He stiffened.

Ashley picked up her head and sat up straight.

He rubbed his chin, looking kindly at her. "You know I'll support whatever you think is best. But, I must warn you that the public health arena has become extremely politicized. I don't know if I ever told you this." He glanced at the doctor figurine on the tree. "Your Mom always reminded me how much I missed my private practice patients." He rose and wistfully stared at the ornament near the pinnacle of the tree. "Before that awful day, she told me that she wanted me to resign my position as Surgeon General." He looked back at Ashley. "I should have listened to her. Maybe things would—." Rogers stopped before completing his thought.

She picked up an ornament of a brown reindeer out of the storage box on the floor. "I've already spoken to my advisor. I'm taking off the rest of this semester." She fastened the reindeer onto an orphan branch near the middle of the tree.

"I see that you're serious about this."

She nodded. "I've been given permission by the dean of my medical school to postpone taking my final classes until next fall. I will graduate with next year's class." She stepped back to admire the newly hung reindeer ornament. "Besides, my mind is just not into studies right now."

"I understand."

"I've been thinking about it ever since Mom passed away. Until my fall semester begins, I've decided that I want to work with you, to learn from you. Besides, with all that we've been through in the last year, someone needs to watch your back until you're able to veto *NeoBloc.*"

He reached into the box and pulled out a gold plated ornament. An intention tremor of his right hand appeared as he hung his favorite decoration on a thick branch. He had given it to Kim a few holidays ago--a plastic mold of two peas in a pod. It brought back a flood of memories.

"That's my favorite Christmas reminder of you and Mom." Ashley rested her hand on his shoulder. She stared at the family heirloom. "I hope one day that I'll find my soul mate."

"When the time is right, you will honey."

"I have my priorities."

Rogers backed away from the tree and faced Ashley. "Well, I'm happy to have you on board. Three days after Christmas, you can accompany me on my return visit to DCP. Beth Murphy went last time but she can't get the time off from work this week."

"Whom will we be meeting?"

"They have a new CEO, Connor Lucas. Their top scientist, Dr. Hussein Nasters, will be joining us as well."

He gawked at the star at the top of the tree. He inhaled deeply. The fresh scent of the Douglas Fir brought back happy memories of past Christmas holidays-----with Kim. He hugged Ashley. Kissing the top of her head, he prayed to God for forgiveness—for what he had not done to protect the love of his life.

******

Connor Lucas held out his hand for his guest. "Dr. Rogers, thank you for coming to DCP." Avoiding direct eye contact with the Surgeon General, Connor's eyes fixated on Ashley while still weakly grasping Rogers's hand. "And, who is this lovely young lady?"

The Surgeon General frowned. He quickly disengaged his hand from the CEO's and turned to his daughter. "This is my newest assistant--Ashley Rogers."

Connor's eyes glistened. His pearly white teeth sparkled in an ear-to-ear smile.

The Surgeon General took a step forward, partially shielding Ashley from the CEO. He whispered into Connor's ear. "You saw her at my wife's funeral. Stop pretending. You know, I'm very suspicious of how you got to be the CEO of DCP and your relationship with that woman—Haley."

The CEO maneuvered closer to where he was able to place his hand on the left shoulder of Ashley. He let his hand linger a moment. "I'm so glad she is here."

She took a few steps to her right, out of his grasp and spun around facing her father and Connor. Ashley seemed to be studying his face. "Have we previously met?"

"Not exactly." He sighed noisily and pointed in the direction of his chief scientist. "Let me introduce you to Dr. Hussein Nasters."

The top scientist walked toward the duo. He stopped a few feet away from them to give a slight bow at the waist. "It's nice to see you again Miss Ashley."

She graciously smiled.

The scientist then nodded at Rogers. "Good day, sir."

Fully conscious of the sheer phoniness of the moment, the Surgeon General took the lead. "Mr. Lucas, let's sit down at the table. We have a lot to discuss."

"Certainly." The CEO ushered the group into the adjacent fifteen by fifteen foot private conference room. Rogers took the seat at the head of the table. Ashley sat to his right, directly opposite Connor, who wore a gray flannel suit, white shirt, and bright red tie. Dr. Nasters, in his laboratory white coat, sat next to his boss.

Once seated, Rogers raised his right hand and spoke up, not waiting for any agreement on protocol. "My goal is to get an early start on the New Year. Hopefully, the strained relations between DCP and me can be put behind us."

Grinning at Ashley, Connor said, "We have already found common ground."

She pushed her chair away from the table as if creating more distance from her new admirer. She looked down and pulled her skirt to cover her knees.

The Surgeon General stared straight ahead. "I see that you follow the business channel," Rogers observed, spotting the large flat panel television screen built into the opposite wall of the conference room.

Connor leaned forward across the table. His dancing eyes surveyed Ashley from head to legs. "My job is to drive profits for DCP."

Ashley swiveled her chair to face her father.

He sensed her negative vibes toward him and twisted his torso to face Rogers. He finished his thought. "To maximize shareholder value----that's why they call me the boss."

The stock symbols streamed across the TV screen. The DOW was down over a hundred points. Rogers glanced back at his host. "Mr. Lucas, I want to ask you---"

The CEO held up his right hand, interrupting. "Please address me as Connor. Everyone else does."

Rogers shifted his sight to Nasters. "My daughter and I want to see the detailed *NeoBloc* human clinical trial data." He added, "All of it."

The scientist's face turned crimson.

Lucas reached over to pat the sleeve of Dr. Nasters. He then landed his gaze on the Surgeon General. "I want to be completely transparent with you. We have decided to outsource seventy-five percent of the human trials on *NeoBloc* to China. America conducts the remaining trials. So, to directly reply to your request, we don't have all the detailed data here but we do have the aggregate summary."

The Surgeon General asked, "Don't you request detailed data from the Chinese scientists?"

"Our mail has been delayed," he replied in a snarky tone.

Ashley pointedly asked Dr. Nasters, "What are your exact quality control processes in China?"

The scientist bristled at the question. "Miss Rogers, our Independent Review Board, National Quality, reviews all of our trials, both in the States and abroad."

Rogers followed up. "Does National Quality have staff that can make unannounced visits to the clinical trial sites in China?"

Nasters's eyebrows flickered up and down as he replied, "I trust that they do."

Connor rubbed his hands together, as if to create a distraction to the building tension. "Dr. Rogers, I have heard that your close friend Beth Murphy is a voting member of this Independent Review Board at National Quality"

"That is correct," he admitted.

"Then we can all rest assured that Beth will ensure that the Board will make the right decision."

He cocked his head. "She's just one vote. Besides, I personally want to see the facts. As you well know, President Williams expects no less than that from me."

Connor abruptly jumped to his feet. "Let's get started. Dr. Nasters, please escort our guests to your office to review the latest human safety data."

With a sharp edge to his voice, the scientist replied, "It will be my pleasure."

******

Dr. Nasters took his seat behind his desk as if he were taking a well-earned seat of honor on a throne. Sitting up as straight as a West Point cadet at dinner, he played with his neatly trimmed moustache. Clean-shaven with jet-black hair, flipped backwards on his head, he stood in stark contrast to the Surgeon General's gray mop of curly hair. A stack of a half dozen manila folders piled almost a foot high in front of the scientist partially hid his face. "Please sit down. Let me know what folders you want to see."

Rogers and Ashley took their seats directly across from the scientist. The Surgeon General changed the subject for the moment and inquired, "Where is Dr. Washington?"

Nasters gazed up at a rack of half a dozen diplomas, each framed in glass and evenly spaced on the wall adjacent to his desk. He stopped his scan to concentrate on the one degree that he earned in Pakistan. "I'm sorry to say that she has left our Company."

"Really! That's quite a surprise. The last time we were here, I was very impressed with her scientific rigor. I thought that you shared my impression."

"As they say in America, things happen." Nasters redirected his eyes to the folders lying on the table between him and his guests.

Rogers murmured under his breath, "You can say that again."

"Excuse me. What did you say?"

"Nothing."

"I accept your word." The scientist picked up the first folder from the top of the pile. He shoved it across the table toward Dr. Rogers. "I've prepared an updated executive summary of all the human trials, both here and abroad." He grabbed for the second folder and added, "In these documents, I have also collated scientific opinions from leading well respected researchers on the efficacy and safety of *NeoBloc* in the human trials."

Rogers exhibited a subtle smirk, watching the scientist trying to put on a believable show.

Nasters pushed over the thick folder with the testimonials toward him.

Ashley intercepted the first folder. She opened it and flipped through a few pages, curtly asking, "What methodology did you use in gathering this data?"

"Standard methods of a randomized trial," he replied in an even matter of fact tone.

The Surgeon General followed up. "How were these clinical trial members enrolled? Were they given the opportunity to opt out after they were given informed consent of the potential risks in participating in the trials?"

"All of the clinical trial subjects are volunteers who pass the customary screening criteria"

"It will save us all time doctor if you would answer my questions?"

"What are you implying?" Nasters asked.

"Don't the trial subjects get paid for allowing DCP to use their bodies to test *NeoBloc*?"

"Of course." Nasters's right eye began to twitch. His upper lip stiffened. "With all due respect, the data and the testimonials are all here. May I ask why you are so interested in these general questions?"

Rogers ignored his query. Ashley picked up the second folder and passed on the executive summary data of folder one to her father. He breezed through the early pages and pointed to the data on volunteer number twenty-seven. "I see that you have some detailed data on this volunteer from Beijing." He pointed toward one line of data. "Why has this particular volunteer lost ten pounds since he started taking *NeoBloc*?"

"Maybe he was overweight and went on a diet."

Rogers shook his head. "Overweight? He weighed only one hundred and fifty pounds."

The scientist's eyes bulged. "What are you getting at doctor?"

He flung the file onto the desk. "You know what I'm after----I want to know about serious adverse events that *NeoBloc* may have caused."

Nasters did not respond. He fidgeted with his collar, blinking repeatedly.

Ashley said, "You look upset."

"I am not upset. I am trying to meet your needs." The scientist's right leg bounced up and down.

"Dr. Nasters, why are you so jumpy?"

Nasters's thundered, "Listen Miss Rogers. I've been conducting clinical research for more years than you've been alive."

Rogers scowled. "Doctor, there is no need to talk in that insulting way to my daughter. And, you will recall that President Williams is counting on a final safety sign off from me before deployment of the vaccine."

The scientist gripped the table and gritted his teeth. "There are tens of thousands of our fellow Americans coming down with nuclear radiation induced cancer every year." He pointed at the strewn pages of data hanging out of the manila folder in front of them. "Here we have a vaccine that could prevent such horrible outcomes. You're a smart physician and yet you persist in asking annoying questions. Don't you see the true value of *NeoBloc*?"

Ashley stood. She placed her hands on her hips. "At least, we know the value of a human life."

Nasters slapped his hand down on his desk. His voice grew louder with each word. "Miss, what exactly are you saying?"

"*NeoBloc* is unsafe." Her chest heaved, pumped by the rising tension of the moment.

"You have no scientific evidence to support that claim."

"How can you deny the truth? Beth Murphy gave us the real monkey data signed by you. It demonstrated that every monkey getting *NeoBloc* died!"

Nasters slowly rose to his feet. "Secretary James has told President Williams that Murphy's data is bogus."

Rogers spoke up. "Quite frankly, with the untimely departure of Dr. Washington from DCP, I have no faith in your so called safety reports. And, I'm prepared to tell the President that DCP is no longer the only game in town."

"You must be referring to W&W." Nasters shot a disdainful look.

"Yes."

"But I hold a trump card. *NeoBloc* will be ready very soon. Our competition at W&W is many, many months behind. America cannot wait that long."

Rogers sprang to his feet. "Let's go Ashley." Walking out with his daughter, he pivoted, honing in on the twitchy face of Dr. Nasters. "Are you a God fearing man?"

"Yes, the will of Allah will always come to pass."

"I sincerely respect all religions. I don't know the details of the Koran but I do know the Bible. It says, "The first shall be last and the last shall be first." Rogers pulled back his shoulders. "And, I'm sure you know the story of the tortoise and the hare."

The scientist's face turned beet red. "You're playing with fire if you try to sabotage the inoculation of every American with *NeoBloc.* "

"Don't fool with me. I'll always do what is right for the American people. It won't be the first time; nor will it be the last," Rogers retorted.

"The President will be disappointed if you try to block the vaccine."

Rogers cast a steely stare at Nasters. "I have one final question for you. Since you so adamantly believe that *NeoBloc* is the savior vaccine, why don't you take it yourself?"

The DCP scientist glared at Rogers. "The vaccine is for the Americans. I don't want to waste even one dose."

Rogers wagged his finger. "That's a strange statement. I thought that *you* were an American!"

The DCP scientist turned his back on Rogers and Ashley. "I'm a naturalized citizen."

They hastily left the conference room. The last to leave, the Surgeon General slammed the door behind them.

CHAPTER THIRTY-FOUR

Connor Lucas commanded that the Secretary of Health sit down. He glared at James from across his office desk. The CEO had already made his decision.

Christian James blinked nervously. "It was a good thing that you had a microphone bug sewn into the inside pocket of Nasters's overcoat."

"Would you have expected anything less from me?" Connor smacked his hands together. "It's obvious that this so called scientist is a freakin madman." He pointed to his head and let his eyes roll back. "Look, I fully expected that *NeoBloc* would have its usual share of minor side effects just like any other biologic product. But, after hearing what he said to the PFF, I snuck into his office one night after he left the building. I found his personal notepad." Connor leaned across his desk and shoved it in front of the Secretary's face, several inches away from the tip of his nose. "Guess what? His notepad gives the details of nineteen deaths, so far, in the *NeoBloc* human clinical trials in China----- out of four hundred and twenty six volunteers."

He threw the note pad across the room, striking the far wall near the base. He hollered, "I may be a lot of things but I'm certainly not a mass murderer of Americans."

His face grew whiter by the second. "Then we have a major problem. Congress, the business community, scientists from the FDA, and to a great extent, the President herself; they are all publicly committed to full deployment of *NeoBloc* to every American."

The Secretary pushed off the arms of his chair, lifting him to a standing position. He began walking in a semi circle around half the perimeter of the room, careful not to walk behind Connor's space.

He blasted, "James, I'm holding you accountable for this mess. Fix these problems or else."

"What about me? I've personally assured the President that the vaccine is safe. My credibility is gone. How am I supposed to convince anyone of anything?"

Connor growled, "Stop pacing. Think!"

The Secretary of Health stopped on a dime. He slammed his eyes shut for a few moments. "Rogers was right all along about *NeoBloc*."

"Just sit down," he snapped. "I've been thinking about our next steps. Weston & Weston is our best option. They have a vaccine in their pipeline very similar to *NeoBloc"*

The Secretary strode toward his seat. He slouched down and held his hand to his forehead. Eyes closed, he mumbled, "How could I have been so dumb?"

Connor ignored his gratuitous attempt to grab some pity. "And, the good news from the word on the street is that their vaccine is actually safe in the early human trials that they began last month."

Mindlessly, James replied in a monotone cadence, "How does that help us?"

"Wake up, you dumb ass!!"

The Secretary sat upright, slapping his face, as if to loosen the cobwebs that were clogging his brain. "I'm sorry."

"OK. Here's my plan. DCP executes a hostile takeover of W&W. We then fast track their research. We then own a safe vaccine that makes us tens of millions. Simultaneously, we do away with both Nasters and *NeoBloc.*" Connor sat back, flexed his hands and cracked his knuckles.

James shook his head. "Why would W&W sell out to DCP?"

"They wouldn't." He laughed. "I have other ways."

"Like------?"

Picking up a ballpoint from his desk, he fired it at James, striking him in the chest. "Like why don't you mind your own damn business?"

"Why do we have to kill Nasters? Why not just turn him into the authorities?"

"So he can finger us?" Connor scrunched his face. "I don't take chances like that. I like closure on all problems---final closure. No witnesses."

The Secretary's face turned beat red. "I don't like the direction we're taking. Money, political influence, and power are one thing but I never signed on to be a murderer."

Connor fired off one of his patented well-rehearsed sinister looks. "It's too late to weasel out now. You're in so deep now that you had better just accept your fate."

James dropped his eyes to the floor. Beads of sweat gathered on his forehead.

"Either you are with me or against me."

The Secretary looked at him but remained motionless.

"I appreciate your honesty. I've got work to do."

"I need to say my prayers," he said disconsolately.

******

Connor rapped on the door of the scientist's private office. He listened carefully. There was no response. He turned the doorknob slowly. The door swung open.

To his amazement, Nasters slouched behind his desk. The scientist's head drooped to one side. His eye sockets appeared sunken and his right eye blinked repeatedly in a staccato manner.

Connor straightened his dark blue suit and walked toward him, wishing that he had a silencer on the Glock that was strapped around his left shoulder under his jacket. He mockingly said, "Just what I need--a drunken scientist!"

Nasters glanced up, tried to stand; but collapsed back into his chair with a heavy thud. Yawning, he leaned forward to grab the near empty beer mug from his desk. After slurping a sip, he asked, while slurring a word or two, "What can I do for you?"

"You can't do a damn thing." Connor pulled up a chair and sat down. "Hey doc! You know what? You look like crap."

Nasters held his hand over his eyes as if they were eyeshades, the green colored ones frequently worn at poker games, and tried to steady his gaze on his boss. "In my faith, we do not abuse our bodies with alcohol."

"You're a disgrace to Islam. You're nothing but a drunken would be mass murderer."

Nasters vigorously rubbed his face. "What are you talking about? I never hurt anyone. Look, I came in at four this morning. I've been on the phone since then, talking to our scientists who are running the *NeoBloc* trials in China."

"The days of your bull shit have run out doc."

"I only opened this one beer thirty minutes ago."

"Then you have a pretty low tolerance for alcohol, judging from the way you look."

The scientist clumsily tried to sit upright in his chair. "Did you come here to insult me?"

"Let's talk business. So, are the clinical trials in China on schedule?" Connor pushed his chair closer to the desk. "Are there any atypical findings?"

The scientist grabbed his beer mug and tried to take another gulp but came up dry.

"There were just some usual side effects."

"Such as?"

"We found cases of decreased appetite and weight loss."

Connor chuckled. "Are you suggesting that DCP markets *NeoBloc* as a weight loss product?"

"I'm trying to be serious."

Quickly pulling out the scientist's private notepad from his pocket, he laid it quietly on the floor, slowly shoving it underneath the scientist's desk with his foot.

He shouted, "I want to change the subject! Where is the elder member of the Pakistani Freedom Fighters? The one you captured----"

"Calm down." Connor laughed aloud, slapping his knee several times. "Now, you're sounding like you've even become afraid of your own shadow."

Nasters demanded, "I want to know. Where is Mugandi?"

The CEO jumped up and stood behind his chair. "Listen to me carefully. I plainly heard what you told the PFF at the Park."

Nasters stretched his arms high above his head. "I told you at the field why I did that. That was only to get them to stop their terrorist plans to detonate another nuclear bomb." He clenched his jaws. "So I could gather further intelligence to hand over to the American government."

Connor sneered, "You're a damn liar." He looked down at the simple frame wood chair. Giving a soccer style boot to it, the chair crashed into the front of Nasters's desk. He picked it up and slammed it to the floor, cracking off two legs. "Look, I know for a fact that nineteen people in China died after taking *NeoBloc*. You hid this from me. Hear me loud and clear, there will be personal consequences for what you have done."

Nasters dropped his head. "You refuse to believe me, a world -wide expert on these scientific matters. Instead, you choose to accept half-truths."

The CEO cast a scornful look at the scientist. "I warned you before. Don't fuck with me!" He heard Nasters mumbling under his breath. *'Where is my notepad?'*

"Oh, by the way, Mugandi wanted me to pass his hello on to you. Yesterday, I spoke with him in our secret location where we are holding him captive. He was placing a phone call to some of his colleagues----- in Pakistan. You might say that he was chatting to your former colleagues—about you."

Connor walked out the door, banging it behind him before slowly re-opening it. Peeking back into the room, Nasters's face was now a whiter shade than freshly fallen snow. Kneeling down, below his desk, the scientist was pulling his notepad toward him.

"Hey doc, I already read it! By the way, I forgot to mention that I overheard Mugandi say to his friend that you and I had killed a few of his Pakistani Freedom Fighting colleagues. Hope his people in Pakistan realize that it was just strictly business for me."

His jaw quivered while tightly gripping his notepad in his trembling hands. With darting eyes, he stared in terror at his boss.

"Your big shot terrorist friend is super pissed! He takes what you did as personal. Watch your back doc."

CHAPTER THIRTY-FIVE

The President hurriedly walked into the Oval Office. Rogers and his daughter were already sitting on the low-backed soft couch. Williams took her customary seat in a high backed red upholstered antique chair.

"I have only a few minutes." She shifted her eyes to Ashley. "I'm glad that you were able to join us. I have wanted to meet you for some time now. Your father speaks of you in glowing terms."

He looked proudly over at his daughter. "President Williams, thank you for inviting her. Ashley is helping me out these days. She wants to be a public health advocate."

Williams smiled at the younger Rogers.

"Madame President, I'm pleased to meet you as well." Ashley reached over and touched her father's hand. "He's the best."

"There is no doubt that he is the best public servant I have ever seen. I completely trust your father." The President now focused her gaze solely on the Surgeon General. "Tell me how the human trials with *NeoBloc* are progressing."

"Well, so far, we haven't discovered any deaths as we did in the monkey clinical trials." Rogers glanced over at his daughter. "But, Dr. Nasters was very evasive when Ashley and I pointed out some potential red flags in the human clinical trials."

"Such as?"

"Unexplained weight loss for one. And, there may be another hitch. China is conducting most of the *NeoBloc* human trials. I worry whether there will be sufficient oversight by any Independent Review Board in that country. A friend of mine, Beth Murphy, sits on our National Quality IRB Board. They oversee DCP operations in North America but have no jurisdiction on clinical trials ongoing in China. I suspect that their CEO, Connor Lucas, outsourced to China not just to save money."

"My understanding is that many American pharmaceutical companies are outsourcing clinical trials to China and India." Williams glanced down at her watch. "I'm sorry but I have a national security meeting." The President stood and extended her hand. Ashley warmly shook her hand.

Williams walked toward her desk. He followed close behind, noting that she picked up a folder titled 'Top Secret" from her desk. She spun around to face him. "Do what you need to do." Glancing at his daughter, she said, "Hope to see you again Ashley."

"Thank you, Madame President."

Williams turned toward the Surgeon General. "Remember, I have publicly announced that you will need to give final sign off on *NeoBloc*. The public trusts you and I do as well."

"Madame President, thank you for your confidence in me but I think I have a bulls -eye painted on my back."

Williams looked at the Oval Office door. Rogers and Ashley took the hint.

When both of them were nearly halfway out the door, the President asked, "By the way, have you ever attended a board meeting at National Quality---to observe how they conduct their oversight of the North American clinical trial reviews?"

"Ashley and I are going to their next meeting."

Williams picked up her desk phone. She waved to Rogers and his daughter. "Report back what you learn."

******

Rogers heard a series of knocks on his door. It was ten 'o clock. He had just gotten into bed and wondered who would be stopping by at this time of night. He slipped on his blue and white robe and shuffled his way to the door. A much louder singular knock soon followed. He stuck his eye into the peephole. A fair-skinned middle-aged blond haired woman wearing a slight smile was looking straight ahead.

He did not recognize her. "Who is it?"

Her reply was gentle but firm. "Cathy Parker."

Cathy Parker. How many years has it been? Rogers snapped open both of the dead bolt locks. The door opened, apparently pushed by his visitor. He ogled her striking hourglass figure. Her bright pink cocktail dress with a plunging V neckline somehow seemed out of place. *She's still a knockout!* Her blue eyes playfully danced. Her pearly white smile that seemed painted on her face was far different from the days when she wore braces well into her sophomore year in college. He remembered how they both changed when he entered medical school. Their interests began to drift apart. He broke up with her during his internship. A month later, he met Kim on a "blind date" and they married less than six months later.

"Well, are you just going to gawk at me in the hallway or are you going to invite a former lover into your apartment."

He snapped out of his daze. "I'm so sorry. It's been so long since I've seen you. I was just going to bed. I must be sleep walking—or something. Come in."

"I tried calling earlier but all I got was a busy signal."

He nervously replied, "The receiver must have been off the hook."

She held out her arms. "Where's my hug?"

Rogers gave her a halfhearted embrace. A quizzical look took hold on Cathy's silky smooth face as he quickly broke their weak clinch to close the door.

Motioning for her to come into the kitchen, he asked in a polite tone, "Would you like something to drink?" He pulled out one of the wooden captain chairs for himself but remained standing. "Cathy, please sit."

In a somewhat annoyed voice, she replied, "A glass of Cabernet would be fine."

He dragged his feet to the wine cabinet. After selecting the right bottle of wine, he carried it over to the counter. "So, what brings you to DC?"

She snapped, "Business."

He used the corkscrew to open the wine and poured the Cabernet into crystal wine goblets for each of them. Once he sat down across from her, he handed her the half-filled one. He offered a toast with his own goblet, filled with no more than two ounces. "Cheers, to good health."

"How boring!" She looked at him seductively. Parker added, "To former lovers."

Rogers set his goblet on the table without actually taking a sip and brushed back his thinning silver hair. He found himself drawn to her full red lips. She quickly drained her goblet.

Parker pointed at his glass. Her eyes sparkled. "I could use another drink but only if you take your first sip."

While pouring the wine into her glass, Rogers felt her sight watching his every move. Her presence was so palpable that he felt a fine tremor of his right hand.

"Jonathan, this time fill mine to the brim." Her voice was gentle and soothing.

He carried out her request and soon took his first sip. Avoiding eye contact with Cathy for more than a few seconds at a time, he glanced up at the kitchen wall clock. *Why is she here?*

"Are you feeling all right? Panini told me you've been through a lot. As you know, he's a neighbor of mine."

Rogers held her gaze for a while before responding. "Panini?" He then gulped down whatever remained in his goblet. "What a coincidence. I hadn't seen him for decades. We lost touch."

Cathy reached out for his hand, resting hers on the back of his hand. "Just like you and me Jonathan." She winked. "We lost touch but here we are—together in your apartment."

He pulled his hand back and picked up the wine bottle. This time he filled his own goblet to the rim. Taking a quick swig, he searched her face. *I'm in no mood for romance lady.*

"Anyway, I've come here to talk about my brother."

He tried to recall Cathy having a brother. He wracked his brain. Then he remembered a much younger boy who always was riding his bike anytime Rogers hung out at her house. "Yes—I remember now. I think I've met him a few times in the old days back in New York. While we were dating before I met---."

Parker sniffled. "My brother and I have gotten very close over the years. He helped me financially when times were rough." Her lips stiffened. "By the way, you know him. You spoke with him not too long ago."

His mental Rolodex sprang into high gear. "Sorry but I'm drawing a blank."

"In fact, you saw him recently. Sean-----Sean Parker."

His hand inadvertently tipped over the nearly empty bottle of wine. A ruby colored pool spilled out onto the balsa wood table. Somewhat ironically, drops of red blood came to his mind. He grabbed a dishcloth from the sink and wiped up the mess while thinking about his prior tense encounters with Sean Parker.

Her face grew somber. "You once met him when he was the CEO of Doctor's Choice Products."

After sitting down, he just shook his head. "He was so young."

"Far too young to have this calamity happen to him." Cathy again reached out for his hand.

He quickly pulled away from the table, leaning back on his chair. "I'm so sorry. The Oldwyck Gazette ran a front-page story of his misfortune. Freak accidents----who could have imagined an accident like a crane falling on him on a city street. You just never know these days."

Her face toughened. "It was no accident. Jonathan, he was murdered."

"What do you mean?"

"He was killed based on a direct order from Zach Miller."

The Surgeon General jerked his head backwards. "Zach Miller? Several years ago, he was blown to shreds in that car accident out by the airport."

She firmed up her eyebrows. "No my friend, he is very much alive and king of the hill---just like the old days.

"How do you know?"

She telegraphed a confident knowing look. "I know."

Oh my God! "That's impossible!"

"I'm telling you the truth. A day before he was killed, Sean called me. Through a slip up---a leak in *The Health Club* communiqués, my brother discovered that Zach was back in Michigan."

Rogers felt like Cathy just dropped kicked him in the stomach. For several years, he had feared that Zach was still alive—especially when the police never found the body of the former leader of The Health Club after the Ferrari that he was driving had exploded after flipping over multiple times while careening down a steep hill. He rubbed away the discomfort on his chest wall—feeling his heart fluttering a few beats. "If you're right about Zach being alive---."

"Take it to the bank dear. He's back."

"Where is he?"

She shivered. "Close by."

Zach Miller! His past flashed before him. Rogers rubbed his temples, wondering how he had somehow survived so many near death experiences---multiple orders to kill him—contracts from *The Health Club*. "Are you sure?" Rogers shuddered.

"There is no doubt in my mind. Look, Zach had Sean killed so he could take over again as CEO of DCP."

"But his Ferrari exploded." The Surgeon General stared at her, not wanting to believe her words.

Her steady eyes confirmed her words. "Trust me!! Zach is now the CEO of DCP."

Rogers blinked several times. "No. Connor Lucas is the CEO!"

"Please listen to me. Sean knew too much. That's why he was killed. Connor is Zach!! His appearance was changed by significant plastic surgery that he had done in Belize."

Suddenly, Rogers could only think of Kim and Ashley. His vocal cords froze. He remained speechless as her words repeatedly echoed in his mind. *Connor is Zach! Connor is Zach!*

CHAPTER THIRTY-SIX

Rogers opened his apartment door. He was pleased to see her quick response to his earlier voice mail. "Beth, it's so good to see you."

"I came right from the hospital."

Entering, she held on to his warmer than usual hug. Rogers lightly kissed her on the cheek.

"Jonathan, I was sorry that I couldn't make the last trip to DCP with you."

"That's okay." He pursed his lips. "Ashley helped me out. But I sure could have used you. Their new CEO, Connor Lucas, is much worse than Sean Parker."

Beth cocked her head a notch. "You can tell that already?"

"It's a gut feeling." Rogers motioned for her to join him at the kitchen table. "Listen, I need to be at your next National Quality Board meeting?"

"It's this Thursday at one PM."

"President Williams suggested that I attend." He pulled out a kitchen chair for Beth around the balsa wood table. "By the way, I had an interesting visitor last night."

She pulled back her medium length brown hair, holding it in a temporary ponytail. "Who was it?" She sat down, arms outstretched across the table.

He took his seat and replied, "An old girlfriend."

She did a double take. "Really." In a heartbeat, she crossed her arms across her chest. "Sounds like your social life is picking up."

"Hardly," he chuckled. "She is a neighbor of a close friend whom I hadn't seen in years. His name is Joey Panini. We were friends growing up in New York. I just recently reconnected with him."

Beth chirped, "Looks like you hit the jackpot. You found a former pal and a former girlfriend." She took off her crème colored glasses and fiddled with them.

Rogers sensed her sarcastic tone. "Anyway-----this woman is the sister of Sean Parker."

"The same guy who was the former head of DCP?"

"Bingo."

A puzzled look emerged on her face. "It's a small world." She unfolded her arms and then pushed her chair a foot away from the table. "The suspense is getting to me," she chided. "And her name is?"

"Cathy Parker." Rogers broke eye contact for a few seconds, looking down at his perspiring palms. "She claims that her brother had once confided in her that he was afraid that he would be a target because of his top position."

She scrunched her face, now more curious than jealous. "And so what is the rest---?"

"You won't believe it."

She snickered, "Hanging out with you for the past few years, I'll believe anything."

"Zach Miller ordered the hit on Sean Parker."

Beth put on her glasses so that they were half way down her nose. "Zach's dead." She peered over the top of her glasses.

"So we thought."

Her complexion flipped to pale. She jumped to her feet. "I don't believe it."

"It's true. Cathy Parker knows that Connor Lucas is Zach Miller."

Beth began pacing the kitchen. "Where's her proof?" She looked over at him with a hard stare.

"She had none."

Beth stopped pacing. "So let me get this straight. An old girlfriend comes over to your apartment and says Zach is alive and you instantly buy her whole story." She placed her hands on both hips in a defiant manner. "Jonathan, you're too smart to swallow this tale."

"I've thought about this all day. She has no reason to lie. Cathy was always straight with me---in the old days. We were very close."

"I'm a little surprised that you said that." Her voice had a snarky inflection. "So you believe her----this Cathy Parker?"

"I don't know for sure." He held his chin in one hand. "But she is completely convinced that her brother was murdered so that Connor Lucas could take over his job as CEO."

"Why would she think that?" She yanked off her glasses and stuffed them in the outside pocket of her nursing uniform. "It sounds to me that she is grasping at straws and is delusional."

He rose to face her. "I don't think so."

"By the way, Jonathan, did Cathy also tell you the moon was made of cheese?"

"Seriously, from what she told me, Sean had picked up some signals through *The Health Club* grapevine that Connor was bucking for his job."

"How is that?

"You know that Sean Parker was once a close confidant of Zach's--- in *The Health Club*. He was, as they say, connected."

She pointed her index finger at him. At five foot eleven in her flat nurses' shoes, Beth was only a few inches shorter. She looked him squarely between his green eyes. "None of this proves that Connor is Zach."

He motioned toward her chair. "Please sit down. We've got more to discuss. Can I get something for you to drink?"

"Well, I could use a beer after your bombshell."

Rogers grabbed two cans from the refrigerator.

Beth stared at the kitchen clock, high on the wall. She blurted out, "To be perfectly honest, I need to come clean myself on something that I haven't told you."

"What's that?" He sat down and pushed her can toward her.

"You're now the second person who told me that Connor is Zach."

His eyes bulged. "After all that you said about Cathy being delusional?"

"Marissa, the roommate of Dr. Virginia Washington, said the same thing."

"Then why were you so surprised when I believed Cathy's story?" Rogers popped his beer can open a second after Beth did the same. "By the way, before I forget, have you spoken lately to the good doctor?"

"I called Virginia a couple of times but she didn't return my calls."

"That's strange. I thought that the two of you were developing a good relationship."

Her face flushed. She took a sip of beer. "I'm getting really nervous about this." Her eyes suddenly welled up.

"You know---you're not the only one who feels that way."

As soon as he said the words, he wished that he hadn't. A tear dropped onto Beth's cheek. She swiped it away, seemingly upset with herself for letting him see how she was feeling.

"Beth, I'll do whatever I can to protect you."

She countered in a flash, "That doesn't make me feel better. You attract killers as honey attracts bees. Who the hell is going to protect you?"

"Hey, I knocked off a professional hit man in self defense," he cackled. "I've survived gunshot wounds, a near drowning in a river, and a false imprisonment to name just a few." Rogers grinned. "I wonder if I could try walking on water."

The tears on her face only increased. She pulled out a tissue and blew hard.

He deeply knitted his eyebrows into a series of furrows. "Trust me. I'll keep us safe---and Ashley as well."

"I hate to say this to you," she said with a painfully obvious reluctance. "It's been on my mind since the funeral." She clenched her teeth. "Please forgive me but you once told Kim to trust you—that everything would be fine."

Rogers looked away.

"I'm sorry I said that."

He hung his head. "You're right. I did fail Kim." He extended his arms across the table. He saw Beth doing the same until their knuckles were almost touching. Looking up, he picked up a gleam in her eyes that he had never seen before. Her dilated pupils sent him an instant message of what Cathy was thinking. Rogers jerked his hands back. "But it's different now. I'm ready for the next attack." Interlocking his fingers around the back of his neck, he thought of his well-concealed semi-automatic pistol as he nervously darted his eyes about the apartment.

She picked up her beer can. "So if you're confident that we'll be safe----." Beth took a long swig. "Why do you seem so agitated?"

"There is more bad news that I haven't told you."

"Well! It seems like both of us have been holding back things from each other."

"It's my fault. This is my mess."

"What do you mean?"

"I should have told you earlier but I recently found out that DCP released Dr. Washington. Nasters said it was just a routine reduction in force."

"That sounds awfully fishy to me."

He nodded.

"Is that all?"

"Just about—I guess that's it." Rogers cast his eyes downward, blinking wildly.

"Jonathan, you're still holding something back—something is eating at you deep inside." Beth searched his face. "I can tell," she said softly.

All that he could think about was stopping the approval of *NeoBloc*. He reflected a moment. "Oh yeah, there's one more thing. Ashley and I went to see the President a few days ago to give her an update. In reviewing the human clinical trial data with Lucas and Nasters, we found a clear case of unexplained weight loss in one study participant."

"That's not what I meant." Her eyes cut sharply away from his.

"Beth, my only concern is this damn killer vaccine."

She rose to her feet, quickly backpedaling towards the door. "So I guess I'll see you at the National Quality Board meeting."

"Ashley and I will be there."

"We'll be reviewing all the *NeoBloc* human data and sending a preliminary report to the FDA."

She already had her hand tightly wrapped on the doorknob, her back angled away from him. Rogers stood. He quickly strode toward her. "Beth thanks for talking with me."

She released her grip on the knob and turned around, directly facing him. "And, there's one more thing that I want to say." She forced a half-smile. Her facial color seemed to have returned. "I'm really worried about you?"

"I'll be fine." He put his hand on her shoulder. "By the way, you'll find out at the National Quality meeting that DCP has outsourced three-quarters of their clinical trials---to India and China."

"Well, aren't you just full of surprises today?" Beth threw her hands in the air. "Is that why you invited me here tonight—just to tell me information?"

"File it away for your Board meeting."

She coldly replied, "Next time just shoot me a text message."

"I didn't mean it that way." He drew closer. "Beth, I know one thing."

"And that would be?"

"I need you---I mean I need your help to solve this *NeoBloc* riddle. Please help me find Virginia Washington."

She pretended to salute him. "Yes sir, doctor general. I will carry out the mission. Business must be tended to at any cost." She rubbed her nose. "Good night Jonathan." Yanking open the door, she appeared to fly through the doorway.

Without success, Rogers tried to get out the words. "Good nigh---."

CHAPTER THIRTY-SEVEN

With the frosty air turning her exhalations into puffs of white smoke, Beth descended the steep flight of stone stairs. She buzzed the rusty doorbell. A not so friendly dog's bark startled her. While the growling grew louder, she instinctively thrust her hands in her deep coat pockets, lest the door open and the canine jump out at her for a few nibbles, an afternoon snack.

She waited. The blue wooden door needed a fresh coat of paint. There was no address number anywhere in sight. Judging from the 4B placard on the street level apartment above, she was most likely standing at the basement door of apartment 4A.

Her call to the administrative assistant at DCP who has previously supported Dr. Virginia Washington had directed her to this location. The AA had bought Beth's story that she was a close friend based upon what she knew about Virginia's special craving for expensive shoes. To find out where Virginia lived, Beth revealed additional details about what she already knew about the scientist's job title and duties at DCP. Under an absolute promise to keep it a secret, the assistant reluctantly gave out this exact address.

She again buzzed the doorbell. It brought on an even louder series of growls. Beth shivered. Her white smoke breaths spewed from her mouth in the sub-zero wind chill temperature. She turned around to crane her neck upward. Cars and trucks whizzed along the avenue, repeatedly honking their horns. In less than a minute, Beth witnessed several episodes of "road rage" that only added to her building anxiety. Combined with the continuous dog barking inside the apartment, she could barely hear herself think.

Amid the clamor, Beth banged on the splintered well-weathered door with her mitten-covered knuckles. A chip of blue paint flew off. Her eyes roamed. Mostly junk mail stuffed the mailbox on the adjacent wall. She was able to tease out a DuPont Public Service electric bill-- addressed to Dr. Virginia Washington at Apartment 4A.

She climbed up the stone stairs to the sidewalk. For no particular reason, she lingered on the avenue. A side alleyway caught her attention when a chime hanging from the porch of Apartment 4B rang out. She walked over and took several steps into the alley. The afternoon sun streamed through the four-foot wide space between Virginia's building and the adjacent brownstone. Out of the wind and protected by the shelter of the buildings, the sun partially warmed her.

Beth peeked into a narrow window just above the brown dirt stained alley pavement. She spotted a black and white border collie prancing around the kitchen. Saliva drooped from the dog's mouth, interspersed by a series of noisy howls. She recognized the dog. It was Bootsie; the same dog that Marissa had tied up in the van. The collie jumped up onto the kitchen chair before leaping onto the table, knocking over a saltshaker.

Out of the corner of her eye, Beth saw an ill-defined shadow on the ground around her. She looked again though the window. Bootsie was now staring back at her, in utter silence. She glanced back at the shadow. It was moving along the ground. Before she could turn, she felt a hard blow to the top of her head. Instantly, the shadow and Bootsie both vanished from sight as Beth lost consciousness.

***

The pounding in Beth's head was intense. She opened her eyes and realized she was lying in a bed. The panting of a familiar sentry was nearby as Bootsie lay no more than two feet away from her. His brown eyes glued on her, almost daring her to move, he appeared eager to spring into action if she dare look directly into his eyes.

A wall mirror over a cherry wood dresser hung directly on the wall in front of her. She tried to get up but her hands and legs would not budge. A short moment later, she spotted a not so friendly looking familiar face in the doorway. Beth shook.

Dressed in a blue nightgown, Marissa was holding the same pistol that she used in the parking lot kidnapping attempt. But there was one important difference. A silencer mounted at one end of the weapon spoke of untold intentions.

A wave of nausea instantly swept over Beth. She looked around. A one-inch thick braided rope tied around her wrists and ankles led to all four bedposts. A glaring light from an overhead ceiling lamp bore down on her, inducing her to close her eyes, to minimize the gavel that she felt pounding her brain. Abdominal cramps chimed in, grabbing her as if a vice closed around her waist.

She glanced back at Marissa's hardened face. Her stomach exploded. Green bile stained fluid gushed from her mouth. She gasped and turned her head to the side, facing Bootsie. While coughing and spitting uncontrollably, the room began to spin. *Stay awake! Watch Marissa—no matter what!*

Marissa was now walking toward her, gun in hand. A second later, Beth felt the pistol barrel pressing into her left temple.

"I shoot trespassers."

"Please don't---," she begged. "Please don't shoot!"

Marissa shouted, "Why did you come here?"

Beth twisted her neck to lock on Marissa's beady eyes. "I came to see Virginia."

Marissa's neck veins seem to pop. "Why were you snooping through the alleyway window into our apartment?"

"No one answered the door. I heard the dog."

Marissa grimaced. "Do you know who used to own that dog?"

"No."

"You're lucky."

"What do you mean?"

"If you did know the original dog owner, my decision to kill you would be very easy." She pressed the barrel harder into Beth's temple. "But since I do know who used to own the dog, I suspect that you're lying." A wicked snarl sprung up around her mouth. "By the way, did you ever think when no one answered the door that it was a clue that no one wanted your company?"

Beth pleaded, "I'm so sorry.'.

"Cut the crap. You're a troublemaker."

"I only wanted to see my friend Virginia." Beth pulled her head to the right, away from the .380 pistol that Marissa continued to press even harder against her head.

"Look, I've shot people like you. This won't be the first time. It makes life easier." She began jabbing the pistol against Beth's skull bones. "Someone used to drill into me the principle of never leaving a witness."

"Please---can I see Virginia?"

Marissa's face turned crimson. "Shut the hell up." She slapped Beth hard across the mouth with her free hand. "You're really pissing me off big time."

Beth felt the drops falling off her lip. She looked down at her shirt. *Blood.* She slammed her eyes shut and prayed.

Melissa screamed into her victim's ear, "Listen honey, you got what you wanted. I gave you that vaccine research paper." She pulled the pistol away from Beth's temple. "But that wasn't good enough for you. Now, you're just causing trouble."

Beth snuck a peak at her captor's menacing eyes. "I only wanted to----"

The pistol returned to her temple. Marissa's index finger pulled back on the trigger ever so slightly. "I've had it with you," she shouted.

A heartbeat later, a familiar voice rang out. "Drop that pistol. Untie her---now."

Dr. Virginia Washington had walked into the bedroom. "I said drop the pistol!"

Marissa said, "I don't trust her." While saying the words, the .380 pistol drifted slowly to her side.

Dr. Washington saddled up to her roommate. "Well, I do."

"Yeah and what if this bitch leads Zach Miller to me?"

"Give me the pistol," Virginia demanded.

Marissa threw the gun on the bed, near Beth's feet. "Shit, she's not worth shooting. I'm going out for a smoke. When I come back, this loser better be gone," she shouted.

Seconds later, they heard the slam of the outside front door reverberate throughout the room.

"Thank God Virginia you came when you did. She said she was going to kill me."

"Knowing Marissa, I'm afraid she might have done it."

Virginia untied the ropes. Beth stretched her aching arms. With difficulty, she forced herself to a sitting position. The room began spinning around her. She turned away and heaved up a torrent of yellow fluid. Exhausted, her head plunked back down to the pillow.

The scientist leaned over and stroked Beth's hair. "It's over. You'll be safe now."

"But Marissa---"

"Believe me."

Beth tried to regain control of her racing thoughts. "Ok. Give me a minute." She rubbed her eyes, trying to focus on a plan to get out before the volatile Marissa returned.

"Take your time. Don't worry about my roommate."

Beth shot back a look of disbelief. "She was about to shoot me. Virginia, please help me to sit up. I've got to get out of here."

The scientist tugged at Beth's arms. "Go slow. Breathe easy."

She slowed her breathing cycles. Her lightheadedness began to abate. "I need to talk with you but not here—not now."

"Let me help you out of bed." She held onto her and assisted Beth's unsteady steps over to a footrest in front of a Victorian wingback chair.

She stared at the ex-DCP scientist. Virginia's face looked puffy and pasty. Her drawn face looked as though she had aged a lot, even though it was only a couple of weeks since she had last seen her. "Is there a back door to this apartment?" She stood, surprising herself that she could actually stand up without assistance.

"Yes, it leads to the alleyway."

"Show me the way. Then, I want you to go out the front door and call Marissa after I walk out the back entrance."

Exiting the bedroom, Virginia pointed down a long hallway. Her next question seemed somewhat inappropriate, given the dire circumstances. "Did the DCP monkey data help you and Dr. Rogers?"

Beth backpedalled down the hallway. A moment later, the front door squeaked open. Marissa stormed in and spotted her half way toward the backdoor. The crazed roommate ran into the bedroom.

Alone with Beth, Virginia whispered, "Run. I'll distract her. We'll talk soon."

As she reached the back door, she heard the command.

"Stop or I'll shoot you."

She turned around slowly and saw the pistol with the attached silencer tightly embedded in Marissa's hand.

"Start walking back toward me," she yelled.

Washington approached Marissa. She yanked on the arm of her roommate. Beth continued walking straight toward the gun.

"Give me the pistol," Virginia demanded.

"No. This broad is best friends with Rogers. You know Zach wants to kill Rogers---and me. I told you that he's back with a new identity. He's the boss of your former company."

Beth stood frozen in place. *Cathy Parker had told Jonathan the truth.*

Virginia held up her right hand. "Listen to me----"

"No, you listen to me. Zach once told me that business and pleasure don't mix. He was a prick but he was right."

"Please Marissa."

"Your so-called friend will only bring trouble for us. We can't let her go."

With fear building inside her, Beth watched the ping-pong conversation, saying nothing, not moving a muscle.

Virginia placed her arm around the shoulders of her gun-wielding roommate. "Trust me. You once did when I promised you nothing would happen after we brought Jonesy to the police. Now, he's in jail, awaiting trial for attempting to hang you. Please trust me now."

Marissa's face softened a tad. She dropped her pistol to her side.

"Give me the gun."

She gingerly placed the pistol in Virginia's hand. Marissa telegraphed an intimidating stare at Beth. "Get the hell out of here. If I ever see you again, there will be no thinking twice about killing you. Your friend saved you this time but this was your last chance." She turned to walk back into the bedroom, slamming the door behind her.

Beth shook her head. "Your roommate is insane."

"She's completely distraught. Marissa believes Zach Miller is alive. She believes that he put a contract on her life."

"Well, before Annie Oakley comes out of her bat cave, let me answer your question. The monkey data did not help us."

"But it clearly lays out the dangers of *NeoBloc*."

"DCP has forged monkey data. It has been delivered to the President by Secretary of Health James." Beth glanced down at the rope burns on her wrist. "Dr. Rogers and I believe that Nasters and the new CEO— whatever he now calls himself-- are lying about the human trial data as well. But, outside of powerful suspicions, we have no hard evidence that any person has actually died after receiving the vaccine."

Virginia's eyes widened. "I need to tell you something." In a hushed voice, the scientist said, "Just before I was let go, I copied confidential information on the human trials in China. I have seen written proof that thirty people were hospitalized but I am not aware that anyone died."

"Were these people so sick that it would be likely that at least some of them may have died?"

Washington looked away and hesitated. Glancing back at Beth, she replied, "It is possible that they died of natural causes and not the vaccine but I believe that not to be the case." Her eyes welled up. "Besides Dr. Nasters, you are the only person who knows that."

"Look, if you don't intervene, the vaccine might be given to all Americans." She placed her hand on the scientist's shoulder. You're dedicated---you're honest."

"I don't think I can do what you want. Nasters is evil. I fear for my own life."

"Every American will be wiped out if you sit on your hands"

Virginia shook her head. "I'm afraid---I can't."

The bedroom door creaked open. Beth sprinted down the hallway, yanked open the back door and ran as fast as she could away from apartment 4A.

CHAPTER THIRTY-EIGHT

Connor rode the elevator up and after hopping out when the door opened to the executive floor, he strolled up to the executive administrative assistant. "Good morning, I'm here to see Dr. Woodhull."

"Yes." He glanced up from his calendar. "Mr. Connor Lucas, you are exactly on time." The well-built thirty something looking stud reminded Connor of his early days. The young man escorted Connor to the open door. "You can go in—our CEO is ready to see you."

Lucas, dressed in his dark blue Armani three piece suit, white buttoned down collar shirt and paisley tie walked confidently toward the CEO of Weston and Weston. Connor wore an ear-to-ear grin and stuck out his hand. "Dr. Woodhull." He made eye contact with his competitor for a split second before focusing his attention on the antique looking maple wood desk. Connor said in an off-handed manner, "Thanks for seeing me."

Woodhull remained standing behind his desk. He pointed. "Please have a seat. I understand that you wish to discuss your *NeoBloc* vaccine. I must say that I'm extremely surprised by your need to see me."

Ignoring his host, Connor rubbed the finish on the desk. "Nice! I need to get me one of these."

In a curt tone, he snapped back, "This desk is one of a kind and it's not for sale."

Connor laughed. "What do you want for it? I'll give you five thousand dollars."

"It's a priceless family heirloom going back four generations."

Connor smirked. "Everything and everyone has a price."

"I see that you have trouble understanding the meaning of the word no."

"I get what I want."

"Please take a seat. I have a lot of work to accomplish this morning. Let's proceed with our meeting. What's on your mind?"

Connor concentrated on Woodhull's high forehead. *It would be a great place for a bullet to land.* He locked his sight on his opponent's pupils, believing that they appeared constricted out of fear. "Let me get to my demand." Connor sat, slouching down low in the chair. "Our vaccine will pass FDA approval and the President supports it being deployed to every American. You and I both know your compound is way behind *NeoBloc*."

Woodhull shifted in his chair. "Not that far behind your vaccine."

"Pardon me but can we agree to cut the shit. Facts are facts."
"Excuse me. We can at least be civil."
"Look, I have enough capital to take over your company and sufficient research dollars that could fast track your compound to an FDA approval within three months, maybe less."
"Why would you do that if *NeoBloc* is almost ready for FDA approval?"
"First of all, that's my business. But, I'll play nice in the sandbox. Maybe I'll want to market your vaccine for a future date in case people eventually develop resistance to *NeoBloc*."
Woodhull replied quickly, "Your offer is rejected."
Connor scoffed. "I'll go over your head----to your Board. Your shareholders will vote to accept my deal. I'll offer such an exorbitant premium that no one in their right mind would refuse."
"Why would you do that?"
Connor banged his fist on the antique desk. "Because I can!"
Woodhull leaped to his feet. His eyes almost went cross-eyed. "This meeting is over. Good day, Mr. Lucas."
Connor hissed at the CEO. "You'll be hearing from me. I'll be watching you. Think about my generous offer—it will be your last."

***

Connor was in an optimistic mood after his plane landed at Reagan airport, just outside of D.C. Outside the Oval Office, he made small talk with the President's administrative assistant. He was pleased that Secretary James and Chief of Staff Pitnar had paved the way for this impromptu meeting with Williams.
Madison's intercom buzzed. She held her gaze on Connor's deep set blue eyes for several seconds. Catching herself, she blurted out, "President Williams will see you now."
He opened the Oval Office door. The President was already standing at the entrance. Her hands on both hips, she furrowed her eyebrows.
"Good morning, Madame President."
"Mr. Lucas, I was glad that you wanted to see me. I have some important questions on your vaccine." She pointed to the couch. "Please have a seat." Williams sat across from him.
Connor sat, his right arm causally resting on the side armrest. "Thank you for seeing me on such short notice. We do need to discuss *NeoBloc*."
"Secretary James assures me that the FDA will approve it within the month."

Connor leaned forward. "With all due respect Madame President, what do you know about the safety profile and the clinical attributes of the vaccine?"

"Thus far, the DCP human trials show the vaccine to be safe according to what I've been told by many of my scientific advisors."

"May I speak freely?"

"Go on."

Connor smiled. "I'm sure that you're aware of Weston and Weston developing a similar type of vaccine."

"But they're research is a year behind yours. Since the terrorists could strike again at any time, we don't have the luxury of more time."

"You're right. However, let's say for the sake of argument that I believe that we should have a backup just in case *NeoBloc* doesn't prove itself to be effective on all Americans."

Williams looked askance. "What's your point?"

"I have a proposal. DCP will take over Weston and Weston." He paused for a reaction. Seeing none, he continued, "DCP can throw a ton of research dollars at getting the W&W vaccine developed and approved in a fairly quick timeline."

"Mr. Lucas, you're making me wonder if there is something that you are not telling me." The President rubbed her chin. "Is there something wrong with *NeoBloc*?"

"That's up to the FDA and Dr. Rogers to decide." Connor shrugged his shoulders. "I'm certainly no scientist."

"Well, it would not be my decision but I don't think W&W would approve of such an offer by DCP. Most likely, they would probably fight a hostile takeover."

"You're right but we need to make it happen anyway." Connor flexed his fingers. "In the interest of national security-----"

The President's eyes widened. "I can appreciate your point of having a backup vaccine, just in case. As commander-in-chief, I need to do everything we can to protect all our citizens.'

Connor smiled inwardly, believing that he had struck just the right chord.

"However, I have an even better solution. The government could infuse capital and resources into W&W as a joint venture."

"With all due respect, do you think the government should be in the business of propping up private companies?" *I want to control the vaccine not some governmental bureaucrat.*

The President rose quickly. "Give me a week or so. Good day Mr. Lucas."

Connor walked to the door with Williams. He cocked his head in her direction, stating, "I want to sincerely compliment your Surgeon

General. Dr. Rogers is all over the *NeoBloc* research. You made an excellent choice in choosing him to be your "top doc."

She replied, "I trust him."

"I look forward to hearing from you."

"Right now, I'm leaning toward my idea of a private joint venture with our government."

"One fact that might help you decide is that DCP has several scientists with great expertise in making vaccines like this. W&W may not have the bench strength that we do. Our chief scientist is recognized worldwide as the preeminent authority on vaccines of this sort."

"Well, maybe I can hire Dr. Nasters to work for the government."

"Madame President, why would he leave his top position at DCP?"

"He could assist me in my efforts to foster national security."

"Good day. We should talk soon."

CHAPTER THIRTY-NINE

Dr. Peter Ulrich pounded the gavel. "The Board will come to order." The members quickly came to silence. Rogers and Ashley seated along the back wall waved to Beth Murphy, seated at the conference table, along with other voting members of the Board.

"Welcome to the winter meeting of the National Quality Oversight Committee." The chairperson's voice rang out, "Per our agenda, I will entertain a motion to accept the minutes of our fall meeting."

A woman seated next to the chair made the motion. The placard in front of her revealed her identity. She was the vice-chair of the Board, Ms. Lindsay Mason.

"Thank you Ms. Mason."

"Is there a second?"

A bearded well-dressed man with a ruddy complexion and seated next to Beth spoke up. "Michael O' Kane seconds the motion."

"Thank you. The motion passes. Is there any discussion?" Ulrich scanned the members. "Hearing no further comments, the minutes are approved. Let's now get to today's item—a discussion of the human clinical trial data on *NeoBloc*. As we all know, President Williams supports full deployment of this cancer preventing vaccine as soon as possible in the best interests of our national security."

Beth raised her hand.

In a condescending tone, he asked, "Yes, Ms Murphy."

"Thank you Dr. Ulrich. I'm sure I don't have to remind the Board that our duty is to review the clinical data evidence on whether *NeoBloc* is both effective and safe. With all due respect, to the President, we should never let anyone's political likes or dislikes influence our decision to make to the FDA. We need to base our decision solely on the totality of scientific evidence."

O' Kane did not bother to raise his hand. His baritone voice rang out. "I fully support what my colleague has just stated."

"Thank you Beth and Michael for your comments." Ulrich searched the table, pausing a moment at each member. "Let us proceed. Two weeks ago, each of you received through our Board courier a copy of the DCP human clinical trial data. I trust that everyone has had sufficient time to review the data. You will note that besides the clinical trials being held in DuPont Michigan that there is also some data from the clinical trials in China."

A familiar voice spoke up. "I have two questions Mr. Chairman."

Ulrich pulled on his collar. "Ms Murphy, I see that you have more to contribute. Please make your points."

"Are we supposed to simply accept as fact any information that we see before us?"

Ulrich began to speak. "I have no reason to question the validity of the data that we are reviewing. Therefore, I ---."

Beth interrupted him. "Excuse me, Mr. Chairman." She held up her hand, still claiming the floor. "And, why are we not reviewing the animal clinical trial data on *NeoBloc?*"

Rogers nudged Ashley. The Surgeon General watched Chairman Ulrich squirm. He noticed that Ulrich slid his chair a foot closer to his Vice-Chair, Lindsay Mason.

The Chair spoke with conviction. "The answer to your first question is yes. We are an advisory Board. We review all data sent to us. We are not the actual researchers so we trust what has been done by the research scientists."

O Kane stood up. "What I heard from Ms. Murphy is how do we know that the data in front of us is credible?" The Irishman promptly sat down. He winked at Murphy.

Ulrich replied, "This Board has, from time to time, visited pharmaceutical companies. Last year, we made a site inspection visit to DCP."

O Kane boomed, "That was before we looked at the actual monkey *NeoBloc* data. How do we know that this data from clinical trials in China is credible? We've never visited that research institution."

"Your points are duly noted. This Board, with its limited resources, can only do so much." Ulrich paused to whisper something to his Vice-Chair, covering his mouth with his right hand. She leaned toward him, shaking her head, in agreement with what he had said.

The chair straightened his tie and smiled. "I will address Ms. Murphy's second question. After that, we need to move on with our agenda."

Rogers noted Beth's bulging neck veins. *Fireworks are about to begin.*

Ulrich stared at Murphy for several seconds and then cast his eyes down on the papers in front of him. "Beth, as you know, it is customary that human clinical trials are not started before animal trials have proven the compound to be effective and safe. So, why would we once again review the animal data, in this case, the monkey trial data? It would seem to be a waste of our valuable time. We've previously approved the safety and efficacy of the monkey data. More importantly, any delays might jeopardize national security."

Before she could reply, Lindsay Mason chimed in, "I'm concerned that you have some reason to mistrust the human trial data that Dr. Ulrich has given out. Am I correct in my observation?"

Beth shot back, "Actually, it's not only the human trial data that gives me pause but the monkey data is clearly flawed."

Rogers jumped an inch off his chair. A volley of thunderous clunking sounds reverberated throughout the Board Room. He took his eyes off Murphy and tracked the source of the repetitive sounds. It was Ulrich slamming his gavel on the conference room table. "How many times do I have to repeat my statement that this Board has already passed our approval on the monkey data?"

"Dr. Ulrich, we have not reviewed the true clinical trial monkey data."

The Chair responded caustically, "For the last time, we have previously approved the clinical trial monkey data."

"Not the true clinical trial monkey----"

Ulrich slammed down the gavel. "You are making an outrageous and unfounded allegation. You are out of order."

"I stand by my statement."

"You're wasting our time, Ms. Murphy."

The Surgeon General knew where she was going. She had set her hook. Rogers waited for her to reel in her target.

Ulrich rolled his eyes. At that moment, an administrative assistant entered the conference room and handed the Chairman a note.

Rogers watched him rub his neck and then overheard him saying to the messenger, 'Tell Mr. Lucas that I'll call him back in thirty minutes.'

Ulrich dropped the note and pointed at Beth. "Today, we are voting on the human trial data."

Beth leaned back in her seat and peered over at Michael O' Kane.

O Kane raised his hand. "I would like to raise a point of order, Mr. Chairman. My colleague has raised a critical issue before we move forward on the human clinical trial data. As for myself, I would like Ms. Murphy to tell the Board what she means when she says we need to review the true monkey data."

The chairperson bristled. Ulrich glowered at each of the Board members seated around the conference table. "We're moving on with the agenda. Now, I'd like to hear opinions from the rest of the Board on the human trial data."

Mason interjected, "Mr. Chairman, I find the current human data compelling that *NeoBloc* is both effective and safe."

Ulrich stated, "I am pleased that the Board has interest in moving forward. Thank you Lindsay".

Murphy shouted out, "I would like to make a motion."

Gaveling her down, Ulrich shouted, "You're out of order Ms. Murphy."

O' Kane again rose to his feet. Rogers estimated the Irishman to be well over six foot five. His burly chest, ruddy complexion, and muscular physique made him look like someone who didn't take any nonsense from anyone.

"Please excuse me, Mr. Chairman. My back has been acting up lately. I just need to stand to stretch a little. Oh, and I want to state for the record that you can't overrule a motion without even hearing what it is. Maybe, Ms Murphy is going to motion for an early lunch." O Kane looked at the Board members. "Is anyone as hungry as I am?"

Rogers laughed along with everyone else in the room except for Ulrich and Mason. He spotted Beth pulling out a document from her briefcase. The Chairman jerked his head to his right shoulder and then to his left one. Ulrich twisted his neck around in a semi circle. His nostrils flared. "What is your motion?"

Beth held up the document. "I motion to enter the contents of this affidavit into the record."

After sitting down, O'Kane added, "I second the motion."

"The chair rules the motion out of order. I cannot permit a motion without having previously read what you are trying to include into the official record. If you had wanted the Board to read what you have in your hand, you had ample time in the last two weeks to send it to me."

She looked at the unsettled faces of her colleagues around the table. "My motion has been duly seconded and I'm prepared to tell the Board what is in this sworn affidavit per the Chairman's request."

Ulrich droned. "And what does it say?" He rested his chin in his hands, elbows propped on the conference table.

"Thank you for asking. This affidavit contains a statement by Dr. Virginia Washington, who has been working as a high ranking assistant to the top scientist at DCP, Dr. Hussein Nasters."

Beth paused. She made passing eye contact with each of the other ten voting members of the Board and then spoke directly at the chairman. "Dr. Ulrich, I know for a fact that Dr. Washington had been working on the *NeoBloc* vaccine during both the monkey and human clinical trials until she was recently let go without cause."

Mason sighed. "How could you possibly know that? Beth, you are not human resources at DCP, are you? You are speculating and what you are doing is---."

Beth began to speak over Mason. "I'm telling you that Dr. Washington---."

Lindsey's hand shot up. She glanced at Ulrich. "Mr. Chairman, point of order. I was still speaking."

"The chair recognizes Ms. Mason. Please go ahead Lindsay---you have the floor."

Mason nodded. "Miss Murphy, maybe Dr. Washington was let go because she was a bad scientist. None of us really knows why she was let go. And, I strongly object to hearing any statements from a fired, disgruntled employee."

Beth noticed that the eyes of all Board members were fixated back on her. "I understand." She expected a gavel any second but Ulrich seemed frozen in place. "As I was saying, Dr. Virginia Washington has sworn in this statement that every single monkey who received *NeoBloc* in the animal trials has died within a year."

The voting members of the Board sat stone faced. Mason lowered her voice and said something to the Chairman.

Ulrich shifted several times in his seat before speaking. "Ms. Murphy, you are again out of order. You say you understand what Ms Mason just said yet you still persist in trying to persuade us that Dr. Washington has credibility." Ulrich threw his ballpoint onto the table. It bounced up and struck a nearby elderly member of the Board on the shoulder.

He reached over the table, past Lindsay Mason, and gently touched the woman's hand. "I'm so sorry Ms. Hall. Are you all right? "

"I'll be fine Mr. Chairman," Georgette Hall replied, almost bowing in his direction.

Rogers strained to hear the murmurings of the Board. But the Chairman's gavel drowned out his attempt. The Surgeon General looked at his daughter. Ashley was giving Beth a thumb-up sign.

O' Kane bellowed above the chatter. "Ms. Mason and Dr. Ulrich, the point is that any discussion of the safety of *NeoBloc* in humans is a farce if all the monkeys died."

"The Board will come to order," Ulrich demanded. "You may continue Mr. O' Kane."

"Thank you. I was just thinking that since the human data is less than a year in duration then all human trial participants might die just as the monkeys did. Therefore, I motion that we make a unanimous recommendation to the FDA that they do not approve this potentially deadly vaccine."

"The chair rules your motion out of order as it is based upon hearsay from a former employee of DCP. Essentially, Dr. Washington has no standing, given her dismissal from DCP." Ulrich turned to his left, ignoring Beth's waving hand. "The Chair recognizes Ms. Hall."

"I have thoroughly reviewed the clinical human data before us. I suggest that we take a vote."

Lindsay Mason added her thumb to the tipping scale. "Ms. Hall is correct."

Ulrich rose. "This has been a grueling meeting. As chair, I am using my prerogative. This Board meeting is adjourned until this weekend. I just remembered that I have a pressing matter that I must attend to now and tomorrow."

The Board sat in stunned silence. Rogers sensed that Ulrich was playing a game of brinksmanship.

"Unless of course that we would vote now on the human trial data." He scanned the members. Heads were nodding in the affirmative.

"All members who agree that the human data is acceptable please raise your hand." He counted only two hands. He leered at several members who had not yet voted.

"Please let me remind the Board. If we do not vote now, all of you will need to stay in town for two days and come back over the weekend to vote."

The Board members who had until then remained uncommitted glanced at each other, looking obviously upset, probably at the implication that their weekend plans might be ruined.

"Raise your hands please," he commanded. He raised his gavel. "Unless we have a majority of the Board voting, I will adjourn this meeting until Saturday."

Many hands soared into the air. Rogers counted eight hands including Ulrich. He looked over at Beth. A fellow Board member seated to her left was engaged in an intense argument with her while O' Kane was shaking his fist at Lindsay Mason.

The Chairman proclaimed, "The Board has voted. We will recommend full approval and a speedy deployment of *NeoBloc* vaccine to the FDA. This meeting is adjourned. Enjoy your weekend." Ulrich stood and walked toward the door, quietly speaking into his cell phone.

CHAPTER FORTY

Connor stayed in DC overnight at the Marriot on Pennsylvania Avenue. In his mind, it was crucial that he meet with Secretary James as soon as possible.

Connor cursed Woodhull. He had recently discovered that the CEO had added a "poison pen" provision in W &W's documents making a hostile take-over by DCP virtually impossible. Gritting his teeth, he was frustrated with the President's desire to infuse governmental money into the coffers of W&W to fast track their clinical trials as part of a governmental-private industry joint venture.

To him, it was becoming increasingly apparent that both Dr. Woodhull and President Williams appeared to have suspicions about the safety of *NeoBloc* but both wanted to control the W&W trials and exclude DCP. He picked up the phone and dialed the private number of the Secretary of Heath. James answered on the first ring.

"Hello Christian," he said in an off-handed manner. "We need to talk."

Silence.

Connor bit his lower lip. "Are you listening to me?"

James voice quivered. "I can't do this anymore. I will not go down in history as a co-conspirator of the mass murder of millions of Americans just so *The Health Club* can continue to fill their coffers."

"Are you crazy? Of course, we must stop *NeoBloc*. We can't make any money if everyone is dead. Why do you think I met with Woodhull and the President? We need to take over the safe W&W compound."

Sounding dejected, James asked, "So why hasn't Williams torpedoed Project Moon Shot with *NeoBloc?*"

"Give her time. She's under tremendous political pressure to do something, especially in the wake of the nuclear bombing in Atlanta."

"Connor, we can't take the chance. This has gone too far. The National Quality oversight Board just recommended that the FDA approve *NeoBloc*. The FDA will quickly approve the vaccine. Then it will be too late. The dominoes are falling. Even you can't stop this!"

"Listen to me. I called Ulrich before his Board met but he didn't take my call until after they made their decision to recommend approval."

"So I'm right. It's too late!"

"Relax my friend. I just spoke with him. The Board will reverse its decision."

"And, what if they don't?"

Connor heard the fear in the Secretary's voice.

"And did you tell the President that *NeoBloc* is unsafe?"

"Would it matter if I did? That's up to her buddy—Dr. Rogers to decide."

The Secretary screamed, "Shit! So, *NeoBloc* is going forward unless Rogers speaks up! What if something happens to Rogers?"

"Look, calm down. I told you Ulrich would reverse the Board's decision. You can bank on it."

James paused.

The CEO could hear him sighing.

"Connor, things are moving much too quickly--spinning out of control. You don't understand how government works. You can't always put the genie back into the bottle."

He's lost it! The CEO let him continue his ramblings.

"Look, my nerves are shot. I can't sleep. I want out of *The Health Club*. I'm going to offer my resignation to the President." He sighed loudly. "I might need to go to the press and maybe even to the Surgeon General. The truth has to get out. I can't live with myself until I make this right."

Connor slapped his hand on his desk. "Stop it! You will do nothing until we speak. Do you hear me?'

Silence.

The CEO continued, "You have my assurances that *NeoBloc* will not be approved by the FDA. But we're in business, my friend."

"Not to kill Americans."

Connor spoke calmly. "Christian, what you need is a couple of drinks of your favorite Scotch."

"No jokes. What's your latest plan?"

"I want to lead a hostile take -over of W&W."

"They will never let you do it."

"Please listen to me. It can be done."

"Why don't you just tell the truth about *NeoBloc?*"

Connor's face grew contorted. He walked over to the nearest wall and punched hard against it. "You are not thinking clearly. Why would I admit to the President that DCP was a month or so from having a deadly vaccine? And, would you like for me to admit to President Williams that you and I had knowledge about it since we heard the beans spilled back in the Park?"

"Connor, you can sell the truth without getting us in trouble. Hell, you can convince President Williams of anything."

"Look, I'm not risking any chance of going to prison. I just told the President that it's always good to have a back-up vaccine just in the remote possibility that *NeoBloc* doesn't work out."

"But, what if she stays with *NeoBloc*?" James shouted.

"She won't!"

"I can't take that chance. Therefore, I'm going to the *Washington Post* and expose our whole scheme. I've kept copies of the reports of death in the human clinical trials in China that you sent me from the maniac's personal notepad. Only you, Nasters, and I have such information. Even, Rogers does not have this evidence. But we do!"

Connor slapped his forehead. *He needs to go!* Wincing, he faked a friendly tone, "Christian, my friend, listen to me. I think you are right. We should tell the President the truth about our vaccine. Let's go for a drink. We can talk this out. But, there is no reason for you to go to the press. I told you that I won't let *NeoBloc* get deployed."

"You can't stop *NeoBloc* from being deployed unless we get out the truth before every American is inoculated with this killer product."

"My friend, fear not. We have an ace in the hole."

"What ace?"

"Dr. Jonathan Rogers. He will never sign off on *NeoBloc*, given his suspicions."

"That's where you're wrong again Connor. The blogging on the Internet has taken a toll on Dr. Rogers's credibility. The newspapers won't accept any story from him."

Connor's stomach sank. *Maybe, I did discredit the Surgeon General too much.* "You know—you could be right about that. Christian, can't we sit down face to face and talk this through?"

"I have a better plan. I can send the clinical trial data from China to Rogers's daughter. She's almost a physician. Her father could then guide her with what to do about it. She still has credibility-- unlike him. The blogs have hit him too hard. Ashley Rogers can send it to the media. What do you think?"

A medical student? "Hold off until we meet. Then maybe you and I could pay her a friendly visit to show her the data. Agreed?"

James responded as if he didn't even hear the question. "There was a quote that I came across in the *Post* where Dr. Woodhull said that he was impressed with Ashley Rogers's passion for the truth." He stuttered. "We--we nee--need someone like that to bring out the dangers of *NeoBloc* to the public."

"You're right. So let's just stop by her apartment and talk with her."

"Connor, you don't understand, I can't take any chances. I need an absolute guarantee that *NeoBloc* will be destroyed."

"Done! You have my commitment. You have a rock solid assurance."

Connor heard him breathing rapidly. "Are you with me?"

"I've got to think. I'm not sure."

"So, my friend, where should we meet before paying a visit to Ashley Rogers?"

His voice became almost inaudible. Connor strained to hear him. "I think I need to go home. There are many decisions to make. I need time to sort them all out in my head. One decision that I need to make is where to send my story---an unbelievably true story that could wipe out an entire nation."

Connor stomped his right foot on the floor, so hard that he winced with pain in his arthritic right knee. "Hold on. Christian, you promised me that we would talk before you do anything. Deal?"

A groggy -sounding voice spit out a barrage of his true feelings. "I want out Connor. I haven't slept in weeks. Ever since I found out that *NeoBloc* is deadly."

Connor replied in an even tone. "My friend, I'm here for you. You want out. I can make that happen. Now, what's your address?"

"155 Elm Street, apartment 1B," James replied haltingly.

"I'll meet you there."

"OK."

"See you there ole buddy. We'll go to a bar, get smashed and have some fun."

"Look, I'm not kidding around Connor. We need to hand over to the press all of our DCP documents demonstrating the *NeoBloc* induced deaths in China."

"Let's work out a plan to do what is right. I'll be at your home in twenty minutes. Don't worry. You'll be permanently out of our organization by midnight. I promise you a good night's sleep."

Christian weakly replied, "You'll find me at my apartment."

"We'll have a good talk. Trust me."

***

Connor packed a Beretta 9mm semi automatic and silencer in his gym bag. He slung the skin toned sheepskin sack over his shoulder before hopping in a taxi. He directed the cabbie to Christian's apartment. A block away from the Secretary's garden apartment, Connor told the driver to let him out.

Upon disembarking from the cab, he looked around his whereabouts. A few people were scurrying past him, hats pulled down over their foreheads to shield themselves from the bitter winds. *No eye contact,* he thought. He walked quickly down the main road and cut into a side alley.

As he drew closer, he felt on edge. *I usually order the hit! Now I'm the hit man! WTF!* He approached the back window of Christian's ground floor apartment. Surprisingly, it was unlocked. *How uncharacteristic for that worrywart James!*

Need to think! Connor walked back to the main street. He scanned the street several times. James's government car was nowhere in sight. *He should have been here by now. Something is up. Where is his car?* There was no time to find a hit man. *Jonesy is in jail. I have to find Christian James before he goes to the Post or wherever else. It's time!*

Returning to the unlocked window in the rear, he cautiously pulled it up a couple of feet. He listened. *Silence.* Sticking his face inside, he spotted a queen sized bed, draped with a dark blue quilt. He put one leg through the window and then pulled himself through, careful to be as quiet as possible.

The wintry breeze gushed through the open window. It rapidly turned the bedroom into an icebox. Connor shut the window. He sat on the bed and pulled out the Beretta from his gym bag. He attached the silencer. *Three shots to the forehead.*

***

Connor checked his watch. He still had not heard any noise from the front rooms. He began to think that James might have gone directly to *The Post. Plan B. I'll call the police and file a formal complaint. I'll say that the Secretary had just made an improper sexual advance by kissing me.*

He always prided himself by preparing for anything. Yet, his mind was in turmoil. Usually clear thinking, he had an unnerving gut feeling that he had somehow messed up. Nevertheless, as hard as he tried, he drew a blank on any misstep.

He reached into his blazer inside pocket and pulled out two uncorked glass test tubes and a pair of surgical gloves. Donning the gloves, he pulled out a napkin from the test tube. It was a specimen that he had recently collected. It contained the DNA of Christian James. The Secretary had once used the napkin to wipe his mouth after having dinner with Connor a few days earlier. He safely secured the collected evidence while James excused himself to go to the rest room.

With his lips parted and tongue protruding, Connor swiped the stained part of the napkin around his own mouth. Then, he dropped the napkin into another glass tube that he had marked with a red X. Connor removed his gloves and stuffed them as well as both test tubes into his pant pocket.

His plan was clear. He would file a formal complaint with the DC police. The intermingled DNA from both of them on the one napkin in his tube would be compelling. Moreover, his personal willingness to undergo a cavity exam would soon convince the authorities to arrest James on a sexual harassment charge. Connor would claim that James had a mental breakdown. His plan to convince the police that the Secretary was hallucinating about a boxing club called The Health Club would discredit anything James would say or do.

Absentmindedly, from his opposite pocket, he pulled out and donned another pair of gloves. He slowly opened the bedroom door. Trotting straight toward the front door, he unlocked it and pulled it open. *No one.* An instant later, he realized how careless he had been. *Shit!* His fingerprints were on the bedroom window. *No gloves then.* He pulled out a handkerchief from his trouser pocket and turned back toward the bedroom. Despite his laser like focus on the mission at hand, a well-lit computer screen in the far corner of the living room caught his eye.

The bright light in the corner of the dark room caught his full attention. *OMG!* Shuddering, Connor took one glance and then looked away. Christian James was hanging with a rope noose around his neck. A pulley, a kicked over chair and a thick braided rope each played a lethal role in the apparent suicide.

After heaving a deep breath, he approached the body. The Secretary's face, neck, and arms took on a bluish hue. He held his gaze on the Secretary's chest while he glanced down on the minute hand on his Rolex. There was no trace of movement. Through the gloves, he felt the body. It was icebox cold.

The bright computer screen beckoned him. An email program of James was still open. Connor checked the sent box. There it was---the Nasters data on *NeoBloc* with deaths in China. He deleted the email after noting the recipient--Ashley Rogers. He quickly scanned the rest of the sent box and then the inbox. Finding no harmful emails, he ripped the laptop from its cable wire.

Connor ran out of the room, laptop in tow, and headed for the bedroom. This time, he methodically cleaned up his fingerprints anywhere near the window with his handkerchief and exited through his initial entry point, making sure that he tightly closed it before trotting out to the Main Street.

He hailed a local bus and jumped up the stairs. The driver looked at his gloved hands and heavy baggage that he lugged. Connor sensed a clearly telegraphed frightened look. He looked around. The bus was devoid of any passengers. He paid his fare and decided for the moment to chill out. The Secretary's laptop, wires dragging along the floorboards, he held in his hands. Walking to the rear of the bus, he sat down and kept a watchful eye on the driver. *If he pulls out his cell phone, he's a dead man.*

A couple hopped on the bus at the next stop and after paying their fare, they took seats in the middle of the bus without making any eye contact with Connor. Staring at the driver for any false move, he made his plan. He ripped off his gloves and stuffed them in his pants pocket. Five minutes later, he exited the bus.

Connor carried the laptop to his rental car, parked on a side street, a block from his Marriot hotel. He looked around. After ensuring that he had attracted no attention, he buzzed open the trunk, threw in the laptop, and slammed it shut. The dark blue sedan was his get-away. He climbed inside and headed for a previously chosen secluded spot near the Potomac River.

***

Connor parked in a wooded rest area. There was no one in sight. He opened the trunk of the Chevy Camaro and snatched out the laptop. With a final mighty effort, he dislodged a tire iron from the spare wheel holder. With his cargo, he rushed through the woods, running towards the river.

He smashed the laptop against a limestone boulder that he had stumbled upon just short of the riverbank. A crack in the casing appeared. With all of his might, using the tire iron, he cracked wide open the laptop, laying bare its contents. He spotted it. There it was----- the hard drive.

Connor wrenched out the hard drive and ran with it to the edge of the river. He dropped the metal box onto the ground. He then stretched out his right arm several times as if warming up to throw a major league fastball. When his arm felt loose, he picked up the hard drive. Like an Olympic discus athlete, he heaved it as far as he could. It splashed down about fifteen to twenty yards out in the fast moving river. The incriminating evidence immediately sunk.

***

It was time for a double Scotch, maybe two or three. O'Malley's bar was three blocks away. Connor felt that he needed more time to think, to plan, and to find the daughter of his number one nemesis. There was no question in his mind. Clearly, he needed to find Ashley before she saw the email from James. He believed, without any doubt, that she would repeat to the authorities a compelling and credible story that would land Connor in prison for the rest of his life.

******

Speeding back to the Marriot, he parked his rental in the indoor parking garage of the hotel. He used the hotel house phone to notify the DC police that he had been sexually assaulted earlier that day by the Secretary of Health—Christian James. The desk sergeant demanded him to come right down to the station to take down his story. Thinking quickly, Connor fabricated an excuse of a family emergency back in Michigan. He swore on his mother's grave that he would be back in touch with the police as soon as possible. Despite his sincere attempt at lying, the sergeant began asking further questions that he did not want to answer. Connor faked a crying episode. After a few crocodile tears, he hung up the phone, claiming that he was experiencing chest pains.

One more call to a FBI insider provided him with a passport photo and further information. Ashley lived in Michigan. Several minutes later from the Marriot Hotel Business Center, Connor read the fax sent from his friend at the Michigan Department of Motor Vehicles. Ashley name appeared as the registrant of the victory red 2007 Chevy Aveo coupe. His shady contact at the Detroit Police Department even provided Connor with his target's home and email address. His contact threw in her Twitter and Facebook ID's for good measure.

Calling the airport, there was a jetliner to Ford International Airport taking off from Reagan in two hours. He went to his room to pack lightly. Heading toward the front desk, Mr. John Doe paid cash for his room. Outside the hotel, he hopped a cab.

At the airport, he passed through security as Connor Lucas and boarded the plane just before the flight attendant closed the hatch on the Boeing 747. Seat 10A was unoccupied. He buckled himself into the seat. More than any time in his life, he was now almost fanatically determined to do whatever he needed to do back in Michigan.

A few minutes later, the jet roared down the runway. As it took flight, Connor cursed inwardly for far too many mistakes. *NEVER AGAIN!* He would arrive in Michigan, rent a car, pay with cash, and drive to Ashley's apartment. No longer trusting anyone, he resigned himself to being the hit man. He hummed the James Bond theme song, *Nobody Does It Better*, as the plane soared to a cruising altitude.

******

Ashley's apartment was located on the perimeter of the University of Michigan campus, where it intersected with the outskirts of the city of Ann Arbor. It had taken Connor twenty minutes of randomly driving around campus to locate her car. *A red Aveo.*

Connor parked his rented BMW on a side street, several hundred yards from her apartment. Not wanting to attract attention, he shut off the engine even though the wind-chill that day was ten degrees. He would wait an hour, hoping that Ashley would use her car, parked plainly in his cross hairs. His intent was to follow her and eliminate one more witness.

The collar on his black wool overcoat pulled up to eyelevel, he slouched down in his seat. With the motor off, a chill set in quickly. He stared at the clock on the dashboard. Minutes ticked away as he fixed his eyes on Ashley's mud stained red *Aveo*, parked three cars in front of his late model black luxury car.

He checked his Rolex. Four o' clock. The sun was beginning to set. He pulled out a diagram of the winding pathways to her apartment that he had earlier checked on *Google Earth.* Forty-five minutes later, no one had yet approached the *Aveo.* The wind howled. The sun continued to drop on the horizon. He began to shiver. Reaching over to the glove department, he opened it. There was his Beretta. A silencer lay alongside. Attaching the silencer, he placed the weapon in his gym bag and laid it on the front passenger seat.

It's time to find her. He opened his driver side door to begin the hunt after grabbing his loaded gym bag. As he headed toward the pathway leading to her apartment, his eyes popped. An athletic looking young woman with long blond hair was approaching the Aveo. He pulled Ashley's FBI passport photo from his pocket. *It's her!* Connor turned his back on her and nonchalantly ducked back into his BMW.

Ashley opened the driver door and slipped inside. At the same moment, Connor turned on his ignition and flipped on the heat to full blast. She pulled out quickly from her spot on DeWitt Street. In turn, Connor hit his accelerator.

Despite a heavy volume of traffic, her bright red vehicle was easy to track. She made one right turn onto an Ann Arbor main road before driving onto the Freeway. He kept his distance of six or so car lengths. *Did she already forward the email from Christian James to her father? To the Washington Post?*

A string of perspiration beads built a small fortress on his forehead. Connor brushed aside the sweat, dripping into his eyes, with a violent swipe of his right palm. He cursed himself one more time for letting things get out of control, vowing that he would now take whatever steps necessary to side step the tsunami that he felt was headed straight at him.

After a mile down the Freeway, the Aveo slowed down a full ten miles below the speed limit. Connor eased up on his pedal enabling him to fall eight or so car lengths behind the red coupe. Several vans, a few jeeps, and one silver colored pick- up truck now separated him from Ashley. He glanced up at the overhead sign. Just ahead was the exit for DuPont. *Is she meeting her father to make a surprise inspection at DCP?*

In a flash, Ashley shifted to the middle lane from the right lane that she previously shared with Connor. The Aveo slowed down to fifteen miles below the limit. *Did she spot me?* Moments later, she was in the adjacent lane, barely one car length ahead of his BMW. He reached over for his Baretta 9 mm and released the safety latch. Connor evaluated his opportunity. *One less troublemaker!* He looked ahead a few hundred yards, knowing that he had room to maneuver ahead to escape after he took his head shot.

With the hood of his BMW even with her rear bumper, he powered down his driver window. With the Baretta, firmly in his hand, he pulled up even with the back seat of the Aveo. His index finger latched on the trigger—ready to squeeze off at least one bullet. *Two seconds more!* He aimed the gun, targeting the back of her head. Inexplicably, at that moment, the Aveo rocketed forward.

Shit! Out of the corner of his eye, Connor also spotted a Michigan State Police Ford Interceptor two cars over in the fast lane. He looked up ahead. The exit for DuPont was fast approaching. Connor tossed his Beretta on the passenger seat.

Backing off even more on the accelerator, he drifted further back from the Aveo. The Trooper car sped up and seemed to be hanging close to Ashley's car. She passed the DuPont exit. *I can't track her all day. Go back to her apartment, destroy the email, dismantle her computer and take the hard drive—and then----.*Connor slammed on his brakes. His tires screeched. He banked hard to the right, barely making the DuPont exit.

Using his GPS, he was back on DeWitt Street in ten minutes. After parking, he took a quick gander around him. Exiting his car, he slung the stocked gym bag over his shoulders. *Where was Ashley going? Who else knew about the damaging email from Secretary James?*

It was dusk. He walked up to a small window on the side of her two-story garden apartment that bordered the woods. Connor scanned the environment. Seeing no one, he tucked the gym bag into the freshly mowed grass, against the brick wall. He pulled down the sleeve of his black woolen overcoat over his right hand so that his bare skin was protected and punched straight ahead, smashing the window. The echoes of the cracking of the glass died quickly. He listened intently. *No alarm.*

He pushed his hand through the sleeve, shaking off a few pieces of glass. Pleased that his bare hand was unscathed, he walked toward the front of the apartment to case his surroundings. Again, he saw no one.

Connor trotted back to the broken window. After putting on a pair of rubber gloves, he teased out several shards of glass from the lower section of the window frame, enabling him to reach inside and unlock it. He peered inside, spotting a toilet and a shower while musing. *Two window heists in one day!*

He picked up the gym bag from its wedged spot on the ground. Putting his right foot into Ashley's bathroom, he squeezed through the opening. The apartment was eerily quiet. Frigid air swooped in from the busted window. Dropping the gag on the floor, he pulled out the Beretta with the attached silencer.

He peeked out the bathroom door. A small table with an Ivy plant caught his eye as he entered the short hallway. A left turn brought him into the front living room. He scanned around for a computer. *Nope!* Holding the Baretta out in front of him, his finger on the trigger, he walked down the short hallway and entered her bedroom.

A grateful sigh emerged from his mouth upon spotting it. He headed straight for the desktop computer. The screen was dark. After laying the gun on the floor, he pushed down on the enter key. *Hope her account has not timed out.* The screen lit up. "Yes!"

Connor scrolled to the sent button. He pounded it and hoped for the best. The string of email recipients was mostly girl friend stuff. Two emails below BevC, he came across a screen name, JRogers. *Rogers knows!* He clicked on it and read the message. 'Hey Dad, check out the Michigan-Indiana game tonight on channel fourteen. I'll be home by 7PM in time for the game. I'm just going to chill out in my apartment watching Michigan slaughter Indiana. Call me. Love, Ashley.'

He clicked on her inbox. *Crap! CJames.* In her new mailbox, the damaging note appeared as unread. Clicking on it, he read diatribe from James. He saddled back into the bathroom, fully loaded weapon in tow. The frilly pink seat cover tightly attached to the toilet seat caught his eye. He lowered the fluffy seat on the toilet, determined to wait for the right moment to strike.

He looked out at the nearby woods, twenty yards from the window. A few shards of broken glass still rimmed the upper frame of the window. Darkness was setting in rapidly. From his vantage point, he envisioned a potential escape route into the dense woods. And, clearly, he possessed an element of surprise when Ashley returned to her apartment. He checked his watch. *Almost six o clock. Time to think!*

Connor sat on the toilet seat and devised a straightforward plan. *Two bullets through both sides of her brain when she entered the bathroom.* He rationalized that Ashley had never even seen nor sent the Christian James email. His efforts at damage control would then revert back to calling the DC police about the sexual harassment complaint that he had fabricated against the Secretary of Health.

After killing Ashley, he would grab her desktop computer. It would journey with him to another well-chosen wooded rest stop. *Another hard drive for another river—this time for the Dupont.* Connor pursed his lips and fondled his semi-automatic.

At six thirty, he started to convince himself that the longer he delayed calling the local police, the worse it would look for him. He flipped open his cell to call the front desk of the DuPont police department. Without any trace of emotion, he reported to the desk sergeant the unsolicited sexual advance made by Christian James back in D.C. Desk sergeant Tommy Angelo was none too pleased that the accuser had left the Capitol area without signing a formal complaint with the authorities in DC. Angelo was even more irate when Connor asked if he could sign a formal complaint while he was in Michigan even though the alleged crime apparently took place back in the nation's capitol.

Only by promising to report to the DuPont police station to provide full testimony within the hour had Connor been able to placate Angelo. A few choice obscenities from the sergeant for the extra workload and violation of police protocol were easily absorbed for the greater good that Connor sought. *I have less than an hour to kill her and ditch the computer before appearing at the station.*

Impatiently, he waited in ambush for Ashley. *Her email to her father stated that should be home by 7PM. Less than twenty-five minutes to knock off the 2nd loved one of Dr. Jonathan Rogers.* To prepare for his upcoming appearance at the police station, he practiced making faces in the mirror. Connor feigned masks of shock and dismay. He thought that he would need those believable reactions once the DC police would surely notify the DuPont authorities of the fact that Christian James had hung himself in his own apartment.

As time passed, his deadline to show up at the DuPont police station grew closer. He decided to wait until seven. If she were not home by that time, he would race to the DuPont police station and then speed back to her apartment. This plan was far less than ideal as Ashley would most likely notice the broken bathroom window and either call her father or call the police. Connor thought for a second and then grinned. *If she calls her father, I'll kill two birds tonight!*

CHAPTER FORTY-ONE

At the Burger Boy restaurant, Rogers thought about Ashley's earlier email about the basketball game. After just speaking with her on her cell phone, she agreed without any hesitation to ditch her plan of watching the big game in her apartment. He felt bad that she would miss the excitement of enjoying the intense rivalry between Michigan-Indiana and the meeting he had called for tonight was far more important.

The Surgeon General applied a topical anti-viral crème to a canker sore on his lower lip. Feeling unsettled and anxious, his nervous system was in crisis mode. As was typical whenever he felt that way, his appetite became voracious. After all, it was not too often when he was more than ready to load up on a triple Chubby Wubby with all the works. In this neighborhood around the DuPont-Oldwyck area, insiders comically knew this selection by the tag phrase-- "You can't be serious!" In addition to the greasiest burger and fillers that he had ever eaten, it also came with a side dinner plate chock full of supersized French Fries.

Rogers glanced down at the bulging tire around his abdomen. He vowed that this would be his last pig out of the year. As soon as he completed the thought, he got a familiar sinking feeling in the pit of his stomach. *Who am I kidding? It's only February.*

Darkness had fully descended upon the diner. A full moon was shining brightly. He tried to focus on the critical matter at hand. A plan to stop President Williams from deploying *NeoBloc* was his top priority. *Could the current CEO of DCP somehow be his former archenemy, Zach Miller?*

From his corner booth in the Jackson Diner, he glanced out the window to the well-lit parking lot. His advisory team would be coming shortly. A red Aveo pulled up first. While watching his daughter hop out of her coupe, his eye wandered over to a black Ford Ranger pick- up truck rolling in to the lot, closely followed by a silver hard top Mustang.

A brisk wind blew strands of Ashley's long blond hair across her face. She wore a gloomy expression as she approached the diner. Panini tumbled out of his truck like an Olympic gymnast right after an unsteady dismount from the parallel bars. His muscular upper body stood in marked contrast to his short stubby legs. After regaining his balance, Panini scanned the windows of the Burger Boy restaurant. His beady eyes landed squarely on Rogers.

As if performing on stage, Panini instantly adopted a new persona, magically transforming his features into an angelic altar boy face. All of

Panini's close friends, like the Surgeon General, knew by the gleam in his dark brown eyes what he was capable of doing. His typically jovial attitude gave away no hint that Panini was deadly serious, depending on the situation. Not only was he fiercely loyal and highly principled in Rogers's experience but also deeply ingrained into his personality were admirable traits such as being strong willed, humility, an overbearing brutal honesty, as well as a wild streak of humor. From as far back as eighth grade, he knew that Panini was someone who you wanted to protect your back if you ever landed in a wartime foxhole.

Act one brought the first chuckle of the evening. The Surgeon General could barely contain himself when Panini stopped in the parking lot in front of the corner diner window to give him a full military salute. Rogers returned the salute, very amused. *Sadly, sometimes being Surgeon General seems like war!*

Ashley was the first to open the door to the diner. She held it for the rotund five foot eight straggler waddling in behind her. While both of them headed for the corner table where he sat, Rogers spotted Beth jogging up the walkway. In her early thirties, she was his junior by almost three decades. Her graceful antelope looking strides reminded him of a beautiful ice skater. Sam Murphy's attractive stepdaughter had never married, focusing on her nursing career while filling Sam's seat on the National Quality Oversight Board.

Looking over the heads of his daughter and Panini, Rogers waved to Beth as she entered the diner foyer area. Spotting him, she headed in his direction, eyes downcast and looking deadly serious.

Ashley led a parade of hugs. He tightly held onto her as they engaged in a brief private conversation. "I'm sorry that I caused you to miss the Michigan game tonight."

"Dad, it's just a basketball game. No worries."

"But, you were so looking forward to watching it at your apartment. You could use the relaxation."

Ashley pulled away from his hug. "Look, it's not important." Her facial features gyrated in a series of knots in various muscle groups. "Dad, strange things have been happening."

"I know. That's why I called you all together. We need to ----."

Before he completed his sentence, Rogers was on the painful end of a breath-taking bear hug, raising him almost a foot off the floor. "Hey, Johnny Boy, is this your lovely daughter?" His first best friend in life released him so quickly that he stumbled and almost fell on his face.

Rogers regained his footing and put his arms around both his daughter and Panini. "Ashley, this is my ole pal Joey Panini."

His friend smiled from ear to ear but the deeply ingrained yellow stains on his teeth failed to brighten up the room. "Young lady, it's my greatest pleasure to meet you." Panini grasped her hand and kissed it

Rogers noted the troubled look in his daughter's eye while she stared at Panini's black wavy hair, closely flapping against her chest. Heavy stubble on his chin appeared to be untouched by a razor for at least three days. Despite her noticeable discomfort with his overly friendly mannerisms, she courteously replied, "Nice meeting you Mr. Panini."

Preoccupied by banter with Ashley and Panini, Rogers felt a hard tug on his left shoulder. A soft voice murmured, "Jonathan, so are you going to welcome your third guest?"

He turned on his heels. Latching onto her green eyes, he awkwardly stuck out his hand. An instant scowl crossed her face. Beth hesitated for a moment or two but then seemed resigned to let the strained handshake take place. Her warm hand felt good to hold. "Thank you so much for coming. Even on such short notice, I just knew that I could count on you."

"The cause is why I dropped everything else to come here," she tersely replied. She warmly greeted Ashley while waiting for an introduction to the newest member of the team, impatiently tapping her right foot.

Laying a rock-solid hand on Panini's shoulder, Rogers clumsily said, "Joey Panini, meet my---meet my colleague, Beth Murphy."

"Sir, it's nice to meet you."

With as somber a face as he could muster, Panini asked, "Who is this sir?" The transplanted New York City native, who had settled in Detroit in recent years, pretended to be straining his neck in looking up at the trio as if he was a tiny sapling in a small forest of three tall redwoods. "Call me Panini and if you want to really get my attention -- you can even shout Yo Panini."

Rogers, Ashley, and Beth grinned in mild amusement, somehow anticipating that he was not finished with his monologue.

"Hey, can we sit down? My neck is killing me. Look, in my whole life, I've been short changed." He giggled. "It's true. My mom once told me that a managed care company denied payment for my endocrinologist's order for growth hormone. They said my stature was normal, given my ancestry." With a twinkle in his eyes, he added, "Come to think of it, I am the tallest in my family."

After a round of polite laughter, Rogers added, "Knowing you like I do, I'm sure that the rest of our team will soon come to appreciate your many talents." He pointed for Ashley and Panini to file into the semi-circular diner booth. Panini took the far end.

Rogers then turned around to face Beth. She bore an exasperated look plastered on her face, seemingly not in the mood for anything but a full-throated discussion on blocking the approval of *NeoBloc*. He sensed her obvious discomfort and gave her a belated half-hearted hug. She returned the ill at ease gesture by leaning slightly forward without moving her feet an inch.

He eked out a half-smile. "Beth, why don't you sit next to me? I'll sit in the middle, between you and Ashley. That way, Panini can't steal my French Fries so easily."

"Oh yeah! Well-- I've got news for you Doctor Jonathan Rogers. When you're looking out the window to see if anyone is stalking you, I'll just grab a few," he replied with an inviting elfish grin.

The Surgeon General reached over and tapped his pal on the arm. "Since I called this last minute meeting, I'm asking the corner booth to come to order," he said with a half kidding look. Glancing over at his friend, he could not help but notice the position of Panini's hands. He folded them with interlocking fingers on the blue and white Formica tabletop, just like in the old days when both of them were in sixth grade at St Vincent. Memories streamed back to the many times that Mother Superior, the school's tough disciplinarian nun, would make unannounced visits to their class, pulling on the ears of any of the boys, apparently just because she wanted to do so, or more likely to reinforce the message that she was firmly in charge of everything and anything.

Panini twisted his body, put his arm around the back of the booth, and faced his team with an easygoing grin. "OK folks, the fun is over. It looks like the Doctor General has some work for all of us."

Rogers nodded. "I do need all of your help." He glanced at both Ashley and Beth. "You're all I have to trust." The Surgeon General spread his arms behind all of them as if he were a giant eagle, a protector of the flock.

"Sweetie, what's the latest with you?"

Ashley wiped away a tear. "Dad, I'm scared."

Rogers noted the server approaching. "Let's order first so we won't be interrupted. The menu is listed on the far wall."

Panini ordered in a low monotone voice. "I'll have one of those special YCBS's."

His friend queried, "What the hell is that?"

Rolling his eyes, Panini chuckled. "Duh, read the menu—General Doctor or General Hospital or whatever they call you down in DC."

Rogers quickly figured out the acronym. "Make that two," replied the Surgeon General. "Ladies?"

"Grilled chicken salad," added Beth as she shifted her hips a foot away from him in the booth. Ashley shook her head in agreement with the prior selection while keeping her downhearted gaze on her father,

The server repeated the order. "Two- You Can't Be Serious orders with the full works and two chicken salads." The server then marched to the kitchen. Rogers gently placed his hand on Ashley's shoulder. "What's going on?"

"I was leaving my apartment to come here." She hesitated and looked at her father with a frightened side wide glance. Ashley then shut her eyes, recalling the scene. "Anyway, for no particular reason my eyes were attracted to this classy looking blue BMW. It just didn't seem to fit with the other Chevy's and Fords on my campus. So, when I pulled out of my parking space, I noticed the BMW following me down the street and onto the freeway." She opened her eyes with a startled look. "It seemed when I slowed down, the BMW did so as well. For a minute or so, I held my cell. I thought of calling you. While I was contemplating what to do, I lost track of the BMW."

Panini interrupted, "Could be just a coincidence."

Ashley continued, "A few moments later, the other car exited at Oldwyck. Even though nothing happened, it was just a creepy feeling." She shook as if an arctic blast had just pelted her. "Looking back, I guess my imagination may have gotten the best of me."

Panini asked, "Did you get a good look at the driver?"

"No."

Beth chimed in, "I was stalked-----once."

Rogers took a few sips of water and imagined what could have happened. "Ever since what happened to----." He stopped himself in mid-sentence. "Ashley, perhaps it would best if you and Beth to---."

His colleague finished his thought. "Ashley, why don't you move in with me until things settle down? I have a spare room."

Rogers shook his head in full agreement. "That's a terrific idea!"

Panini deadpanned, "How come no one is asking me to room with them?"

Looking over at Beth, Ashley added, "Deal." She asked, "How about if we all go back to my apartment tonight for me to gather my stuff?"

"Honey, we'll go back after our meeting. Maybe, we'll catch the end of the Michigan game."

"Three in an apartment would still work better than two," Panini contributed with a twinkle in his eye. "Cheaper rent for one thing."

Beth chirped up, "Glad to have you as a roommate. It will be fun. We'll all help you to pack tonight."

Rogers shot a wink at his pal, and guessed where he would probably take the conversation. "We need to focus on this deadly vaccine that is likely to be approved for mass deployment among all Americans if we don't stop it. I've been thinking. We need to starting thinking and acting like detectives."

Panini took the bait. "Listen, I watch CSI. The secret to solving any Sherlock situation is to grab a DNA specimen."

The Surgeon General thought about Sally Parker's claim that Connor was Zach. "DNA could help us." He turned toward Beth. "One of our jobs is that we need to gather evidence to prove that Connor Lucas is really Zach Miller."

Ashley looked apprehensively at her father. "But Zach Miller is dead. What are you saying?"

"Sweetie, I'm sorry to say that we have good reason to believe that Zach never died in that explosion of his Ferrari. And, we have an informed source stating that Zach had plastic surgery in South America and returned in the person of Connor Lucas."

"That's really bad news if it's true." She clenched her fist. "That guy was a monster!"

Panini scratched his forehead. "Who are all these people? All I know is that Chuck Connors was the Rifleman. Is this guy Connor somehow related to the western cowboy TV star?"

Ashley replied to his attempt at humor. "Even if he had plastic surgery, Connor doesn't look at all like Zach."

Panini interjected, "Duh. That would be too easy. A TV show would be over in the first five minutes if it were that simple. I'm telling you my friends; the answer is blowing in the DNA."

"Ashley, I've seen unbelievable changes from plastic surgery. It's certainly possible." Rogers leaned over, past his daughter and tapped his friend's wrist. "OK, smarty pants, how are we going to get DNA from a supposedly dead guy who was blown to smithereens when his car flipped down the hill at Baker's Field Airport over a year ago?"

Panini covered his eyes with his right hand, resting his palm on his forehead. After withdrawing all of his digits from his head, he snapped his fingers. "Karnack says we could swab any part of the Ferrari that still remains where ole Zach might have touched."

Rogers grinned. "It sounds so simple. But I'm not sure that any DNA sample would still be viable—after all that time and exposure to the elements."

Before anyone could reply, the server approached with a tray of entrées. Beth called out. "The boys get that greasy thing---whatever you called it and the ladies get the healthy salads."

The Surgeon General took a hearty chew of his Chubby Wubby. The ketchup dripped down his hand past his wrist. He didn't attempt to wipe it off, seemingly engrossed with his tasty meal. "This is living."

Panini took a series of chomps. "You can say that again, Johnny Boy. Just like the old days."

Beth glanced up from digging into piles of lettuce interspersed with a few slices of cucumber and tomato and asked, "Most importantly, what about the President's later decision on the vaccine?"

Rogers pointed to her. "Thanks for bringing us back to reality." He looked over at Ashley and Panini. "How we can stop Project Moon Shot before a rifle is aimed at the ultimate decision maker----me."

Panini choked on his burger. "It seems to me that President Williams won't stop this vaccine program. Could it be just because she is the mooner-in-chief?"

Rogers could see Ashley's carotid artery pulsating as her cheeks grew redder. In a few seconds, the building of her temper would explode down the tracks like a runaway freight train.

She unleashed her anger on time, as expected. "This is not funny." Her usually soft voice sounded more like the shrill bark of a boardwalk caller, selling something. Ashley turned her back on Panini. "My Dad's been through enough. This is serious."

The lonesome voice from the end of the table persisted in his banter. "I recommend that we all become Canadians. At least, we can be sure the President of the United States won't inoculate them with *NeoBloc.*"

As soon as Panini said it, Rogers felt pangs of guilt. He looked at his daughter and Beth. "Listen guys, my friend here is at an unfair disadvantage. He is not fully aware of the gravity of the situation. He's only heard bits and pieces. That's my fault. Let me summarize how we got here for everyone's benefit."

"Thanks Johnny Boy. Start with the Rifleman—Chuck whatever his name is."

***

After hearing the whole story in precision detail, Panini's demeanor turned completely somber. Rogers looked at each appointed deputy. "So, what do you all think?"

Beth's fork clanked off her plate. "We need to find Connor Lucas as soon as possible."

"He's the key," Ashley agreed.

"All in favor?" Rogers counted three hands. Dissuading President Williams from her mission to deploy *NeoBloc* would be challenging. But, for now, Beth was right. Connor was their obvious target. He slapped a high five with each of them.

******

Connor waited five minutes past seven but Ashley was a definite no-show at her apartment. He knew that the patience of law enforcement in DuPont was rapidly cascading toward the tipping point. Ashley had obviously changed her plans. It was time to move to plan B. He would return to Miss Rogers's apartment after he gave his formal complaint to Sergeant Angelo.

He crawled out the raised bathroom window sash with his weapon in the gym bag held close to his chest. In the blackness of the night, only the full moon provided guidance while he cut across the winding pathways of her apartment complex. With his BMW coming into sight on the street, he jumped into the driver's seat and sped his way to the police station.

Arriving just five minutes before Angelo's arbitrary deadline, he bounded up the flight of stone stairs, after double-parking his car. He sprinted to the front desk. Sergeant Angelo exuded arrogance, shouting at Connor for his last minute arrival.

He profusely apologized on why he didn't come into the DC police station immediately after his first call and why he chose to make his official complaint in DuPont Michigan.

Angelo, the desk sergeant launched some verbal barbs at him. Minutes later, the cop finally stopped his tirade and allowed Connor to speak. He reminded the sergeant that he needed to rush home from DC to attend to a sick family member. His excuse won him a reprieve.

For the next twenty-five minutes, he articulated an utterly fabricated tale. Angelo captured on tape every exquisite lie. He then signed a formal complaint against Secretary James while answering some basic questions from the detective assigned to the case. When asked about the DNA evidence linking James and himself, Connor cleverly posed a question of whether the police lab would be able to process the specimen at this late hour, repeatedly emphasizing that he had the critical evidence securely refrigerated at his home in order to preserve it. Breathing a deep sigh of relief after the detective approved of a daytime delivery of the DNA proof within the next three days, he knew that he had dodged another bullet.

Pleased that he was free to leave, he drove back to Ashley's apartment. He checked his watch after pulling into a space on the barren street. *9PM.* He made his way back to her place. Heading toward the bathroom window, he heard nothing. After slipping on a pair of gloves that he pulled out of his gym bag, Connor raised the window sash even higher, providing enough clearance space for him to slip easily inside, but equally important, so that he would be able to hastily exit once he killed Ashley. For a full thirty seconds, he counted off, intently listening for any sound coming from within the apartment. *Silence.*

Inside the apartment, he dropped the gym bag to the bathroom floor. He pulled out his 9mm and ensured that the silencer was firmly in place. From room to room, he searched, finding no one. He walked back into the bathroom. The frigid night air rushed through the window opening, dropping the temperature even lower since he had left two hours earlier. Connor sat down on the cover of the toilet seat, shaking himself and crossing his arms over his chest to maintain as much body heat as possible, all the while maintaining a firm grip on his pistol. He wished that he was wearing his thick winter jacket but he took comfort in knowing that his mark would be arriving sometime that night. *Plan B is working.*

Rogers barreled down the road toward Ashley's apartment. His daughter rode shotgun. Beth and Panini each planted themselves against their respective doors in the back seat of the Lexus. Golden Oldies music blared on the radio. Panini, who lip sang his favorite Beatles song, *Yesterday,* was in a great mood, reliving the poetry of his teenage favorite lyrics.

Approaching DeWitt Street, Rogers heard a breaking news story on the national news station. Turning up the volume, he listened carefully. Half-way through the dreadful report that Christian James had hung himself; he pulled into a spot on the street close to Apartment Nine. The DuPont Commons apartment complex sprawled over many acres. Distracted from the small talk of his advisors in the car, he reflected on the potential implications of the Secretary's apparent suicide with regard to the political dynamics swirling around the *NeoBloc* vortex.

Deep in thought, Rogers jumped out of his Lexus and hastily walked toward his daughter's apartment, leaving the rest of them temporarily in the dust. He was a dozen steps ahead of them when Ashley began her trot to catch up with her father. She then sprinted ahead of him, actually being the first to arrive at her front door.

From the rear of the pack, Panini yelled, "Hurry up and open the door. It's freezing out here. The wind chill temperature must be in the teens."

Jumping up and down to keep as warm as possible, Rogers impatiently waited for Ashley to unlock the door. She inserted her key and pushed it open. He followed her into the apartment. A surge of frosty air from inside the living room smacked them in their faces, sending chills down their spines.

He turned around to see Beth and Panini fast approaching, half dozen steps away from the front door. He yelled, "It seems as cold in here as it is outside."

Ashley took two steps from the living room down the hallway toward her bathroom just as Panini entered the living room. He instantly called her name. She stopped dead in her tracks. "Hey, what temp do you keep your thermostat on?" Panini asked while he checked the actual room temperature.

"Sixty eight," Ashley replied, looking somewhat confused as she met his hard gaze.

"Really!" Panini stared warily down the hallway. He then motioned for her to come back toward him.

"I need to make a pit stop. I'll be right back."

He sprinted after her and grabbed her arm. She turned around with a stunned look. He covered her mouth with his hand and whispered, "Don't say a word." A moment later, he frantically pushed the trio toward the front door. "Let's go----now!"

"What the hell are you doing?" Rogers protested while being corralled out the front door.

"Shut up! I'll explain in a few minutes. He slammed the door shut. "Run as fast as you can toward that building," he whispered, pointing in a westerly direction.

Ashley and Beth led the sprint----twenty yards or so to the next building. Soon, they were all standing behind a corner wall of the next set of garden apartments. Once gathered, Rogers poked his head out, looking back toward Ashley's front door. "OK, Panini, let's hear it."

Panini took several full breaths before beginning. "Something is wrong in there. The thermostat is registering thirty nine degrees but its set at sixty eight."

Ashley offered, "Maybe my furnace broke."

Panini squared up to her. "I see that you get your logical thinking from your dad. But I saw something suspicious in there. You have a small table half way down the hallway that leads from the living room. The table had a leafy Ivy plant on it."

"So?"

"I saw an open door right directly across from your plant."

"What's your point?"

"Humor me." Rogers and Beth huddled closer around them. "What room is across from the plant?"

"It's my bathroom," she replied.

"Ashley," Panini continued, "I'm sure you don't keep your bathroom window open in the dead of winter when you set your thermostat at sixty eight degrees."

"Why would you say that?"

"The leaves on the Ivy plant were swaying as if a stiff breeze was blowing at them. I would bet my life that your bathroom window is open or busted."

Rogers put his arm around Ashley, sending her a knowing look. "My friend is street smart. I think he's right."

Beth whipped out her cell and waited for it to power up. "I'm calling the police."

Panini puffed his chest. "I once saw a TV show where a criminal broke an apartment window on a night like tonight. The intended victim saved her life by feeling the chill when she opened the front door. The woman smartly ran out of the apartment. Otherwise, she would have been stabbed to death."

Rogers shook his head in agreement. "Makes sense to be careful, especially under our circumstances."

Ashley shivered as another north wind kicked up. "Beth, did you get the police?"

"Shit, my battery must have died."

Rogers pulled out his Blackberry.

Panini held up both hands. "I've been thinking. If someone were still in your bathroom with a gun, the intruder would have simply walked out while we were in the living room. Clearly, he would have heard all of our voices as we entered the apartment. But, if the intruder had a knife, he would wait until someone actually entered the bathroom. And, it's also possible that whoever broke in has already left the premises."

Rogers began dialing the police with his Blackberry on the speaker function.

"DuPont police."

"I am reporting a break-in at the DuPont Commons off DeWitt. Apartment nine."

"Your name, sir."

"Jonathan Rogers."

"Are you currently inside the apartment?"

"No."

"Good. Do not go inside. I'll dispatch a car. I'll stay on the call with you."

"OK."

Panini began to backpedal toward Ashley's apartment.

"Where do you think you're going?"

"Guys, I want all of you to walk over to the central courtyard. It's far enough away to be safe but you'll have a direct line of sight to the apartment. I want to check around the back of Ashley's apartment. I'll be right back."

Instinctively, Rogers reached out and grabbed Panini by the arm. "Are you crazy? Let's wait until the police come. They can handle it."

"Listen General Doctor, I'm not going inside the apartment. I just want to get a closer look. Do you want him to escape while we just stand hear waiting for the authorities? And, if they put their sirens on, the guy will just escape into the surrounding woods."

"How do we know it's a guy?"

"Good point. We don't." Panini turned and began walking toward the opposite side of the apartment, away from the bathroom window.

"I'm going with you." He pointed at the women. "Do as he said." He gave the Blackberry to his daughter.

Beth and Ashley ran to the courtyard while Rogers stayed with his friend.

"Panini, I'm right behind you. Staying a few steps behind, he mimicked his every move as they both sneaked beneath the living room window, slithering alongside the aluminum siding. As they made their way around the back, the dense woods came into view. Ashley's bedroom window was intact. They turned the corner toward the other side of her apartment. A small window came into view. Panini placed his index finger over his mouth while pointing to the broken window. Holding his hand up, he said in quiet voice. "Stay put. I just want to get a little closer."

He reached out and tapped Panini's shoulder. "No. Let's get out of here."

"OK. Start heading back to the women. I'll be with you in a few seconds."

Rogers retraced his steps and headed for the central courtyard. Beth and Ashley were peeking behind the corner of the next building.

"Dad, thank God you're back. Where's Panini?"

"He said that he would be right behind me. I'm going back to get him."

"No," Ashley shouted. "If someone is in my apartment, I bet it's the driver of the BMW that trailed me." "Sweetie, it will be OK. The police are on the way."

She pointed to the Blackberry. "No, the dispatcher just told me they are delayed five minutes."

"Panini needs to let the police handle this." Rogers glanced down at his watch. *Five minutes to ten.* He hoped the police would not use their sirens. "I'm going back to get him."

"Dad, promise me that you'll be careful." Ashley pulled his sleeve toward her, roping him toward herself. "I don't have a good feeling about this."

"I'll be fine. Stay here with Beth." He kissed her forehead and then dashed back toward her apartment. He reached the back bedroom window, near the woods, but saw no sign of his friend.

The boom of a single gunshot cracked the night air. The sound seemed to come from around the corner of the apartment. Reflexively, he sprinted toward the bathroom. Turning the corner, he saw Panini writhing on the ground, flat on his back. Bright red blood stained both of his hands and his slacks were soaked with blood near the groin area.

A gun barrel with a silencer protruded from the bathroom window, pointed directly at Panini. Rogers lurched toward it. Grabbing the white-hot barrel, he tried to wrench it away. His hand immediately felt the burn from the fiery metal, forcing him to release his grip. He looked up at the contorted face of the shooter. *Connor Lucas.*

He elbowed Connor's hand, forcing the gun to be directed skyward. His long time sworn enemy roared with hatred as his mouth twisted into an evil sneer. An idea popped to mind. Rogers pulled down the right sleeve of his jacket, placing his now covered right hand firmly on the barrel. In wrestling for control of the gun, a moment later, the Baretta pointed at his right ribcage. He fought to push the barrel of the weapon toward the ground. Connor's finger was on the trigger.

"You're dead meat Rogers. Just like when I killed Kim."

Upon hearing those words, something primal went off in his brain. Kim's image instantly planted itself—right between him and the killer as if she were trying to protect him. The Surgeon General heaved a violent karate chop to Connor's right hand, dislodging the Baretta. The gun fell onto the grass.

Rogers lunged at him, grabbing Connor's shirt just below the neckline. He planted his feet against the apartment outside wall for leverage and heaved as hard as he could, pulling the killer out of the bathroom and toward him.

Tumbling in the grass, Connor hollered, "You're like a cat." But, with his superior strength, he pinned the Surgeon General flat on his back. "But, even cats don't have ten lives. And the string has finally run out for you doc."

Desperate to push Connor off his body, the shooter's powerful legs held down him down. From the corner of his eye, he saw Panini badly faltering when he attempted to stand.

The killer leaned to the right and was able to get his hand around the Baretta. A wad of Connor's spit hit Rogers in his right eye. He reacted with a burst of adrenalin, hammering the gun barrel to point in the direction of the ground with one vicious swipe of his hand. That only enraged Connor. By now, his face resembled a deranged psycho. He looked like a maniacal killer, struggling with all of his might to point the gun barrel back toward his target.

The Surgeon General felt his strength ebbing. The barrel moved in an erratic arc, at times the younger and more muscular Connor was closer to gaining the deadly edge in a furious struggle. Rogers saw that his eyes carried a demonic glaze. *Fight! Never give up!* As if in a slow motion movie, he spotted Panini's blood soaked hands now tightly gripping the gun. With overpowering revenge exploding in Connor's darting eyes, the Baretta wavered from side to side. An instant later, the left side of Rogers's head felt as if a fire iron torched it.

After the 9 mm. shot was fired, Panini's hands flew off the smoldering silencer. Dazed, Rogers heard booming police sirens. Everything seemed jumbled in a whirling blur. He spotted Connor leaping to his feet. The blaring of the sirens grew louder, as if they were already at the scene. He picked up his head and caught a glimpse of the shooter dashing away into the woods. His mind turned fuzzy, no longer able to think clearly. He dropped his head to one side, watching Panini collapse to his knees after attempting a few steps, unable to chase the fugitive. Ashley appeared to be running toward his side. When she touched him, the severe crushing pain inside Rogers's temple appeared to subside just as he began a peaceful dream-- with Kim. She was floating on a billowy cloud and blowing a tender kiss in his direction. Peace had arrived.

CHAPTER FORTY-TWO

Ashley bounced off the wall in the back of the Med-Evac helicopter as it banked hard left. Strapped into a seat, she stared fearfully at her father and held his right hand. An intravenous line of fluids dripped into a vein in his left arm. He had been unconscious ever since she found him lying on the grass just outside her bathroom window.

Just before the helicopter took off, paramedic named Tracey inserted a flexible plastic tube into her father's airways, connecting the opposite end to a mechanical respirator.

Another paramedic named Mandy spoke on an overhead speaker to the closest tier 1 hospital trauma neurosurgeon. "Dr. Fisher, our patient is a sixty two year old male. The patient has remained unconscious since we first arrived on the scene. Past medical history is unremarkable except for an upper lobectomy of the right lung due to a gunshot wound in the chest just below his clavicle almost two years ago. He is taking Cozaar for mild hypertension. Fifteen minutes ago, he suffered an open gunshot wound to his left temple. I'm applying gentle pressure to a deep scalp wound. There is bright red blood oozing through a Bacitracin soaked gauze pad. I've used a new pad every two minutes. His pulse oximeter measures 88% O2 saturation. Blood pressure is 95 over 60. His Glasgow neurological score is 9 with an E2V3M4 breakdown. D5W/Normal saline is pouring in his vein at 150 cc per hour. A few minutes ago, both pupils were fully reactive to light. Now, the left pupil is no longer reacting as well as the contralateral right pupil. Our clinical impression is that he may have third nerve dysfunction secondary to a possible subdural hematoma."

The neurosurgeon responded on the intercom. "Good work Mandy. From the departure time your pilot gave us, you should be landing at our helipad at Detroit Metro in twelve minutes. Technicians are standing by for an emergency CT exam. We'll need to operate as soon as possible in order to evacuate any blood clots, remove the bullet, and reduce the intracranial pressure. I want you to administer mannitol 20% solution over thirty minutes at one gram per kilogram of body weight. That should reduce his building intracranial pressure. You should be here at the Medical Center before the solution runs through."

"Tracey," Mandy relayed, "Begin intravenous mannitol per Dr. Fisher's order. Is there anything else, doctor?"

"If he becomes combative, push five milligrams of diazepam. Continue to monitor his Glasgow score every minute and call me immediately if you observe any further deterioration."

"Will do doctor. Over and out."

Ashley interrupted. "Tracey, I'm a fourth year medical student at the University. I know that a Glasgow score is a composite of specific neurological findings. But I'm no expert on the specifics."

Tracey, while grabbing for the mannitol, responded. "The Glasgow score acronym is EVM. It measures eye reactions to voice and pain. The score is a useful tool to measure a range of verbal abilities and motor skills as well."

"I know you're very busy. If you can talk to me while you're working, what's my father's current condition?"

"Just before I intubated your dad with his breathing tube, he was blurting out random words but he was not coherent. He was not making any sense. So his verbal or V score was 3. And, his M4 score measures motor function. He was able to respond to hard pressure applied to his heel by trying to withdraw his leg."

Ashley wiped away the streaming tears cascading down her cheeks. "Thank you so much. My dad's all I have."

Tracey smiled and hung a bag of mannitol and connected it to the intravenous line. She adjusted the drip frequency into Rogers's veins after doing the body weight calculations per Dr Fisher's order.

Ashley realized that she was being intrusive. "I apologize for my questions." She touched Tracey's hand.

"No problem. Fire away."

"Why did you give him an E2 score?"

"His eyelid moved slightly when I pressed hard on his nail bed to cause him pain."

"How bad is his overall Glasgow score?"

"His overall score of nine is a sign of very serious head trauma. A lower score generally means a worse prognosis." Tracey began to pump up the blood pressure cuff. She put the listening pieces of the stethoscope into her ears. "Please excuse me."

Ashley watched the paramedic repeat the neurologic testing every minute. Each time, she recorded the results on her notepad. By now, Beth and Panini would be at the local Mercy Hospital in DuPont. She had overheard the conversation of the EMS worker who evaluated Panini while he was lying on the ground next to her dad. Judging from the entry wound, the bullet to his groin just missed his femoral artery. One less worry----Panini was going to survive.

A few minutes later, Ashley could not restrain herself. "What's the latest on my dad?"

Mandy frowned. "Not now, his pulse oximeter just showed a drop in oxygen in his blood. I think he's building up more intracranial pressure." The EMS worker looked away. "We'll be landing in several minutes. I need to call Dr. Fisher with an update."

The paramedic pressed number one on the intercom buttons. Ashley heard Dr. Fisher's voice on speaker. Mandy calmly whispered the latest findings. Ashley noticed one spoken fact----her dad's overall neurological score had dropped to an eight. *Not good!*

While holding his hand tightly, her dad moaned several times. Soon, he began to thrash about--his arms flailing wildly. Mandy held down both arms. Tracey pushed a bolus of diazepam into the intravenous port. After he quieted down, Mandy pulled back his eyelids and flashed a penlight into his eyes.

The pilot yelled out from the cockpit. "Seat belts on! We'll be landing in approximately one minute."

Ashley glanced out the side window of the BK-117 helicopter and saw the Detroit Metro landing port a thousand feet below. Tracey and Mandy buckled themselves into adjacent seats. Rogers's chest rhythmically expanded and contracted with each cycle of the respirator. The repetitive sounds of the oxygen being forced into his lungs seemed to grow louder. *Whoosh----whoosh-----whoosh.*

She turned toward Tracy. "Before you intubated my dad, you said that he was speaking random words. What were they?"

The paramedic hesitated a second or two and then whispered, "I believe he was calling out your name Ashley and also someone named Kim."

CHAPTER FORTY-THREE

Beth slumped in a straight-backed chair alongside Panini's bed. His surgeon had left the room twenty minutes ago. Panini had drifted off to sleep. But the last call from Ashley had further darkened her mood. Her mind wandered to a place far away from Mercy Medical Center in DuPont.

A full recovery by Jonathan weighed heavily on her mind. Profoundly worried that he might not make it this time, she hoped that the patient in front of her would recuperate soon so she could head toward Detroit Metro—to see her friend.

Panini stirred. He asked, "Any word from Ashley?"

Beth continued to stare at the floor, deep in thought, not hearing his voice.

He stifled a wince of pain from his bandaged hands, burned while he had gripped the white-hot silencer on Connor's Baretta. He bellowed, "Hello Earth to Beth. I said, how is Johnny Boy doing?"

Startled, Beth's eyes popped open. "Ashley called me after you fell asleep. He's in surgery. His condition deteriorated just before he underwent the emergency CT scan."

"Shit! I should have kicked the gun out of that guy's hand instead of going for it."

Beth reached over and touched the section of sheet covering his leg. "You were shot yourself. You did the best you could. Don't beat yourself up."

"A flesh wound. No big deal."

"We'll both go to Detroit Metro Medical Center tomorrow after you're released."

"Somehow, I'm going to find the guy who shot us and when I do---."

Beth rose slowly as if trying to shake off the cobwebs. "I'm going for some coffee. Want me to bring back one for you?"

Panini kept his eyes downcast. "Thanks. I take mine black."

Walking out of the room, she met two DuPont detectives who flashed their badges. Beth turned around and resumed her seat. The detectives hovered at the foot of Panini's bed.

"Good morning. I'm Detective Roman. This is my partner, Detective Scott."

"Where's Sergeant Joe Friday," Panini joked. "Bet you gentlemen have a bazillion questions for me."

Scott asked, "Did you get a good look at the suspect?"

"Yep, I sure did. When will you be sending a police sketch artist over?"

Roman said, "She'll be here this afternoon." He wrinkled his forehead. "I see that you know the drill."

"I watch a lot of movies."

Pulling out a notepad, Scott asked Panini for a complete statement of what had transpired. "After, I record what you say; Special Agent Susan Masters will be taking over the case of the double shootings.

"Well gents, this is what happened----sad but true---."

******

Panini was impressed. "You're black and white drawing is coming alive."

The artist asked, "What about the shooter's eye color?"

"Light blue." He scratched his beard, growing as a goatee on his chin. "His eyes looked strange—phony. I'll just bet that asshole was wearing contacts."

"I'll make a note of the color at the bottom of the sketch." She drew the shape of the suspect's nose per Panini's recollection. She glanced over at him. "Are we there yet?"

"Not quite. The jaw needs to be much fuller. And, the eyes need a more devilish look to them."

"Gotcha." The artist penciled in the additional changes. She rolled her chair back to view her work. "How is this version?"

Beth held her hand to her forehead and cried out, "It's him. That's Connor Lucas"

CHAPTER FORTY-FOUR

Connor spent a restless night in an off the beaten path DuPont hotel. Last night, he checked in as John Smith and paid with cash in advance. He was unwilling to risk staying at his Tudor style home in the upscale area of DuPont; for fear, the local police would be paying him an unwanted visit. He was certain that he was already a "person of interest" in the Christian James hanging case given his prior calls to the police departments in DC and DuPont and his signed complaint for sexual harassment in DuPont against James. He thrashed about in his bed, torturing himself for being so stupid as to trust the Secretary of Health.

Now, with the double shootings at Ashley apartment on his mind, he became alarmed. Two people could place him at the crime scene. It was time to lay low. Time was what he needed---time to sort things through.

While tossing about, he had changed his mind. For the time being, he decided to hold off delivering the test tube with the DNA profiles of both Christian James and himself to either the DuPont police. *I'll use it when the time is right!* The napkin in the marked glass tube was going to be the forensic evidence to discredit James and any adverse allegations the Secretary might have previously made about him and *The Health Club.*

After rising early, he drove to his office, arriving at five. He flashed his ID and passed through the one guard manned security gate. Once inside, he saw no one and he walked to his office and locked the door. On a 9 X 11 yellow sheet, he wrote down his challenges and on another sheet, he penned a directive note for his administrative assistant. Clearly, James's email to Ashley exposing Connor and *The Health Club* was at the top of his worry list. Just below that trepidation was his concern that he had himself left behind incriminating forensic evidence of his own DNA by spitting in the Surgeon General's face and of course—the eyewitness.

Connor flipped on his Apple laptop. He brought up the web site of the local newspaper, The *DuPont Gazette.* The front-page headline screamed the news. Surgeon General Shot: Comatose. He read further. He slammed his fist on his desk, fuming that he had not finished Rogers off when he had him in the cross hairs. *An inch more toward the center of his forehead and he'd be gone for good.* While reading on, the story in the *Gazette* revealed the name of the man he shot in the leg. Goose bumps sprang up all over his skin. Dante Joseph Panzzanini was reportedly in stable condition at Mercy Hospital.

As mounting problems paraded across his mind, he had already pictured Panzzanini as an eyewitness sitting up in his Mercy hospital bed and talking to local DuPont detectives and then the FBI. Lower down on page one was a story about the discovery of the body of Secretary of State Christian James. The paper quoted the police as labeling the hanging as a suicide. A wry smile emerged on his face when there was no mention of any allegations regarding Connor, DCP or *NeoBloc*. He opened his desk drawer and pulled out a marked manila folder. This was his emergency plan he had drawn up for dire situations like this. *Execute the plan---execute the plan!*

He leaped up, unlocked his door, walking out with the folder under his left arm. Dropping off his note on the chair of his administrative assistant, the message informed her that he would be traveling on business for a few days and that she should not try to contact him under any circumstances. He had added the words in large letters---no matter what!

Connor settled into the plush leather bucket seat of his BMW. Still unable to forgive himself for his lack of critical decision-making judgment, he punched the rawhide-covered steering wheel several times. *No more mistakes! Kill anyone who can hurt me!*

Within minutes after snaking his way through local streets, he drove onto Highway 96 West. Grand Rapids, Michigan, was his destination. He had loyal friends there; the type of friends who would do anything for money.

As he headed due west, Connor weaved his way through the highway traffic, changing lanes as though he was driving at a NASCAR event. In response to his aggressive driving, at one time, another driver tried to get even by exhibiting his own road rage. He returned the mutual finger exchange after both drivers tried sideswiping each other.

Not having slept well for the last couple of days, he nodded off several times, almost drifting off the highway on two occasions. Thankful that he had averted these near mishaps on the highway; his adrenalin flowed at breakneck speed. Cascading through his blood, his own natural hormone, was the only difference in keeping him alert—and alive!

A half mile ahead, parked in the center divider by the overhead lamppost, he spotted a Michigan State Police car. He looked down at his speed. *Eighty.* Connor slammed on the brakes and glanced in his rear view mirror. He covered the left side of his face by pulling up the collar of his black down winter coat. His heart felt like it was going to burst from his chest. As he passed the lamppost, he prayed to his gods. The police car did not budge. He sighed deeply and made a mental note for the remainder of his road trip.

Once he was able to calm down, he was able to finalize a plan of action in his mind. He admitted to himself that it was extremely risky. If it worked, he assured himself that he would remain king of the hill. If it failed, he knew that he would soon be a dead man.

CHAPTER FORTY-FIVE

Ashley was barely listening to her cell conversation while she waited outside the neurosurgical operating room. An attendant had wheeled her father into surgery hours ago and she had not yet heard a word from his physician. From speaking with Beth, she learned of tomorrow's discharge from Mercy Hospital for Panini. Both had planned to come to Detroit Metro as soon as they could.

She gazed out the window, lost in her thoughts, watching big snowflakes, tiny snowflakes, each crisscrossing other flecks, a maze of particles blown by swirling winds. The flakes zoomed horizontally, vertically, and randomly exploding against each other, sometimes avoiding a head on collision, blotting out the adjacent hospital wing. Gravity began winning out, melding each flake as it reached its ultimate destiny, nesting softy in a blanket of pure white snow in the huge parking lot of Detroit Metro.

The peacefulness of the pure snow stood in marked contrast to the vortex of turmoil that she was feeling. Ashley stood to stretch. Her neck muscles pulled in every direction as if she were sitting on a spinning top. The clock on the wall revealed how long it had been since she had spoke to the neurosurgeon. While she began walking to the nearest nurses' station, the door to the waiting room outside the surgical suite opened slowly. Her heart pounded. It was her father's neurosurgeon.

Dr. Adrian Fisher strode in her direction. It had been ten hours since he first told her that the CT scan revealed a large expanding blood clot with an embedded 9 mm bullet in his temporal lobe. As she watched him advancing toward her, she felt paralyzed, unable to move a muscle.

Yanking off his surgical mask, his eyes were mere slits just below a heavily perspiring forehead. His mouth drooped down while he moistened his chapped lips with a short swig from a bottle of water that he carried in his right hand. Fisher drew in a deep breath that he noisily exhaled just as he reached her side.

The neurosurgeon motioned for them to sit down. She anxiously searched his face for answers. Ashley said a quick prayer. *Please dear God, don't let him say what I fear!* He sat alongside her, in an adjacent chair, looking completely drained.

He squinted, clearing his voice. "Your father is one tough hombre. He is still in a coma but, considering all factors, he is doing as well as possible. He'll be in the recovery room for another hour or so before going to the intensive care unit."

She reached out for Fisher's hand. "Doc-----." Unable to finish, she squeezed his hand. *Is he going to be all right?*

"I understand what you're going through." Fisher pulled away, stood, and let his steady hand linger for several moments on her shoulder. "He is stable for the moment. That is all that I can say at this time. I'll speak with you again in an hour or so."

"What----what can I do for him?"

"Hope and pray for the best."

She covered her face. Her cell phone rang but she ignored the ring tones of "Wind beneath my wings" and resumed her prayer to God.

******

A familiar sounding voice awakened Ashley. She rubbed her eyes. The bright light streaming from the overhead fixtures in the family waiting room outside the ICU forced her to blink repeatedly, to focus. She looked up from the leather-cushioned couch where she had slept the entire night

Beth said, "We came as fast as we could. How is he doing?"

Ashley shielded her eyes. She spotted Panini standing alongside her roommate. "Dad is still in a coma." Feeling weak, she searched for her water bottle on the adjacent table. Beth handed it to her and Ashley took a long gulp.

"His latest Glasgow coma score is a nine, a slight improvement over where he was pre-op."

Panini made a face. "What's a Glasgow?"

"It's a combination of factors that doctors use to measure brain function. Just remember that the higher the number, the better the prognosis."

"Got it. Nine out of what?

"15."

"Thanks." Frowning, Panini sat down alongside Ashley. "I'm so sorry. I tried to get the gun away from that guy but I was too weak." A slight grimace blanketed his face as he gently rubbed his right groin. "No excuse. I should have done better."

"It's not your fault." Ashley patted his hand. "What actually happened? Did you get a good look at the shooter?"

Beth interjected, "Panini, I don't think we should be discussing these things now." She sat down and hugged Ashley. "I know your dad. He's tough. If anyone can make it, he will."

"All I do is pray. I can't even think straight." She put her arms around Beth and Panini and drew them closer to her. A moment later, she looked up and saw Dr. Fisher walking toward her. He was wearing a huge grin. Ashley leaped to her feet.

"Good news! Your dad is awake. You can see him but only for a moment."

"Thank you God. Thank you God." Ashley squeezed Beth and Panini's hands. Dr. Fisher, can my friends come?"

He hesitated. "OK but only for a minute."

All of them trailed behind the neurosurgeon in entering the ICU. They walked past several rooms until the surgeon stopped just short of room number seven.

Fisher whispered, "We were able to remove his breathing tube. He's now breathing on his own." His face softened. "That's a great sign."

Beth whimpered. "Ashley, I told you that he would make it."

Fisher issued a stern order. "Remember, we can't let him get excited. One minute and you leave."

Ashley took a deep breath. "We promise."

Upon entering his room, she saw her father's bloodshot eyes smiling at her. She ran toward him, holding back her pent up tears. Barely noticing the multiple intravenous lines and the nasal cannula providing oxygen, she grabbed his hand, intertwining their fingers.

"Daddy, I love you so much."

Rogers looked straight ahead at the door, unable to shift his eyes to her side. After slowly opening his mouth, he ran his tongue over his lower lip. "Ash---Ashley." His mouth appeared to be twisted toward the right. His pallor lightened a few shades, blending in with the white hospital sheets, as he struggled to speak.

Ashley looked at the neurosurgeon. Fisher pointed toward the door. She slipped her hand from her father's weak grasp. "Daddy, you're going to be OK. Remember I love you."

The neurosurgeon put his arm around her and escorted her to the doorway. She looked back at her Dad. She read his lips. Rogers mouthed the words--*I love you*. With a gentle tug on her arm, Fisher led her out of the room with Beth and Panini closely following.

***

Ashley half opened her eyes. A shiny badge held a few feet from her face picked up a ray of sunshine and prompted her to shut her eyes. She nodded off, believing that she was dreaming. A hand on her shoulder, gently nudging her, seemed part of her dream. A soft voice said, "Ms. Rogers, I need to speak with you." Believing that she was now in the throes of a nightmare, she cried out, 'Leave my Daddy alone.'

The prodding against her shoulder became stronger. She awoke with a start. A fuzzy outline of a middle-aged woman dressed in a black business suit began to take shape.

"Ms. Rogers, I'm Special Agent Susan Masters. We need to talk."

She stretched her back, just now realizing that she had fallen asleep in a chair after last night's visiting hours were over. "Talk about what?" "I'm the FBI agent in charge of the investigation of the shooting of your father and Mr. Joseph Panini."

Upon hearing his name, she felt herself drifting back to the scene where she cradled her father's head in her hands, lying on the blood-covered grass just outside of her apartment. Still reliving the nightmare, she recalled the police arriving but the shooter had already escaped.

"Are you all right? Ms. Rogers, can I get you some coffee? You look like you could use some."

Ashley rubbed her eyes, trying to focus. "I'll be fine." She squinted but was able to make out the number on the agent's badge. *Number six twenty.* "So, you're from the FBI?"

"Yes."

The agent's face looked hard-edged, worrisome.

"I also want to speak with Mr. Panini and Beth Murphy. Do you know where they are?"

"They'll be back tomorrow morning---to visit my Dad." The black and white clock on the wall helped to orient her. Shrugging her shoulders, she added, "Guess it's already morning." Wrinkling her nose, a yawn emerged; she massaged her neck. "Then, they should be here any minute."

"How is your Dad doing?"

"Dr. Fisher is optimistic."

"I understand from the statements that Mr. Panini and Ms. Murphy gave to the local police that a man named Mr. Connor Lucas is the prime suspect."

Ashley bolted straight up from her slouched position. "What!"

"Mr. Panini had a police artist sketch the likeness of the suspect. The FBI presently has a nationwide manhunt underway for Mr. Lucas."

"I've been so upset about my Dad; I didn't hear what actually happened that night. Ashley felt dazed, even thirty-six hours after the shooting. "I think I'm still in shock."

"I fully understand. You and your family have been through a lot." Masters paused a moment or two. "I'm sorry to trouble you, but I need to ask you about an email that you received from Secretary of Health Christian James."

Her mind suddenly clicked, as if she had thrown a light switch. She stared up at the ceiling. "His email was quite long. It was rambling and full of self-loathing statements for what he had done." Unable to suppress a yawn, she apologized. "At the time, I wasn't completely concentrating on it." She shook her head. Her eyes locked on the agent. "At the time, I was totally outraged that the National Quality Board had just approved the human clinical trial data on *NeoBloc*."

"Go on."

Ashley noticed the FBI agent's apprehensive gaze. "I do remember that Secretary James believed that *NeoBloc* would kill all Americans who received it." Her head began to pound. She slammed her eyes shut; rubbing her forehead. "Sorry, my head is killing me."

"You're doing fine." Masters motioned for her to continue.

"Secretary James stated in his email that the group responsible for trying to push the deadly vaccine through FDA approval was called *The Health Club*." Ashley's eyes were now blinking wildly. "James named two people as being responsible." She looked upward, searching for the right words.

"Take your time. It will come to you."

She snapped her fingers. "Now I remember---he mentioned Connor Lucas and Dr. Hussein Nasters. With the shock of my father getting shot, I guess I had subconsciously blotted out reading the Secretary's email."

"You're doing fine."

"Anyway, while I was reading the Secretary of Health's email, I now remember doing something that I normally don't do. I checked on the 'keep as new' option so I would remember to read the email when I was fully ready to process it. Like I said, I was so distraught that the National Quality Board had just recommended approval of *NeoBloc* to the FDA."

"I understand. Does the name Jonsey ring a bell?"

Her eye twitched. "No."

Masters stood. "Why don't we take a break?"

"Panini and Beth should be here soon. I want to see my Dad."

The agent nodded. "Of course. We have a lot more work to do."

"I'll meet you back here in twenty minutes."

***

Ashley and Masters were sitting in the ICU waiting room when Panini and Beth strolled toward them.

The young Rogers did the introductions. "Good to see you guys. This is Agent Susan Masters of the FBI. She is in charge of the investigation into the shootings. The agent has some questions for us."

Beth pulled over a chair, as did Panini. The four of them sat in a close-knit square.

"Mr. Panini, as you already know, from your statement to the police and the sketch that you helped the artist create, Mr. Connor Lucas is our main suspect."

He cocked his head to the side. "I'll never forget his face. Evil personified."

Beth chimed in. "All of this has to be about *NeoBloc*. Agent Masters, have you questioned Dr. Nasters?"

"He is under close observation. I can't divulge what I know about him, but I can say that there are other issues pending as well."

Panini leaned forward. "What issues? Why haven't you brought him in for questioning?"

"I'm not permitted to discuss that."

He slapped his forehead. "Why not?"

"National Security is involved. That is all that I can say."

Ashley's eyes drifted lower. "Dad told me you said the same words the last time he was shot."

"I promise you that if I come across any information that your father's life is in any jeopardy, I will inform you immediately." The agent lowered her voice. "It's not FBI protocol to call a family member on such matters of national security but I'm in charge of this investigation. Rest assured that I'll do as much as I can to keep you informed."

Ashley handed her a piece of paper after she scribbled her number on it. "Call me on this number---it's my cell."

Agent Masters stuffed the note into her wallet.

Ashley glanced over at Panini's face. It seemed about to erupt. He hollered, "Why isn't this Lucas gangster under custody? After all, he is the prime suspect. I'm an eyewitness. I saw him shoot me and Dr. Rogers."

"I understand, Mr. Panini. The agent nodded in his direction but ignored his questions. "Excuse me Ms. Murphy; does the name Jonesy sound familiar to you?"

She replied as if a light bulb had instantly turned on in her brain. "Yes."

"What about the name, Dr. Virginia Washington?"

She nodded. "What about her?"

"First, what do you know about Jonesy?"

Beth paused. "I just heard his name in passing, nothing more."

Masters cocked her head, looking at her from a sideways disbelieving stare. "When I mentioned his name, your face lit up. Are you telling me everything you know?"

Panini blasted, "I hope you're not suggesting that Beth is lying."

"No, of course not."

Ashley interrupted, "Do these people have anything to do with the shooting of my father and Mr. Panini?"

Agent Masters abruptly rose to her feet. "I'm investigating all angles." She handed her business card to each of them. "Call me directly if you remember any information---no matter how far -fetched."

Beth examined the card. The faces of Ginny and Jonathan came to her mind. "To save me a phone call, what do you want to know about Jonesy?"

"Whatever information that you can provide."

"All I know is that I heard that he was a hit man who tried to kill the roommate of Dr. Virginia Washington."

"Who told you that?"

Ashley sensed that Beth was growing uncomfortable talking about this guy. She spoke up. "Ms. Masters, can this wait? We all want to see how my father is doing."

"It can wait for now. I'll call you if I find out any information."

After Masters walked out of the room, Ashley looked at Panini and Beth. "Where is Connor Lucas? If there's a nationwide search for him, why can't they find him?"

Panini pounded one fist into the open palm of his other hand. "This bastard will be found---even if we have to do it ourselves."

CHAPTER FORTY-SIX

Nasters persistently questioned Connor's administrative assistant, Andrea, as to the whereabouts of her boss. By now, news of the twin shooting outside of the Surgeon General daughter's apartment had been widely reported by the national media. Following her confidential directive on the yellow sheet of paper that her CEO left at her workstation, Andrea told the scientist that Connor was traveling on unscheduled business but she did not know where or how to contact him. Sensing that he was not hearing the real story, he headed back to his office to make an extremely important call.

******

Nasters phoned DCP Board Member Xavier Rudolf and set up a meeting for later that day at a local coffee bar. He picked up a copy of the *DuPont Gazette*, noting a follow up story about the hospital release of one of the men shot outside Ashley Rogers's apartment. The article on page four also gave brief mention that of the continued hospitalization of Dr. Jonathan Rogers at Detroit Metro Medical Center. The story said nothing about his prognosis. *The Detroit Free Press* gave superficial coverage as well; saying nothing more than the Surgeon General was stable after undergoing emergency surgery to remove a 9mm bullet from his brain.

Unable to concentrate on his summarization of the results of the ongoing clinical trials in China for the FDA, he prepared for his noontime Muslim prayer by covering his body with a loose fitting cotton white pull over robe. Nasters then performed a ritual ablution by washing himself with water from a canter that he kept on a nearby bookshelf. A faithful member of the Sunni sect, he washed his hands, mouth, nose, face, arms, forehead and hair, ears and feet --three times each, in that order. He stood in his usual spot, facing in the general direction of Mecca. Reciting the first chapter of the Qur'an, he thanked and praised Allah, asking for guidance along the Straight Path.

After concluding his prayer, his mind cleared. A thought registered. There was a good reason the rogue cell leader has not contacted me after what happened at the Park. *They are planning to execute me as a traitor.* Fully expecting what he now believed was inevitable, he found himself unable to control a recurrent facial tic involving a twitching of his left eyelid.

******

"Mr. Rudolf, thank you for making the time to meet."

Sitting directly across from Nasters, he sat ramrod straight in the corner booth of the *"Daily Mug,"* The Board chair was neatly dressed in a gray flannel Brooks Brother's three-piece suit. He took a long sip from his coffee cup, maintaining constant eye contact with his host.

Nasters looked away; feeling invaded and uncomfortable by the intense stare of his piercing light blue eyes. He patiently waited for the board member to put his coffee mug back on the table.

"Dr. Nasters, why are we meeting without Connor Lucas?"

He leered. "That's an odd question. I'm sure that you know that no one knows where he is at the moment. His assistant tells me that he's traveling out of town on business. Andrea says she knows nothing more than that."

"So, you asked me to have coffee with you just to find out what I know about your boss?"

Nasters squirmed. He did not answer immediately. "Look, I'm only concerned about what happens to DCP and our vaccine, *NeoBloc*. I'm also worried about our CEO." The scientist leaned across the table. "Do you know where he is Mr. Rudolf?"

"The newspapers say that these matters are all under FBI investigation." His eyes searched every corner of the scientist's face. "Of course, its public knowledge based on the story in the *Washington Post* that Connor is a "person of interest" after they obtained the Secretary of Health's email to Ashley Rogers under the Freedom of Information Act."

He felt his underarms getting moist. "Even before the Secretary's email, I was under the distinct impression that Connor had changed his mind on *NeoBloc*. I don't believe that he was going to sign off on final submission to the FDA approval."

"Really!" Rudolf grinned. "If that were true, I would have imagined that Connor might have contacted you to discuss the affirmative recommendation of the National Quality Board to move forward."

No longer able to hold back his feelings, he replied in a testy tone. "I can assure you that I have not heard a word from him."

"So, what do you know? What exactly is the latest on our vaccine?"

"Connor wants DCP to take over W&W so we can use our scientific expertise and financial resources to speed up the last phase of research on their similar compound."

Wrinkling his forehead, the senior asked, "Why would he do that?"

"He is mistaken. I have told him so." Nasters softened his face. "I have assured him that *NeoBloc* is safe. However, Connor doesn't understand science. Neither did Secretary James. What Christian James wrote in his email to Ashley Rogers is simply untrue."

Rudolf leaned back. "Educate me."

"There are pre-existing medical reasons why those volunteers taking *NeoBloc* in the clinical trials in China died----reasons that have nothing at all to do with the vaccine."

"And, how do you know this?"

"I understand cause and effect. I know biologic processes. With all due respect, to Connor and Secretary James, they just didn't understand. They believed whatever they heard from ill informed people."

Rudolf leaned across the table, his face barely a foot from his host's face. "Let's stop the bullshitting! I just happen to be aware that nineteen people in China died after taking *NeoBloc*. You expect me to believe that nineteen young volunteers in their twenties were all going to die anyway before they got the vaccine?"

"You must understand the details. The volunteers were desperate for money. I have information that showed half of them were suffering from AIDS. Staph pneumonia had hospitalized another quarter of the clinical trial enrollees. Their immune systems were already severely compromised."

Rudolf frowned. "Then, they simply should have been excluded from the trial."

Nasters crossed his arms in front of his chest. "But they weren't. Volunteers for clinical drug trials are getting harder and harder to recruit. Why do you think we moved most of the trials from America to China? The American volunteers wanted much more money. It was a DCP business decision made by Connor himself."

Rudolf pointed his finger in Nasters's face. "I think you know a lot more than you're telling me."

"Please drop your finger. I will not be disrespected by anyone."

Lowering his hand, he apologized. "Doctor, I meant no rudeness."

Coldly, he asked, "Where do we go from here?"

"Connor has previously told me that you have been meeting with the Pakistani Freedom Fighters. Are they paying you to do something?"

Nasters shook his head from side to side. "My relationship with them is purely personal. I would rather not discuss them."

"Is that so?"

In a louder octave, he spoke firmly, "Respect my wishes."

"That's not good enough for me. If the truth be known, I am aware of where Connor is hiding their leader. Good day, Dr. Nasters."

He pointedly asked, "Can you tell me where to find Mugandi?"

Rudolf rose slowly. "Ha. First tell me why you are working with the PFF."

"I'm only trying to deceive the PFF so we can proceed with *NeoBloc*."

"The PFF are terrorists. Why would you work with people committed to killing Americans?"

Nasters blurted out, "I'm totally opposed to their plan." He lightly slapped the table. "Please sit down."

Rudolf slid back into his seat. "What plan?"

"It's an ill conceived plan to destroy America."

"So you do know what they are planning."

"I never said that. I only said they have a plan—not what the plan entails."

"Hold on doctor. You called their plan ill conceived. If you don't know what it is, how do you know it's ill conceived? And, why would you risk your life deceiving your own colleagues?"

"Mr. Rudolf, you must trust me. Selling three hundred million doses of *NeoBloc* will make us all extremely wealthy. *NeoBloc* is the savior vaccine for all Americans! Just ask the President, Congress, and the American opinion polls."

The Chairman stood and cast a disdainful look at the scientist. "You better not be found working to hurt our great country."

Nasters rose quickly and stood toe to toe with Rudolf. "Sir, I am a proud American citizen."

Rudolf sharply replied, "You wouldn't be our first traitor."

The scientist's face turned crimson. "For the last time, I only want *NeoBloc* to succeed. The American National Quality Board approved the vaccine as safe and effective. I repeat. Our President wants it. So does Congress, and so do the captains of American industry." His chest heaved as he sucked in a series of rapid breaths. "Our country has suffered two major nuclear attacks and a series of smaller attacks using radioactive cesium. We must inoculate all of our citizens before a third strike."

Rudolf cocked his head. "Who said anything about a third strike?"

Responding rapidly, he said in a matter of fact tone, "I am only speculating."

"What does Connor know about all of this?"

Nasters paused. "He is convinced that *NeoBloc* is deadly."

"Not that. I'm talking about another nuclear hit."

"I know nothing about any details of another nuclear strike on America----nor does Connor."

He half cocked his head and narrowed his eyes. "Dr. Nasters, I think that I'll pay a visit to Mugandi. Perhaps, he will tell me what you won't----perhaps, all he needs is a little persuasion."

Rudolf walked outside and hailed a cab.

The scientist flashed back to his initial meeting with the PFF. *I trust no American!* "I need to do away with them before they kill me and destroy my jihad." *Allah, guide me to kill all the infidels.*

CHAPTER FORTY-SEVEN

Connor stumbled into his hotel room. For the last half hour, he had hung out at the local bar, downing three shots of double whiskeys. He dialed Rudolph's private number. The room was spinning just as he plopped down on the bed. His cell plastered to his right ear, he yelled, "Pick up the damn phone." For sure, the Chairman of the Board's opinion was of utmost importance.

On the sixth ring, Rudolph picked up. "Glad you called."

"Hey Xavier, what the hell is Nasters up to?"

Rudolf replied, "He's covering up on the deaths with *NeoBloc*. He argues that those who say the vaccine is deadly are misinterpreting the data. Essentially, he blames you."

"Nasters will be done in by his own people. The unanswered question is whether the nineteen deaths in the *NeoBloc* clinical trials is a real trend or not. Lord knows, I'm no scientist. That's why we depend on doctors."

The Chairman was emphatic in his point. "We're businessmen, not mass murderers."

"Right now, the wise course is to hedge our bets and take over W&W just in case our vaccine really is deadly."

"It makes good business sense to always have a backup plan."

"We agree. On another point, just how bad is the situation for me?"

"I guess being the center of a national manhunt by law enforcement would not be considered good news no matter how much I might like to favorably spin it.

Connor covered his face with a pillow. "Let's get back to Nasters for the moment."

"I told him that I know where you stashed the Pakistani leader."

He paused a moment and thought of Rudolf's face on one of his playing cards. "Must have made him freak."

"I believe that he's expecting a knock on his door any night. He must sit at home in the dark facing his front door, holding a fully loaded Uzi."

"Besides wanting to get revenge on their treacherous countryman, what else do these so called "freedom fighters" want?"

"Nasters said they want to destroy America."

Connor pushed himself to an upright position. He staggered over to his gym bag and pulled out a favorite Cuban cigar. Using a pocket lighter, he lit the stogie and began puffing rings. "What's the plan to stop that from happening?"

"Well, I have his home address from HR records at DCP. I could leak his whereabouts on the street----in the Muslim sections. Once he's dead, we can move on W&W. Then, we'll need to convince the President that fast tracking out a new compound is the only way to go."

"Let's get back to me. What are your thoughts about the Christian James email implicating me and *The Health Club*?" Connor sucked a long draw on the cigar and exhaled slowly

"First of all, I think it's a mistake playing defense, hoping the police don't find you. I think you need to go to the Michigan police with hard DNA evidence that backs up your claim that James sexually harassed you. You need to somehow discredit his story."

"Look, I just gave a written complaint to the DuPont police but I decided not to present the DNA evidence."

"Why not? A loud moan came through the phone line. "Why would you not go on the offensive and play hard ball?"

"Let's just call it a gut feeling."

"Then you need to do something else to discredit James before his story takes hold in the news cycle. Unless you act swiftly, the media will soon be in a feeding frenzy. Someone will see your picture somewhere and report your whereabouts to the police."

"I'm working on some ideas." Connor walked over to the tiny bathroom and threw his half-smoked stogie into the toilet bowl. "I'm concerned that my delay in filing a formal signed complaint against our loser will raise eyebrows."

"That's easy to explain away. Here is your story. After you thought about it, you were too embarrassed to come into the police station to say that James kissed you at work. You can always force Andrea to back up your story."

"She's always been loyal to me. I have no doubts about her. Andrea has covered my ass on more than one occasion."

"Just make it sound as though James was having a nervous breakdown and that he was acting paranoid, making crazy accusations that you were the leader of a DuPont boxing club called *The Health Club*. Maybe send in Andrea to the DuPont police station to back up your story."

Connor cleared his voice. "That might discredit him. What else do we have to do?"

Rudolf's voice turned somber. "That was the easy part. Now, let's discuss your real problem. You better hope the police can't link you to the shootings at that woman's apartment."

"What can we do about that?"

The DCP Board leader hesitated. Several moments passed by. Connor listened carefully. He could hear heavy breathing followed by a series of muffled coughs.

"Xavier----are you still there?"

The reply was brusque. "Look, what's done is done. To be blunt, you can only hope that all relevant parties are as dumb or as corrupt as we need them to be."

"I don't like risking my life on the possibility that the police and the Rogers crowd will screw up. The Surgeon General is far from dumb. That is if he even survives."

"You have another eyewitness to the shootings."

"You mean that friend of Rogers?"

"So, what's you plan for him."

"I have my ideas. What do you think?"

"There are far too many uncertainties—too many loose ends. Frankly, I don't like the mess you created. Why kill Rogers yourself? Ego?"

"That's not it. How was I to know that James would set this chain of events into motion? I was reacting to what he had done. What else was I to do?"

Silence.

"Xavier, we need to work together."

"From my perspective, I'm not implicated nor is DCP directly involved in the shootings---other than through you."

"Listen, I don't want my fate determined by events that I can't control."

"Hey Connor, neither do I. That's why I always have an ace up my sleeve."

Silence.

"Well, so what the hell is it Mr. Rudolf?" Connor felt his blood pressure rising. He sensed that he was being isolated. He asked, "So what's the ace that will put this crap behind both of us, my friend?"

"It's my ace, not yours"

Connor roared, "What the hell does that mean?"

Silence.

"Rudolph, answer me dammit." Hearing the dial tone, Connor ran over to the couch, kicking it repeatedly.

CHAPTER FORTY-EIGHT

Beth drove to her apartment. Her new roommate rode alongside her. In the back seat, their new best friend, Joey Panini, spread out like an eagle. Ashley was hesitant to leave the hospital. Nevertheless, with her father out of his coma, she felt better about her decision to spend the night at her new digs.

Panini had convinced Ashley and Beth that in Jonathan's absence that it was up to them to plan what to do next to stop the likely FDA approval and deployment of the lethal *NeoBloc*. He also insisted on doing whatever they could to figure out the whereabouts of Connor. "Beth, park down the street, about a hundred feet from your door."

She grinned. "I already know why?" She brought her car to a standstill on the quiet street.

He asked for Beth's apartment key. "Ladies, wait here."

Handing her key to him, she asked, "Do you suspect anything?"

"Always!" He walked up a stone staircase to the front door at 22 Meridian Drive. Using the key, he unlocked and pushed the door in, quickly stepping to the side. He took a deep sniff before entering the walkup garden apartment. Panini pulled a .38 snub nose revolver from a sheath strapped to his right calf and entered the apartment. Standing motionless for a full minute, he closely listened for creaky floorboards.

As he scanned the foyer, he held his revolver in front of him. His trained eye carefully searched each room. He checked the thermostat. The room temperature matched the setting. All windows were intact and firmly locked. Nothing seemed amiss.

He ran back down the front stairs and trotted around to the back of the apartment. Panini climbed the fire escape ladder and tried to open a back window to the apartment. *Locked.* He descended the ladder and walked back to the street. Whistling to the women in the car, he shouted, "All clear. Come on up."

Minutes later, all three of them congregated in the kitchen. Beth boiled water and shouted out a choice of teabags. Panini searched the freezer, pleased to find a half gallon of butter pecan ice cream.

Ashley sat behind the white Formica table, her elbows propping up her chin, facing the locked front door. She pulled out a paper from her handbag. "Mr. Panini, I have a couple of questions for you."

"Unless you are having a séance with my deceased father, there is no need to address me as mister. Just call me Panini." He sat down after grabbing three large bowls and tablespoons. He peeled off the cover on the store brand ice cream. "Is anyone going to join me?"

Beth and Ashley both declined, indicating that he should still feel free to enjoy the butter pecan. Panini shoved a huge spoonful into his mouth. "Ashley, don't wait for me. I'm enjoying a little part of heaven." He dished up another tablespoon of the ice cream.

"OK. Here are my two main questions. How do we nail Connor Lucas based on the Christian James email to me? And, how do we convince President Williams not to deploy NeoBloc?"

Beth poured boiled water into each of their teacups. "Could we hold those questions for a moment?" She picked out her favorite organic tea bag. "Let me know if you both think this is off topic but I wonder if Virginia Washington is still living with Marissa. Ever since the FBI agent, Susan Masters, asked me about her at the hospital, I can't seem to get her off my mind. I tried calling Ginny's cell but she doesn't get back to me. I'm really worried."

Panini dipped his tea bag into his cup. "Masters asked you about a guy named Jonesy? How is he connected to your friend Dr. Washington?"

Beth dunked her tea bag into the steaming cup. "Jonesy tried to hang Ginny's roommate—Marissa Jones."

"How do you know all of this?" Panini took a sip before he carved out two more hefty sized scoops of ice cream into his bowl.

"Marissa used to be the main squeeze of a man named Zach Miller. And, as Ashley and I painfully remember, Zach had tried more than once to kill Jonathan." Beth looked over .A twitch appeared in Ashley's right eye. "I'm sorry for interrupting your questions and for dredging up the past."

"It's OK. Tell him the story." Ashley sipped on her tea, looking increasingly pensive.

"Marissa believed that Zach sent Jonesy to kill her since she was once disloyal to her former lover. She thought that if I could take her to Dr. Rogers----that maybe Ashley's dad knew something about Miller. Essentially, Marissa wanted to do away with Zach before he turned the tables on her."

Panini stuck another glob of ice cream into his mouth. "I got it." He smacked his lips, savoring the creamy taste. "The rest of the story is that Jonathan told you guys that Zach is Connor. My neighbor Cathy Parker essentially told me the same thing after her brother was murdered. I just never got around to telling Johnny Boy."

"It's so strange to hear you call my father that name."

He chuckled. "It's from the old days---when dinosaurs walked the earth."

"In any case, we need to prove that Zach is Connor. We need to prove it with DNA."

Ashley added, "Maybe we can get a DNA swab from the Ferrari that Zach Miller once drove and compare it to DNA from Connor Lucas. That will totally discredit DCP if we can prove that Connor Lucas is the fugitive Zach Miller. I just don't know where the Ferrari is located. I heard that it was pretty well blown up."

Panini leaned back. "I know where we can look." He looked over at Beth. "But first, tell me about this guy Dr. Nasters. Is it money that motivates him?"

"Don't know but I'm totally convinced that he's lying about the safety of *NeoBloc*."

Ashley stood and paced the kitchen. "The way I see it, it all comes down to Connor Lucas---he's the key to everything. Then, we can focus on the President's support of *NeoBloc*."

Panini nodded in approval while shoving another spoonful of ice cream down the hatch. "Tomorrow, we're going to the local police junk yard. I'll just bet Zach Miller's Ferrari is still there." He winked. "Let's hope we're lucky enough to get inside the yard to find it."

"Why would the police let us in?" asked Ashley, still moving about the perimeter of the kitchen.

"They won't. In fact, they'll be pissed off that it wasn't their idea if we find something. It's just the nature of the beast."

Beth said, "Everyone assumed Zach was dead. That's probably why the FBI didn't swab down the Ferrari at the time of the accident"

Panini took another sip of tea. "Bingo. Everyone presumed that Zach died. Case closed."

Ashley stopped dead in her tracks. "We now know otherwise."

"Yep, the junk yard will be shutting down around four thirty. I'll pick the lock when they close up for the day."

Beth murmured, "That's illegal."

Panini laughed so hard that he rocked the kitchen table, causing Beth's cup of tea to topple over. She grabbed for a dishtowel and wiped up the spill. "What I said is funny?"

"Yeah it's a total gas! You women from the 'burbs are so formal----by the numbers. Me, I got street smarts. Johnny Boy--I mean Dr. Rogers used to have these same skills."

"Won't they have security cameras in the junk yard?"

Panini slapped his knee. "Guarding what---junk?" Smirking, he drained his cup.

******

For the last hour, on a nearby hill, Ashley observed the routine at the junkyard with the aid of a pair of binoculars. She asked Panini, "When do we go in"

"When the guards leave?"

"So, I guess the guards are there during the day just to let in new loads of junked cars."

"Yep." He grabbed the binoculars. "Let's get back in your car. It looks like they're locking the gate for the night." He hopped into the passenger seat while Ashley took the wheel of Beth's car. Panini poked her in the arm. "So, did you see any security cameras guarding the junk?"

"No. I guess they believe that the eight foot high chain link fence topped by barbed wire is enough."

He made a scary face. "But there might be a prowling guard dog." Ashley rolled her eyes.

"Probably not—would cost too much to take care of the German Sheppard."

"Question?"

Holding his hands up with palms facing out, he pretended being held up at gunpoint. "Shoot."

"Are you ever serious?"

"Don't ever worry about me. When the time is right, I'm deadly serious."

"I hope so." She leaned over to pick up the binoculars off the floorboards. After another quick scan of the junkyard, she twisted her neck to face Panini. "Where will we get a non-corrupted sample of DNA from Connor?"

"You've been spending too much time with your medical textbooks. The answer is obvious."

Ashley scrunched her face.

"Connor spat in your father's face. Don't you remember?"

"I guess I missed that."

"It was in the police report that I gave you. After we're done here, we'll go to the police. I'm sure they confiscated the towel used by EMS in cleaning up your father's face."

Ashley let a subtle grin sneak onto her face. She reached out and patted his shoulder. "I'll tell you what I think." She held her gaze on him for several seconds before speaking. "If my father didn't bring you into our lives, we'd all be up a creek."

Panini looked down to the gate. "Start paddling. See them all jumping into the truck. Wait a minute and then we'll go."

She turned on the key and drove slowly to the outside gate of the junk yard. Turning off the motor, she and Panini got out of the car and approached the huge gate to the chain link fence.

"I'll pick the lock. You stand guard." While picking the padlock on the gate, he recalled the old days when he would use his street skills in the church sacristy to pry open the lock to the wine cabinet. Before

Mass, some priests would ask the altar boys to fill up several cruets of wine. But, after the Mass was over and the priest had left, I would do my thing, open the cabinet again and take several swigs. After several unsuccessful tries, he kicked a mound of dirt—spraying a plume of dust in the air. "Dammit, I used to be much better at this."

"Relax, you can do it." She craned her neck, looking back at the access road. "I guess that I'm worried that the security guards will be back."

He re-focused on the padlock with newly found confidence. On this attempt, the tumbler moved and he was able to get the bolt out of the lock. He tugged on the gate just enough to allow both of them to gain access inside the junkyard.

"Good job," she proudly declared. "Let's pray that Zach's Ferrari is still here."

"You go left. I'll look on the other side."

"Remember it's a blue convertible." She scanned the piled heaps of scrap iron. Vertically stacked rusted black and red chassis's came into view. Crushed cars and trucks were loaded one on top of the other to a height of thirty feet or so.

Panini searched his neck of the junkyard. Behind a white Ford pick-up truck, he thought he spotted it. He yelled out, "Think I found it." He began climbing up the pile, over a silver RV, a white van, and a yellow Hummer.

Ashley ran to him.

He pointed. "It looks like the one buried underneath the red Dodge sedan."

Panini placed one foot on the rusted roof of the Hummer. He squeezed himself under the sedan and wedged himself into the front seat of the blue convertible. He looked up. The red Dodge and a black Ford pick- up truck were piled over the Ferrari. With his added weight to the stack of vehicles, the occasional crunching noises of metal on metal were a constant reminder of the precarious nature of what he was doing. "Most of the Ferrari survived the accident and fire."

"Be careful," she pleaded.

"Don't worry. I may look dumb but I've got street smarts. You dad and I used to jump over an alleyway that was two stories high just to get to a roof where we had hit a fifteen cent pinkie rubber ball."

"You guys were crazy to do that."

Panini pulled out a plastic bag and a pair of surgical gloves that were in the pocket of his trousers. He looked down at Ashley. "Whoever said I wasn't serious?" He pulled the gloves over each hand. "By the way, I guess it's a safe bet that you didn't bring a pair of gloves."

"Touche."

"And, before you ask—yes the plastic bag is sterile." He lifted a cotton swab out of the bag and held it in his left hand. With his free hand, he unhooked a pocketknife from his belt. Probing the dashboard of the charred Ferrari, he pried the glove compartment open just enough to reach inside. "Well, look what I just found." Panini pulled out a small tin box. "Looks like an air tight container." With some degree of effort, he used his knife to pry open the rusty lid. "Ah ha! I'm looking at two half-smoked cigars. And, these stogies look and smell like Cubans". Using a small roll of sterile gauze from inside the plastic bag, he grabbed the cigar box, dropping it into the plastic bag. He leaped off the pile of stacked up cars. "We just struck pay dirt."

A heartbeat later, she heard a thunderous creaking sound. Stacked on top of the blue convertible, the higher sitting Dodge sedan and Ford pick-up truck moved a few inches before they tumbled down in a blink of the eye, smashing the Ferrari dashboard at the exact spot where Panini had been working a few scant seconds earlier.

"Whoa that was close." He pointed toward the heavens. "It's better to be lucky than good."

Ashley beamed. "You rock Panini."

"It's all about street smarts," my friend. Yet, one needs good fortune for success."

CHAPTER FORTY-NINE

Williams spoke on the Oval Office intercom. "Madison, please get in touch with Dr. Rob Woodhull from Weston and Weston. I must speak with him immediately."

"Yes, Madame President, I'll buzz you when he's on the line."

She dropped her daily national security briefing on her desk. She swiveled her chair to scan the Rose Garden. Rubbing her forehead, it was obvious to her that events were getting more out of control by the day. Just minutes earlier, her national security advisor had dropped the latest bombshell on her.

Buzz. She pushed around her executive style leather chair to face the intercom, clicking on. "Yes."

"Dr. Woodhull is on line two."

She cleared her voice and pressed the button. "Good morning, Dr. Woodhull."

"Madame President."

"Let me get right to why I called you. Recently, I spoke with Mr. Connor Lucas, the CEO of Doctor's Choice Products. He told me that the two of you have discussed a potential merger or take –over of W&W by DCP."

His voice was without a trace of emotion, steady. "If the truth be known, it was not the most pleasant meeting. After reading what the late Secretary of Health wrote before he died. Lucas knows that the DCP vaccine is bad news."

"The FBI is currently looking for Lucas as you know by reading the papers." She paused. "Doctor, I need your help. Your compound, if it receives FDA approval, can protect tens of millions of Americans from getting radiation induced cancers."

"We're making sound progress." The CEO hesitated a few seconds. "But we certainly don't have the scientific resources that DCP has to fast track the appropriate research through the clinical trials. At W&W, we are committed to doing sound research. We would never submit a compound for FDA approval until we were absolutely positive that it's safe."

"Here is my challenge. It's imperative to get a vaccine preventing radiation induced cancers deployed as soon as possible." She paused to see if he would jump in. He remained silent. Williams continued. "And, the vaccine must be safe."

"Our human trials could be done much quicker if we had more money to hire more expert staff."

Williams gritted her teeth. She raised her voice an octave. "I've got to stop the radiation induced suffering and deaths. It is my duty as the commander in chief."

"I fully understand. But, with all due respect, Madame President, what can I do about it?"

"I propose a governmental joint venture with your Company. The United States government can drive your clinical trials through a 'fast track' process to get FDA approval."

Woodhull hesitated. He began slowly, as if thinking through all the issues if he accepted the offer. "President Williams, I don't think having the government as a partner is a good idea. Essentially, it would turn over the management of the Company to the political process in order to meet the forced deadlines set by non-scientists.

"Safety is my issue as well but time is running out on the American people."

"What about *NeoBloc*?"

"The National Quality Board approved *NeoBloc* for submission to the FDA. However, my Surgeon General has communicated to me his strong concerns on the safety of that vaccine."

"Madame President, it is not my place to say this."

Williams fired back. "Say it—and don't mince words."

"*NeoBloc* is not a savior vaccine. It is a killer vaccine." He paused. "I'm sure you've seen the charge from your late Secretary of Health that appeared in the *Post*. Many people in China have died soon after receiving *NeoBloc*?"

"Not to be argumentative Dr. Woodhull but things are sometimes much more complex than they seem. Apparently, there were mitigating factors. Dr. Nasters emailed me with information that seventy five percent of those Chinese volunteers in the *NeoBloc* clinical trials were already critically ill." Her eyes widened. "Could they have died from other causes, unrelated to *NeoBloc*?"

"You raise a valid point. If the volunteers were already ill, this might change my impression. Yet, I'm still troubled by reports that all monkeys died after getting *NeoBloc*."

The President countered, "Is it possible that all the monkeys died because of a lethal virus?"

"Madame President, anything is possible."

"If we are hit with another nuclear bomb, countless innocent citizens will develop cancer and die from the radiation. Would you rather have me sit on my hands and do nothing?"

"I just don't think the W&W Board will accept a governmental joint venture with our Company."

"Then it is you who must convince them. Dr. Woodhull, our national security interests are at stake. We can't put all our eggs in one basket---in *NeoBloc.*"

"Madame President, give me some time."

"Let's talk within the next one to two days." Reaching over, she clicked off the intercom.

******

President Williams looked down the length of the glass topped conference table in the National Security Conference Room. Seated next to Marcia David, Secretary of State was Bill Stapelton, the Secretary of Defense. Homeland Security Secretary Justin Lenz sat at the far end of the table, next to Vice-President Chester Stockard.

The President exchanged furtive looks with her Vice-President. Stockard slouched in his seat. His nostrils flared with each heave of his chest. Ten minutes earlier, in the Oval Office, he had engaged in a private heated conversation with the President regarding options to pursue. Williams had cut off his rant so that this national security meeting could proceed, on time. The VP threatened to express his divergent views in front of her inner circle of advisors. The President stormed out of the hostile meeting with the VP. Her parting words— "Do what you must do."

Williams pulled out a note from the top-secret file in front of her. It was from her Chief of Staff. As she read Pitnar's message, a sinking feeling grabbed her stomach. The President's face grew somber. She turned toward her Secretary of Defense and called the meeting to order. "Bill, what's the latest?"

"Under intense interrogation, a terrorist from the rogue call in Atlanta confessed that there will be another nuclear strike within the next week or so."

Stockard let out an exasperated sigh. All eyes were cast in his direction. Feigning embarrassment, he dramatically placed his hand over his mouth. He bolted ramrod straight in his seat, lips parted, clearly waiting for the right moment to enter the fray.

The President leaned forward. "What intelligence do we have as to location of the next possible attack?"

Stapelton pointed to a large four-foot square wall map, hanging at one end of the conference room. "Justin, I'll defer to you on the details."

Lenz stood and walked over to the map of the United States. "We've picked up a cluster of relevant chatter on the web." He used a pocket pointer to shine a laser beam of light at Denver and Detroit. "We don't know which city will be hit but we're fairly confident that one of them is a target."

Williams asked, "Tell us about the role of weather in assessing collateral damage."

"At present, the winds in the Detroit area are blowing westerly while the Denver atmosphere is calm. So there would be more down -wind radiation exposure if the terrorists strike Detroit—at least under present wind conditions."

Williams joined Lenz at the map, her eyes visually outlining a one hundred mile radius around Denver and Detroit. *More deaths,* she feared. She sharply pivoted to face the Secretary of State.

"Marcia, what's the latest on your end?"

"The Russians and the Chinese have made it crystal clear that if we attack Pakistan, they will intervene. Our prior military engagements across the Middle East, Afghanistan, and North Africa have led to widespread distrust of America. To be frank, they are worried for their own survival. Lastly, the Government in Islamabad has demanded that we steeply reduce the number of CIA and Special Operations forces and that we halt our CIA drone strikes aimed at suspected militants in the northwest quadrant of their nation."

"While I have been President, as you all know, I have made a major course change in our foreign policy. We are no longer doing what my predecessors have done. America has charted a way forward that now recognizes the right of all sovereign countries to govern without intervention from us. But, I will not draw back our CIA, Special Ops, or drone attacks on probable terrorist camps."

Secretary of State David nodded. "If we respect all of the positive interests of nations in the region, we can continue the healing process of our relations with the international community." She then clenched her fist. "But, if we do not begin treating them as an ally, we will be pulling the scab off unhealed feelings of antipathy toward our nation. Only God knows the world wide hell that might break loose if we actually bombed Pakistan."

The President angled herself to face her Vice-President. His scrunched up face told a story that she didn't want to hear but knew would be forthcoming—and soon. She shuffled her feet while making her way back to her seat at the head of the conference table. Williams pointed at the VP.

"Jane, we keep coming back to the same point I raised weeks ago. With all due respect to the Secretary of State, we need to act. We're sitting ducks. America has truly become a paper tiger."

"Chester, thank you once again for reminding me that we disagree. And, let me return the favor by reminding you that the Pakistani government has killed more terrorists than any other nation."

Stockard's jaw visibly tightened. He smacked his lips, apparently enjoying the spotlight. "That's because they allow the terrorists to multiply in their country. You can do the math. Let us not forget that the number one terrorist in the world was caught and killed by U.S. Navy

Seals in Pakistan---just down the road from the major Pakistani army base akin to our own *West Point."*

"My decision stands," Williams rebutted. "We shall pursue our Homeland Security Intelligence and we shall pursue international diplomacy."

The Vice-President bristled. "Let me change the subject to one of your defense strategies. You're putting a lot of your political capital in depending on your so-called savior vaccine to mitigate the fallout from further nuclear attacks. What exactly is the current status on *NeoBloc?"*

"Phase 3 clinical trials are nearly complete," The President replied in a confident manner. "A FDA decision should be coming shortly. However, there's the latest charge from the late Secretary of Health that there have been deaths in the *NeoBloc* clinical trials in China."

All eyes remained focused on the VP as if it was his turn in the point—counterpoint dialogue. Stockard did not disappoint.

"Why would we trust what he said? In the *Post* story, Christian James sounded like he was mixed up with some shady characters."

The President steadied her gaze on the VP. "We are not physicians. We need to trust our FDA scientists----and, Surgeon General Rogers."

He shook his head. "I heard that Dr. Rogers just came out of a coma. Don't think he's ready yet to weigh in." He threw his hands into the air. "Well, based on our Homeland Security intelligence that we're going to be hit again, we damn better have *NeoBloc* deployed soon."

"Mr. Vice-President, as you well know, we are actively working to prevent and I emphasize the word prevent any nuclear strikes----the vaccine is a backup---just in case."

Stockard looked appalled. "That wasn't your initial plan. You said that you wanted all Americans inoculated before any future nuclear attacks. *NeoBloc* has always been your first line of defense. You called it—the savior vaccine. Now, I don't think you even have a plan B."

Williams did not flinch. She glared at the VP. "Are you done?"

"Actually, I'm just getting started." Stockard pounded his fist into the table and then cast a wary eye at Secretary of Defense. "The PFF seems to have checkmated us. If we strike the border between Afghanistan and Pakistan, we'll be accused of starting World War Three. If we don't, we have to hope that our intelligence enables us to stop the next nuclear attack and that our scientists eventually come up with a safe vaccine. It seems to me that our plan to save our country is based purely on hope."

Williams crossed her arms in front of her chest. As she scanned each of the faces around the conference table, she thought of her late sister Maryann as well as Cassie and Emma back at the Minneapolis Medical Center. We must deploy *NeoBloc ---we need a vaccine to be a backup*

The VP's nostrils flared. "Let me remind everyone about the Pakistani Inter-Services Intelligence or as it is widely known-- the ISI." He looked squarely at Williams. "As we know, the ISI is their intelligence agency—like our CIA." He clenched his fist. "In 2010, there was a report from the London School of Economics that gave concrete evidence that the ISI is providing the funding, training, and sanctuary for the Taliban." He grunted, "They must be stopped. What more evidence do you need?"

The President dismissed his plea. "As you know, our commander of the US Central Command refused to endorse that report in congressional hearings. Our General stated that contacts between the ISI and the terrorists are for legitimate intelligence gathering purposes. If the ISI didn't have any contact with the Taliban, how would they gather any intelligence?"

"I don't give a hoot about any country except the United States of America," Stockard blasted.

Williams fired back, "That's because you're not the President of the United States. I care deeply about America but I will not shoot from the hip, endangering the whole world. Whoever sits in the chair of the American presidency bears global responsibilities."

"Jane, we have no vaccine to protect our people, we are unwilling to go on offense, and we know we are about to be hit once again with a nuclear bomb." His voice tightened, his brow deeply furrowed. "What are you going to do for America?"

The Secretary of State received her first order. The President's voice was strong, her cadence quick. "Contact the Afghanistan and Pakistani ambassadors," Williams commanded. "Tell them that the current situation is intolerable. From this point on, I am holding their governments accountable to stop any PFF rogue cell that threatens another attack on America. My timeline is five days, to deliver the terrorists to us. All options will remain open to me. Ensure that the ambassadors understand that I mean business."

"I will carry out your orders. Nevertheless, by issuing an ultimatum, I want to go on record as registering my strong disagreement given the lack of any specific evidence against the Afghan or Pakistani government in these grave matters. We would be a violation of the sovereignty of an ally."

"Marcia, I respect your judgment. However, if you will not publicly support my decision as the Commander in Chief, I will accept your resignation."

The Secretary of State nodded, saying nothing further, and looked down at her folded hands that rested on the conference table.

Williams glanced over at Stockard. His face had softened more than a trifle. The President then locked her sight at the Secretary of Defense.

"Effective immediately, I am authorizing a full scale targeted cyber attack on previously selected military targets within that region. By launching our computer viruses, we will shut down twenty-five percent of their electrical power grid. They will get the message that we mean business."

Stapelton nodded. "I will ensure that your order is promptly carried out."

Williams's eyes locked on the disbelieving gawk of the Secretary of State. "Marcia, do not mince words. Let the ambassadors know that I will protect America. Remind them that I will suspend the distribution of billions of dollars in foreign aid that we give to their nations each year."

Stockard grinned broadly while the rest of the senior advisors sat stone faced.

"Does anyone want to venture any final comments? Offer any resignations?" The room fell silent. "Hearing none, this meeting is adjourned."

The President rose. Everyone else remained in their seats, looking down at the conference table. Williams made no further eye contact. She marched out of the national security bunker room, praying that she had not just set the clock ticking to start World War Three.

CHAPTER FIFTY

The conference call with the FBI had just concluded. The DNA from both the Ferrari and the saliva retrieved from the towel cleaning the face of Jonathan Rogers were a perfect match. Connor Lucas was definitely Zach Miller.

Under orders from Agent Masters, it was communicated to Ashley, Beth, and Panini, through Agent Phil Donaldson, that the government had unique technological equipment to find missing persons. Using Wi-Fi and GPS satellites, the Department of Defense was currently tracking the whereabouts of Connor by latching onto a personalized signal from his mobile phone.

Yet, to their dismay, the Agent claimed that he was not at liberty of disclosing where Connor was at that particular moment. Donaldson went on to confirm that Special Agent Masters would be the final decision maker on all matters related to the shootings.

***

The horn blared outside of Beth's apartment. Beth and Ashley rushed out the front door to meet their driver. Panini was behind the wheel, giving a thumbs-up sign.

Ashley's eyes bulged when she saw the make and model that he was driving. "Where did you get this hot car?"

Panini laughed, saying nothing.

Beth opened the back door of the silver Bentley. "Come on. Tell us. Who owns this piece of heaven and what are you doing with it?"

Sheepishly, he replied, "OK. A well to do friend of mine loaned it to me. He manages a hedge fund."

Ashley and Beth both plowed onto the plush leather rear seats of the luxury town car. They met his squinting eyes in the rear view mirror.

"My friend's name is Brent Symanski, born to the right crusty set of parents. Bet he slept at a nicer place than I did last night." He paused. "My place—the Holiday Inn---Oldwyck's finest!" Panini twisted his neck around to see Ashley. "Any further word on how your Dad is doing?"

"This morning, the nurse called me. He's making slow but definite progress."

He put the luxury town car in gear. "Glad to hear Johnny Boy will be back in action." The Bentley moved forward. Unable to avoid a few potholes, he felt as though he was navigating a powerful machine that seemed to float down the road as if a soft silky blanket had cushioned each wheel.

Beth poked his shoulder. "Are we headed for Detroit to pay Jonathan a visit?"

"Not yet. I'm hungry."

Beth rolled her eyes and looked at Ashley.

She shook her head. "As much as I want to see my Dad, we need to find Connor Lucas." She rubbed her forehead. "I just can't get it out of my head. Connor Lucas is really Zach Miller."

He snuck a peek in the mirror. "This Miller is a real psycho. I can't wait to put him out of his misery. And I mean permanently."

"Panini, you may not have heard the whole story. Not only did Zach Miller try to kill my father on many occasions but he also had his nephew kidnap me. I thought the guy was going to kill me for sure." Ashley began to shake, recalling her chained in a dungeon nightmare. "Thinking about it still gives me----"

Beth patted her shoulder. "We need to find Connor before he finds Jonathan."

"Could be a little difficult," he said. "Has anyone ever found a needle in a haystack?"

"What if we contact the DuPont police?" Beth offered.

"Whoa, let's not get too crazy here. First, we get lunch at the DuPont Diner," Panini added. "I think better with a full stomach."

Ashley glanced at her watch. "It's only ten forty in the morning. So, you can call it brunch if that floats your boat."

"Works for me," he replied.

"Panini", Ashley asked in a serious tone, "Have you spoken to your underground contacts?"

"I sure have." He rubbed his abdomen. "After we eat, we can discuss that. Right now, my stomach is growling."

******

The trio sat at a table near the back of the restaurant. Ashley pushed away half of her Cobb salad. "I'm too nervous to eat."

Panini swallowed a humungous mouthful of a corned beef and pastrami sandwich on rye. "Good thing that I eat fast." He looked past Ashley. "Beth, another order of French fries?"

She pretended to retch. "So, what's our plan?"

"I'll take that as a no." He took the measure of both women, searching their faces. "Now, I'm ready to do business." Panini put on his game face. "Look, I know some people that might make each of you ladies a little nervous. So, I'll take the point in dealing with them."

"Before you make us barf our entire brunch, let's start with what we know," Ashley began. "You said that your sources traced Connor to

Grand Rapids, Michigan." She leaned forward. "How did you find that out?"

He glanced over, admiring the sparkle in her innocent looking blue eyes. "How I learned it is not important. It's what I learned that will help us."

"Gotcha."

"My sources confirm that Connor has hooked up with two vicious members of a Russian gang. These ghouls usually hang out in Grand Rapids. My insider contacts are trying to pinpoint exactly where the asshole is at this time."

"Go on," Beth added.

He slurped a diet Pepsi through a bent straw that had served as his chewing stick. "I have a question. Knowing what we know, if you ladies were Connor, what would you do?"

In exasperation, Ashley looked over at Beth. Both shrugged her shoulders. They replied in unison, "Tell us."

He munched on his last super sized French fry. "All right, let me ask my question a little different. Who are Connor's principal enemies?"

Ashley slumped down in her seat and sighed, "My Dad."

Panini just stared at her and said nothing further.

"What about Nasters?" Beth asked.

Finally, Panini replied, "You're both correct." He motioned to the server to bring the check. "Who else must Connor hunt down?"

He drew a blank look from Beth and Ashley.

Beth sighed deeply. "Just tell us already."

"Who else?" He plastered a smile from ear to ear, revealing his coffee stained crooked front teeth. "That would be me-----Joey Panini. Remember, I saw his face. Lucas knows that. Trust me; he'll be gunning for me."

Ashley quivered. "Are you armed?"

Turning his back on the restaurant patrons, under the table, he flashed a *Glock* semi-automatic, pulled out of an inside pocket sewn into his bulky navy winter coat. "And, I'm fully trained to use it."

"Have you ever shot anyone?" Beth queried.

Panini narrowed his gaze. "Let's just say that the doc would trust me to protect the both of you."

"Beyond finding Lucas and making sure all of us and my Dad are safe, let's not forget something else. We need to ensure that the President doesn't deploy *NeoBloc*."

He nodded toward Ashley while taking another sip from his diet Pepsi. "First, I recommend that we pay a visit to Dr. Hussein Nasters. He may be easier to crack than Connor Lucas."

Beth motioned for him to holster his *Glock*. "Let's get out of here. Somehow, we need to stop the mad scientist before he wipes out every American."

"We still have time." Panini blinked several times while shoving his weapon back into his pocket. "Don't worry about me. I know how to handle myself." He paused. "Force is always my last resort," he said, almost as an afterthought.

"Guns make me nervous," Beth replied.

Ashley shuddered. "I've already seen too much bloodshed."

"Maybe you ladies would like to try to befriend Nasters on *Facebook* and build a working relationship. As for me, if he doesn't cooperate and tell us what he knows, I may have to resort to other tactics—even though I'm basically a kind and forgiving type of person."

Ashley clenched her jaws. "We've got to do whatever it takes."

CHAPTER FIFTY-ONE

Connor awoke with a splitting headache. He looked around his shabby twenty dollar a night room. With just three hours of piecemeal sleep, he could barely contain a series of uncontrollable yawns. He downed three aspirins without any aid other than shoving them into the back of his throat and swallowing hard.

Packing into his briefcase his semi-automatic pistol, three Blackberries, and a clown costume, he laid it down on the bed. He shaved, showered, and dressed in gray slacks and a navy sport jacket. Connor buttoned his white collared shirt and straightened his paisley tie. *I'm ready for an appearance on TV, not radio.* He headed downstairs and out the tiny hotel lobby.

The bright sun nearly blinded him. He shielded his eyes and strode into a breakfast café across Forrest Avenue. The overheard lights in the café were dim. He counted less than a half dozen patrons. He walked toward the rear with his briefcase in hand; spotting two middle- aged men, each of whom sported a full-length graying beard. He sat down at their table after ordering a pot of coffee from a passing server.

Plunking himself down, opposite the two men, he kept his briefcase on his lap. "Gentlemen, this is your lucky day if you do right by me."

In a thick Russian accent, the older and stockier of the two men mumbled, "Our interests are similar."

Connor held back any appearance of friendliness toward them. "From the scars I can see under your beards, you both look like you've been through a few battles."

The younger looking man said harshly, "You will obey our rules. First, we have no use for small talk. Code names will identify each of us to one another. You will be called Fuzzy."

The server brought a steaming pot of coffee to the table. Connor winked at the busty young woman. He held up his cup. "Fill it up," he said in a condescending manner. "Leave the pot on the table."

"So, what do I call you hoodlums?" He blew on the coffee. Peeking through the rising steam of the scolding hot coffee, he saw the younger man scowling at him. "Excuse me. There is no need to get upset." He grinned. "I meant to say—what are your names?"

The older man touched the sleeve of his colleague. Deep pockmarks covered his face. A craggy skin that had leather -like quality and a deep scar that ran across his entire forehead led to the obvious conclusion that he was the elder statesman among his newly hired friends. "Fuzzy, that's much better. We prefer to think of ourselves as respectable executives. My name is Charger."

Connor reached out to shake hands. Charger weakly grasped his hand and then added, "My friend is Scout."

Scout nodded. The CEO soon dropped his hand after Scout let it linger in mid air.

Connor pulled out a piece of paper from the inside pocket of his blazer. Slapping the one page summary of roles and responsibilities of everyone on the table, he flipped his plan around so they could read it. He drained the remainder of his black coffee in two gulps and poured himself a second. "I'm paying you very well to make my plan work. Are we clear?"

Scout motioned for him to lean across the table. He murmured, "Do you want us to kill someone or do you want to just keep talking?"

Charger then pointed a finger in Connor's face. "You'll obey our rules."

"Got it. No small talk."

"I see three targets," replied Scout, glancing down at the plan of attack.

"There's one target for each of us. I want Rogers for myself. Charger, you have Panini. Scout, Dr. Nasters is yours."

Connor pushed back his chair. He opened his briefcase, careful to shield the contents from their sight. He pulled out the three mobile devices and laid them on the table. "We will each use one of these Blackberries's. We need to communicate flawlessly for this to work." From a hidden pocket in the briefcase, he drew two stacks of one hundred dollar bills. "Remember I'm in charge of this operation. Do you understand?" He pushed a stack for each of them across the table and stood.

Charger rose. "You have paid us well Fuzzy. Count on us. Back in Russia, we were both known as the angels of death."

"You each have your orders. I'm heading down to the local radio station." He roared, "I'll see both of you in hell." After slinging his blue blazer over his shoulders, he walked behind the Russians as they left the café.

Once the trio hit the street, he spotted his BMW fifty feet away and trotted towards it. He looked back after reaching his car. The Russians were nowhere in sight. After getting behind the steering wheel, he sent a separate text to each of the hit men. The message was for them to acknowledge on their BlackBerry who was the boss. He ordered them to reply immediately. Charger responded within seconds. Scout took a little over a minute to reply.

A derisive smile broke out on his face. Connor did not bother to reply to either of them. What the Russians didn't know was that each of their Blackberries carried a tracking device that anyone in law enforcement could use to follow them. They would at least create decoys so he could personally finish off his business. If they could actually kill Panini and Nasters, that would be pure gravy.

His clean-shaven face appeared in the rear mirror. "DCP doesn't pay me well enough for how good I really am." He turned on his GPS, noting the route. The Grand Junction radio station, The Vantage Point, was his next destination.

******

Connor pulled up to the Grand Rapids radio studio and meandered inside. He addressed the receptionist. "Good morning, I'm Connor Lucas. Your morning drive time anchor is an old friend of mine. May I speak with Quincy Wall when he gets a break?" He smiled broadly. "Please tell him my nickname----Zach. That's how he'll remember me."

"Certainly, Mr. Lucas. I'll pass him a note to see if he can come out of the recording studio at the next commercial break. Please take a seat."

"Sure." He sat down on one of two rickety looking wooden chairs. *What a dump!* He pulled out his handwritten notes from the inside pocket of his blazer. He glanced down at them. *I'm ready for prime time!*

For a moment, he closed his eyes, thinking about his radio friend. Quincy Wall, besides being an old high school friend, was known professionally as the kind of guy who would take on controversial stands as the host of his drive time radio talk show. With a large listening audience, Quincy would provide the precise forum that he needed to get out his propaganda.

Connor heard the creaky floorboards squeaking and looked up. He stared at a slender bespectacled man with acne scars dotting his long, narrow, and sallow looking face.

Breathing heavily, Quincy blurted out, "Zach, I wouldn't have recognized you." His eyes were bloodshot and his face grizzled. The radio show host's elongated nose reminded him of a ski slope. Quincy ran his finger down the incline repeatedly, nervously blinking.

"What brings a city slicker like you out to this neck of woods?"

He bounced out of his seat and pointed to the door marked private. "My friend, can we go into your office to talk?"

The five foot seven host of WOOP radio motioned Connor to follow. "I only have three minutes before I'm back on the air. We run five minutes of weather and commercials on the half hour."

"Thanks for your hospitality."

"That's what friends are for Zach."

***

Inside the radio anchor's inner sanctum, Connor sat on a metal fold up chair across from Quincy. His host leaned back on a wobbly red upholstered chair. His black leather boots quickly appeared on top of a cluttered dusty looking desk. A pile of newspapers met a swift boot. The sheets of paper tumbled to the floor and scattered in all directions. "Sorry for all the clutter."

Connor needed to find out if he could trust his old friend. He checked his Tag Heuer gold plated watch. *Two minutes before airtime!* Grinning at his childhood friend from Brooklyn, he stated, "Let me get right to why I'm here. I need your help. Listen carefully my friend. The man you knew as Zach died in a car crash." Connor winked. "Do we understand each other?"

"You and I go way back," he drawled. He rubbed his chin slowly. "You must have you're reasons and they aren't any business of mine." He chuckled. "So, Connor, what can I do for you?"

Reaching over the small desk, he put his hand on the anchor's shoulder. "Put me on your show. I have a blockbuster story to tell your listeners. I promise you that it will make the network news."

The radio host leaned back so far that he was afraid the chair would tip over. Quincy caught his balance and paused while stealing a look at the wall clock.

"I guarantee your ratings will zoom."

A twinkle gleamed in his weary looking eyes. Nodding his head, he spoke up. "I trust you. I always have." Quincy pointed to the door leading to the recording studio. "Follow me. You're on."

Connor had no sooner settled into his seat in front of his own microphone than he saw the producer point to the host that they were on the air. *What timing!*

"Good morning. You are listening to the Quincy Wall Show on The Vantage Point WOOP radio station. Folks, you are about to hear important breaking news. At the commercial break, an old friend stopped by. He is an amazing man. His name is Connor Lucas and I'd like to welcome him to my show."

He smiled into the microphone. "Hello Quincy and hello to all of your listeners."

"We're pretty informal at this station. Tell us what is on your mind! What brings you to Grand Rapids?"

"It's a long story but I'll try to be brief. I'm the current CEO of a pharmaceutical company called Doctor's Choice Products. We're based in DuPont."

"Our company has been working on a vaccine that will prevent cancers secondary to radiation. Unfortunately, our scientists have recently informed me that volunteer subjects taking our vaccine died in the clinical trials." Connor lassoed Quincy's empathy by covering his heart with his right hand as he spoke.

"Sorry to hear that."

"I'm heartbroken because our vaccine could have saved tens of thousands of lives. However, there is good news. Another company is producing a similar product that appears to be safe. I think all Americans should support our competitor company's vaccine."

"Wow! Did everyone just hear this? How often do we ever hear or read of a CEO supporting a competitor just because it is the right thing to do? Connor, I applaud you patriotism and sense of fair play."

"Side effects can be lethal. Unfortunately, the DCP vaccine—*NeoBloc*—is deadly."

"This is breaking news!"

"Vaccines are to be used only if they are proven to be safe. It is my understanding that our Surgeon General—Dr Jonathan Rogers—is extremely concerned about the clinical trial deaths in China for those volunteers inoculated with *NeoBloc*. I completely agree with the good doctor. He is a voice of reason. We need more physicians like him."

Quincy's eyes popped wide open, revealing two deeply set red globes. "Didn't I hear that Dr. Rogers is currently hospitalized after being shot?"

"I read about that in the papers. What a shame. Let's all pray for his recovery," Connor said, almost choking on his words. "Dr. Rogers and I just want to do what is best for America."

He glanced down at three blinking lights on his phone lines. "We got some callers."

Connor held up his hand and mouthed, *Hold on a second.* "I've been completely honest about this situation. I just want what is best for the American people. However, to my dismay, certain events have transpired beyond my control and a process set into motion to tarnish my good intentions. It's distressing to think this, but there are some misguided scientists at DCP who are simply not looking out for the public good and are still pushing the deadly *NeoBloc* vaccine despite the objections of the good doctor—our Surgeon General—and myself."

"That's disgraceful. Thanks so much for warning my audience. Folks get on your social media connections and immediately get out the word about this dangerous vaccine. And, if you believe it's warranted, maybe you could tweet or post something positive about a courageous American—Connor Lucas."

"Thank you for allowing me this opportunity to formally go on the record before you hear my good name trashed in the media."

Quincy tracked where he was going. "Are you saying that powerbrokers at your drug company and others elsewhere are trying to scapegoat you in order to line their own pockets with blood money?"

Connor gave him a thumbs-up sign. "You hit the nail on the head." An unopened can of diet Pepsi was lying on the table. He grabbed it and pulled back the tab, taking a brief swig. "After DCP made me their CEO, I recently found out that my predecessor actually knew about the real dangers associated with the vaccine. I had no idea."

Quincy piled on the praise. "All Americans are blessed to be living in a God fearing great country like ours. It is my humble view that it's up to fair-minded people out there to stand up for those who are working in the public interest. Unfortunately, the politicians and even some of the prescribing doctors don't always do what is right when they get paid to support unsafe vaccines and medications."

The host scribbled a message and passed it to Connor.

Give me thirty seconds, the guest mouthed.

The host agreed to let his friend stay on his message. "Your words certainly ring true. Before I take a few calls, please go on with your shocking story."

"I hate to bring this sad story up but it is already in the newspapers. In my travels as an executive for our biotech company, I've had the occasion to meet the late Christian James, the Secretary of Health. His recent suicide came as a great shock to all Americans. All life is precious."

"Right on, Connor."

"The whole truth must come out. That's why I'm here. To let the American people know the facts."

Quincy asked, "I have to ask you this question. Did the Secretary of Health work with you before his suicide to try to stop the passage of this killer vaccine?"

Let the story come to me. "It's complicated but the short answer to your question is no." Connor plastered a dejected expression on his face, looking down at the strewn newspapers.

The host glanced down at the flashing lights on his panel. "I have a caller from Detroit on the line." Quincy pressed the panel button all the way to the right. "Go ahead caller."

"Hey, my name is Smitty. I've been a long time listener to your show. But, this is my first call. I just want to say that I totally agree with the comments of your guest. I have been reading the newspaper accounts about the late Secretary of Health. Can Mr. Lucas offer any insights into why Secretary James killed himself?"

"Sir, thanks for your question." Connor hesitated. He pulled out a handkerchief and pretended to blow his nose. "I guess as someone who stands for pro-life in cases, I feel deeply that all life is precious. And, I also feel bad discussing anything personal about Mr. James on the radio out of respect for his grieving family."

Smitty replied, "I can relate to that sentiment. But the Secretary was a public figure. Americans depend on the honesty of public servants to protect us. We deserve to know if he was trustworthy or not."

Make them beg me to tell them the lies.

Quincy's face turned somewhat perplexed. The host took charge. "Thanks Smitty for calling. I agree with you. Mr. Lucas, please tell us what happened and whether you have information that Mr. James may have broken the public trust."

"I'll do my best." He lowered his voice, making it sound as somber as he could. "I'm just concerned for his family." *Reel them in!*

"I'm sure that you'll be sensitive to the feelings of the James family while still telling us what the Secretary might have done in his public role that would concern all of us, especially if he didn't do what you have rightfully done in opposing a deadly vaccine."

"Well, there was a recent unfortunate incident involving Mr. James and myself. It's embarrassing to talk about. But, I assure you and your listeners that I did nothing wrong."

"By your coming forward," Quincy explained, "it tells me that you're only interested in doing what's right. Clearly, it sounds to me that the Secretary of Health was somehow involved in some impropriety. And if that is true, the public has a right to know."

Connor covered his face with both hands for a second or two, rubbing his eyes. He took a deep breath, audibly exhaling into the microphone. "This is hard to talk about given his recent passing but the fact is that the Secretary was strongly attracted to other men. Now, others may disagree, but I believe that we are all God's children and that we should not judge one another in matters such as sexual orientation."

"I happen to agree with you. It's not right for me but I don't judge the behavior of others. To me, it's a matter between that man and his God."

"Quincy, you said it well. However, what is upsetting is that his advances were not consensual. It has come to my knowledge, that many others rebuked his overtures. Sadly, he persisted and simply could not take no for an answer." He paused to take another gulp of Pepsi. *I would have made it in Hollywood,* he mused to himself.

"Take your time. We understand that it's difficult to talk about what another human being may have done, even more so if his actions would have been hurtful to America as well as to you personally."

Time to lower the boom! "Though it will be damaging to the reputation of the late Secretary, I must be perfectly candid. Several days ago, I was a victim of sexual harassment at the hands of Mr. Christian James."

"Did you go to the police?"

"I did," he replied with sadness in his voice.

"What can you tell us about what happened and whether this may be connected to the Secretary's role in regard to the public health of our nation?

"If I may, I would like to back up a little. I'm a recent widower. My loving wife of twenty years recently passed away from a long suffering bout with cancer."

The talk show populist interrupted. "I'm sorry for your loss. I understand what you are going through. I'm a recent widower myself. Please continue with your story."

"Well, when I was in DC at the request of President Williams to discuss the DCP vaccine *NeoBloc*, I personally warned her how deadly it is. After our meeting, the President asked me to meet with Mr. James in his office at the Department of Health to discuss my concerns. We were in the middle of a discussion on a safer vaccine manufactured by a company called Weston & Weston when he made a sudden improper advance on me. It caught me by total surprise. I was quite upset. I've never before had a man kiss me on my lips." Connor paused a few seconds. He raised his voice to sound indignant. "I told him that I was quite upset by his unwanted behavior and that I was going to call the police to file a formal complaint."

Connor took another mouthful of Pepsi. "Who knows what he was thinking when he subsequently hung himself? I hate to speculate but he might have panicked, knowing that he was going to be publicly disgraced, lose his powerful government job, and possibly land in prison after I filed charges with the DC police."

Quincy asked, "Why do you think he picked you, especially in light of the fact that I'm sure you told him that the President herself asked you to meet with him on the issue of vaccine safety?"

"I have no idea what he was thinking Quincy. He must have just snapped. Maybe, he thought that he could make me go along with his views on the DCP vaccine if we were close friends. But I told him before he attacked me that I was strongly opposed to the deployment of NeoBloc—despite the fact that I was the CEO of the actual manufacturer of that product."

"I understand. Let's get back to *his* position on the deadly vaccine— *NeoBloc.*"

"To be blunt, before he attacked me, he confided in me that he only recently came to be aware that *Neobloc* was a killer vaccine." Connor paused to let his words sink in. "I told him in light of what he found out that it was not too late for him to work with Dr. Rogers to fight for the safe vaccine from W&W.

"That makes a lot of sense."

"Mr. James told me that he had opposed Dr. Rogers on the vaccine issue but he was afraid the President would fire him. So, to save his career he did not want to admit the truth."

"But millions of Americans would have died had he been successful in covering up what he knew."

"You're absolutely correct. Clearly, the President was seeking a safe vaccine. However, I do not think that Mr. James was acting rationally, especially since he fought so hard for *NeoBloc*. But, let us all pray to God for his soul."

The studio door opened. The producer walked in and handed the host a note. Quincy read it to himself. He pressed line four. "Folks our first caller wanted to make another comment. "You're back on Smitty."

"Hey thanks. I called the studio and spoke to your producer. I just had to come back on the air. First, let me be perfectly clear that I don't know your guest from Adam. I just want to talk from my heart after listening to him. It's a damn shame that people like Mr. James got into a position of power and then tried to bring down a good and innocent American as Mr. Connor Lucas."

"Thank you for your strong feelings." The host clicked off the connection with Smitty. He looked directly at Connor. "While I've been listening to your story, one question popped into my head. In all fairness, Mr. Lucas, do you have any evidence to back up your claim?"

"I do." Connor took another mouthful of Pepsi. "I have DNA evidence that I'll be handing over to the authorities like any law abiding citizen would do. At the time of this unfortunate incident, I had immediately notified the DC police. Subsequent to my return to Michigan, I have also issued a formal complaint to the authorities in DuPont."

The host leaned back and just shook his head in amazement. Quincy's face told Connor everything he wanted to know. He was convinced that he had just pulled off the biggest lie of his life.

"Mr. Lucas, we have one more minute before I need to break for another segment. Is there anything else you would like to tell our Michigan audience?"

"I sincerely hope that the top scientist at DCP, Dr. Hussein Nasters, the FDA, the National Quality Board and President Williams will all have a change of heart. They need to stop pursuing the lethal vaccine—*NeoBloc*. We must always put the public interest before the rapacious private interest. As the esteemed physician, Dr. Jonathan Rogers is so fond of saying: *First, do no harm.* Let me say how much I admire the Surgeon General. He always does what is right. We need more physicians like him."

He sat back and poured the remainder of the Pepsi down his throat.

Quincy spoke into his microphone. "Ladies and Gentlemen, I hope you have appreciated hearing directly from Mr. Connor Lucas, CEO of Doctor's Choice products on this breaking story. Start calling the TV networks, post a Facebook status and tweet the story that you heard right here on the Quincy Wall Show on WOOP."

Connor raised his hand and held the microphone in his hands. The host acknowledged his request, "One final comment from our guest."

"Thank you for the opportunity to speak directly to the people of our great land, unfiltered by the left wing media and heartless politicians. God Bless America."

******

Once in his BMW, Connor smacked his hands together and let out a deafening holler, *Yes.* Within the hour, every major network in the country would be broadcasting his story. A million tweets and posts would proclaim him some sort of a national hero. Feeling that he had just inoculated himself from any political damage from the Christian James email, he gleefully headed east in his BMW to finish a job that had waited far too long to consummate.

CHAPTER FIFTY-TWO

Nasters's was in the middle of saying his afternoon prayers when he received a phone call. As he listened, his mood turned sour. It was from Mugandi. The leader of the rogue PFF cell reported hearing a breaking news story, just been picked up by the major networks. The reports stated that Connor Lucas tore the safety of *NeoBloc* to shreds on a local western Michigan radio talk show.

Nasters sat down, closed his eyes, as he listened to the rest of Mugandi's rant. His tone was decidedly accusatory toward the scientist.

The PFF leader chided Nasters. "You said the President and the FDA was in favor of deployment of *NeoBloc*. You said every American would receive this vaccine. You said that every American who received the vaccine would die."

He weakly replied, "I stand by my statements."

"Hussein, I am not a fool. Based on the public comments about you, the late Secretary of Health, and *NeoBloc* by Connor Lucas, you are viewed as a liar in the eyes of the American people."

"It is he who is lying. I am being truthful."

"Do you expect me to believe that your greedy capitalists would inoculate every American with a deadly vaccine? He breathed deeply into the phone. "Let me spell it out for you. There is no profit if every American is dead."

"Listen to me. I am the scientist who developed this vaccine. No one knows what I know. I have told everyone but you, my brother, that *NeoBloc* is safe."

"By your own words just now you have just confirmed what I just called you—a liar. You previously told everyone that the vaccine is safe but according to Connor and you, the vaccine is deadly. You have been caught in your own web of deception."

"You are missing the larger point. I had previously explained to you that I lied in order to trick--."

Mugandi interrupted him in mid sentence. "Allah may forgive your lies but the PFF will not. If we can, we will dismember each of your limbs while keeping you alive—just so we can inflict more torture on you."

"But—"

"Say no more. Prepare to explain your disloyal deceit to Allah."

Nasters heard the slam of the phone. He slumped at his desk. *It's time to buy a Browning high power pistol. I'm a dead man.*

Two hard knocks on his office door broke his personal terror. He shuffled over to open it. He saw Ashley, Beth, and Panini glaring at him. "What do you want?" Nasters coldly asked.

Ashley took the lead. "Before we begin, let me introduce you to Mr. Joseph Panini."

"Is this a joke? You dare to come here to have me meet people who mean nothing to me."

"Mr. Panini has been a lifelong friend of my father."

Nasters turned his back on them and plopped down in his chair behind his desk. He shouted over his shoulder, "Ms. Rogers, why are you and your companions here?"

"To clear the air."

She pulled up a chair and sat next to the scientist. Panini and Beth sat across the desk. Nasters turned to Ashley. "You have two minutes."

Panini pounded the table. "Listen doc, the three of us are prepared to go to the press after we leave your office and show them the valid monkey data from Dr. Washington. That data combined with the *Post* story of Secretary James's email disclosure of nineteen deaths in the clinical trials in China after receiving *NeoBloc* should elevate more than a few eyebrows."

Nasters rose slowly from his seat. "You do not understand science. The subjects in the clinical trials had pre-existing conditions that should have precluded their acceptance into the trial. That's the fault of the Chinese researchers, not a problem with *NeoBloc*." By now, the veins in his neck were pulsating. "Do you have nothing better to do than to annoy me with your ignorance of the scientific facts?"

He yelled, "Where's Connor Lucas?"

"I have no clue. Frankly, I don't care since even he has turned against *NeoBloc*." He pointed toward the open door. "All Americans are stupid!"

Panini took two steps toward Nasters but Beth blocked his path. Ashley pulled out her digital camera and placed it on the windowsill. She directed the lens toward the scientist who was now standing. His face was contorted. A second later, the flash went off. Panini ran to retrieve the camera.

"I have asked you to leave me alone Ms. Rogers."

"Your picture will be plastered on the web and television within the hour. Actually, I'm surprised that every reporter in town is'nt already here, given what Connor Lucas said today about you and *NeoBloc*."

"You are a troublemaker. I will report you to President Williams. She believes me." The scientist raised his fist above Ashley's head.

Panini intercepted the forearm before it struck. He shouted, "Dr. Nasters, how dare you try to hit the daughter of the Surgeon General?"

Nasters already beat red face began to sweat. Perspiration beads trickled off his forehead. "Get out," he shouted. "Americans all deserve to die. Every one of you is an arrogant infidel. I hate every single one of you."

Beth walked over to the scientist. Panini stood between the two of them. He motioned for Ashley to begin walking toward the door.

Beth pulled out her miniature tape recorder from an inner pocket of her navy pants suit. "I'll be handing over this tape to the media to add to the rest of the evidence against *NeoBloc*---and you—you son of a bitch."

"You are trying to blackmail me."

"Not at all," Beth said, "I just recorded your own words." *'Americans all deserve to die.'* She pretended to spit at him. "If you had an ounce of decency, you would pick up the phone and pull *NeoBloc* from FDA consideration."

"Never! It will be over my dead body if *NeoBloc* is not injected into three hundred million Americans."

Panini headed toward the scientist. He saddled up to his face. "Mom once told me to be careful of what I wish for."

The scientist cursed under his breath. He ushered them toward the door. Panini sharply pivoted and faced Nasters. "Oh, one more point. Mom was always right."

CHAPTER FIFTY-THREE

Panini parked the silver Bentley in a no parking zone in front of the DuPont Herald building. Ionic marble columns flanked the three dozen concrete steps. Impassioned, he felt himself flying up the stairs, leaving Beth and Ashley in his wake. With the digital camera and Beth's audio tape in hand, he waited for the duo to catch up before heading for the office of Mr. Larry Pequod, chief editor of the flagship newspaper for the past thirty two years.

Outside a corner office on the newsroom floor, Panini knocked. He stuck his nose a foot from the door. A middle-aged African-American man in an open collar blue shirt yanked it open. "Can I help you?"

"Mr. Pequod, I'd like you to meet Ashley Rogers, daughter of the Surgeon General. She has a tape recording and photo that I believe will be of great interest to your readers."

"Come in."

Ashley handed the editor the evidence just as her Blackberry beeped. She walked away as Panini and Beth began conversing with the editor.

"Hi, my name is Beth Murphy. I'm a member of the National Quality Board that makes recommendations to the FDA on drugs and vaccines that are in the pipeline of pharmaceutical companies." She presented a manila folder to the editor. "Dr. Virginia Washington was one of the scientists working on a vaccine to prevent cancers from radiation."

Pequod dropped the camera and tape on his cluttered desk. He quickly perused the document that she gave him. "I'm well aware of the controversy swirling around *NeoBloc*."

"It's been all over the news as the next savior vaccine."

He continued to scan the document. "Where did you get this?"

"Inside the folder, you'll find a sworn affidavit from Dr. Washington that the data you are looking at is the real monkey trial data on *NeoBloc*."

His eyes shifted back and forth to the two of them. "I see the executive summary."

Beth searched for her roommate. She spotted her hunched over a cubicle in the hallway outside the editor's office. "Ashley, come back in."

Panini spoke up. "Mr Pequod, we need you to print this story."

Pequod covered his mouth. He sat down in his chair, leaning forward, and looked at the two of them. "This data shows that every monkey died after receiving *NeoBloc* and that it took a year to occur."

Beth glanced over to the open doorway. It was Ashley. Her eyes were devoid of any feeling.

Speechless, she pointed to the message on her Blackberry. Panini grabbed the mobile device and began reading the email aloud. "It's a confidential email from FBI Special Agent Masters." He paused and shot a worried looking glance at Ashley. "It says the FBI is currently tracking Connor Lucas. He is now forty miles due east of DuPont, apparently headed for Detroit."

"He's going toward my father—to finish him off—for good."

"Let's go," Beth exclaimed as fear exploded in her eyes.

Panini's eyes squinted. "Lieutenant Masters states that police guards are now stationed outside the hospital room of-----." He stopped reading, glancing up to see Ashley. She was already gone.

Beth and Panini ran out of the office, trying to catch up with her. Half way down the hall to the large foyer of the Herald Building, Panini shouted to Beth. "We have to stop Connor before he kills Jonathan."

***

Panini looked at the dashboard mounted GPS. He keyed in the coordinates. "He's at least a half hour east of us, even if I break the speed limit."

In the backseat, Beth reached over to Ashley. "Don't worry about your dad. He has police protection."

Ashley looked out the window as Panini drove onto the outside shoulder and passed two vans before diving back into the fast lane. "I've heard that before." She rubbed her forehead. "How far are we from the hospital?"

"We'll be there in seventy minutes, more or less, that is if I don't get caught for speeding by the State Police."

Ashley fired off a text message to the FBI Lieutenant. *How far is Connor from my Dad?*

Seconds later, the reply came. *Less than an hour.*

Accelerating, Panini swerved to avoid a blue Cadillac sedan that tried cutting them off. "What the hell is he doing?" He honked the horn as the sedan dropped back into the adjacent lane. From the corner of his eye, he saw the Cadillac accelerating forward, veering toward the rear bumper guard of the Bentley. "Brace yourself."

The sedan banked hard into the luxury town car, causing it to scrape along the concrete median divider. Panini hit the brakes. Just as he tried to read the sedan's plate number, the front windshield shattered on the passenger side. He recognized the pattern of the cracking of the glass. He yelled, "That was a bullet. Get down!"

The Bentley coasted along the divider. The Cadillac sped ahead. "Did anyone get hit?"

Beth replied, "We're OK. However, you had better stop. That State Trooper behind us is flashing his overhead lights."

The unmarked trooper vehicle pulled up behind the town car. In the rearview mirror, Panini could see the officer calling for back up on his radio.

Ashley cried out, "We need to get to the hospital. We're wasting time."

Beth put her arms around Ashley. "A second Trooper just pulled up."

One slender looking trooper approached the Bentley from the driver's side and another heavyset officer came from the passenger side. Panini noticed that each of them had their Smith and Wesson compact .40 caliber pistol aimed at each of them.

The trooper on the driver's side, hollered, "Slowly exit the car. Keep your hands above your head at all times."

Panini opened his door and raised his hands above his head. "Ashley, Beth, do the same." They followed his instructions and walked toward him.

Both troopers continued to close in even more. "Keep your hands up."

Ashley spoke up. "My father is Dr. Jonathan Rogers, the Surgeon General and former Commissioner of Health from this state."

One trooper replied, "Quiet, Miss. Are any of you carrying a weapon?"

Panini said, "Someone just shot at us. That's why I crashed off the divider."

The other trooper raised his voice. "I repeat. Are any of you carrying any weapons?"

Panini confessed. "I have a Glock semi-automatic strapped to my right calf."

Ashley could not help herself. "Can I please show you a message from FBI Special Agent Susan Masters? There is a man named Connor Lucas driving right now to Detroit to kill my father-----Dr. Rogers. Her email is on my Blackberry. If you check with the FBI, they will tell you that Lucas is the subject of a national manhunt by all law enforcement."

The next order came from the tall slender trooper. "Everyone lie face down on the pavement. Do it slowly. And sir, do not reach for your gun or I'll shoot you."

The trio followed orders. When all were face down, the husky trooper removed the gun from Panini's calf. "Where is the Blackberry?"

"On the back seat."

The trooper opened the back door. Ashley craned her neck. She could see him reading the message from Agent Masters. He shouted to his partner, "Cover them. I need to make a call."

Ashley looked up. She saw the barrel of the trooper's Smith & Wesson pointed at her head. She shouted, "We're wasting time."

The thin faced trooper yelled back, "Don't move. Put your face down on the pavement."

***

After making the call, the trooper returned. Ashley observed his holstered pistol. "Miss, your story checks out with the FBI. I spoke directly with Special Agent Susan Masters." He then ordered the other trooper to put away his weapon. "You folks are free to leave."

He walked over to Panini who by now was on his feet. "Sir, I can't return the Glock to you."

The trio ran toward the Bentley. Panini waved to the trooper. "Can you give us an escort to Hockeytown?"

The trooper tipped his hat. "Follow me."

Ashley shrieked, "Did Agent Masters say anything else?"

His response was chilling. "She said you should check with the Detroit police before going near your father's hospital room."

CHAPTER FIFTY-FOUR

Connor felt orgasmic. He was within ten minutes of his arch
nemesis. *Dr. Rogers will soon be a dead man!* At a red light on Center
Line just off the Chrysler Freeway, he glanced down at his Blackberry.
He scrolled a page of unread emails. Charger had just sent him a text
message. Connor hit reply and berated him for his failed attempt to
crash the Bentley and his failed attempt to kill any of the passengers. He
scrolled down further. Scout left a message. The PFF and FBI were
both trailing Nasters.

The light changed and Connor pulled off to the side of the road. He
typed quickly, ordering Scout to back off and merely observe the
scientist. Sending a second message to Charger, he ordered him to find
and kill all three occupants of the town car. He then spotted a lone
phone booth. Hopping out, he called Andrea. She informed him that the
FBI had stopped by asking a lot questions.

"Andrea, what did they say?"

"Just wanted to know where you were. A woman—a special agent
named Susan Masters---is in charge of some investigation."

"Just keep to your story that you haven't seen or talked to me in
days."

"Don't worry. I'll be discreet. However, you will be interested to
know that hundreds of listeners, who heard you speaking on the WOOP
radio show, are calling into our DCP switchboard. They are calling you
the champion of drug safety—a national hero."

He smiled broadly. "I'll call you if I need you."

He jumped back into his BMW and pulled back into traffic.
Laughing to the point of tears, he glanced over to the Groucho Marx
facemask that was lying on the front seat. His plan was to go to the
nurses' station in the children's ward and pretend that he was a clown.
He would use his well-honed persuasion skills to convince the head
nurse that he was a hospital volunteer. He would convince everyone that
he was there solely to amuse the children. Connor would ask the
pediatric nurses to fill out a hospital badge, displaying the name Fuzzy.
Then he would meander over to Jonathan Rogers's room and carry out
his own mandate. An order to kill!

******

Parking in the Medical Center lot nearest to the main road, Connor stuffed his big nose, furry eyebrow mask, Blackberry, and Baretta into his briefcase. He strolled into a side entrance of Detroit Metro carrying the leather case. Told where the children's ward was, he quickly found the nurses' station.

A twenty- something looking nurse was writing in a hospital chart behind the counter. As he arrived in front of her, he gently lowered his briefcase. Turning around, he opened it, pulling out the mask. He giggled as he plastered on a zany looking face. He pivoted back, displaying his full costume.

With his dimples on full display, he faked a childish voice, "Good afternoon, young lady. My name is Fuzzy."

She cackled. "And, what can I do for you today Mr. Fuzzy?"

"I'm here to entertain the kids." He spun himself around in a three hundred and sixty degree circle on the sole of his right foot. He then dropped to the floor, pretending that he was break dancing. Clumsily rising to his feet, he faked reeling in the slack of an imaginary fishing pole.

The nurse frowned. "The kids are getting their meds. This is not a good time."

Connor pulled off his mask, smiling broadly. "I see. Perhaps I can come back later." A glint in her eye flashed back. Her nametag was in full view. "I see your name is Susie." He covered his face with his left hand while stretching out his other hand. "I've always been on the shy side." The nurse went along with his gig. He kissed her wrist after doing a curtsy.

He spotted the envious looking smiles of other nurses passing by, who appeared to be somewhat impressed by his gallantry. Susie's eyes widened, as she seemed to bask in the personal attention that she was receiving.

Connor stretched out his arms as if they were wings on a jet airliner. "I'm just a humble hospital volunteer. Can you do a humungous favor for me and write out one of those hospital visitor name badges?" He turned his mouth into a pout. "The security guard downstairs ran out of tags."

Susie looked down at the patient chart in her hands. "I'm not supposed to do those kinds of things."

"I'm so sorry to ask you to do this one simple thing." He feigned a cascade of tears. "Pretty please—a favor for a clown—a clown trying to bring smiles to the faces of the cute kids." He assumed a saddened face, a final thrust to achieve victory.

Susie nodded. "Oh, I guess so." She picked up an official Detroit Metro Medical Center badge from a drawer below the counter. Writing out his name in flamboyant red letters with a felt tipped pen, she proudly held it up for all to see. *Detroit Metro Volunteer- Fuzzy.*

Connor covered his heart with his right hand. "Didn't I see you in the final of the Miss Michigan Pageant last year?"

Giggling, she replied, "You're such a tease."

"I'll be back sweetie to entertain the children after the meds are given out."

She waved. "The kids will love you. You're such a nice man. See you later Fuzzy."

Connor ripped off the cellophane. The official looking badge stuck nicely to his left lapel. He bowed one last time, bringing a loud guffaw from the young nurse.

"Are the nurses in the medical ICU as kind as you?"

"They are even nicer. By the way, do you know how to get there?"

He crossed his eyes and shrugged his shoulders. "What do you think?"

Susie gave him directions. He picked up his briefcase and marched off wearing his Groucho Marx mask, proudly wearing his hospital badge that proclaimed him to the world as Fuzzy the Detroit Metro volunteer.

***

Connor typed in follow up messages for Charger and Scout. Their replies came back quickly. Scout texted that a PFF cell seemed to be closing the noose around Nasters by placing lookouts strategically nearer to his office. He cursed Charger for reporting that Panini's whereabouts was still unknown. *Dammit!* He fired off a final email to the Russians, ordering them to have no further contact with him. *I can't trust anybody but myself.* Striding past several ICU rooms, he looked inside each, trying to locate his target.

He began picking up worrisome vibes from passing hospital staff. Rather than continually appearing to be searching for Rogers's room, he approached an elderly nurse in the hallway. "Excuse me, young lady." He read her nametag. His beady eyes squinted just below his gyrating hairy eyebrows. "Good morning, Miss March."

She tried hard to contain her laughter within herself. "Nice mask," she offered.

Connor played it straight. "I'm a dear friend of Jonathan Rogers. I'm currently volunteering on the children's ward." He pointed to his badge. "I was so upset to hear what happened to him that I just had to come here to pay him a visit. How is he doing?"

"He's holding his own. You'll find him in room seven." She pointed. "It's the one with the policewoman standing watch on the outside."

"Well, Miss March, thank you so much. I really wanted some private time with him to reminisce about the good 'ole days. I wasn't expecting a party." He raised his hands over his head. He pretended as if a robber had pointed a gun at him. "Will the guard want to frisk me?"

Her focus no longer on his face, the nurse began to read his nametag. She laughed aloud. "You're Fuzzy?"

"Not so loud, please, I'm embarrassed enough." He pointed to his mask. "The policewoman will give me one chastising look and all my years of psychological therapy trying to regain my self esteem will be gone."

Her lips parted, revealing a sly grin. "Maybe I can help you."

"I would be eternally grateful for whatever small favors you can do for a homeless clown."

She spoke in a low pitch. "I can't promise anything but I happen to know that the guard is due for a five minute break. I'll speak with her. If she agrees to keep the door unlocked in her absence, that will give you time with your friend. You know, private time---just you and Dr. Rogers. Just don't stay too long. He is still very weak from his ordeal but he is breathing on his own. He slips in and out of consciousness. Just remember, do not say anything about what happened to him. He still has not been told."

"Mum is the word."

Miss March walked toward the guard outside of Rogers's room.

Connor took two deep breaths. *It's working!* He observed the police officer's body language. The nurse pointed back at him. The guard laughed when he knelt down on the hospital floor and pretended to be pleading his case. Yet, the police officer shook her head in the negative. He picked up his briefcase from the floor and set it down on a nearby hospital cart. He unlatched the briefcase. *I didn't want to kill innocent people.*

Connor opened the case and reached inside for his gun. By now, Miss March had left the guard's side. The police officer took a seat in a corridor chair, no longer looking in his direction. He looked around. Seeing no one observing him, he quickly attached the silencer on his Baretta. He flicked off the safety latch and tightened his right hand around the gunstock. *I'll whack the policewoman first---then Rogers--- and then anyone else who dares to get in the way.*

A split second later, he heard ear piercing sounds of a fire alarm ringing out. His hand still gripping the gunstock, the police officer ran off down the corridor in the opposite direction. Miss March began walking toward him. Connor released his grip on the Baretta. He slipped it back into the briefcase and slammed it shut.

Drawing within ten feet of him, the nurse shouted above the din, "It's probably a false alarm. But you're lucky. This is your chance to see your friend---alone. Just close the door behind you—to lessen the noise from the alarm."

Connor telegraphed a peaceful look. He raised his eyes to the ceiling. "God certainly works his will in wondrous ways."

"I don't know why the policewoman is even here. She just appeared an hour ago." March stared down the hallway. "From the direction she took off, it looks like she believed the alarm was coming from the adjacent hospital wing. But, she'll be back soon."

Miss March does not know who the lucky one is. "I just want to see my close friend." Connor held both hands over his ears, trying to block out the thunderous clanging of the alarm.

"You might get five minutes of private time with Dr. Rogers if you go in now. Don't forget to pull the curtain and close the door for privacy. By the way, he is much more alert today."

He kissed the nurse on the cheek.

"Five minutes," she shouted above the din of the clanging alarm and then walked away.

He entered room number seven. His eyes grew large. Rogers was fast asleep. He saw an oxygen cannula, affixed to his nostrils. An intravenous line connected to his left forearm dripped in a green liquid. A heart monitor revealed the rhythmic beating. An occasional run of snores unnerved Connor, fearing that his victim would awaken before he was ready to kill.

Connor quietly closed the door and drew the curtains. He glanced down at his watch. The guard would be back any minute. And, Miss March might even decide to crash his private farewell party.

He approached Rogers from the left side of his bed. His heart pounded. *At last!* Connor sensed his victim's complete vulnerability. The Surgeon General arms looked flabby. There was no way that he would be able to fight off anyone. Now, a foot from his face, he watched carefully for any signs of awakening. The eyes fluttered but did not open. *How can he sleep with this damn alarm blasting?*

Rogers was now breathing deeply, a slight snore punctuated every few cycles. Connor opened his briefcase. He searched inside and donned a pair of surgical gloves. The patient stirred, opening his eyes for a split-second and then quickly closed them. The snoring intensified.

Connor drew a few deep breaths, recalling all the misery that he had caused him over many years. The CEO was trying to work himself up into a rage. He thought of missed opportunities for untold wealth, always stymied by Dr. Jonathan Rogers. Jealous that the lovely Kim Rogers had preferred her husband over him had always pissed him off as well. He tightened his mask. *I have killed before.* A second later, he viciously pounced on his victim; his strong hands began choking the Surgeon General's neck as hard as he could.

The patient's eyes popped open, possibly recognizing Connor despite the Groucho Marx mask. Rogers squirmed and attempted to shout but his feeble attempts were easily defeated. His eyes began to flutter. His face turned whiter than the hospital sheet. Connor was surprised that it was this easy. His eyes finally closed and remained shut. The chest of his victim became still. The cardiac monitor hummed as a flat line ran across the screen. Connor checked the carotid artery--- no pulse. He thought he heard his own heart pounding as he became acutely aware that the room had became mostly quiet. *The fire alarm is off!*

He hoped that he had another minute before the guard would return from the adjacent wing. But he had to be sure Rogers was dead. He opened his briefcase and laid his Baretta at the foot of the bed. He resumed his chokehold. *Twenty more seconds of choking -- make sure he's gone forever.* He silently counted to himself. *Nineteen---eighteen- seventeen.* Each second was one moment closer to victory. Rogers didn't move. Connor savored the moment. Revenge was sweet. Suddenly, the heart monitor alarm was beeping loudly—a signal to the staff that something was wrong.

Connor pounced on his Baretta but fumbled his grip. In a state of frenzy, he knew doctors and nurses would be streaming through the door any second. He made a second unsuccessful attempt to corral his gun from the foot of the bed. He sensed someone watching him. He glanced up, spotting a man standing in the open doorway, roaring like a lion. *Shit! It's the guy I shot outside of Ashley's apartment.*

Enraged, Panini leaped toward him as if he were Superman flying through the air. A moment later, Panini squeezed Connor's neck with all of his might. In the struggle, his mask ripped off his face. Fuzzy made another futile attempt to grab the Baretta lying inside the briefcase. Panini kicked it off the bed. Connor received two hard knee kicks to his groin and he fell on the floor.

In the hallway, Fuzzy spotted Miss March. She was pointing toward the room, yelling for the police officer to run towards her. Panini jumped on top of him. His neck felt like it was in a vise, gasping for a breath but no air was forthcoming. Each second, the pressure on his neck tightened harder and harder. Panini gave him two more knee chops to his stomach. *I can't breathe.* He looked into the eyes of the brave defender of Dr. Rogers. They burned with revenge. Panini jammed his thumb into Connor's Adam's apple. *He's gonna bust open my neck.*

Two wads of Panini's spit hit him in his eyes. After shutting them, he tried to re-open them but they no longer responded to his command. It was almost as if the spit was holding his eyes shut like glue. *Where is the police officer?* Connor tried to think, unable to fight any longer. He could not pry his attacker's hands loose.

Connor's thoughts rambled. He imagined that his hands were still choking Rogers. Rapidly weakening, he began dreaming of raging fires around him. His skin appeared to be burning. It seemed to be peeling off his bones. Screeching sounds coming from all directions were hellish. A moment or two later, Connor Lucas---Zach Miller was gone.

Panini released his death grip. Ashley and Beth were yelling for help. Panini pushed himself up, grabbing his groin at the spot of his gunshot wound. His chest heaving, he stepped over the body of Connor Lucas toward the other lifeless body on the bed.

Ashley put her face next to her father's mouth. Beth tried to get a carotid pulse. *Nothing.* Panini felt paralyzed. His worst fear hit him, smack in his face. Had he been too late?

CHAPTER FIFTY-FIVE

Ashley tossed Miss March the intubation set up. The corridor loudspeakers blared. *Code Blue--ICU Room Three.* Ashley pushed the bed forward and stood at the head, behind her father. Tilting back his head, the head nurse was able to insert the breathing tube down his throat.

Trembling, Ashley saw house staff physicians and nurses pouring into the room. One nurse rolled her father onto his side while another slipped a board underneath him. A young male doctor began pumping on the Surgeon General's chest. A nurse hooked up the intubation tube to a respirator-----pouring in life demanded oxygen into his lungs.

The chief resident barked out orders. "I need a bolus of epi." A nurse handed him a syringe with a three-inch needle. "Hook him up to the monitor. What's his rhythm?"

"Flat line, Doctor Hastings."

The chief resident felt for the sternum. After moving his fingers two inches to the left in the fifth interspace of ribs, he aimed the long needle toward the second right costochondral junction, plunging it directly into the Surgeon General's heart. He pulled back on the plunger---drops of red blood floated into the syringe. He injected the epinephrine in the hope that it would stimulate his heart to beat.

Hastings looked at the monitor. "I see an occasional beat. Keep pumping Torrance. Nurse, push a bolus of sodium bicarbonate." The house doctor rechecked the monitor. "It's working. He's back in regular sinus rhythm."

The doctor in charge shouted, "Get the family out of here, now."

The nurse pulled Ashley's hand away from Rogers. *I can't leave him.* She felt Miss March's hands on her shoulders---firmly steering her out of the room. Panini and Beth tried to console her. She jerked her head back when she heard Hastings yell out, "He's flat lining again."

Once again, the doctor stabbed the three-inch needle straight into her father's heart, sending the heart-stimulating hormone into his system. The monitor blipped once, showing a solitary heartbeat followed by a flat line.

"It's not working. Push a bolus of 3mg of atropine and another syringe of sodium bicarbonate. Get the paddles ready to shock his heart."

The steady drone of the cardiac monitor was Ashley's last memory. The door slammed shut, blocked by the security guard. Both Panini and Beth tried to hold back their tears but succumbed to the inevitable urge to break down.

The world was vanishing before her disbelieving eyes. Unable to walk away from her father's room, Ashley collapsed to the hospital corridor floor, adjacent to his room and prayed.

CHAPTER FIFTY-SIX

Nasters cheered the news. The lead story on a local TV news show, announced the death of Connor Lucas. Within five minutes, the national media broke the news because of his connection to the late Secretary of Health and President Williams.

In recent days, the DCP scientist had come to hate Connor for opposing *NeoBloc* and for wanting the President to favor an alternative vaccine from W&W. *My jihad will now survive! Praise Allah!*

A phone call from Xavier Rudolf interrupted his prayers. As he listened, the news got even better. He hung up the phone and began dancing around his apartment. Nasters could hardly wait for dawn to arrive.

******

Rudolf was already waiting for Nasters when the scientist walked into his own private office. The scientist was not surprised. It was widely accepted throughout all of DCP that the Board leader had full authority to move freely throughout the Company, even to private offices of senior management.

The visitor rose to his feet and took charge. "President Williams called me. She has spoken with the FDA chief, Tom Lake. It appears that upon investigation of the *NeoBloc* trials in China that many of the volunteers were previously sick, as you have claimed all along."

"You see." Nasters quickly concocted a logical scenario. "If Connor was truly convinced that *NeoBloc* was deadly then why would he have tried to kill Dr. Rogers---the most outspoken critic of the vaccine and the only one the President empowered with cancelling deployment of our vaccine?"

Nasters waited as the logic embedded in his clear statement fully sunk into Rudolf's consciousness. "Does my statement not make perfect sense?"

The Chair of the Board cleared his throat. "Your point is well taken."

"I'm glad that you're beginning to see the light. Permit me to return to your comment on our phone conversation from last night. You freely admitted that I have been well recognized by my scientific peers as being an expert in biologics---in vaccines."

"That fact is well established. If you weren't respected for your scientific knowledge and experience, I never would have recommended your initial appointment at DCP."

"Thank you. So, after all is said and done and through the deceit of Connor Lucas, we have come to two powerful conclusions---that I am a well respected scientist on vaccine matters and that if I was wrong about *NeoBloc* then Connor never would have tried to kill the number one opponent of DCP's vaccine—Dr. Rogers."

"Don't mix science and business. Connor did not know crap about science. He was only interested in making a profit." The chairperson took one-step closer to Nasters. "It's not that simple. I've known that there was bad blood between him and Rogers going back for years. He may have hunted down the Surgeon General for personal reasons totally unrelated to *NeoBloc.*"

Nasters smiled. "There are credible rumors that the President has returned to supporting *NeoBloc* after W&W turned down her offer and after she realized that their compound is far from ready." The scientist sneered. "The safety points on my vaccine cannot be refuted."

"Look doc, I'm a businessman. We need scientists like you to produce these damn products." Rudolf sent a warm gaze at Nasters. "So, I'm beginning to lean toward recommending that you be named CEO of DCP in the wake of Connor Lucas's untimely death."

"Mr. Rudolf, I am deeply humbled by your confidence in me and profoundly saddened by the passing of Connor Lucas----however misguided that he was about *NeoBloc.*"

Rudolf walked up and almost bumped the chest of Nasters. "Doctor, can you absolutely assure me that *NeoBloc* is safe? As you know, an imminent FDA decision is pending."

"I believe in full transparency. To answer your question, there have been no deaths in any of the human clinical trials conducted in America. And, the National Quality Board has recommended to the FDA that *NeoBloc* be approved for public distribution."

"I must admit that the lack of deaths in the United States clinical trials with the vaccine is rather compelling."

"That's because in America, immune-compromised sick volunteers are excluded from our *NeoBloc* trials. It is standard industry practice in the United States. So, you see when the rules are followed, our vaccine is very safe."

"Please don't get me wrong. I truly hope that you are correct in your assessment."

"By the way, did you know that it was Connor's decision to outsource the majority of clinical trials to China?"

"We both know that he did it solely based on economic reasons. It was cheaper getting paid volunteers in Asia."

"While that is true, in China, we do not have the oversight as we do at home to exclude those who should not be in the study. Connor knew that all along."

"You don't believe he outsourced the vaccine to China to make *NeoBloc* look bad, knowing that they would not exclude sick volunteers."

"It is sad to say but that thought has crossed my mind. Is it conceivable that he wanted W&W to succeed over DCP? Was he promised a special deal by their Board that you and I did not know about?"

"That would be highly unlikely."

Nasters shrugged his shoulders. "We'll never know for sure. Dead men don't talk."

Rudolf nodded. "You are correct that President Williams has been fully supportive of deployment of our vaccine and the National Quality Board is in complete agreement that the vaccine is safe."

"Our brave national leader is proceeding along a path that makes total sense for America."

Rudolf stood and extended his hand to Nasters. "So, the bottom line is that if the vaccine is not proven to be harmful in healthy volunteers then this product will be the blockbuster that DCP has long awaited." The chair's face brightened. "Our stock price will zoom!"

"Sir, my primary interest is the safety of the American public and my secondary interest is making DCP a successful and well respected pharmaceutical company."

"The Board will meet tomorrow. I fully expect that you will be confirmed as CEO of Doctor's Choice Products."

Nasters walked Rudolf toward the door. "Thank you, Mr. Chairman. This is truly a dream come true. I come from humble roots back in Pakistan. I just wish my father—Ali—was alive to see my success."

"Just execute on maximizing our shareholder value and keeping our patients safe!"

"It will be my highest privilege as an American scientist."

***

Nasters prayed. He faced the back wall at DCP, which as the crow flies would lead in the direction of Mecca. After a full hour, he rose from the floor. He glanced outside his window. Three stories below, lurking on a street in back of his office, he spotted several Middle Eastern looking men. *I need to buy time. Time to buy protection from the PFF until NeoBloc wipes out America.*

CHAPTER FIFTY-SEVEN

Rogers felt shooting pains radiating down his neck. Something was stuck in his throat. He tried to clear it but whatever it was that was pinching his vocal cords, it would not go away. Unable to move, his hands felt tied to something.

The last thing he remembered was seeing Connor's maniacal face. It seemed like a dream. As though he was watching a movie, he pictured both Connor and Nasters chasing him in an open meadow of rolling hills and green grass. Sporadic gunfire shots shattered the creepy quiet on the open pasture. Rogers saw himself running to save his life, running from those trying to kill him and millions of Americans as well, running from evil.

Warm skin touched his face. He forced his eyes to open. Beams from a mass of pocket lights on the ceiling partially blinded him. He blinked several times. A dark haze seemed to prevent him focusing. Then he heard her voice calling his name. Rogers struggled to free his hands. The image that appeared to be in front of him was elusive, disappearing whenever he thought he was seeing who was actually there—someone calling him Jonathan. Increasingly frustrated, he thrashed about, swinging his body wildly from side to side.

An authoritative voice rang out. *Five milligrams of diazepam.* He dreamed of seeing Ashley crossing the finish line in her marathon in Alaska. Kim was holding his hand.

******

Intermingled, distant vague memories were returning more and more. Alternating passages of periodic daylight or moonlight streaming into his room subconsciously seemed to Rogers as vague evidence of passing time. Still particularly groggy throughout this entire period, nevertheless, he had a growing sense that he was slowly awakening from a long winter's hibernation from reality. During the last period of darkness, he felt like an incoming baby, being born into a world comprised of both love and hate.

Today, Rogers fully opened his eyes. For the first time since he remembered struggling with Connor at his daughter's apartment, he spotted Ashley. Tears streamed down his cheeks. He felt euphoric.

Despite his overwhelming sense of happiness in seeing her standing alongside his bed, the pain in his bandaged left temple area intensified. He no longer felt any tube sticking in his throat. When he tried to speak, his mouth felt stuffed with cotton balls. Ashley moistened his mouth with a wet towel. Smacking his lips, he ran his tongue around his mouth like a wet mop.

"Daddy, I love you." She wiped away his tears as her own also dripped down to her chin.

He looked into her gleaming blue eyes and tried to speak. It was an effort to utter her name. "Ash—Ash---Ashley." It felt good to be squeezing her hand. He winced in pain as he turned his head to the other side of the room. Familiar faces appeared. "Beth----Panini."

"Hey----." Looking back at his daughter, Rogers asked, "What happened?"

She hesitated. Ashley looked at Panini and Beth for support. They both walked toward the bed and touched his arm.

He asked his question again. This time he added some emotion. "Ashley, what the hell happened to me?"

"First, you were shot."

Rogers moaned. "Again?"

Ironically, the trio found it hard to stifle a slight chuckle. Given the way in which he said the word—again—his survival of two separate shootings that were usually fatal was indeed—a miracle.

"Dad, the doctors say you're making good progress."

He remained confused. "I don't remember much. Who shot me?"

Ashley glanced over at Beth and Panini. "We can go over this some other time. You need your rest. Just remember that we all love you and that everything will be all right."

Rogers felt a wave of agitation growing within him. He looked at Ashley. "I really want to know. Who shot me?" He held her gaze as seconds passed.

She said quietly, "It was Connor Lucas."

He slapped his hand on the bed. "Why?" He looked over at Beth. "Why did Connor shoot me?"

His friend paused before speaking. "Jonathan, I don't think this is a good time to be discussing this subject."

"Tell me. I want to know. If you don't, I'll ask Panini. He won't bullshit me."

Ashley interrupted. "Dad, you may not be remembering but Connor Lucas is actually Zach Miller."

Connor is Zach. How could that be? He attempted to center his mind. Recollections were beginning to trickle back. *Connor is Zach.* He looked at Panini.

"Where is Zach?"

He saw his friend bending down, coming closer to his face. "Let's just get you better old friend." Panini gave him a light kiss on his cheek. Rogers searched Panini's eyes. "Tell me. Tell me."

"Zach, and Connor, whatever you folks call that fuckin bastard----
he's dead. You do not have to worry anymore about the prick. He's
burning in hell."

Rogers searched his friend's twisted grimace. He cleared his voice.
"Who killed him? Was it the FBI?"

Panini gripped his lifelong friend's hand. "I killed Connor with my
hands."

The patient eyes widened, wanting to believe. "Are you sure that
he's dead?"

"I would never lie to you. It's finally over Jonathan."

The Surgeon General closed his eyes, exhaling a loud sigh. "It's
never over!"

CHAPTER FIFTY-EIGHT

Ashley, Beth, and Panini each rented a room at the local Marriot Hotel in Detroit to be close to the recovering patient. That night, they sat in the business center, off the lobby, huddled around a computer. A Blackberry found in the briefcase of Connor Lucas was the center attraction. A copy of the *Herald* lay on the floor. Ashley had just finished reading the story written by Larry Pequod, the editor of the newspaper.

She held the Blackberry. "Look at these emails that Connor----I mean Zach Miller sent and received on his last day. Panini, it looks like this Charger guy is the one who tried to run us off the road. One day, I'll share these with my father."

"With all this information, we need to get to the newspapers and hold a press conference with the media." Panini opened another email on the Blackberry. "It looks like Connor has paid this creep Scout to finish Nasters off."

"Look at this saved email." Ashley shook her head. "This one confirms the nineteen deaths in China from taking *NeoBloc*. You know, this is like finding the Dead Sea Scrolls."

Beth slapped the desk. "But look here. This is new data. There were more deaths in China after the initial cohort. In addition, these volunteers were healthy before they took the vaccine. It was like the monkey trials—it took time for them to die. Nasters was lying about all of them being ill before receiving the vaccine. Only some of them were sick."

"That guy is a crazed zealot," Panini exclaimed.

Beth added, "For our media blitz, we need to get Dr. Ulrich from the National Quality Board to put out a statement condemning this killer vaccine."

"Do you believe that this Ulrich doc was unaware of all these deaths until now? " Panini asked.

"I'm not really sure," Beth replied. "Until I spoke with Dr. Washington yesterday, I had assumed that Ulrich didn't know the full story. Therefore, Ginny called the researchers who were working on the human clinical trials in China and confirmed what Connor's Blackberry states. Last night, I emailed Dr. Ulrich with the information on what Virginia reported. He has not responded to my email."

"Let's call him," Ashley said.

Beth placed the landline call for Ulrich at his full time position at Chester Labs. She put the call on speakerphone so Ashley and Panini could also hear.

"Hello, this is Dr. Peter Ulrich." His voice was crisp, sounding distracted.

"Hello, this is Beth Murphy." She waited for his reply.

"Look, I'm extremely busy. Why are you calling me? The next Board meeting is not for another two months."

"Don't tell me that you haven't seen the newspapers?"

"You mean about Connor Lucas?"

"For starters. What are your comments about the latest story in the Herald quoting Dr. Nasters on his threats to all Americans? But, most importantly, is the National Quality Board going to respond to Dr. Washington's affidavit that I forwarded to you?" Beth waited and heard nothing. "And what about the late Secretary of Health's confession about *NeoBloc* that appeared in the *Post?*"

His voice quivered. "Neither I nor the Board, when we decided to support *NeoBloc,* was aware of the recently released information."

"It's never too late to do what is right."

"Look, it's in the hands of the FDA now." He paused. "Understand that President Williams is fully supportive of *NeoBloc* being deployed as soon as possible to every American. Those, Ms. Murphy, are also facts."

She began to shout, "What about the email I forwarded you last night from Connor's Blackberry? It confirms that even healthy volunteers died after taking *NeoBloc.*"

"The FDA makes the final decision."

"Aren't you, as the chair of the Board, going to make a public announcement based upon what we all now know? You need to inform the FDA of the new facts that have surfaced. It changes everything."

"I need to think about that. Sorry, but I am working on an important project. I have to go. Goodbye."

"I'll make you regret your decision."

"I said goodbye." The dial tone droned.

******

"Panini, what are you reading?"

"Boy, this Connor Lucas asshole really tried to cover his tracks." Pointing to an article in today's *Post,* he said, "His appearance on that radio show in Grand Rapids really brought out some crazy folks who believed him when he almost was willing to be proclaimed the savior of America."

"My Dad tells me stories all the time about how gullible folks are to con artists like Connor."

"Ashley, if his neurosurgeon is agreeable, do you think it would be appropriate for your father to be part of our press conference?"

"I'm worried about him. He still looks so frail. It's only been two days since he fully awoke from his coma. Any stress could cause a setback. I just don't know if he can handle any more."

Panini touched her hand. "I knew your dad when we were little boys. He has always believed in doing what is right. He would want to do this."

CHAPTER FIFTY-NINE

Rogers awakened early with an ice pick like splitting headache. On his morning rounds, Dr. Adrian Fisher had decided that he was not ready to participate in the planned press conference at noon. Among many medical concerns, the neurosurgeon feared that the added excitement could raise his blood pressure and trigger a devastating re-bleed of his already traumatized brain.

Yet, the Surgeon General had tried to bargain with his doctor. He was fine with not participating in any press conference if, as the morning progressed, he had any symptoms or if his blood pressure was elevated. Dr. Fisher was not pleased at the pushback but did not want to argue and add to the stress load of a determined man like Jonathan Rogers.

The patient thought of a beach scene while the nurse listened with her stethoscope. "Grace, how's my blood pressure?"

"One twenty over eighty. How's your headache? Is the Tylenol working?"

Rogers smiled. "I feel fine. My daughter will be here around eleven 'o clock. Dr. Fisher has not completely ruled out the possibility of my joining Ashley in a scheduled noon time televised press conference from my room."

Grace cast a sideways glance at him and slowed down the rate of his intravenous infusion of saline. "I see from your empty tray that your appetite is back in full force. In addition, it seems as though your energy level is getting better each day. Let's see how you do over the next few hours."

******

Rogers's mid-morning nap lasted one hour. Opening his eyes, he spotted Grace walking in the corridor outside his room. His headache felt much worse. He looked up at the clock. *Ten fifty*. Ashley will be here any minute. He meditated by closing his eyes. In the past, the word *ocean* had always brought him peace. Slowly repeating the word to himself, he envisioned blue waves crashing onto a sandy beach. The sun was shining brightly in his mental picture. Minutes later, he had convinced himself that his headache had lessened somewhat.

Soon, Ashley and Beth walked into his room. A TV camera operator with his hand held equipment followed close behind them.

"Good morning Daddy." She kissed him on his forehead.

"Hi sweetie."

"Jonathan, how do you feel?"

He reached out for her hand. Beth held onto it.

"Great. I'm just terrific."

Ashley asked, "Is Dr. Fisher going to approve of your participation in the conference?"

"He'll probably want one last exam before he permits me to go on the air." He forced a half-smile. "Stop worrying you two. I'm fine."

Grace walked in and addressed the camera operator. "I think it would be better if you waited outside in the corridor until it's time."

He nodded and immediately left the room.

The nurse questioned her patient. "Dr. Rogers, tell me the truth, is your headache completely gone?"

"For a guy who almost had his head blown off, I couldn't be better."

Grace cast a suspicious look in his direction. "Let me check your blood pressure."

The Surgeon General immediately went into full mediation mode. After the nurse removed the cuff, he waited for the verdict.

"One eighteen over sixty five."

Rogers thrust his hand over his head. "Yes."

"Not so fast doc. Dr. Fisher will want last licks."

"I'm sure," he added, smiling at the nurse. "Ashley and Beth, so what's our game plan for the TV interview?"

"If Dr Fisher agrees that you are OK, I thought that you should start off by introducing yourself, Beth and me. Then, I will show a copy of Dr. Virginia Washington's sworn affidavit attesting that all monkeys died from *NeoBloc* and that there have been many more human deaths from the vaccine in China, even among healthy volunteers."

Rogers asked, "What about the National Quality Board? I hope they are finally on board with the truth. It would mean a lot if they admit that they made a mistake by recommending NeoBloc."

Beth's upper lip stiffened. "I'm still waiting to hear from Dr. Ulrich. Actually, I would love to talk into the TV camera and state that he does not really care at all about what's right. Sadly, he's become a political and corporate puppet."

"He'll have you removed from your seat on the Board if you publicly expose him."

"Let him just try. Jonathan, as you well know, the price of honesty is steep but well worth it."

"Dad, a reporter from the *Detroit Free Press* will be here to ask us questions. His name is Billy Snodgrass. The video feed will go out on a local cable channel. Mr. Snodgrass told me that CNN will also pick up the feed so we'll be live on national TV."

Rogers took hold of each of their hands. He lowered his voice. "If anything ever happens to me, I want each of you to carry on the mission to do what is right on behalf of the public."

"Dad, don't talk like that."

He looked at both of them, wrinkling his forehead. "I'm serious. Promise me that you'll all carry out my wishes."

Beth looked at Rogers's daughter. "We're a team. Each of us should know that we're all in this situation together."

Rogers raised his index finger. "Make sure Panini is in that foxhole with you. You always want a guy like that. I trust him with my life."

"Do you absolutely swear to carry on—no matter what happens to me?"

In unison, Beth and Ashley replied, "Yes."

***

The reporter walked in and introduced himself. "Hello, I'm Billy Snodgrass from the *Free Press*. I'm pleased to meet you Dr. Rogers."

"It's nice to meet you as well Billy."

The Surgeon General pointed to the corridor outside his room. "Ashley, please get Beth and the cameraman."

"Beth just received an important cell phone call. She'll be here soon."

A minute later, the reporter directed the camera operator where to stand and addressed the Surgeon General and Ashley. "After you make your opening statements, I'll ask a few questions. Dr. Rogers, I've been told by your doctor to limit my time to a maximum of two minutes."

The Surgeon General nodded. A moment later, Beth rushed into the room.

"Jonathan, good news," she said, waving a paper in her hand. "This is a fax from Dr. Ulrich of the National Quality Board. He is attesting to verification of the report of nineteen deaths in the *NeoBloc* clinical trial in China. Better yet, he wants me to use his name as a supporter on a complete halt to all further testing of the vaccine. Ulrich is also sending a personal note to the FDA recommending non-approval of *NeoBloc*. Lastly, he apologized to me, admitting that I have been right all along. It's a grand slam."

"Wow. As they say, better late than never."

Snodgrass spoke up. "We're on in four minutes. Camera operator, can you get a wide angle on the three of them? Ashley, please take a seat on one side of your father and Beth a seat on the other side."

Rogers's grin turned to a pursed lips frown when he saw Dr. Fisher and Grace enter the room. By now, his headache had slightly worsened.

Fisher gave the orders. "Grace, take his blood pressure." The neurosurgeon held up his index finger. "Jonathan, please follow my finger with your eyes but don't move your head."

"Good. Now grip both of my hands with yours."

"Can we wait until Grace is done?

"Doctor, his blood pressure is fine."

After removal of the blood pressure cuff, he grasped each of his neurosurgeon's hands.

"Come on. Squeeze as hard as you can."

"Terrific. So, are you sure that you're up to this news conference?"

"It will be a walk on the beach." He glanced over at the reporter. Snodgrass held up two fingers.

"All right, I'll be outside the room if you need me." Fisher looked over at Snodgrass.

"Remember, two minutes."

The reporter nodded. "Ok, we're sixty seconds to air time. Everyone, take a deep breath."

Ashley rested her head on her father's shoulder as the seconds ticked off. Rogers felt at peace except for the nagging headache that began to increase in intensity.

The camera operator pointed to the reporter.

"Good afternoon, ladies and gentlemen. I'm Billy Snodgrass from the *Detroit Free Press.* We are at Detroit Metro Medical Center in the hospital room of Dr. Jonathan Rogers. The Surgeon General and his team will each make a brief statement and then I will follow up with questions." The reporter gestured toward Rogers.

The Surgeon General mustered all his energy and sat up straight, looking directly into the camera lens. "Thank you all for listening in today. I'm not going to spend time on how I ended up in this hospital bed. That, you may have read about in the newspapers."

He looked at Panini, stationed by the doorway to his hospital room, wearing a *Detroit Tigers* baseball cap. His life- long friend gave him a thumbs-up sign. "Before I start this press conference, I want to thank my good friend Joey Panini for saving my life, at least twice in the last week or so." He paused as the camera operator turned to capture a brief shot of his friend. Panini tipped his cap in appreciation.

Rogers refocused on the camera. "My daughter, Ashley and my colleague, Beth Murphy will join me in addressing you about a most important subject for every American." He paused and took a deep breath. The pain in his temple was pulsating more rapidly. He chose to ignore it and continued, "We're here to let the American people know that we have solid evidence that the vaccine all of you have been reading and hearing about to prevent radiation induced cancer is unsafe. I repeat *NeoBloc* is a killer vaccine."

He gritted his teeth. A drowsy feeling was coming on fast. He felt drugged. Looking over at Ashley, he sensed that she could see that something was wrong. He gave her a forced smile. A new symptom of light-headedness caused him to steady himself by gripping the rails to his hospital bed. He continued, "I've asked Ashley and Beth to present the complete evidence."

Ashley looked at the open doorway, trying to make contact with anyone in the corridor. *Where's Dr. Fisher*

Rogers motioned for her to start. She shot a worried look to Beth before beginning her statement. "At the end of this conference, I will pass out to the press copies of a sworn affidavit from one of the scientists who used to work on this deadly vaccine at Doctors Choice Products. Dr. Virginia Washington has the original data signed by the DCP top scientist, Dr Hussein Nasters, which proves *NeoBloc* to be lethal." Ashley glanced over at her father. A deepening frown crossed her face. "We all want to thank the *Detroit Free Press* for the opportunity to present our story directly to the American people."

Rogers was about to point to Beth but he could not control the gross tremor in his hand that had just developed. Dropping it underneath the blanket, he introduced her. "Miss Murphy will now present additional information."

Beth looked into the camera and held up the second document. "This is a signed statement from the chairman of the National Quality oversight board on *NeoBloc*. Dr. Peter Ulrich believes that the vaccine manufacturer should declare an immediate halt on all clinical trials with the vaccine. We're calling upon Dr. Hussein Nasters, the current CEO of Doctor's Choice Products, to issue the order."

Rogers took a deep breath. He rationalized that this would be over in a few minutes. *Just need a couple of Tylenol.* "We'll now take— we'll now take a couple of quests fro the puess," he said, slurring the last couple of words.

Snodgrass asked, "Dr. Rogers, what do you think President Williams will do, now that *NeoBloc* has been totally discredited? She has always been such a staunch supporter of *NeoBloc*. Doesn't this create a political nightmare for her?"

Rogers pressed on his temple, near the area of the bullet wound. He felt the booming pulsations of his temporal artery. "The President is a decent and thoughtful leader. She is trying her best to defend our country. Another Company has a promising vaccine in this space. Soon, we will have a safe vaccine to protect our people against the nuclear radiation."

The Surgeon General looked up. Dr. Fisher and Grace were standing in the doorway. The neurosurgeon put up one finger and pointed at the reporter. Snodgrass nodded in compliance.

Rogers felt a wave of nausea. He swallowed hard. The image of Fisher in his white coat grew fuzzier by the moment.

"Dr. Rogers," the reporter asked, "In our final minute, can you give our audience a taste of the ordeal that you've been through as our Surgeon General?"

The ringing in his ears drowned out the question. Squinting, he replied, "I guess the lights from the camera are causing me to see stars." He suppressed an urge to retch. To Rogers, it felt as though the left side of his head was about to blow off. "Can you repeat what you said?"

"Sure, this will be my last question. Let me ask it a little differently. In the last year, you've been shot twice, survived a strangulation attempt, pushed off a bridge into a raging river, your wife, Kim, has been murdered in cold blood, and your daughter Ashley has been kidnapped. Sir you have undergone far more than what most people could possibly endure. Yet, you are still here talking with us about an important public health issue. Please tell us what keeps you moving forward despite the tragedies that you and your family have undergone."

Rogers only heard Kim's name before closing his eyes. He dreamed of walking with her in an open grassy field. He reached over for Ashley's hand but she was not there. His throat felt like something was being jammed down it. Explosions seemed to be rocketing throughout his brain. In his mind, Rogers saw himself holding hands with Kim lying down on a grassy hill in Turkey Knoll Park. Ashley was throwing a Frisbee to a cute golden retriever.

CHAPTER SIXTY

President Williams glared at her Vice President. Stockard had just barged into the Oval Office. He sat down next to her on the couch. She clicked off the CNN live broadcast of her Surgeon General's press conference.

"Dr. Rogers got very sick at the end," the VP stated, in a worried tone.

Williams stared at the blank screen. "He didn't look well. In any case, it's now crystal clear that *NeoBloc* is finished."

"You've changed your mind on the vaccine before. I'm glad you're coming around to see what needs to be done."

"Listen, you are no better than me to judge the science around these vaccines. We both depend on physicians like Dr .Rogers and scientists like Dr. Nasters and Dr. Ulrich."

"Point well taken." Stockard scratched his nose. "I understand that W&W turned down your offer for the government to go into a joint venture with them to "fast track" their vaccine."

Williams rose and began pacing in front of the couch. She looked down at Stockard. "I believe Dr. Woodhull is a good man. He just needs to be convinced that our government will not force W&W to abandon their principle of safety first just to get a vaccine out there. However, we desperately do need a vaccine to prevent tens of thousands or more cases of cancer in case we suffer another nuclear attack. It's a matter of national security."

Stockard leaped to his feet and stood toe to toe with the President. "Excuse me for my bluntness. But, you're still missing the bigger picture. You are still playing defense. We need to take out a military target in Afghanistan or Pakistan before the terrorists strike us again."

Williams held her ground. "All you talk is war!"

He shouted, "And, all you talk about is a vaccine that's not even ready should the terrorists strike tonight. And, until recently all you talked about was *NeoBloc*, a vaccine that would have killed us."

"Our national guard is fully mobilized. Homeland Security is doing everything they can to find the terrorists." Williams pointed to the couch. "Please sit. Let's lower our voices."

Stockard resumed his spot on the couch. He began speaking calmly. "Jane, I'm talking about saving American lives. Secretary of State David informed me this morning that both ambassadors are threatening us.

Unless we offer them an iron clad guarantee that we will not bomb them, their army will no longer defend our embassies. Marcia told me that you were informed about this last night."

"I'm aware."

He pumped his fist. Raising his voice, he thundered, "This morning, I heard a report that Pakistani and Afghan soldiers have exchanged fire with two NATO helicopters that crossed into their airspace." The VP pursed his lips. "Jane, they are shooting at NATO. This is intolerable. You must act to send a message that we will not accept them shooting at NATO and we will not accept their ISI working with the Taliban."

Williams continued to pace, glancing up from time to time at the Vice-President. "There is no doubt that the streets in the region are teeming with terrorists who already hate us. Dropping bombs on them will make them hate us even more. The people are innocent. It is the few radicals that are doing this to America."

"It's us or them. Americans will die of cancer and radiation sickness caused by further radiation if we don't stop the next terrorist attack." Stockard slapped his hands together. "How can you possibly sleep at night knowing that your only option is many months away from FDA approval and deployment among the public. Most importantly, we must stop the attacks!"

The President took a seat in her customary chair, across from the couch. Her voice dropped an octave. "My sister, Maryann, was instantly vaporized after the first nuclear bomb fell in Minneapolis. I made a promise after her death that I would prevent others from suffering like that. I intend to act. Make no mistake about that."

"You have an option that's available right now----you are the Commander in Chief." The VP leaned forward. "Give the order, Madame President. It is our best chance to save our citizens. It is time to take the battle to the enemy. With all respect to our homeland security defenses, I fear they will not be able to stop another nuclear strike."

Williams ran her hands through her hair and hung her head.

"Jane, America is being held hostage by these terrorists. The Pakistani government has not lifted even one finger to stop them. Only you can save us. It's that simple."

The President stood and fired a steely- eyed stare at the VP. "Without *NeoBloc*, without a viable vaccine at this time, I must admit that we are defenseless unless we can stop these attacks. We have nothing to defend America if we cannot find the terrorists first. They must be stopped."

His voice softened, "Now, you're talking like the President that America needs. Great leaders take us where we ought to go."

"America cannot risk another nuclear strike on our homeland-----I will do what I can to stop the terrorists, to stop the cancers, to save our Country."

"We need to act." Stockard slapped his hand on the couch. "God only help us that we're not too late. What is your decision?"

Williams walked toward her desk. She pressed the intercom. "Madison, have Mac call an emergency meeting of the national security team. Have them assembled within the hour."

She clicked off the intercom. The President stood tall and pulled back her shoulders.

"We will strike high value military targets in the region unless the latest terrorist plot to bomb another America city is uncovered and stopped."

******

Within the hour, the Chief of Staff had called together the Security Council on the President's order. Seated at the head of the conference table in a room just off the Oval Office, Williams initially singled out the Secretary of Defense.

"Bill," the President, declared, "Before this meeting, I've consulted with the Joint Chiefs and others." Williams glanced over at VP Stockard. "My decision is to launch a major strike against high value military targets within seventy-two hours. There will be no bombing of any areas with non-military civilians. We do not intend to hurt any innocent people. We will give both governments ample warning of our intent. They will still have time to rein in these rogue terrorist cells."

Marcia David gawked in disbelief at Williams. "I recall the Joint Chiefs stating if you launched a pre-emptive strike that you'd be starting World War III."

"The war has already begun. World War III started the day we were attacked with nuclear weapons." She pointed to a security briefing that lay in front of her. "The Vice-President and I have decided that we need to take the offensive in view of current facts. We have given them sufficient warning to rein in the terrorists. They have not acted. Therefore—we must."

Secretary of State David said calmly, "Let the record show that I disagree with that decision."

"Marcia, though it pains me to say this, I expect your resignation on my desk within the hour." The President stood. "It is time for America to act! God Bless America!"

The Vice President and the Chief of Staff both nodded in full agreement. Pitnar asked, "Can you get this done in time Bill?"

Secretary of Defense Bill Stapleton replied in a subdued yet firm voice. "Yes."

Buzz.

The President bent down and picked up the receiver from the phone on the conference table. Her face drooped a few seconds into the message. After several rounds of shaking her head, she hung up.

She tersely announced, "Dr. Rogers has slipped back into another coma. He's to undergo a second urgent operation on his brain to remove a blood clot."

No member of the Security Council stirred. The tension was palpable. Heads dropped. The silence in the room was deafening.

With her voice cracking, Williams murmured, "The latest prognosis from his doctors is that he is unlikely to recover. His doctors believe at this time that the Surgeon General may never regain consciousness. Based on his current clinical condition, Dr. Jonathan Rogers is essentially brain dead. It will take a miracle for him to survive."

CHAPTER SIXTY-ONE

After watching the CNN broadcast of the Surgeon General's press conference in the corner office of Connor Lucas, Dr. Nasters kicked over his portable TV set off its wooden stand. It crashed on the floor, cracking the screen. A minute later, he slammed down the receiver after a fierce shouting match with Dr. Ulrich. He prayed to Allah for guidance.

The ring of the phone interrupted his prayer. "Nasters, this is Xavier Rudolf."

"Yes, sir."

"Don't give me that yes sir bull shit. You tried to screw America and me with that killer vaccine of yours. I saw the TV broadcast. Dr. Washington and Dr. Ulrich both threw you under the bus."

"You can't believe what you hear. It's all lies."

"Before I heard the latest information from the Surgeon General's press conference, I was starting to believe you. Now, I know that you played me for a fool. I am calling an emergency meeting of the Board. You'll be fired within two hours. Start packing."

Nasters tore at his hair. He ripped the wire out of his desk phone and heaved the phone across the room. *Whom can I trust? My brothers!* He wished he could reach the PFF leadership. *How?* Then, it came to him. He went out to the administrative assistant's desk. By now, Andrea was gone. Clicking one by one, he scrolled down the list of incoming calls. He redialed Xavier Rudolf's number.

The scientist cursed when the voice message came on. He left a terse message. *'Call me. You'll want to know what I have learned.'* Nasters sat down and waited. One minute later, the phone rang. "It took you long enough."

"Talk!"

"I have a deal for you. And, don't worry; I'm not going to put up a fight when Human Resources comes knocking on my door."

"Listen to me you damn terrorist, I don't make deals with madmen. I'm calling the FBI after I hang up on you."

"Then you and the FBI can just guess what American city will be nuked."

"You don't know. You're bluffing to save your ass." Rudolf shouted, "Why should I believe you? You've lied about everything."

"Then why did you return my call?"

He hesitated. "Why would you give me information about which city you assholes are bombing next?

"I have my reasons." He inhaled deeply. "Stop saying I've been lying about *NeoBloc*. I've given you my honest clinical judgment as a well respected scientist."

"I don't trust a word out of you. I hope Mugandi gets his revenge on your sorry ass."

Nasters sighed. "Look, my capitalist pig. The better question is how can you risk not trusting me? Remember, the Afghanistan and Pakistani Freedom Fighters are my brothers. We may squabble from time to time but their blood flows through them and me. A rogue cell will soon annihilate an American city."

Rudolf hollered, "This is your last chance. I'll be right over."

"Come alone or else."

******

Nasters prepared himself for the showdown. In the CEO's corner office, he sat patiently behind the desk of his former boss and prayed to Allah.

Rudolf stomped into the corner office thirty minutes later, practically foaming at the mouth. "What's your fuckin deal?" he blasted.

Nasters leaned back in his chair. "When we had coffee at the *Daily Mug*, I recall you saying that you knew where the leader of the PFF was stashed away."

"So what," he defiantly replied

"Sit down."

Nasters smirked as Rudolf took a seat on the other side of the desk. "I see that you take commands. That is good. And, since I haven't been thrown out of our Company, I would predict that you've not shared your negative feelings about me with the full Board."

Rudolf asked evenly, "What do you want?"

"If you bring me to Mugandi, I'll tell you what American city is going to be hit."

Rudolf held out both of hands, palms upward. "How would you possibly know?"

Nasters leaned closer to Rudolf. "Why don't we forget this whole matter?" His nostrils flared. "The blood of an American city is on your hands. Get out of my office old man."

"Don't screw around with me Nasters."

The scientist rose and walked around the desk. He pressed his hand down on Rudolf's shoulder. He yelled into his ear, "For the last time, where's Mugandi?"

The Board member jumped to his feet. Rudolf stood toe to toe with the scientist. "You better not plan on double crossing me."

"Shut up old man." Nasters pointed his finger into Rudolf's chest. "If you want to save an American city from nuclear annihilation, don't ever back a rat into a corner."

"I'll drive. I'll take you to Mugandi."

"Hey Rudolf, remember, this is *your* last chance. Don't ever threaten me again."

******

Nasters grew increasingly leery of where Rudolf was driving. On the outskirts of DuPont, the Board chief pulled his white Mercedes coup up to an abandoned warehouse. Surrounding them was a junk yard and a large storage facility. The scientist glanced over at Rudolf. His face appeared to be petrified in place, a determined look in his glassy looking eyes.

Rudolf turned off the ignition and muttered, "Let's go."

"Where's Mugandi?"

He pointed toward the warehouse. "Inside." Rudolf exited the car and began walking toward a landing next to an entrance door.

"How do I know you're not setting me up?" Nasters anxiously scanned the grounds.

"Stop your crap! You're lucky that I haven't asked my friends to cut you up into a thousand pieces for trying to sell a killer vaccine to the President of the United States."

"That issue remains a matter of scientific opinion. For the last time, *NeoBloc* is not dangerous."

Rudolf scowled at Nasters. "Only a madman like you would still spout that bullshit after reading Dr. Washington's affadavit."

The chair scaled the four wooden steps to the small landing and pulled open the warehouse door. He shouted back at the scientist. "Dr. Washington publicly sold you out."

Nasters said in a mocking tone, "She was a disgruntled employee who was dismissed for scientific incompetence. And, you choose to believe her? No, Mr. Rudolf, it is you who has lost his mind."

***

Once inside, Nasters found himself in a small room stocked with a few simple wooden chairs and a Spartan appearing four by four foot metal desk.

"Wait here," Rudolf barked.

Moments later, Dr. Nasters saw Mugandi's livid face appear in the doorway. The Chairman of the Board led his blood brother into the room. Thick ropes shackled Mugandi's ankles and wrists. The PFF leader shuffled his feet toward Nasters. He stopped, less than a foot from the scientist. Cursing under his breath, the captive spat in his face.

Nasters bowed toward his brother. "I am to blame for everything. I deserve to die. Allah is my savior. I beg forgiveness. The Americans deceived me. I did not know of their plan in the Park." His eyes met those of Mugandi. "I lay myself at your feet. Do as you will." Nasters knelt on his knees, hanging his head.

Rudolf shrieked, "Get up you freakin terrorist!"

Nasters slowly rose to his feet, keeping his eyes fixed on Mugandi.

Rudolf ordered the PFF leader and the scientist to sit down on two rickety wooden chairs. They both complied. Rudolf leaned against the wall and pulled out a cigarette. Blowing rings across the room, he pointed at Nasters.

"Doctor, it's your meeting."

The scientist turned his chair on the dusty wood floor and faced his fellow Pakistani. "My I address you by name?"

A curt reply boomeranged back. "You seem to do as you please anyway so why do you ask me?"

"Brother Mugandi, if I may. You and I are aware of secret things that Mr. Rudolf knows nothing about. Despite what you think of me, we are both Pakistani blood brothers."

The PFF leader smirked and said nothing.

"Our tactics may differ but we are one. I think you know what I mean."

Mugandi remained unmoved.

Rudolf interrupted. "No more code talk. Speak straight English on exactly what you mean."

Nasters rose to his feet. He walked over and grabbed the cigarette from Rudolf's mouth. He took a long drag. Forcefully blowing out the smoke, he whispered in Rudolf's ear. "Do you want to hear everything I know?"

"Why else would I be here with you two terrorists."

"Then I need you to do something."

"Name your price."

Nasters grinned. "Shoot me in the foot." He stuffed the cigarette back into Rudolf's mouth and waited.

"Are you nuts?" Rudolf asked, throwing his half-smoked cigarette butt on the wooden floor.

Nasters lowered his voice even more. Drawing closer to Rudolf's ear, he murmured, "Shoot me in the foot."

"You *are* fuckin crazy!"

He pulled on Rudolf's earlobe. "I said shoot me in my foot or it's no deal."

The Board chief shook his head. He looked at him and yelled out, "I would need a gun to do that."

Nasters feigned a look of shock. "I told you I don't have a gun." The scientist backed away and walked over to the PFF leader. "Mugandi, this American asked me if I had a gun. He wanted me to shoot you. That is why he brought me here. He offered me the position of CEO of DCP if I would kill you. Of course, he is badly mistaken. I would never do any harm to you."

Rudolf boomed, "You lying son of a bitch. If I had a gun, I'd kill both of you without blinking an eye."

The eyes of the Pakistani prisoner brightened. Nasters winked at Mugandi and then walked backwards toward Rudolf, kick boxing him in the stomach.

The chair reached underneath his right pant leg. He pulled out a four-inch knife that opened into a stiletto. Rudolf lashed out and howled. "You're a terrorist."

He took a quick backward step, avoiding the slow arc of the knife. "You are a stupid old man. You came here without a real weapon and expected to take on two Pakistani warriors?"

Nasters grabbed Rudolf's right hand before it swung back. He slammed it against the wall. The stiletto fell to the floor. The scientist grabbed the chair by the throat and dragged him toward Mugandi. Nasters pinned Rudolf against the wall, unleashing a short right upper cut that sent him to the floor, crawling on his stomach.

The scientist stomped on him, landing on his low back with his full body weight, led by his knee. Rudolf screamed out in pain. On his knees, he crawled over to the PFF leader. His head now lay between the knees of Mugandi, who with one quick snap of the American's neck, killed him on the spot.

Nasters knelt down and presented his head to Mugandi. "It is my turn. Kill me. I do not deserve to live."

The Pakistani grabbed the scientist by the head. His fingers moved toward Naster's neck. Mugandi then kissed the scientist's head. He released his grip on him and pounded his own chest with flailing hands. He shouted, "I will not kill you. We are one. We are brothers. You and I will annihilate the infidels!"

CHAPTER SIXTY-TWO

In her father's ICU room, Ashley awakened from her nap. Dr. Fisher was in the midst of an examination of his patient. After several minutes, he put his penlight into his white coat pocket. The neurosurgeon's face was drawn. He sat down next to her and gently rested his hand on her shoulder.

"Your father's Glasgow score is a six. He has suffered another major insult to his brain. Evacuating the last clot may have saved his life but I cannot even say that with certainty. I am sorry to tell you but his coma is extremely deep."

"How bad is his prognosis?"

"It is unlikely that he will ever regain consciousness and even more remote is the slim chance that he will ever return to his baseline functionality or personality."

Hearing those words crushed her. "Doctor, he's all I have." She reached out for his hand.

Fisher clung to it for a few moments. "He's stable for the moment. The intubation tube will need to remain until he shows he can breathe on his own. The intravenous mannitol and corticosteroids will decrease his intracranial pressure. For his mental state to have any chance of healing, any more pressure on his brain must be avoided."

"Based on all factors, do you have any idea of how long his coma will last?"

Fisher withdrew his hand and looked away. "There is no way to predict. It could take weeks---months--maybe much longer." The neurosurgeon stood and began checking Rogers for any sign of an ankle reflex. "It's up to a higher power than me."

Ashley slipped away from Dr. Fisher and headed toward the hospital chapel. After a prayer to Saint Jude, she knew exactly what she needed to do.

******

Ashley sat across from the CEO of Weston and Weston. "Dr. Woodhull, I'm sure that you've heard about the President's decision to stop all work on *NeoBloc*. That deadly vaccine is finally history."

The CEO of W&W unfolded his hands and leaned across his desk. "We would have had a national catastrophe were it not for your father's courageous leadership."

Ashley looked down, thinking of him, lying in a coma. She worried that the President would now feel that she needed to launch a preemptive strike on Pakistan since she no longer had *NeoBloc* as a defense against the nuclear radiation from further nuclear attacks.

She raised her head and looked at the CEO. "I'm sorry. Your comment made me think of my father." She blinked away a tear. "Dr. Woodhull, America needs your compound to be approved by the FDA."

"It will be approved----in five to seven months."

"From what I've learned from my father, we don't have that long."

Woodhull leaned back. "We can't rush science. In fact, we just lost two of our leading scientists to another competitor."

"Hire them back."

The CEO hesitated before speaking. "Miss Rogers, we fired them over a confidential sexual harassment suit with another employee. They're not coming back."

"What about the scientists at DCP? Can't they help expedite the process?"

"I suppose we could try to lure them with money and advancement in their career."

"Then, let's do it. We need your compound on the fast track."

"President Williams told me that I needed to accept the joint venture from the government in the name of national security."

"Are you willing to accept her challenge?"

"I told the President that I wanted to think about her offer. An hour ago, I spoke to my Board about the President's request. They left the decision up to me." He reached out to shake Ashley's hand. "I'll accept the President's offer. It is my intention that our compound can be ready before---before---. He hesitated and then said the word. "Armageddon!"

******

Ashley had not slept all night. Stopping at DCP, she had convinced Nasters's new admin to give her the boss's apartment phone number. After dialing, she waited as each ring tone banged louder on her eardrums. On the seventh ring, she heard the click---but the line was silent.

"Hello, Dr. Nasters. This is Ashley Rogers. Please speak to me. It's urgent."

A gruff reply came her way. "What do you want?"

"We need your scientific expertise to help W&W to fast track their compound."

In a sarcastic tone, he replied, "Why would I help the competition?"

"Give it up Dr. Nasters. *NeoBloc* is history. You're the only scientist in the world who believes that it's safe."

"That's because I am the world expert in cancer preventing vaccines. I know best. Do you doubt that? If so, hang up and don't ever call me again."

"You may be an expert but I believe the facts are clear. *NeoBloc* is lethal."

"You're dead wrong. The vaccine works and it is safe."

"That makes no sense in view of what happened in the Chinese clinical trials." Ashley shook her head. "Can't you see that you're acting irrationally? I have a way out for you."

Ashley heard him curse under his breath. A second later, she heard a dial tone.

***

Undeterred, she redialed his number a few minutes later. She heard him pick up. "I hope you've thought about what I've said." He was reciting a Muslim prayer. "Dr. Nasters, please. We need your help. You are the worldwide expert in these matters. It wasn't your fault that *NeoBloc* turned out to be a killer vaccine." She stopped to listen. There was silence. "Your professional reputation can be redeemed if you help us with the W&W compound."

Nasters painfully uttered, "Much as I hate to agree with you, I concede your point----*NeoBloc* is over. I will no longer pursue my vaccine, not because it's dangerous and ineffective but because of politics and the ignorance of its detractors."

Ashley picked up the pace. "The good news is that you and Dr. Washington know more about organic chemistry and the molecular pathways to develop a vaccine that will prevent radiation induced cancer than any other scientists in the world."

"I'm listening. What do you propose?"

"Meet me at DuPont square in one hour. I'll have something that will make you feel better."

"I'll be there," he snapped.

******

Waiting at DuPont Square, Ashley covered her eyes with her hands. The blinding early spring sun had made searching for the scientist a challenge. As she turned to her left, he came into view. Nasters swaggered while maneuvering among a flock of Canadian geese. Dressed in his DCP lab coat, he looked like he was officially reporting for work.

"Since our conversation, I have prayed long and hard. I need to put my world class scientific talents to work."

She tensed every muscle in her body. "Thank you. Why did it have to come to this? Until now, you were pushing a killer vaccine."

"That is a matter of scientific interpretation. Until Dr. Ulrich changed his mind, the National Quality Board that oversees our clinical trials found no wrongdoing. In fact, they voted to recommend *NeoBloc* to the FDA. True or not?"

"The Board was misled."

"Nonsense. How many times do I have to explain that the clinical trial volunteers in China who died all had pre-existing conditions that probably caused their death? All you have is circumstantial evidence. The relationship between *NeoBloc* and every death represents, at best, a correlation. No one has ever proved cause and effect. "True or not?"

Ashley responded with a sharp edge to her voice. "Not exactly but we can squabble all day. Let's move on."

"Miss Rogers, I'm a proud scientist. Before we "move on" as you Americans are so fond of saying, I want to make it clear that I have done no harm to anyone. I have committed no crime. If Dr. Ulrich had a scientific backbone; I would still be the CEO at DCP and *NeoBloc* would have been approved by the FDA in a couple of weeks."

"Dr. Washington would not agree. And, if you insist on prolonging this discussion, I can counterpoint your argument."

Nasters held up his hands in front of him. "Medicine is not exact. Many drugs produced and subsequently approved by the FDA end up killing people. Why are you holding *NeoBloc* to this higher standard?"

"Our country is at war and your vaccine was believed to be able to fill a critical need to save lives. However, my father was the first to see the truth---*NeoBloc* killed monkeys and finally the full truth came out that it also killed people. If the vaccine had not been touted the savior of America, more people may have agreed much earlier with my father."

Nasters covered his heart with his hand. "I believe in this country. You value every single life."

"We certainly do."

"Then why do you allow drugs to be approved by your government through the FDA process that kill more people in one year than all the Americans who died in the entire Vietnam War?"

"I see your point. Those drug companies believed their drug was safe. Their intentions were honorable."

"As are mine. I believe NeoBloc is safe just as other pharmaceutical company CEO's believes that their own anti-hypertensive, their anti-lipid, and their anti-depressive medications save lives."

"We've gone over this many times before." Ashley pumped her fist into the air.

Nasters held her steady gaze. "Every scientist at every drug company in America wakes up each day and works to develop drugs, many of which kill people even after they have been fully researched and approved by the FDA. Why don't you interview all of them and ask them the same questions you just asked me."

"OK. OK. You have convinced me that you truly believed that *NeoBloc* was initially safe. Nevertheless, now we know that it is not safe. Research has proved that W&W has a similar compound that works and is not dangerous. What the manufacturer needs is a dedicated and passionate scientist like you to ensure that the vaccine gets quickly to market."

"I wish them luck. They are a long way from getting approval. I have read public information about their compound. One of their challenges of W&W is that they will need to find a way to store the vaccine---a method to preserve the potency of the product until it is fully distributed across America."

"I believe that process is already underway at W&W."

Nasters glanced at his watch. "Look, I was in the process of updating my resume when you called me. Before I leave, answer one question. Did you invite me here just so we could quibble back and forth like school children?"

Ashley counted to herself, up to ten, holding back her intense desire to have Nasters admit just once that her father was correct about *NeoBloc*. But she saw that it was futile. She locked her eyes on his. "Pardon my directness but would you consider an offer to work with the W&W scientists? You could work side by side with them."

He sneered. "Miss Rogers, I have been the top scientist at DCP. I would only consider a similar scientific position at W&W. Nothing less will be acceptable."

Ashley motioned toward her Aveo coupe. "Let's take a ride Doctor."

******

Ashley did the introductions. "Dr. Woodhull, this is Dr. Nasters."

The scientist and the CEO both nodded toward each other but neither extended his hand.

Woodhull said in a matter of fact tone. "Thank you for coming Dr. Nasters."

"Miss Rogers has invited me. I'm here to listen to what you have to say."

The W&W CEO pointed to his small conference table in the corner of his office. "Let's sit. Can I get anything for either one of you?"

"No thank you," Nasters replied, taking his seat across from Woodhull.

Ashley studied the scientist. He was fidgeting in his seat. His left eyebrow was fluttering. Woodhull exhibited a rigid posture, facing her and avoiding making eye contact with the former DCP scientist.

"Gentlemen, to tell you the truth, I think that we could all use a bottle of tequila. However, since that is not realistic, let us all realize what is at stake here. Pardon my saying so but we do need to lighten up."

The CEO met his guarded gaze. "Doctor, I'm offering you an opportunity to use your scientific expertise in molecular oncology to help W&W advance our cancer prevention vaccine through phase two and three human trials."

Nasters replied, "No one knows more about cancer preventing vaccines. Listen carefully to my words--no one in the world knows more." He plastered a smug look on his face. "Would you agree?"

"We clearly respect you're scientific expertise in this area. As I have said already, I want you to join our team at W&W."

"I was the lead scientist at DCP. I will not be demoted to join your team because of a scientific squabble over the value of *NeoBloc*"

Ashley watched Woodhull swallow twice, the last one causing his throat to ripple. "You will be our lead scientist on this project."

"I was not prepared to take action today. I wanted to think over any offer you might make. However, I realize that my country comes first. I cannot let down America. When do I start?"

"I'll take you to your lab so you can meet your subordinates. Welcome aboard doctor."

"I will take the lead to ensure that Americans receive a safe and effective vaccine." After saying that, Nasters looked up above his head and publicly chanted a brief prayer to Allah. *The fate of America is now in my hands.*

CHAPTER SIXTY-THREE

W&W rolled out the red carpet for him. Nasters had complete access to all of their research. On this night, he was all alone in their lab. As the new lead scientist at W&W, Nasters poured over the vaccine data. Flipping pages on the isomers and the exact molecular structure of the W&W compound, he expected it to be somewhat similar to *NeoBloc*. In his vast clinical experiences, it was logical, the compound needed to affect the same cellular pathways to prevent the cancerous process.

It was ten at night. Bleary eyed, he saw something on page three hundred and sixty-six that jumped off the page. He shut his eyes, concentrating. His mind rambled through various isomers and atomic positions on the molecule. *It can't be!*

Nasters dropped the W&W research manual on his bench. He ran to the laboratory blackboard. Organic chemistry equations rattled around in his head. Scribbling the symbol for water next to the molecular structure of the W&W pipeline compound, he vigorously rubbed his chin. *Not yet.*

His heart felt like he was running a one hundred yard dash. He held the chalk so tightly that it snapped in two. Picking up a small piece from the floor, he added hydrochloric acid to his equation. There is something still missing. The chemicals must be boiling hot for the molecular structures to change.

He stood back from the blackboard, casting disbelieving eyes. He had stumbled upon what he wanted all along. There it was. By mixing boiling water and acid to the W&W compound, he had changed the molecular structure of the presumed safe W&W compound to the feared and lethal *NeoBloc*.

Nasters dropped to his knees. *Allah is great!* My jihad will happen after all. *No one will ever know until it is too late!*

CHAPTER SIXTY-FOUR

Ashley waited patiently outside the Oval office. Out of deference to her father's precarious condition, the President had given her five minutes. After meeting with Williams, her plan was to return to Detroit Metro Medical Center--to room seven in the ICU---to stand vigil.

"You can go in now," Madison said.

She opened the door to see President Williams staring out on the rose garden. An unexpected late spring snowfall had sent chills all day through Ashley. The dismal cloudy day matched how she was feeling.

"Good morning, Madame President."

Williams turned slowly. She pointed to the couch. "Hello Miss Rogers. How is your father doing?"

Ashley walked alongside the President, not looking at her, staring straight ahead. She cleared her throat. "He's still in a deep coma, responsive only to pain. His last brain wave test showed minimal activity." She eased onto the soft cushions at the far end of the couch.

The President inched over to Ashley. "He's in my prayers." Williams rested her hand on Ashley's while staring blankly at the Ben Franklin clock, on the wall across from the couch. "Madison said it was important for you to talk with me."

"Dr. Hussein Nasters called me late last night. He has made a major scientific breakthrough. He discovered a way for them to store the vaccine without inactivating it. This critical discovery now enables them to fast track their compound."

"How long will it take?"

"Dr. Nasters said that the clinical trials will be speeded up. The earliest dates for FDA approval would probably be within a month."

Williams sighed. "I wish it was ready at this time like *NeoBloc* would have been."

"Madame President, *NeoBloc* is history and thirty days is not that far away"

"Miss Rogers, I wish it were that simple. My deadline is at hand. That's all I will say." The President rose and returned to her spot behind her desk, pensively looking out at the garden.

"Thank you for your time, Madame President."

"Tell Dr. Nasters God speed on creating a safe and effective vaccine ASAP."

"I'll let him know that you're counting on him."

"It would better put to say that America is counting on his success."

Ashley could not help but notice that Williams' body language telegraphed a message that the President's mind seemed many miles away. She left the Oval Office wondering what period the President had in mind for deployment of a safe and effective vaccine and why had she not shared her deadline? *Something big is in the wings!*

******

Ashley observed her father's chest, rising and falling with each cycle of the respirator. *Whoosh Whoosh.* The intubation tube protruding from his mouth was providing him a remote chance, as life sustaining oxygen streamed to every cell in his body. A central venous port below his left collarbone dripped in vital nutrients to sustain his organs. An occasional twitch of his right eyebrow and an intermittent fine tremor of his left hand gave Ashley barely a glimpse into the central nervous system of her father, a system in chaos. Given his deep coma, she speculated whether her father had any sense of her presence. Ashley promptly answered her own question in the negative, as she believed her father's spirit was as a man of action, not merely a physical body, passively existing with the aid of mechanical interventions. Ashley pulled her chair closer to his bed. She gently dropped her head onto his chest.

CHAPTER SIXTY-FIVE

Beth thought it was the right thing to do to give Ashley more time with her father. So she met with Panini at the DuPont diner. Sipping her Diet Coke, she could not help but recall the last time that she sat in this very same booth. In somewhat of a daze, she remembered the day that she was supposed to have met Dr. Washington---only to meet Marissa and a pocket sized .380.

After he drained his second Coke with one prolonged chug, Panini broke the silence. "My buddies have found out something that just went down. Two teenagers playing in an abandoned warehouse outside of town found the body of an elderly man. His neck had been broken. The kids had called the police. The deceased is Xavier Rudolf." He motioned for a passing server to bring back a refill. "And wouldn't you know it, Rudolf just happens to be the chairman of the Board of Trustees at DCP."

Beth's interest was piqued. "Those damn DCP people get around. But, what would a Chairman of the Board be doing in a place like that?"

The server plunked down a refill, complete with a straw. "The police found a cigarette butt at the scene. It had Rudolf's fingerprints."

"And, --."

Panini twirled his straw in his glass of Coke. "There also were prints and DNA from two other people at the scene. No one knows who they are although the FBI is running these prints through their master file."

"Did the kids find anything else?"

"Earlier that day, they remembered seeing two dark skinned men walking away from the warehouse. One wore a beard. From his recollection of TV news, one of the kids said both men looked like shorter versions of Bin Laden."

Beth shot off a knowing look at Panini. "Are you thinking what I'm thing?"

Panini grabbed her hand and winked. "Maybe I can read your mind if we're connected somehow."

Beth pulled her hand away. "I'm serious. You're not being funny."

Panini chuckled. "Relax; I can feel your tension." He reached below the table. She saw it vibrating. "Unless we're having an earthquake, it must be you that's making this table twitch."

"I hate when people tell me to relax," she fired back. Beth looked down at her legs. Her right one was pumping like a car piston firing on all cylinders.

Panini looked below the table. "Ha, I was right. It is you."

"Can we get focused?"

"Look, tens of thousands of good law-abiding American citizens are Muslims. Our problem is finding the one rogue terrorist cell."

"I agree." Beth's eyes reddened. "Look, I'm just so upset at what's happening to Jonathan."

"I can see that you and Johnny Boy are close friends." Panini flung his right eyebrow up. "I picked up on good vibrations going on between the both of you."

She pulled out her straw, picked up her glass and gulped down the remainder of her Coke. "What do you mean?"

"You like him. Don't you."

She returned his gaze and held it. "We've been friends---that's all. He was happily married until Kim was---"

Her words hung in the air. Beth turned away, gazing out at the parking lot.

Panini cast his eyes downward. "It's only been a few months since her passing. Sometimes, Johnny Boy gets that faraway look in his eye. I believe that he's always thinking of Kim."

Beth scooted out of her side of the booth and rose to her feet. "I think we should pay a visit to Xavier Rudolf's office. Ashley told me as Board Chair at DCP, he has a small place to hang his hat. Let's call her. Perhaps, we can find a clue."

"I'm one step ahead of you." Panini pulled a small piece of paper from his wallet. "My friends gave me Rudolf's home address." He threw a five-dollar bill on the table and followed her to the foyer of the diner.

She stopped and faced Panini. "Who are these friends you keep talking about?"

"You don't want to know."

******

It was a rainy dreary day in DuPont. Beth drove Panini to Rudolf's apartment building. He led Beth to apartment two on the first floor. After using his handy skill to pick locks, the door creaked open. The blinds were drawn. No lights burned. An answering machine red light flickered.

Beth pressed the button. It was a woman's voice wanting to know when she could come over for her monthly cleaning. Panini pressed rewind. *Three old messages.* The first message was from a guy named Robin wanting to know when Rudolf was able to play golf. The second was his same friend calling back and leaving a tee time. Panini played the third message.

'Call me. You'll want to know what I have learned.'

Beth shouted, "That's Nasters. I recognize his voice."

"Let's call Ashley."

CHAPTER SIXTY-SIX

A cold front from Canada had turned yesterday's overnight rain into a heavy snowfall. Six inches of snow had already fallen. While most of the locals stayed indoors, Nasters drove his beige Toyota sedan to his meeting in Turkey Knoll Park.

He parked on the side of the road due north of the football field. There were no other cars within sight. A red scarf around his neck and a winter down jacket would keep him warm. Wearing two pairs of sweat pants, he wished he had worn a ski cap. He secured his Browning high power 9 mm in an ankle harness, inside loose fitting black sweat pants.

Nasters almost slipped on the icy pavement upon exiting his Toyota. He scanned the soccer and football fields. The goal posts were his guide. Following Mugandi's instructions, he was still puzzled why they were meeting here. *I have learned my lesson. Ask no questions.*

The crunching sounds of his high backed leather boots indenting the drifts of snow were a sharp contrast against the eerie quiet of the field that he soon approached. When he reached the goal posts, he turned around. He saw only his tracks. Nasters shivered. He plodded forward until he stood amid the swirling snow on the fifty-yard line.

The driving snowfall had limited visibility to twenty yards. He scanned the horizon in all directions. Seemingly, out of nowhere, from the south, a bearded man advanced. He was walking straight at him. Five yards away, Nasters noticed the tall man brandishing a three-foot long machete.

"Brother Nasters," Mugandi called out. "Kneel down!"

I have no choice but to follow the will of Allah!

He acted on the command. On his knees, Nasters glanced up. The Pakistani Freedom Fighter leader hovered silently over him. Mugandi held the machete directly over his head. The scientist closed his eyes. *I will accept the will of Allah!* He anticipated being with his father—Ali. A crooked smile crossed his lips.

Mugandi spoke softly, "You may now rise."

The scientist profusely thanked Allah for sparing his life. He rose slowly. His ice cold soaked knees brought on another chill. The wind howled, driving the snow horizontally, directly in his face. He wiped away a build- up of clinging snow from his forehead, wondering why his brother had brought a machete which he still held tightly in his hand.

Nasters noted Mugandi's eyes rapidly darting around the field. The PFF cell leader quietly asked, "This time---can I trust you?"

"Yes." Nasters drew closer to his Pakistani brother. "Our mutual goal to kill the Americans has always been aligned"

"But, from the start, our tactics have been different. You wanted to kill Americans with your vaccine—your biological warfare. We have always wanted to destroy them with repeated nuclear attacks—one after another. That is why I intervened to behead Lauren Timmons. I wanted to infuriate Dr. Rogers so he would take up our cause to fight you on *NeoBloc*."

"You have enlightened me. Now, it all makes sense. Dr. Rogers was opposed to *NeoBloc* before I ever met him. I had a premonition that someone was feeding him information on the vaccine. Now, based on what you have said, it was obviously Ms. Timmons."

Mugandi dropped the machete. The blade sliced through the deep snow burying itself except for the red plastic handle. The PFF leader stuck out his hand.

Nasters grasped Mugandi's hand and kissed it. "*NeoBloc* is history. Now your nuclear tactic to kill the infidels is also my tactic."

"My brother, our time is at hand. You must leave Michigan today. From the latest weather forecast, the radiation from the nuclear blast is expected to blow this way."

"When?"

"The nuclear bomb will explode precisely at ten 'o clock tomorrow morning."

The scientist looked up at the heavens. "To show my loyalty to you, please grant me the privilege to press the nuclear button."

Mugandi brushed a build up of snow from his eyelids. He circled Nasters twice before coming to a sudden halt. "I believe in you. Our half-way house is in Columbus, Ohio. Forty One Turtleback Street. Arrive by nine. You're code name is California Sunshine 13579. After you detonate the nuclear blast, Detroit will be smashed into oblivion."

Nasters said with as much reference as he could muster. "Allah! Thank you for the trust that you have placed in me by convincing my holy brother of my loyalty to our divine cause."

Mugandi bowed at his brother. "I will meet you at the half-way house. There will be no further communications until then. Peace my brother." He turned and began walking south, toward the opposite goal post.

Without a second thought, Nasters bent down and pulled out his Browning. He fired twice at point blank range at the back of Mugandi's head. The PFF leader went down. Red blood poured out onto the white snow. Nasters kicked the body over. His eyes were fixed, lifeless. The scientist calmly stuck the 9mm in his coat pocket and trotted back to his car.

******

Nasters had previously done his homework. It was as simple as checking the Internet Department of Defense website. By calling 000-545-6000, the switchboard operator would connect him. With his newly learned national security intelligence in hand, he had no doubt the operator would connect him to the appropriate channels so that he could report the planned attack. Driving to a secure place, he would carry out his plan.

He believed that President Williams would proclaim him a national hero, averting a major terrorist nuclear attack. Most importantly, he would be free to continue his work on the W&W compound. Free to work on converting the safe W&W compound into lethal *NeoBloc.* He pulled out his cell and dialed.

On the seventh ring, a low-pitched voice whispered, "Good afternoon. This is the operator at the Pentagon."

"Hello, my name is Dr. Hussein Nasters. I am the chief scientist at W&W in DuPont, Michigan. It is urgent that I speak immediately to your agent working on the shooting of Dr. Jonathan Rogers. I have vital information that will prevent a nuclear disaster in America."

The operator replied, "Please hold on."

Nasters drove over the Pigeon River. He pressed the window button. Once opened, he tossed his Browning into the rapid flow of the deep river.

On his cell, he heard a muffled voice. The static in the cell increased. "Is this Dr. Nasters?"

"I'm here," he shouted, skidding in the snow to stop for a red light.

"I'll connect you now."

"Thank you."

A woman introduced herself. "I am Special Agent Susan Masters. How may I help you?"

"This is Dr. Hussein Nasters."

"I know who you are. You are the scientist at DCP."

"Correction, I'm now the top scientist at W&W."

Interrupting, she said, "You called saying you had information about a nuclear disaster."

"This is my story. Recently, I was having coffee at the *Daily Mug* in DuPont. I overheard two men talking about a plan to blow up Detroit. I listened closely. I heard where the terrorists are hiding. Please take down this detailed information and send agents immediately. The terrorists are located at-----"

******

Nasters checked into a hotel in Oldwyck under the name of Anthony Hochkiss. He connected his laptop, sipped a cup a tea and waited. After full deployment of *NeoBloc*, it would be a good idea, he believed, to accept Special Agent Masters's offer to put him into the witness protection program. He would request safe passage to a foreign country, probably Africa. By the time the vaccine began to kill, he would just disappear into the jungle where he could savor the sheer destruction he had reeked upon America. To be the one who brought the killer *NeoBloc* to all Americans, that would be his reward for the freedom that he would abandon without any hesitation.

His cell phone rang. "This is Dr. Nasters."

"Where are you now?"

"You know where I work."

"President Williams will be most pleased by your vigilance toward saving our nation."

"Glad to be of service to America."

CHAPTER SIXTY-SEVEN

President Williams took an urgent call from Secretary of Defense, Bill Stapleton. He informed her of the capture of the rogue terrorist cell. The FBI had confirmed their plan to set off a nuclear device in Detroit. Surprisingly, Dr .Hussein Nasters was the informant.

"I am pleased to hear that we have captured this cell. I need to thank Dr. Nasters." She exhaled a breath of relief. "How many other rogue cells are out there? Minneapolis and Atlanta have been nuked and many other cities have been exposed to cesium radiation from "suitcase" bombs placed at strategic locations around our nation."

"Madame President, I understand the absolute need for America to do something to stop this terrorism. I just pray that the global community of nations doesn't start World War Three if we attack military targets in Afghanistan and Pakistan."

"Bill, after the stadium in Atlanta was bombed; we caught one of the terrorists. She admitted responsibility for the attack. She was a member of the Pakistani Freedom Fighters. Since then, the State Department has tried to involve the global community to addressing this issue. We have tried to get the ambassadors in the region to convince their governments to intervene and do something about the terrorists who are being trained in their country."

"That is all true."

"Yet, were it not for the assistance of Dr. Nasters, the city of Detroit would have been leveled by another terrorist attack. What is your response to this fact?"

Stapleton said tersely, "Madame President, our plan is on schedule. Per your direct order, our non-nuclear bombers will strike in the early morning."

"Thank you Bill. Keep me posted. That is all!"

Hanging up, the initial prediction of the Joint Chiefs that dropping a nuclear warhead on the region would lead to World War III weighed heavily on her mind. Her plan was to start with conventional type of bombs only on military targets.

Ashley Rogers had just told her that the safe W&W vaccine could be available in approximately thirty to sixty days, now that they had the expertise of Dr. Hussein Nasters. She closed her eyes and prayed that her decision was right. Williams hit the intercom, "Madison, hold all calls. I do not want to be disturbed by anyone."

"Yes, Madame President."

Williams began pacing the Oval Office. The gravity of her decision to strike the high value military targets in the region with conventional bombs touched off a migraine. She wished that she could hide somewhere—to escape—to be alone in her prayers. Yet, at this moment, she realized she needed people more than ever. She needed input. *Whoever said it was lonely at the top was right!*

Williams hit the intercom. "Madison, please summon the Vice-President to my office. It is imperative that I see him right away. I know he's in town."

"Actually, Vice-President Stockard is standing right next to me. He had just arrived a few minutes ago to see you. I was going to buzz you but you said not to interrupt you.

"Send him in."

***

Stockard stood in front of the President's desk. He looked down at her, wearing an unsettled face. "I heard the great news from the FBI that they caught the rogue terrorist cell in Columbus."

The President rose quickly. "We really owe Dr. Nasters a debt of gratitude for tipping off the FBI."

"He's a true patriot." The VP pointed to the couch. "Jane, I have something important to say to you."

Williams sat at the near end of the couch, twisting her torso to face Stockard. "Chester, I've been thinking that W&W is now so close to a vaccine and that any imminent threat by the terrorists may have been averted. Homeland Security has been monitoring the chatter on the web and they feel confident that no further nuclear attacks are likely in the near future."

He nodded. "I knew that you would be thinking that. That's why I came to convince you not to change your mind---again!"

"You must agree that some critical facts have changed."

"I don't agree. The main fact, as you refer to it, is that the terrorists have declared war on our nation."

The President paused. "That may be true but tell me why we should not hold off on tomorrow's attacks pending further intelligence reports from Homeland Security."

"It would indicate to the terrorists that our President is a weak leader," he said, scrunching his face. "It would be a terrible mistake. You will never win re-election."

"I don't give a damn about elections. It is easy for you to say that discretion would be a mistake. If I ever gave the command to launch American bombs to devastate those military targets, no one will ask *you* a damn question."

"That's why you, and not me, is the President. It is your call."

She countered with force. "You do not have to remind me that I am the Commander-in-Chief."

The Vice President's face relaxed a bit. "Jane, do not back down now. You do not know what other rogue terrorist cells are still out there. Catching one cell doesn't end the war against America."

"Let me play devil's advocate with you."

Stockard rolled his eyes. "If you must, I'll go along."

"I have given this much thought. In my view, there is no longer a compelling reason for us to lash out. We have thwarted the plot to destroy an American city. It buys us time."

He shook his head. "Time until they nuke us again. That could be in two--three days. I state unequivocally that time has run out. It's time to act."

"If we've learned anything from our ongoing war on terrorism is that bombing the mountains of Afghanistan won't guarantee that America will not be hit again."

"It will send a powerful message that America will not stand idly by while our citizens are killed by terrorists." The VP clenched his jaws. "If you back down now, everyone will view you as weak."

"Look Chester, I was never an ideologue. Knee jerk reactions are not my style. I carefully weigh my decisions based on the risk and benefits to America and to others. Frankly, I don't understand why you refuse to accept the fact that since the plot to annihilate Detroit has been foiled that things are different today than they were yesterday."

"Your only responsibility is toward the people of our nation. You seem to want to please others in the rest of the world. A strong leader protects our own people. Call me an ideologue if it makes you feel better. I am proud to unequivocally state that I believe in America first."

Williams listened carefully. She rubbed her forehead. Her intestines felt squeezed. She held steady eye contact with Stockard.

Raising his voice, he fired away. "Look, nothing has changed. I'm wasting my time talking to you. I'm sorry but I cannot sit back and let America be in constant jeopardy."

Stockard leaped to his feet and stormed out of the Oval Office. While Williams walked back to her desk, the VP reappeared in the doorway. He shouted, "For the record, you are a weak leader and I intend to resign as your Vice-President. I will challenge you in the upcoming primary for the upcoming nomination of our party. You will go down in history as the worst President of all time."

The President buzzed Madison to place a call to Bill Stapleton. Williams hung her head and prayed. She thought of Maryann and the other American victims—all completely innocent civilians.

Buzz

"The Secretary of Defense is on line two".

Pressing the intercom, Jane Williams gave the order in a decisive tone. "Bill, cancel all attacks."

He hesitated. "Madame President, I don't---I don't understand."

She elevated her voice a few octaves and spoke distinctly. "Cancel the attacks. Maintain our current heighted state of vigilance."

"Thank you, Madame President. I will pass on your order."

CHAPTER SIXTY-EIGHT

Ashley led Beth and Panini into Nasters's laboratory office at
W&W. She knocked on his door. Wearing surgical gloves, she held a
steaming hot coffee mug in her other hand. A special agent from the FBI
opened the door.

She was surprised to see that the scientist now had an FBI agent
guarding him. "Hi, I'm Ashley Rogers. My friends and I have an
appointment with Dr. Nasters."

The agent checked their ID badges. "You are expected."

Ashley spotted Nasters at his desk, looking down at several papers
strewn in front of him. Beth and Panini soon surrounded him.

The scientist looked up. "Oh no! I hope you don't want to discuss
NeoBloc anymore." Nasters smirked, feigning that he was about to pass
out.

Ashley sat down on an adjacent chair. Beth and Panini stood.

"Miss Rogers, I hope this will be quick. I have much work to do.
Our President is counting on me." Nasters stared at her hands. "Why
are you wearing gloves?"

"I have a ricketsial infection of both palms. I was hunting in the
woods. I suffered a tick bite. I'm on a couple of antibiotics but my
hands are raw to touch."

"It's always something, as you Americans are so fond of saying."

Ashley nodded. "I'll survive. In any case, we came by to thank you
for saving the people of Detroit. As you know, my father is at Detroit
Metro Medical. So, your heroic actions to tip off the FBI are deeply
personal for me and many others."

Nasters looked up at Beth and Panini. "Are those your bodyguards or
your fellow hunters? I'm glad you two didn't get bitten by a tick." He
winked at Panini. "As you saw, I have my guard as well. You have
already met Special Agent Nelson."

Ashley glanced over at the FBI agent who merely nodded. She took
a long sip of her coffee, noting Panini's subtle nod.

He swiveled his seat toward Ashley. "I'm sorry to hear that your
father had a recent setback."

"Thank you. By the way, Dr. Nasters, you never told us the name of
the W&W vaccine."

"Far be it from me to give it a name. Right now it's just a compound
until the FDA approves it."

She replied, "Perhaps the Nasters vaccine?"

His eyes twinkled. "I am too modest to celebrate for my own benefit. Perhaps, it would best be remembered as the Rogers vaccine."

"My Dad would never let that happen. He's far too humble. But, I would not be opposed to you sending him a brief note to try to convince him."

Nasters beamed. He picked up his ballpoint pen. "I would be honored to do so."

"I have a pen." Ashley pulled out a felt tip pen from her suit pocket. "This will show up better. My father's eyesight is weak."

The scientist took her pen and quickly penned a one-paragraph message to the Surgeon General. He folded the paper and handed it to Ashley. "I personally informed the President this morning that we are only twenty days away from FDA approval of the new vaccine. Then we can start full scale manufacturing of the compound and inoculation of every American."

Ashley pulled out a tissue from a small red box and pretended to blow her nose. Instead, she grabbed the felt tipped pen with the tissue and dropped it into the red box that she deposited in her pants suit pocket.

"Miss Rogers, if it were not for you, I would not be here at W&W. I can see much of your father in you. You may not realize now what you have done. Because of your efforts a new vaccine will be ready in time to save millions of Americans from further radiation induced cancers."

"Dr. Nasters, we'll let you get back to your work."

******

Ashley opened her apartment door. Beth and Panini stepped inside. Earlier, she had called Agent Susan Masters who arranged for a pickup of the potential evidence to see if it was possible to match up the fingerprints on the body of the late Mr. Rudolf with Nasters's print on the felt tipped pen.

"Panini, you were right. The FBI has confirmed a DNA fingerprint of Dr. Nasters on the hand and earlobe of Mr. Rudolf."

He responded, "So, that places our brilliant scientist at the warehouse scene when Rudolf's neck was broken."

Beth added, "And, there is more. The DuPont police just found the body of a Pakistani man in Turkey Knoll Park. They ran the dead man's prints against the fingerprints on the skin on Rudolf's neck. Guess what?"

"Our scientist sure spends a lot of time in parks and warehouses." Panini's eyes darted to both women. "The web is tightening. So, the man most likely killed Rudolf while Nasters was at the murder scene."

"What's the connection?" Ashley asked.

"Based on what we now know, I think we need to pay another visit to Dr. Nasters," Panini said. "Let's see if we can get an appointment for later today."

Ashley put her clenched hand in front of her. Beth and Panini put their fists before them as well so that all fists now were touching. "My father is near death because of these evil powerbrokers. We need to shut them all down."

******

Entering the lobby of W&W, Ashley saw VP Stockard pacing the floor. "I'm Ashley Rogers and these are my---"

"I know who you are", he angrily replied.

"Mr. Vice-President, I'm surprised to run into you here. Do you have an appointment with Dr. Nasters?"

"It seems as though you've convinced the President that this vaccine is the new savior of America. I came because I want to ensure that this W&W vaccine is the real thing." Stockard glanced over to his own two Secret Service agents.

Ashley replied, "My friends and I are meeting with Dr. Nasters." She introduced Beth and Panini to the Vice-President.

Stockard tapped his foot while waiting outside the door to the W&W lab. With his arms folded across his barrel chest, he seemed like he was stoking for a fight with someone.

An assistant scientist, dressed in a full-length white lab coat opened the laboratory door. She checked for authorized badges. Looking at the Vice-President and the Secret Service bodyguards, she stated, "I don't have any of you listed for an appointment."

Stockard's face exploded with rage. "There must be some mistake here. I personally spoke with Dr. Nasters a few hours ago."

"I have no record of an appointment with you. But, I will speak with him. He is very busy. I cannot promise that he has time to see you today. Perhaps we can reschedule."

He shouted, "Listen to me. I am the Vice-President of this country. Doesn't that mean anything?"

The assistant scientist kept her cool. "Mr. Vice-President, I'm extremely sorry. Please let me usher in people who have been patiently waiting for their appointment. I promise to be back shortly after I confirm with Dr. Nasters on whether he has time to see you. I apologize for any inconvenience."

Surprisingly, the VP looked disarmed. "These things happen. I'll wait a few minutes."

***

While following the assistant scientist into the lab, Ashley noticed that they were going right past Nasters's office---heading toward what appeared to be a huge manufacturing section of W&W. An overhead concrete walkway opened up to a myriad of ventilation pipes and one large twelve foot high stainless steel vat inside a three story high ceiling room half the size of a football field.

Ashley spotted Nasters standing on the twenty-foot high walkway, leaning over a safety railing. He was wearing a large protective eye facemask and yellow rubber gloves. Standing on steel scaffolding, he peered across the steamy vat, painted black. An odor of rotten eggs permeated the air.

The assistant scientist waved up at him. She caught his attention. He yelled back, "I'll be right down."

The assistant yelled, "The Vice-President is here in the lobby. He wants to see you."

The top scientist descended the metallic ladder. He ripped off his gloves and plastic see through facemask and tossed them into a barrel. As he approached the trio, Nasters glanced at his assistant. "Please tell the Vice-President that I'm working on a critical step. I can see him tomorrow. Please apologize for me."

"I will ask him to re-schedule."

Nasters glared at Ashley. "Back so soon?" the scientist asked. "You have five minutes--no more. My assistant told me this visit was really important."

"I guarantee you that it is vital."

Nasters pointed toward a small conference room with glass paneled walls. "Let's sit in there. Through the glass, I must observe the technicians and the chemical reaction-taking place in the vats. We're presently working on a key step in developing a preservative for the vaccine."

"It should be named the Nasters vaccine!"

The top scientist at W&W countered quickly, "No, I will recommend to President Williams that it be named the Rogers vaccine---in honor of your father."

Beth asked, "What's in that vat? It is huge. It must be more than five feet across and twice as deep."

"Smells like hydrogen sulfide," Panini contributed.

"It's hydrochloric acid. Both the mist and the solution have a corrosive effect on human tissue, with the potential to damage respiratory organs, eyes, skin, and intestines."

Beth coughed as if on cue. She reached for a tissue from a box of Kleenex. Covering her mouth, she tried to clear her throat.

"You must be very sensitive to the acid." Nasters rose and walked over to a vertical file cabinet. He pulled out a surgical mask from the top drawer. "Put this on. It should help."

"What happens if that acid comes in contact with your skin?" Ashley asked.

"Severe burns, ulcerations, and scarring. That's why I wear these rubber gloves." Nasters compassionately looked over at Murphy. "Is the mask helping?"

"Yes, thank you."

"Good. Too much inhalation of the hydrochloric acid fumes can induce swelling of the larynx and lungs. It can be pretty nasty stuff if you come in direct or even indirect contact." Nasters turned toward Ashley. "Look, I don't have much time."

Ashley stood to pace the floor. She pivoted sharply. "Dr. Nasters, do you know anything about the death of Xavier Rudolf?"

Nasters kept his frozen gaze fixated on the vat. "Only what I read in the newspapers and see on local cable TV news."

Panini waved his hand in front of the scientist's vacant stare. "Do you think you can take your eyes off the damn vat for a second? Are you expecting an explosion?"

"The President wants our vaccine as soon as possible. She personally called yesterday to thank me for averting a nuclear disaster in Detroit." He reached out and grabbed Ashley's arm. "Please stop walking around. Are you on another fishing expedition? Just tell me what you want."

She sat down and took his measure. "DuPont police found a man in Turkey Knoll Park. He had been shot twice in the head."

Nasters looked out at the vat. His expression was unmoved. "So, why are you giving me these useless local news updates?"

"Maybe this will grab your attention," Ashley added, "Your DNA has been found at the scene where Xavier Rudolf was murdered."

Dr. Nasters glanced down at his watch and waved his arms in the air, grabbing the attention of a young scientist who was walking by the translucent window of the conference room. Nasters pointed to a bucket near the boiling vat. His colleague acted upon seeing his boss's signal, climbed the ladder and emptied a bucket of clear liquid into the smoldering cauldron. A smug look appeared on his face. The assistant scientist looked toward the conference room and gave a thumb- up sign.

Nasters returned the sign. "Excuse me, Ms. Rogers, what did you say?"

"Your DNA was found at the scene where the police found the body of Mr. Rudolf. His neck was broken."

The scientist's eyes seemed to glaze over. "It must be a DNA mismatch. These things happen. I know. Remember, I am a physician— and a trusted physician of President Williams."

Beth interjected, "Our story gets worse."

"I feel bad for anyone who dies. But you are wasting my time." He bolted upright in his chair and jumped to his feet. "I gave you time. It's now my time to work to save America."

"No, Dr Nasters. What I meant is that our story gets worse for *you"*
Just as he was about to leave the room, he turned. "What do you mean?"

"The FBI also found your finger prints on the hand of a Pakistani man who was recently shot in the Park. His name is Mugandi. He was a leader of a Pakistani Freedom Fighter rogue terrorist cell."

"This is sheer nonsense." Nasters stood. "I don't have time to hear of every bad person who you are tracking."

Ashley held up her hand as the scientist was about to turn to open the door. "Strange that Rudolf's, Mugandi's, and your DNA were all found in the front room of the warehouse."

"Not that it matters but where would you get my DNA?"

"Were you at the warehouse when Xavier Rudolf was murdered?" Panini asked, reaching out for the scientist's arm.

Nasters shook off his firm grip. "When President Williams called me, she said that I am the savior of America. If you don't let me return to my work, I'll have no other choice but to ask my Secret Service agent to escort all of you out of the building."

He stormed out the door, stopping off at the shower near the huge vat to wash off any contamination particles that may have been floating in the air. He opened a decontamination cabinet and donned a fresh pair of gloves and new facemask. Waving to the young scientist already on the walkway, Nasters headed back up the ladder.

A moment later, Ashley heard shouts coming from the direction of Nasters's office. She turned around and there was the Vice-President accompanied by his Secret Service agents. Stockard was yelling, "Where's Nasters? He agreed to meet me. Where the hell is he?"

As the VP passed Ashley, she pointed upward. The top scientist was writing on a yellow pad and leaning against the five-foot high cast iron guardrail of the steel scaffolding. Just underneath the walkway, three scientists in lab coats were working at a lab bench in one corner of the huge room. Several foot high flasks and a Bunsen burner clogged their work area.

Stockard stared up at Nasters. "We need to talk," the Vice-President ordered.

"Sir, with all due respect, I've no time to waste. President Williams wants the vaccine available for mass inoculations within several weeks of FDA approval. Now that Dr. Rogers is essentially brain dead, as soon as the FDA approves my vaccine, it needs to be ready for shipment to every county health department in the country. I'm working on the final reactions to store the vaccine at various distribution centers around our country. "

The Vice-President hollered back, "If it wasn't for your latest vaccine, President Williams wouldn't have changed her mind to issue a terrible decision that puts America back into the cross hares of terrorists."

"I admire President Williams. Now, please excuse me. I have a lot of work to do on my new vaccine."

"*NeoBloc* fails and now you come up with son of *NeoBloc*. Without your damn vaccine, the President would have acted. America would have ridden our country of a hateful enemy. But when she learned that your W&W vaccine would soon be ready, she held off."

"Bombing the border of Afghanistan and Pakistan would have been shear madness. On the other hand, making a vaccine that prevents radiation induced cancer will win me the Nobel Peace Prize."

Stockard shot a quizzical look. "Who said anything about our military plans?'

Nasters waved to one of the scientists in the corner. "Please escort our guests out of this laboratory."

A tall well-built man in a white lab coat gently placed his flask on his workbench and headed toward the four of them. He stopped five yards short of the Vice President and froze in his tracks, looking down the long hallway.

A second later, Ashley heard gunfire and then footsteps running toward her. She craned her neck. Two masked men were running toward them. They were shouting, 'Praise be to Allah.' Each man carried an AK-47. One intruder fired a round into Stockard's right calf.

Tumbling hard to the floor, the Vice President screamed out in pain, "Who the hell are you?"

Ashley grabbed a towel from the decon station and applied firm pressure to Stockard's calf. "Mr. Vice-President, it's a superficial wound. But, I'll tie this towel around it. Please lay down."

He glared at the masked men and indignantly shouted, "I'm the Vice-President of the United States. I'll have you men hanged."

One of the masked men screamed, "Shut up or I'll blow off your head. I already did that to one of your bodyguards." A second Secret Service agent jumped in front of the Vice-President, the bulge in his jacket was obvious to Ashley.

The taller of the masked men took charge. He looked up at the scaffold. "Nasters, you have killed Mugandi, our brother. You are a traitor in the eyes of Allah!"

Ashley stepped in front of the shorter man who was walking toward the ladder. The masked man pointed the AK-47 assault rifle into her chest. She backed up, praying the entire time. "Ok, please don't shoot."

The other invader began rounding up the three scientists, Panini, Beth, and Ashley. He called out to his brother, "Shalya, kill our brother by having him jump into the vat."

Nasters backpedaled fifty yards along the scaffolding from the ladder.

By now, Shalya had climbed the ladder and was already standing on the scaffolding. "Stop sneaking away like a coward Dr. Nasters. Come towards me."

Ashley's mind was whirling. She heard additional footsteps coming from down the corridor near Nasters's office. A man wearing a bulletproof vest snaked his way toward them. She noticed that Beth had also seen him approach. It appeared that he was carrying a Glock semi-automatic pistol. Ashley spotted two women right behind the armed man. She looked over at Beth. Her roommate mouthed the words, *Virginia Washington and Marissa.*

Shalya called out, "Oman, I have a clear shot to fill the traitor with holes."

"No, that would be too quick. I want to hear his skin sizzling in the acid. I want to inhale the smell of the acid eating into his traitorous heart."

Ashley made eye contact with Panini. Her eye movements led him to spot the approaching two women and the man bearing the Glock. She pleaded, "Please Oman, spare our lives. We have done nothing."

The tall masked man walked toward her. "I can see the resemblance. You must be the daughter of the famous Dr. Jonathan Rogers. Perhaps, I will kill you first."

"We mean you no harm." Ashley covered her mouth.

"You are a liar! We have discovered that your American government was about to launch a military strike on our bases. And, you have the nerve to tell me that you mean us no harm."

Ashley took a step back. Oman used the stock of his AK-47 to hit her in the jaw, opening a two-inch superficial gash. She fell on her back. The terrorist stuck his weapon in her face. Blood dripped down her neck.

"I will make an example of you. You will be the first to die."

With one giant leap, Panini dropkicked Oman in his back causing him to lose his grip on the AK-47. Beth grabbed the assault rifle from the floor. Oman then kicked Panini in the groin several times sending him reeling. The masked man forcefully grabbed the weapon from Beth's weak grip. He shot Panini once in his left ankle, leading him to fall to the floor, writhing in pain.

Oman's eyes darted. He walked over to Panini. "Say your prayers." Suddenly, he stopped and pivoted. "While you suffer, my brother and I will fry Natsers. Then Shalya and I will come back and kill everyone."

Oman headed for the ladder to climb toward the walkway. Nasters shouted out, "Help me. The President needs me. America needs me."

Vice President Stockard whispered, "We need to let these men kill Dr. Nasters."

"What are you saying Mr. Vice President?" Ashley screamed. "Once Nasters dies, this vaccine doesn't get produced as quickly as the President wants."

Stockard yelled, "Who knows if this new savior vaccine will be any better than NeoBloc? Don't you get it? Without any vaccine, the President will feel exposed again. If there was no damn vaccine, President Williams will give the order that we all need."

Oman backpedaled down the stairs. He headed straight to the Vice President. "I overheard what you said." He pointed the AK-47 at Stockard's head, between his eyes. Oman squeezed off a round of bullets. The right side of the Vice President's head flew off, exposing a bloody cavity.

The terrorist fired a few rounds into the air, to punctuate what he was about to say. "You Americans will all die. Do you think we will stop just because you kill a few of us?"

Ashley looked up at the scaffolding. Nasters was down on his knees. Shayla was pulling his hair and dragging him closer to where the scaffolding hovered over the boiling vat. Oman was staring up, savoring the moment. A shot rang out. Oman grabbed his right shoulder. He whirled and aimed his weapon at Ashley just as a second bullet smashed through the back of his skull. Oman fell to the ground as a pool of blood gathered around his head.

A moment later, a shower of bullets from Shayla killed the three scientists, the remaining Secret Service agent and one of the women who were with the man with the Glock. Virginia Washington took cover. She dived to the concrete walkway. A three-foot high wall of cement protected her and Ashley.

Ashley hugged her, "Virginia, oh my God." She then felt a tap on her shoulder. Ashley jerked her head around, about to scream.

Pointing his Glock at the walkway, he whispered, "I am a security guard for W&W."

"What are we going to do?"

Forbes spoke into his shoulder radio. 'I'm requesting immediate backup at the W&W manufacturing plant. There are six dead. Six are still alive and a terrorist named Shalya. He is armed with an AK-47 assault rifle."

Ashley took a quick glance at Virginia. "Who was that with you?"

"Marissa. She insisted on coming. She wanted to make up for what she and Zach Miller had once done." Dr. Washington covered her mouth. "Now, she's dead."

Ashley searched for Beth and Panini. Both of them were under the scaffolding. So far, Shayla had not seen them. Ashley took a peek upward. She drew his attention. A heavy rain of bullets smashed the concrete wall barely an inch above her head.

Forbes's voice rang out. "Keep down. He has too much firepower. I'm going to try to retrieve Oman's AK-47." He began snaking along the concrete wall just as his radio blasted.

The W&W security guard repeated the message aloud for all to hear. "Yes, Madame President, we will do everything we can to save Dr. Nasters."

Nasters was now hanging on to the scaffolding. He was screaming. His feet dangled just a yard above the deadly corrosive hydrochloric acid. Shayla was viciously stepping on his fingers, trying to force him to let go.

Seeing Shayla distracted, Forbes made a run for the AK-47. He picked it up and ran for cover toward Panini and Beth. Forbes looked upward. Shayla was walking along the walkway, toward them. The security guard shouted, "President Williams has ordered us to save Dr. Nasters so he can develop the savior vaccine." No sooner had he repeated the presidential demand than a salvo of bullets sliced into his abdomen. Blood poured out of a half dozen one inch in diameter holes. Seconds later, he collapsed, dropping the AK-47.

Panini picked up Oman's weapon and squeezed a few rounds off in Shayla's direction. With Shalya returning fire, Beth ran toward Ashley and Virginia.

Ashley watched Panini hobble on one foot under the scaffolding. He tore off his shirt and wrapped it tightly around his bleeding ankle. By now, Shayla's attention was back on Nasters.

Panini somehow began climbing the criss- crossing beams until he pulled himself up on the scaffolding. He slowly crawled on the metal walkway toward Shyla and Nasters. His feet clanged on the metal. The masked man shot off a few rounds at Panini, freezing his position as the bullets ricocheted off the iron railing.

Nasters cried out, "Save me. The President needs me to save America. There is no one else to develop the savior vaccine."

Shyla aimed the assault rifle at Nasters fingers on his left hand and fired off a couple of rounds. The scientist howled out in agony as his hand shattered. His severed left hand fell into the boiling vat, instantly decimated by the acid.

Nasters was barely hanging on with his remaining right hand. "Help me. I'm the savior of America."

Panini pulled himself up and dragged his left foot, making another hobble toward Shayla while firing the entire time. Return fire by the terrorist ripped a salvo through Panini's right thigh. He fell to the metal walkway and ripped off his tee shirt, tightly wrapping it around his upper leg.

Screaming *Praise to Allah*, Shayla aimed the AK-47 at Nasters right hand. Before he could squeeze off a round, a salvo of bullets from Panini ripped into the masked man's head, toppling him in to the vat of acid. Shayla yelled out his agony while bobbing up and down in the scolding acid. Panini crawled as fast as he could toward Nasters. The terrorist screamed while his head surfaced above the acid. Seconds later, all cries from Shalya had ebbed as his body sank in the vat.

Ashley felt helpless. Nasters's voice grew weaker by the second. "Help me, I can't hold on any more."

Panini lunged for Nasters's hand and grabbed it. But, the sweat on their hands was too much to get a grip. The scientist shouted, "Ali, Ali," while falling feet first into the vat of acid. He surfaced twice and each time yelled out in agony, "No. No. I'm the savior of America."

Ashley jumped to her feet and climbed the scaffolding toward Panini. She grabbed a quick glance into the vat. Seeing the horror reeked on Nasters body by the hydrochloric acid, she watched him sink for the last time.

CHAPTER SIXTY-NINE

Beth felt an overwhelming urge to take charge. She had driven
Ashley to visit Panini at Mercy Hospital. He was recovering from a
delayed elective surgery to remove three bullets from his right thigh and
one from his ankle.

His nurse had just left his room when Beth spoke. "Panini, you
saved our lives."

Ashley began crying. "And, that day at my apartment, my dad
would already be dead if you hadn't leaped to knock the gun from
Connor's hand. And, if you had not warned me that someone was hiding
in my bathroom—and---."

"I should have done better." He grimaced as he tried to change
positions. "Ashley, we all did good things. How is Johnny Boy---I
mean-- how is your Dad doing?"

"No change." Hanging her head, Ashley leaned into Beth's
embrace. "I'll be renting an apartment next to Detroit Metro."

"Your dad would be so proud to know what you've done in his
absence."

Beth said, "With Dr. Nasters gone, this will only delay the vaccine
program. In fact, I'm meeting with Virginia Washington today. The
CEO of W&W hired her as one of their high ranking scientists,
specifically to pick up where Nasters left off, to work on the savior
vaccine."

Panini moaned. "You guys think I'm some sort of hero. But I'm not.
Look, can I trouble you women to scout me up a Chubby Wubby burger?
This hospital food is making me sick."

Ashley let herself smile for the first time in a long time while she
and Beth came to his bedside.

He added, "Make the order-- three Chubby Wubby burgers."

Beth hugged Ashley and Panini while they all wept to release the
biting awful pain they had endured.

******

Inside Dr Nasters's old office at DCP, Beth met with Virginia
Washington. The scientist reviewed the notes previously written by the
slain scientist while he developed the necessary storage properties for the
new vaccine. As she turned each page, her eyes seemed to jump across
the passages with increasing alacrity.

"Virginia, where do we go from here? Can you pick up where Dr. Nasters left off?"

Washington began shaking her head. "I can't believe it. I just can't believe it."

"Can't believe what?"

"I've reviewed his notes for making changes to the vaccine. They indicate that he modified the W&W formula. That was the reason why we saw that huge vat of hydrochloric acid."

"Why would he do that?"

"His new formula indicates by mixing heated water with the acid stabilized the vaccine so it could be stored while it is being deployed over the country." She pointed to a pertinent passage. "He states here that the heat and acid when mixed with the chemical structure of the vaccine would act as a preservative."

"Scientifically speaking, can that happen?"

"I've never heard of that possibility but he is the world expert on this type of vaccine."

"Despite what he did to save a nuclear attack on Detroit, I never quite trusted him. Remember, we have DNA evidence that Nasters was at the warehouse when Mugandi killed Rudolf. And, his DNA was found on the PFF leader's body in the park." Beth narrowed her eyes. "I smell something rotten."

"Give me some time to review all this clinical data. I'll call you."

"Call me on my cell. I'll be driving over to visit Jonathan Rogers."

******

Beth slowly opened the hospital room door. Rogers remained tethered to a respirator, unable to breathe on his own. A nurse conducted a Glasgow coma neurological exam. With his composite score somewhat improved at seven, he remained in a deep coma.

Beth recalled all that had happened since *The Health Club* murdered her stepfather, Sam Murphy, for being a whistleblower on DCP. Jonathan has been a force to right many wrongs. He was a powerful ally for improving the public health of America.

Seeing the tranquility plastered over Jonathan's face, she wished that her good friend would once again be able to enjoy peace. She prayed he knew he succeeded in doing what was right. Beth began to doze off just as her cell awakened her. It played her favorite tune, '*There's a place for us.*'

"Hello,"

"It's Virginia. I have stunning news."

Beth jumped to her feet and anxiously began pacing the room. "What did you find?"

"I studied Nasters organic equations. Something didn't seem right. So, I went back to his original formula for making *NeoBloc*."

"Get to your point."

"If you mix the safe W&W formula in boiling water and add hydrochloric acid, you get a deadly vaccine."

"What?" Beth slapped her cheek, trying to become more alert. *What is Ginny saying?* "I'm not tracking with you. Why would he develop another vaccine that would be lethal?"

"By adding the acid and boiling water, Dr. Nasters changed the molecular structure of the safe W&W compound to make a lethal vaccine that we already knew about."

"What are you talking about?" Beth pinched herself. *Ouch!* "Please be specific. What lethal vaccine was Dr. Nasters developing at W&W?"

"*NeoBloc*! He was turning the safe W&W compound into the same deadly *NeoBloc* vaccine."

Beth dropped her cell. She covered her mouth. Recovering, she picked up the phone. "Are you certain?"

"Absolutely certain!"

"Oh my God! This is huge. Virginia, I'll call Ashley. We need to call the President right away. We need to advance the actual W&W compound. It will be up to you."

Ginny replied, "We're finally going down the right path for a safe and effective vaccine. So many lives have already been lost in getting to this place."

"So many more will be saved."

******

Four months later, Dr. Ulrich smiled at Beth Murphy and Michael 'O Kane. So much had happened. Beth glanced over to the newest plaque on the National Quality Board conference room wall. The award was given posthumously for the pharmaceutical company investigative activities of her late stepfather, Sam Murphy.

Goosebumps rippled over her skin. "I motion that we unconditionally support the approval of the actual W&W vaccine for FDA approval. It has been proven safe and effective in all the clinical trials."

She believed that the arduous journey had been worth it. Yet, her mood turned south when she thought of the probability of America losing a healthcare advocate—giant force for positive change. Someone she trusted implicitly---someone who fought to make a difference in the lives of so many people. *Jonathan.*

Her friend, O 'Kane, raised his hand. "I second Beth's motion."

Ulrich grinned. All in favor of the motion?"

Every hand went up. Lost in her thoughts, Beth's hand raised her hand.

'O Kane made a motion that was quickly seconded. "I motion and ask for unanimous consent that we recommend to W&W that the savior vaccine be called "The Sam Murphy Vaccine."

Except for Beth and 'O Kane, everyone in the room stood in applause. Beth leaned toward her loyal Irish friend. Her emotions had been pent up long enough. Not in the least concerned that she was at a public National Quality Board meeting, she openly wept on Michael 'O Kane's shoulder. *If only Jonathan could be here.*

EPILOGUE

"It's better to light one candle than to curse the darkness."
Chinese proverb attributed to Confucius

The doctors transferred Dr. Jonathan Rogers to a private hospital bed from the ICU of Detroit Metro. Though still in a coma for months, Ashley took some solace in the fact that his Glasgow neurological score had gradually improved to an eight. *My dad always said where there is life there is hope.*

She warmly greeted Beth, Panini, and Virginia as they came to pay a visit to Rogers. After a series of long hugs, the women sat around his hospital bed.

Panini walked over to his boyhood friend and stood in silence. He then bent down and kissed him on the cheek. He then took a seat, blowing his nose. Panini looked up as they all stared at him. "What? It's just allergies."

Ashley reached over and patted his hand.

"Sweetie, I knew your dad from the streets. Growing up together, we were fearless. Your dad never lost that courage to plow forward no matter how hard the consequences as long as he believed in what he was doing. Don't worry. He is a fighter. They don't make them any tougher than ole Johnny Boy."

Beth's eyes flickered. She glanced over at Jonathan, seemingly about to lose it. She bit her lower lip and took a long deep breath.

Ashley broke the moment. "All of us need to work for the President's re-election. There was a news report today about positive diplomatic ties with Islamabad. The Pakistani government is now pro-actively working with us to stamp out the terrorists."

The crusading trio each took a deep breath. Once again, they focused their eyes on the man in front of them—a man that all of them truly loved. No one spoke for several minutes, each lost in memories of happier times.

A child's cute giggle outside the hospital room broke the peace. Ashley looked at the doorway. A woman stood with her arms around the shoulders of a young girl holding a teddy bear.

"Come in." Ashley motioned.

The woman spoke, "Excuse us. We've met Dr. Rogers before. When we heard what happened, we just had to visit him. We wanted to wait until he was stable to come. He was there for us when we needed it most. It was right after the nuclear bombing of Minneapolis." Ashley stood and hugged the young woman.

"We wanted to show our respect by being here today for him. My name is Cassie. This is my daughter Emma. We're both survivors of the Minneapolis nuclear bombing."

Ashley held out her arms to the child.

Emma walked slowly toward her. "This is Waggles, my friend."

"Well, it's very nice to meet you and your cute little friend."

Emma encouraged Waggles to give Ashley a high-five.

The young girl pointed to Dr. Rogers. She looked into Ashley's eyes. "Mr. Waggles remembers your dad. He told me last night after mom tucked us into bed that you're dad would be OK. Waggles just whispered to me. We both think that your daddy is just sleeping. My mom said that he's been working really hard. He deserves a rest."

Cassie wiped away a tear. "It was determined subsequent to meeting with Dr .Rogers and the President that the both of us were actually three kilometers away from the primary blast site. The doctors decided that we were candidates to receive the Sam Murphy vaccine since our exposure was less than the guideline cut off for inoculation. We hope they are right. Therefore, if it weren't for people like your dad and President Williams, we never would have received the Murphy vaccine. Neither would have the other tens of millions of Americans who will live because of what he did for all of us."

Cassie held up Emma. Emma held Waggles. Everyone put their hands together, high in the air, each knowing their own particular challenges that lay ahead. Everyone laughed when Waggle's fuzzy paw patted each of them.

******

Today was the first day of the fifth month of her father's coma. It was midnight. The hospital corridors were completely still. Ashley gripped her father's warm hand, feeling the close bond. His face was serene. A gratifying thought came to her. Her father had accomplished what God wanted him to do.

She sat alongside his bedside, unwilling to let go of his hand, her singular connection to her beloved hero who had taught her everything by just being himself, through simply standing up for what was right. Her dad would be so proud, knowing that she was following in his path by becoming a physician. In one more month, she would graduate--Dr. Ashley Rogers.

She had once promised him to carry on his work as a champion for the public good. Evil versus good were at war, a daily battle. People had choices to make. Her father had always sided with fighting evil. Fighting to achieve the greater good was where she would cast her lot. Difficult days lay ahead.

Leaving his side that night, she walked toward St. Joseph's Church. She leaped up the granite steps, surprised but pleased to find the main door open, as the hour neared midnight.

Ashley bowed in the direction of the altar and walked toward the vigil candles. She knelt down on the black marble floor after lighting two candles. A sense of calmness descended upon her. She looked up at the ceiling. Angels and saints were hand -painted on the rounded dome mural. Instinctively, the words to the Lord's Prayer began flowing from her mouth as she imagined the angels blowing trumpets in joyful jubilation.

It finally dawned upon Ashley. Her dad and mom were forever to be part of her inner fiber, her spirit. That would never change. *Everything is going to be all right.*

Made in the USA
Lexington, KY
04 October 2012